Heartbeat

ISBN 1-59113-105-7

Published 2002

Manufactured in the United States of America.

Booklocker.com, Inc.
2002

Heartbeat

Samuel Finn

Heartbeat

Chapter One

A face, almost a century old, asleep, or is it dead? No, not dead. Pale, translucent skin slack over bone, purple threads of veins, fine creases spreading from the hollows of its eyes and toothless mouth. Zach, look at it, imagine yourself so old, so many years of life.

The eyes pop open, startling me. The creases distort into a smile. "Where am I?" she rasps.

"Where are you? Well, this is the emergency room. Are you, um—" I glance down at the chart for a name, "Frieda Goldberg?"

The smile persists, her eyes cling to mine. Finally, "What did you say?"

Louder this time, "Are you Mrs. Goldberg?"

"Yes." Her voice wavers. "Who are you?"

"I'm Dr. Mendel. You're in the emergency room."

"I am?"

"An ambulance brought you here from the—" I fumble again with the chart, from some nursing home. "—from Covenant Manor. Is that where you live?"

She stares vacantly. "What time is it?"

"It's about nine o'clock."

"Oh, in the morning?"

"No, it's evening," I shout in her ear.

She nods again, apparently unsurprised.

"Have you been sick?"

"Oh, yes."

"What's been bothering you?" Again she stares, another stumper. The transfer form mentions cough and fever, loss of appetite, and lethargy.

I examine her quickly, gently. She smells of urine. Her ribs raise stony ridges across her thin chest. My stethoscope brings me the distant whir of calcified valves. She rapidly sinks back to sleep.

This face, Zach, this old woman's wilted face, so old, imagine so many years of life. And being so close to death.

Zach, I keep thinking of you. Why do you keep coming to mind? I talk to you now, in my head, like you're here. I used to do that, didn't I? Back when we were kids, or when I was a kid and you were dead. I talked to you in my head then, too.

"Leon," a nurse approaches. "The kid in Bed 14, the one with the forearm fracture. The parents are getting upset because it's taking so long."

"Haven't the ortho residents come down yet?"

"They're still in surgery with that femur fracture. And the kid's in a lot of pain."

"I told Patterson to order some Demerol for him."

"The kid wouldn't let me give it."

"He refused it?"

She nods. "Scared of needles."

"The kid's hurt but he won't let us give him a shot cause he's afraid of needles. Okay, give the syringe to Patterson and tell him to go talk to them and give the kid his shot. It's his patient."

She nods, moving away.

"Wait, Susanne, the lady on the backboard in trauma C, how does she look?"

"Good. She's stable. Sore back and neck. She's a walker for sure."

"Okay, then move her to another room and get her neck X-rayed. Keep those trauma beds clear. What's happening in trauma A?"

"The surgery team, Beauregard and his intern, are with that kid who got shot. They're putting in a chest tube."

"Okay, then they're off to the operating room. Where's Icky?"

"He's sewing up a little girl's face in Bed 11. There's a new intern here."

At the nurses station a chubby young woman in a clean white coat smiles politely. She has a round face with wide hazel eyes that give away nothing.

"I'm Lydia Neuman." She holds out a dry, firm hand. "I'm a family practice R-1."

"Leon Mendel. Glad to have you with us. Is this your first month in the E.D.?"

"In the what?" She has freckles. Freckles on a doctor?

"In the emergency department?"

She nods. "Well, it is July, so this is my first month on any rotation here."

"Yes, I guess that's true. Silly question, wasn't it? So, are you scared?"

She smiles again, meeting my eye. "Should I be? The patients should probably be scared of me."

A sense of humor, good, we need that around here. And freckles. Have you come to terms with your freckles?, I want to say.

"Okay, here's the two-minute rap, and then I'll get one of the residents to show you around. We are a level one trauma center, one of two in Cincinnati, the other one being University Hospital across town, so anything and everything is brought here. And not just trauma. We get all the bums and the homeless off the streets when they get sick, all the people on welfare who can't find any other doctors to take care of them, all the schizophrenics and psychotics who wander the boulevards of our fair city. We have 25 beds and a 10-bed holding area over there."

I wave a hand, pointing over the counter-tops of the nurses station at the cavernous room surrounding us, partitioned and curtained, harshly lit. Nurses in green scrubs move about.

"There are usually two attendings here. Tonight it's myself and Icarus Polyzarin. We're both board certified in the specialty of Emergency—"

The radio on the counter sounds its long tone, then, "Medic 7 to Municipal Emergency."

I pick up the receiver. "This is Municipal. Go ahead, Medic 7."

"We are proceeding Code 2 to your facility with a seventeen-year-old female who ingested an unknown amount of Sinequan and Tylenol pills belonging to her mother. She also has been drinking alcohol. She is delirious and combative, requiring restraints. Vital signs are stable at this point. We have started an IV and the patient is in sinus rhythm." Shrieks are audible behind his voice. "We will be at your facility in approximately 12 minutes. Over."

"Okay Medic 7. We will be expecting you. Good luck. Municipal Emergency clear."

I turn to the white Patient Control Board on the wall and find a magnetized tag that says MEDIC from the rows of square tags at the bottom. I move it to the space marked Bed 10, a single bed room where her howls won't disturb the whole department.

"Overdoses are always such fun. Okay, where was I?"

"She must be hurting very badly to want to kill herself," Lydia says.

"You're right," I say. "We tend to get cynical here, and I am as guilty of it as anyone. It's just that with a lot of these teenage girls it's a gesture. Their boyfriend looks cross-eyed at them, or doesn't ask them to the dance, so they go home and take Mommy's pills and then we have to knock ourselves out to save them or at least to make sure they're not going to get real sick, and then they go back home giggling and carrying on like nothing ever happened. Okay, so…"

"You were saying something about you and the other attending."

"Oh, yeah, Icky and I are both faculty of the Emergency Medicine Residency Program. So there are Emergency Medicine residents down here all the time, too. As you know, the whole hospital depends on you residents to function, and the E.D. is no exception."

Her hazel eyes watch mine. She is pale beneath the freckles. These poor kids, no summer vacation, straight from medical school to internship, the frying pan into the fire. She probably graduated two weeks ago, laughing with her friends in their caps and gowns on a lawn somewhere—

"Dr. Mendel?" she says.

I realize I've stopped talking. "Oh, I'm sorry. I was thinking of something else." I feel my face redden. "So half the residents down here each month are from the Emergency Medicine program and the others are from other services like yourself. You should try to see—"

"We are the shock troops, the marines of modern medicine." Icarus swaggers into the nurses station. "From the halls of the Mayo Clinic to the shores of the welfare state."

"Icarus, this is our new Family Practice intern, Lydia Neuman."

"Glad to have you aboard, my dear. Watch out for young Mendel there. Behind that dark Slavic countenance lurks a lecher beyond belief. And take careful note of the recent absence of a wedding ring on his left hand. Thirty-three years old and already one marriage to the wind."

"This is Icarus Polyzarin," I tell her, "a Greek name, so you don't need to ask. He's six feet four inches tall, so don't ask that either, and yes, he is balding above that rat's nest of hair, so don't mention that either, and yes, if he were any skinnier we would test him for AIDS, but he's been monotonously monogamous since kindergarten. So what are you having your troops call you these days, Commander Polyzarin?" I ask.

"Icarus will be fine," he smiles down at her.

"Not Icky," I say, "anything but Icky."

"Please, Leon, one cannot help one's name, or one's height, or one's hair pattern. Do I tease you about your dubious intellect or your diminutive stature?"

"My stature's hardly—"

"Dr. Mendel!" Ruby, the secretary, shouts at me, pointing. "Trauma A, stat!"

"LEON!" Across the department I see Matt Beauregard's head around the curtain. "C'MERE!" He waves a frenzied hand.

"Something's up. C'mon," I say to Lydia.

Nurses are moving that way.

"CODE BLUE, EMERGENCY DEPARTMENT," the hospital P.A. sounds, "CODE BLUE, EMERGENCY DEPARTMENT."

Beauregard called a Code Blue. That's a cardiac code. Jesus, what's he doing? The kid's been shot in the stomach. He was awake and talking a few minutes ago.

Around the curtain the boy's muscular body lies limp. His skin has the grayish cast of black skin with no blood flowing through it. Someone has started CPR A clear plastic chest tube protrudes from his right chest. Each chest compression pumps a thick stream of bright blood into a growing puddle on the floor.

“What the hell’s going on, Matt?” I grab a hemostat from the open instrument tray and ratchet it tight on the tube, stopping the red river.

“He has a pneumo and Finkel was putting in a chest tube,” Beauregard's face is pale above the paper mask covering his mouth. “Look, there's the X-ray. There's no blood in his chest. Where's it coming from?”

A chest X-ray glows on the wall viewbox. A moment's study reveals the error. Someone hands me a pair of gloves.

“You gonna intubate this guy, Leon?” the respiratory therapist asks urgently. He's breathing for the boy with an Ambu bag and mask.

“Shit, Matt, look at that film!” I step to the head of the bed.

“He's in v-fib, Leon,” a nurse says.

“Course he's in v-fib. He's got a chest tube in his heart.”

“What about it?” Beauregard yells, staring at the X-ray. He is tall, sandy-haired, but his usual self-confidence is shaken.

“C’mon, Matt. What's the matter with that film?” I lean down with the laryngoscope in hand and slide its curved metal blade into the boy's mouth. His body quakes with the rhythm of the chest compressions. Lifting the instrument opens his mouth, raises the limp tongue clear of his throat. The tiny light shows his vocal cords and the dark slit between them that is the opening of the trachea. The R.T. hands me a plastic endotracheal tube, which I slide into the slit. Now we can breath for him. The R.T. hooks the bag to the tube and begins pumping oxygen directly into the boy's lungs.

“Did you figure it out, Matt?” I straighten up, eyeing Beauregard and his intern. Matt is a big rock-jawed football type, Finkel gangling and awkward. I'll give him five seconds more.

The Internal Medicine team arrives from upstairs, Todd Pinehurst, an insipid senior resident, and his intern. They are supposed to run cardiac codes.

“What's happening, Leon?” Pinehurst says, breathing hard. His pudgy face is pale.

“This one's a Trauma Code, Todd. I don't know who called the Code Blue.”

“Internal Medicine responds to Trauma Codes, too.”

“Fine, but you don't run them.”

“He's in v-fib, Leon!”

“Good, Todd, I'm pleased you can read the monitor. How 'bout it, Matt?”

“The film's reversed,” Beauregard says. “Somebody put it up backwards cause the heart’s pushed over.”

“Right, now what are you going to do about it?”

“Aren't you going to shock him, Leon?” Pinehurst says.

"Cool it, Todd. Beauregard's running this one."

"Jesus Christ." Beauregard stands shaking his head. "I can't believe—"

"C'mon, senior surgery resident," I say. "You screwed up. That happens. Now what are you going to do to fix it? You're a smart boy."

"Leon," Pinehurst persists, "why don't you guys work out your troubles later. This kid needs to be shocked."

"Pinehurst, shut the fuck up. This is a Trauma Code and you can either watch quietly and learn something or go back upstairs."

"Okay, okay," Beauregard says, moving now. "We gotta crack his chest. Tell surgery we need the cardiac room now, pump team, the whole crew. Call Mandrill, the chief, and tell him we need him down here stat. Tell the lab we need two units of O-negative blood right now and six more typed and crossed stat."

Two nurses move away. Another opens the sterile-wrapped thoracotomy tray. I slather the boy's smooth chest with brown Betadine solution. A nurse slides a rubber nasogastric tube down the back of his throat into his stomach.

Beauregard moves to the boy's left side. With a large scalpel his gloved hands make a long curved incision parallel to the ribs. The skin opens like a smile, fat and muscle gleam beneath. He incises again, deeper between the ribs. A whoosh of air relieves the pressure built up inside.

"How did you get the chest tube into his heart?" I ask him, handing the rib spreader to Finkel.

Beauregard shakes his head, breathing hard behind his mask. "Shit, Leon, you don't want to know." His fingers move rapidly.

I glance across the bed. A chest tube trocar, like a short bloodied spear, lies on the instrument tray.

"You used a trocar?"

Beauregard nods. He holds the rib spreader while Finkel turns its short crank. Like the metal fingers of a pair of hands, the instrument pulls the ribs apart. Cartilage pops and gives way.

"Why the hell'd you use a trocar?"

"C'mon, Leon, not now," he says angrily. Sweat beads his forehead.

Blood spills onto the bed and the floor. With the pressure of the pneumothorax relieved, the boy's heart moves back to its normal position, deep in the hole Beauregard has made. In fibrillation its muscle crawls like a sack of tiny worms, and it pumps no blood. His fingers close around it and the tube skewering it. He slides the chest tube out of the heart and stoppers the hole with a finger. Now his hands begin to squeeze, pumping for the wounded organ.

"Open up the fluids wide." Self-assurance has returned to his voice. The nurses open the valves on the IVs. Warm saline pours into the boy's veins.

He looks at me.

“Incise the pericardium, in case there’s any tamponade.”

With his free hand he reaches for a smaller scalpel.

“Vertical incision, watch out for the phrenic nerve.”

He slices through the tough layer of tissue that covers the heart. Jelly-like blood clots spill out.

“Now take the Foley and put it in the hole.”

He nods. Finkel passes a thick rubber catheter to Matt’s hands inside the boy's chest. His blue-gowned arms are dark red to the elbows. He threads the catheter tip into the hole.

“Don't let any air in. You'll get an embolus.” I want to reach into the boy's warm body myself, save this life with my own hands.

There is a man staring from the glass partition, staring across the room at me. He has a mustache, tangled dark hair, and wire-rim glasses. A haggard face, tired eyes holding my gaze with a concerned expression, a stranger who looks like he needs to tell me something, bad news perhaps. Who is that, Zach, do we know him?

“Okay, Finkel, fill the balloon,” Beauregard says.

The intern squirts a syringe full of saline into the valve on the catheter, filling the small balloon inside the heart. His hands shake terribly. He looks close to tears. His hands made the hole in that heart, his hands pushed the trocar into this kid’s chest, Beauregard directing him, teaching him.

I look again at the man’s face behind the glass and it looks back. My own reflection I realize, from the odd angle of the overhead light.

“Now, let it fill with blood,” I say, “and then clamp it right where it comes out with a little tension.”

“I know, Leon, I know,” Beauregard says. Good, he's back to his old self.

The face in the glass shakes its head at my foolishness. Is it me, Zach, or is it you watching me? That could be you. We were twins, identical twins, the same genes. We would still look alike. The image of that black station wagon comes to me, the Cadillac hearse they took you away in, with the sharp tail fins and the chrome curlicue on the side.

“Okay, internal paddles,” Beauregard says, “charge to five joules.”

A nurse hands him the defibrillator paddles, small black spatulas with cables leading to the squat machine on the crash cart. He slides one behind the heart and one in front. A shrill tone sounds from the machine.

“Clear,” he says. Everyone around the gurney steps back. The machine clicks and the boy's body shivers.

I watch the fist-sized lump of muscle begin its gentle motion again, its millions of fibers shocked into synchrony.

A firm hand on my shoulder belongs to Mike Mandrill, the chief surgery resident. "What's happening, Leon? This kid get a bullet in the chest?"

"He got a bullet in the belly."

"Looks like it went up into his chest." His face has creases from a pillow, his hair needs combing.

"He got a chest tube trocar in his chest."

"What? What the hell are you talking about?"

"Look at that X-ray." I point to the film on the wall.

"What about it?" Mandrill says, irritated.

"Read it."

Finkel speaks, "That X-ray got—"

"Shut up, Finkel." He eyes me, aghast. I'm trying to save his butt.

"He's got a pulse," a nurse says.

"You better sedate him, Matt," I say. "He might wake up."

I turn back to Mandrill. "What do you see, Mike?"

Lydia watches me. Am I showing off? No, I'm trying to save Beauregard and Finkel.

"He's got a big right pneumothorax," Mandrill says.

"Which side?"

"Right. So what, Leon?"

"That's how Beauregard and Finkel read it, too."

"Operating room's ready," someone announces.

"Let's go," Beauregard says. He looks at me gratefully.

They gather the IV fluid bags and a portable heart monitor. With a clunk the wheels of the gurney are unlocked and they move off toward surgery.

"Good luck in the O.R., you guys." Beauregard will have some explaining to do when their attending arrives. I take off my gloves and start to move away.

"How could you let this happen, Leon?" Mandrill has figured out the X-ray.

"I wasn't in the room. I figured your boys could figure out which side to stick a chest tube in."

He opens and closes his mouth, pale with anger. "You're responsible for resuscitations down here. You're supposed—"

"He was resuscitated, Mike," I feel my own voice rising. "He was stable the whole time, from the moment the medics picked him up. Look, why don't you go sew up his heart and come on back and we'll talk about it. Who's your surgery attending tonight?"

"Graffen. He's gonna love this." He walks quickly off to the operating room.

Lydia is still with me. "I don't understand," she says. "How did that happen?" We move back to the nurses station.

"Well, that kid got shot in the belly. Who knows why, probably some drug deal, or they wanted his sneakers or something. So Ted and I evaluated him before the surgery guys arrived. They get called for every gunshot wound anyway. It was obvious he needed surgery. He was stable and had a collapsed lung on the left. The bullet must have gone up through his diaphragm and punctured his left lung. He needed a chest tube but we figured we'd let the surgery team do it. They were here anyway and we've got plenty to do ourselves, as you can see." I gesture toward the board, which is filling up fast.

"Dr. Mendel," Ruby says. "The overdose is in Room 10."

"Okay, would you find Rohit and ask him to go in there."

She pushes a button on the department intercom and pages, "Dr. Medari to Room 10, please. Dr. Medari to Room 10."

I turn back to Lydia's freckles. "So the air in the left chest from the pneumothorax had pushed his heart over toward the right. When Beauregard or Finkel put up the chest x-ray on the viewbox they put it up backwards because the heart was on the right side instead of the left. They didn't look at the left-right markers on the film.

"So with the film up backwards they thought he had a pneumo on the right. Of course they could have listened to his breath sounds like they're supposed to, but they were in a hurry and it all seemed pretty straightforward, I guess.

"So they put the chest tube into the right side of his chest instead of the left where the pneumothorax was. But then they did the thing I can't understand. They used a damn trocar to put in the tube. Those haven't been used for years in trauma cases. You're supposed to make an incision through the chest wall and stick your finger in first to make sure you're in the right place and there's nothing in the way. But I guess they jammed it in with the trocar and sure enough with the heart pushed over to that side the trocar pierced the heart.

"Bad move. Very bad move, in fact. I'm gonna be hearing about this one for a long time. And you can bet Beauregard and Finkel are gonna get roasted for it."

"Leon," Ted Watanabe joins us, resting his broad behind in a chair. "Can you believe that? They stuck a trocar into that kid's heart." Two charts on metal clipboards dangle from his hand.

"That kid, Dr. Watanabe, was our patient, too. You and I had initial responsibility for treating him."

"But they were right there, Leon. We hardly said boo to the guy."

"Wrong. Would you tell the court who initially examined the patient, Dr. Watanabe?"

His Japanese eyes narrow, his smile vanishes. The residents hate this game.

"I did."

"And what did you find to be the patient's injuries?"

"He had a gunshot wound to the abdomen and a left pneumothorax."

"And did you then obtain surgical consultation, Dr. Watanabe?"

"Yes, immediately, the surgeons were there within five minutes of the patient's arrival."

Beyond a countertop I see a respiratory therapist scurry across the department and disappear behind a curtain.

"What's going on in Bed 3, Ruby?" I ask the secretary.

"Dr. P gotta guy havin' a heart attack, sounds like." The department intercom speaker is on in front of her. I can hear Icky's voice talking rapidly, a patient coughing in the background.

"Has he got a resident with him?"

"Sounds like Dr. Patterson be in there."

I turn back to Ted. "And did you inform the surgeons of your findings?"

"C'mon, Leon."

"C'mon yourself, Ted. There's lawyers that would sell their children to get hold of a case like this. Chances are the kid's family, if he has one, will never get it together to talk to a lawyer. He'll probably be okay and they'll never understand all this. But if they did, my friend, you and I would fry along with the surgeons."

"But we didn't—"

"Stop, Theodore. We've got patients to see. Dictate a thorough note on exactly what you did, step by step. State that I was your attending on the case and was present in the room. State exactly at what point the surgeons took over and exactly what you said to them. Do you recall if you told them which side that pneumo was on?"

"I did. I know I did."

"Did you tell Finkel or Beauregard?"

"Finkel. Beauregard was on the phone calling for an operating room."

"Okay, do the note, tell transcription we need it now, and then let me see it."

He stands, tapping a chart in his hand. "Okay, I've got this asthmatic girl I'm ordering some Albuterol for. She's in Bed 7."

I glance at the bank of heart monitors that makes one wall of the nurses station. The number next to the green tracing for Bed 7 is 138, very fast for an adult, not bad for a child. "How old?"

"She's eight." He taps the second chart. "And there's a good-looking lady over in 12 says she knows you."

"Probably wants narcotics. What's the matter with her?"

“Nothing. Her daughter's got cystic fibrosis, fever, and vomiting.” I take the charts from him. “Okay. Ted, this is Lydia Neuman, our Family Practice R-1 for the month. Lydia, this is Ted Watanabe, a second year Emergency Medicine Resident; a seasoned veteran of the Emergency Department who with diligence and perseverance may someday be an exemplary ER doc.”

“Like you?” Ted says.

“Like me if you're lucky. Anyway, would you give Dr. Neuman the fifty-cent tour, brief her on the board, and introduce her to the charge nurse?”

They start to move away. “Lydia,” I stop her. “Listen, two things are important down here. First is honesty. Don't ever fake it. If you don't know something about your patient, or forgot to do something, then say so. Don't ever pretend or fake it. The whole system breaks down and that's when patients get hurt.”

“Give it a rest, Leon,” Ted says. “She's a big girl.”

“What's the second thing, Leon?” Lydia says.

“Listen to the nurses. They know what they're doing and they'll keep you out of trouble.”

Watanabe shrugs as they walk away, speaking to her, making her laugh.

I glance at the chart for Room 12, a thirteen-year-old girl named Britnie Zeller. The mom knows me? Britnie? Didn’t her parents know how to spell? Under mother's name it says Rita Thal. Different last names, not unusual around here, but neither name is familiar.

* * *

These rooms, they’re so awful. I forgot what it’s like, sitting, waiting, wondering what’s gonna happen. God, I could use a cigarette. And you’re so helpless, sick people all around, and drunks, always somebody angry, yelling.

That baby across the hall sounds terrible. And there’s blood on the floor there in the corner, and the trash can, don’t look in the trash can. It makes me shiver.

Or a glass of wine, some wine would be good. Why can’t they go ahead and give Britnie a breathing treatment. It’s obvious she needs—

“Was he Chinese?” Britnie says.

“Who, that doctor? Well, he wasn’t Mexican.” I try to laugh. “I’m sorry, that was silly. I don’t know. He didn’t speak with an accent. He must have been born here, don’t you think?”

“Yeah, but he looked Chinese.” She sits like Camille used to, on the side of the bed, leaning forward to breathe. But she’s not so skinny like Camille got, not so pinched.

"Well, obviously," I say. "I mean I guess he could have been Japanese, or Vietnamese. No, I think Vietnamese look different. Their eyes aren't so narrow."

"He's obviously not Vietnamese, Rita," she says, the expert all of a sudden.

"Those people are very smart, I've read, Chinese and Japanese. Their kids do better in school." At least they could put her on some oxygen. I could do that, get one of those little tubes out myself and plug it in that little thing on the wall.

"Smart?" Britnie says, "You mean smarter than white kids? That wouldn't take much, would it? So now what? What are they going to do?" She is tired, impatient. "You said there's another doctor? Why do they need another doctor?"

I move over and sit by her on the bed. It's awkward, we don't know each other still. "Sometimes it takes a long time here, sweetheart. They get so busy and they have to take care of really bad patients first. That doctor was a resident. He's like a student. I mean I guess he's a doctor but he's still learning to be a specialist or something. Now he has to go and talk to the real doctor, Dr. Mendel, I hope. You'll like him. He's very kind. He's even good looking. Some of these doctors are so dorkey looking."

"Dorkey looking, right. Nobody says dorkey anymore, Rita. Did he take care of Camille?" she watches my face.

There is a shriek somewhere.

"What was that?" she says.

A white coat appears. It's him.

"Hello, I'm Dr. Mendel. Are you Britnie?"

Will he remember me? He looks busy, preoccupied, that poker face they wear.

"Dr. Mendel," I say, "I was hoping you'd be here." Stand, smile, take his hand. His eyes flicker over me the way men do. That's okay. "I'm Rita Thal. Do you remember me? You helped my other daughter, Camille. About a year ago she kept coming in here—I mean when she started getting sick all the time. She had cystic fibrosis also." God, what am I saying, in front of Britnie.

"I do remember," he smiles, "quite clearly, in fact." His hand draws back. Still the steady calm gaze, those brown eyes behind the wire rims, the way they watch for your feelings. They don't all do that, but he does.

"Yes, I'm sure," I say. "You and I went round and round for a while 'til we reached an understanding. But you were so helpful to us. So patient and kind with Camille."

He is pale, tired. "Camille. That's right, Camille was her name."

And he responded with feeling to Camille, and even for a moment to me. He's probably forgotten, but he did.

"This is Britnie. Britnie, this is Dr. Mendel."

"Hey," she nods.

"Hi, Britnie," he says, "it looks like you're not breathing too well today." Then to me, "I didn't realize you had another child with C.F."

"I didn't. Britnie is a new addition to my family." Put an arm around her, hug her. "Isn't that right?"

She nods again, looking at the floor, stiff, not quite leaning away, drawn in. I can't blame her.

Now the poker face again as he realizes what I just said. Does he think I'm crazy? He must.

"Okay, so..." He looks at her chart in his hand. "So you're thirteen years old and you've been coughing and having trouble breathing?"

He checks her over quickly, those hands are so quick, so sure.

Those hands held me once. He held me as we watched Camille die. He helped her die a peaceful death, no tube in her throat, no ventilator. Down the hall someplace, in one of those rooms, in the middle of the night. He had them give her morphine. Just Camille and me, and him, nobody else, and he understood. He let me sit in the room afterward.

And oh, my, no ring now, no ring on his left hand. He used to have a wedding ring. Hmm, think of that.

He talks about breathing treatments, IV fluids, antibiotics. I love his jaw, lean, almost delicate. Britnie sits dumb, letting it fall about her ears. I'll help her with it all, this child I don't know very well.

"Have you gotten involved with the Cystic Fibrosis Clinic over at Children's Hospital?" he says to me.

Don't you remember? "I don't get along very well with the people over there. Camille and I had such bad experiences there."

The poker face again. He looks thinner than before. He must be working too much. "Right, I remember. But you do get continuity of care there. You get one doctor who really gets to know you, the two of you."

Which is bull, I want to say. The residents there change all the time. The real docs stay the same but you hardly ever see them.

He pats Britnie's shoulder but avoids her eye. "Well, Britnie, it's nice to meet you. We're going to do some things to make you feel better, okay?"

I follow him into the hall, people moving about. "Dr. Mendel." Maybe here I can make contact, get past the doctor face.

He turns. Take his hand. "You know, I've thought about you a lot." How lame. Keep going. "You were so wonderful with Camille."

His face, there is more than fatigue. He's unhappy. Does he smell the wine on me? They all get so sensitive to it here.

He says, “You went through...um...you were wonderful with her yourself. It must have been difficult for you.” He lets my hand go.

“No, it was the most important event in my life. It taught me the strength of love.” The words are out before I realize what I’ve said.

He nods, watching me. Is he going to laugh? “I’ve never heard anyone say that before. That’s remarkable.”

So now what am I supposed to say? Something, ask him—

“So Britnie is not your own daughter?” He says, his eyes still on mine.

“I adopted her.”

“Did you know...you must have known she had C.F.”

“Of course. I went through the Cystic Fibrosis Foundation to find her. I know what you're thinking. You're thinking I must be nuts to do this again.”

“More or less,” he says, trying to smile. “Either nuts or you are a truly unique kind of person.”

“Prob’ly nuts.” Okay, take the plunge. “You have no wedding ring. You used to have one.”

“You're right. It's true.”

“I’m being too forward, aren't I?”

“No, not really. I do remember you. You've got quite a temper, as I recall.” Such a smile he has, I’d forgotten it.

“Yes, well, it's important sometimes. It's the red hair. Redheads are very passionate, you know. Passionate in many ways.” Oh, please, did I say that?

“Leon, phone call,” someone calls him from the nurses station. Thank God.

“I have to go.”

“Will you be back before we leave?”

“I'll be back.”

“Dr. Mendel, have you been ill?”

He gazes at me. Was it the wrong thing?

“You could say I've recently been under stress.”

“Perhaps I...I'm sorry for you.” Almost said it, should have said it, offered.

“I'll be fine,” he says, turning away.

Chapter Two

Rita Thal, she's very pretty, I'd forgotten how pretty. Maybe I didn't notice before. That short red hair and those eyes, so perfectly made up. That quick, warm smile. She smells like she's been drinking. I think she smelled that way before, too. Have I been ill, she said. Ill, do I look ill?

And I don't feel ill, but something seems different tonight, here, in the department. Fear, foreboding, like a bus wreck about to happen. Does anyone else feel it?

"Dr. Mendel, the nurse wants an attending in Bed 10," Ruby says to me.

In Bed 10 lies a delirious teenage girl, twisting and moaning. Stephanie, the nurse, and the paramedics who brought her are tying white cloth restraints around her wrists.

Rohit Medari, one of my first year Emergency Medicine residents, tries to help them. He looks scared.

"What's up, Rohit?"

"She has overdosed on Sinequan and Tylenol. She has been drinking, too."

"How long ago?"

A paramedic turns to me. "Boyfriend came over to her house, said he found her this way. Said she called him a couple hours before but he doesn't think she had taken anything then."

"Anyone else there?"

"Nope. Boyfriend said he found these bottles out on the floor when he got there. Says he just told her yesterday he was movin' on, didn't want to see her anymore."

He hands me two plastic pill bottles. The girl squirms on the gurney; her pale pimpled face contorts.

"How about parents?"

"Mom's out for the evening. Nobody knows where, but from the looks of the house she doesn't hang around much."

"How about Dad?"

"What dad?"

What dad, the usual situation. "You guys do a chemstick?"

The paramedic nods. "Blood sugar was 135. Gave Narcan with no response."

I look at Rohit's face. He is East Indian, dark, delicately handsome. "What's Sinequan, Rohit?" I hold up the bottles.

"It is a tricyclic antidepressant."

"Right. Is it dangerous?"

He nods. "It has strong cardiotoxicity."

"Good, what do you think we should do?"

He eyes me. "She needs gastric lavage."

"Sounds good. Anything else?"

"Toxic screen?"

"Well, probably, but that won't come back for hours. Won't help us much now. Looks like we probably know what she took, Sinequan and Tylenol. Does she have a gag reflex?"

"No gag. You think we should intubate her?"

"What do you think?"

He glances about the room. "Yes, I guess so."

"Damn right. What if she vomits when you pass the lavage tube, and then aspirates? You're only wrong if you don't."

"Should we paralyze her?"

"Well, you've got two tubes to pass in a delirious, uncooperative patient. Your choice."

"Okay," he turns to Stephanie. "Get some Anectine, please."

She holds up the syringe, the medicine drawn up and ready. She's several steps ahead of him, but he's learning fast.

Injected into her IV line, the Anectine renders the girl flaccid, paralyzed for about ten minutes. I help Rohit find her vocal cords and intubate her. Now the respiratory therapist can breathe for the girl, and her lungs are protected should she vomit.

Then Rohit slides an even thicker tube along the back of her throat into her esophagus and down into her stomach. Now we can pour water into her stomach and let it flow out again, hopefully washing out any remaining pills. It's a miserable procedure with a conscious patient but this girl won't remember it in her current state, and it may save her life.

"Okay, what about the Tylenol she took? Pretty harmless stuff, right?"

"Right. No, wait, not harmless. Liver toxicity. We have to get a level four hours after the time of ingestion, then look at the nomogram for—"

I hold up a hand. "Okay, you pass. Stephanie will help you lavage her. Get labs ordered and watch the monitor. Call me if you need me."

Stephanie waves me away with the back of her hand. She knows what to do.

I find Frieda Goldberg's chest X-ray. Her right lung shows streaks of white, pneumonia.

"Dr. Mendel, your wife is on the phone," Ruby calls to me across the nurses station.

"My wife? My former wife? Tell her I've checked out to the Carlton Hotel with two of the nurses."

Ruby laughs, teeth flashing in her pretty black face. "I ain't gonna lie to the woman. You want to talk to her?"

"No, hell, it's ten-thirty. What's she calling about now? Tell her I'm too busy. That's not a lie."

I write a prescription for Frieda's antibiotics, her discharge instructions, and put the chart back in the rack, then I write a red "DC" by her name on the board. DC for discharge so the next available nurse can call the nursing home to come and take her back.

Watanabe approaches, singing to himself, "Oh, it's another Saturday night and I ain't got nobody—"

"What are you in such a good mood about?"

"Hey, it's Saturday night at Cincinnati Municipal Trauma Center and Welfare Reclamation Department. What's your problem, Leon? Don't worry, be happy." He holds up another chart.

"You be happy. What have you got?"

"Boy, that Lydia, she's pretty funny."

"Funny haha or funny weird like you?" I hear the radio tone.

"Funny haha. She is." He presents a four-year-old boy with an ear infection.

Jenna, one of the nurses, takes the radio call. "Eighteen year old with vaginal bleeding," she says to us. "Probably pregnant. Sounds stable."

"Gee, something new," Ted says.

I look in on Watanabe's four year old. The mother struggles with a younger child, a chubby toddler who screams and waves his dirty hands.

"Get out of the damn wastebasket," she shouts at him. She looks about twenty, so fat her face is distorted. The patient sits on the gurney, laughing, egging on his brother. One glance tells me he is a healthy child, safe to send home on antibiotics for his ear. They are on welfare, like nearly half our patients, the mother unwed, the two children probably from different fathers.

Then the asthmatic eight year old, a skinny black girl. She coughs and stares, bored, at the ceiling. She has pulled off her monitor lead wires.

"Hi. Where's your Mom?"

"She went out to have a cigarette." She picks her nose with dirty fingers.

"How do you feel?"

"Okay. Can I go home now?"

"Let me listen to your breathing."

She turns her back to me, taking deep breaths. She knows the routine. I listen with my stethoscope.

"Better?" she says.

"Sounds pretty good. How long have you been sick?"

She shrugs.

"Stay here 'til your Mom comes back and then you can go home. Tell your mother to stop smoking. It's bad for—"

"Thanks a lot." Her mother comes around the curtain. "Who are you?" Her sullen face throws an angry glance at me. Her hair, tinged with purple, is shaved close around her lean head, making prominent the shape of her skull. She is maybe twenty-two, with a silver nose ring.

"I'm Dr. Mendel. I work with Dr. Watanabe to—"

"Can we get outta here? She breathin' good now." She knows who I am. She's been here many times. We are her family doctor.

"Do you know about smoking and asthma? It makes her asthma worse if you smoke at home."

"I know. Y'all done told me that before."

I wait, watching her.

"I know the shit, man. Y'all preach it to me every time. I be careful. I go outside or in the other room. Ain't that right, child?"

Her daughter ignores her.

So what can I do? Call Child Protective Services? Is it neglect? Take the kid out of the home and put her in foster care? Right.

At the nurses station Wanda puts an electrocardiogram in my hand. She looks tired, frustrated. "Here, Leon, I just ran this on the guy in Bed 6. He's got chest pain, looks like the real thing to me." The tracing has inverted T-waves, an abnormality, but it may be old, even years old. I'll need one of his old EKGs to compare.

"Ruby, I need the old chart on Bed 6, please."

"Honey, Medical Records ain't answered their phone in two hours. They either asleep or dead."

"Well, then call the nursing supervisor. Let her work on it. Would you page that new intern, Dr. Neuman, and point her to Bed 6?"

Bed 6 is Fred Skilkin, fifty-eight years old according to the chart. He lies ashen on the bed, frightened and sweating.

"Mr. Skilkin, I'm Dr. Mendel. How long have you had this pain?"

He glances at his wife who sits next to the bed. "I never felt anything like this before, Doc. Been going on about an hour, I guess."

"What were you doing when it started?"

"Nothing. Just watchin' TV."

"Can you describe what you're feeling for me?"

"It just hurts like hell." He holds a tight fist over his chest.

"What kind of pain is it?"

"Like somebody got a knot tied around my insides and is pulling it tighter and tighter." He's panting.

"Does it hurt to breathe in and out?"

He shakes his head.

"Can't you help him, Doctor?" his wife says. "Can't you see how much he hurts?"

"Yes, I will. I just need to get a little information first so I don't do him any harm. Fred, have you ever had any heart trouble?"

He shakes his head again.

"Okay." I punch the intercom button. "Ruby, I need a nurse in Bed 6 right away."

"Soon's I find one," she says.

It's a judgment call, as usual, but he looks to me like a man having a heart attack. I ask the nurse to begin giving intravenous nitroglycerin and morphine to relieve his pain. The nitro will relax the tiny muscles of his coronary arteries and let more blood flow to his heart. Also an aspirin for its blood-thinning effect.

"What's going on, Doc?" he says. "Guess it's time to stop smoking, huh."

I ignore the opportunity for retort. This man needs sympathy and reassurance. "Fred, I don't even know if this pain is coming from your heart at all. It may be entirely unrelated to your heart. But we have to assume it is your heart and treat you that way. I'm going to call your doctor and talk to him about putting you in the hospital. That way we can find out if it is your heart and keep you as safe as possible until we know."

He nods. A simple explanation, but the cardiologist will have plenty of time to talk to him. People in pain don't remember much anyway. The man's doctor is Hiram Rothman, an older internist, one of the downtown crowd who avoid Muni, don't like hobnobbing with lower class patients and having residents looking over their shoulders. Back at the nurses station I ask Ruby to page him for me.

"There's a trauma coming, Leon," a nurse tells me, turning from the radio. "Sounds pretty bad." She hands me the scribbled radio call report and hurries off.

How bad? The note says a twenty-four-year-old woman from a car accident with chest pain, a broken leg, and very low blood pressure. They'll arrive in ten minutes.

Lydia appears. "Okay, you've got ten minutes to do a quick history and physical on the guy in Bed 6. He's having chest pain. Here's his ECG. I asked the nurse to start nitro and morphine, but see what you think."

"Ten whole minutes? What should I do with the extra time?" She grins and walks off with the chart.

The slots on the board are filling fast. Each red tag means a patient in a bed waiting to be taken care of and there are eight of them. The triage nurses out in front check them in and call us to see the ones who need immediate care. I hate to think what the waiting room looks like now.

Two policemen bang through the double doors of the ambulance entrance, struggling with a handcuffed drunk. He is shouting obscenities and dripping blood from his pant leg along the floor. A nurse points them to a trauma bay.

"Where's he hurt?" I ask.

"Not sure," says one of the cops. "He got stabbed in a fight downtown at some bar. Looks like he got it in the groin or his thigh."

"LEMME GO. I'M GONNA GET THAT FUCKER."

"All right," I say, "put the leathers on."

Claudette and Roxanne, our police security guards, appear. Tall, stout women, like twin rhinos, but they can move like cats. Rapidly they imprison the man with thick leather cuffs around his wrists and ankles, strapped to the steel bars of the gurney. I help the nurses cut away his clothes. We need to know how badly he is hurt.

"What's your name?" I ask in a friendly voice.

"FUCK YOU. UNTIE ME, ASSHOLE." He starts to spit. Claudette's heavy hand slams his mouth shut. I hear teeth crumbling. She doesn't like spitting. The surprised man struggles to breathe through his nose. A nurse puts a paper mask over his mouth with strings looped over his ears. We have all done this before.

The doors swing open again and three paramedics push a stretcher toward us; a limp body strapped to a wooden backboard, a bloodless face with eyes closed above a hard plastic neck collar.

"Pressure's 80, Leon," one of them yells as they pass.

I push the intercom button. "Ruby, get Patterson and Watanabe over here and call a Trauma Code."

"The trauma team's still in O.R.," she says.

"Team 2 will come. Go on and call it."

A curtain away from the drunk, they lift the backboard and patient, littered with equipment, onto the gurney.

"Is she awake?"

"She was for a while," one of the paramedics answers. His partner breathes for her, pushing oxygen in and out of her lungs with a blue Ambu bag. IV's flow rapidly into each arm.

"What's her name?"

"Leanne something."

HEARTBEAT

I lean over the pale face and shout her name. A purple bruise pushes up the skin above her ear. The plastic endotracheal tube snakes into her mouth. I slap her cheek gently, then hard. No response.

The Trauma Code sounds over the hospital P.A. Soon the thundering herd will be upon us; surgery residents, internal medicine residents, respiratory therapist, pharmacist, X-ray techs, and a chaplain. “Okay, 2 milligrams of Narcan IV and a chemstick, please,” I say to a nurse. I slide the girl's eyelids up. She has clear blue eyes. The tiny black pools of her pupils shrink in the light.

“Pupils?” the recording nurse asks, staring at a trauma flow sheet in front of her.

“Equal, round and reactive, about 3 millimeters,” I say. Then to the paramedic, “Anybody with her?”

“Yeah, boyfriend's dead and another girl in the back they're still trying to get out of the car.”

“How'd she look?” If she’s alive they will bring her to us.

“Bad.”

Watanabe appears by my side with Lydia.

“Okay, Ted, twenty-four-year-old female from an MVA. Go for it, buddy.”

“Just like that, huh.” He glares at me.

“Trauma Code's been called and I'm right behind you.”

He moves close to the bed, taking off his white coat, draping his stethoscope over his neck. Someone hands us gloves and masks.

“Okay, what happened?” Ted says.

“Car was an old Chevy Malibu,” the paramedic says. “Looks like they went down the Ludlow Boulevard off-ramp way too fast, didn't make the curve, and flipped over the guardrail. Landed nose down. She was the driver, no seat belt. Initially conscious and complaining of chest and right leg pain, also head pain. Steering wheel badly bent and windshield shattered. Took about thirty minutes to get her out. Initial blood pressure was 90. Decreased breath sounds on the right and subcutaneous air. Obvious right femur fracture. We put on a Hare traction splint and started two lines, 14 gauge in each side. Level of consciousness went down fast. We intubated her about five minutes out. She's had about a liter and a half of fluid.”

“Her pressure's 85,” a nurse says, “pulse 134.”

Another nurse and I are undoing straps and cutting away her clothes. She is a plump girl with cold moist skin. Monitor leads are attached and her heartbeat appears above us.

The X-ray camera rumbles into place on its overhead rail.

Ted shouts at her as I did, but the Narcan has done nothing. Then he listens on each side with his stethoscope. “No breath sounds on the right. Set up for a chest tube.” His voice is high pitched, urgent.

He presses on her abdomen. “Shit, Leon, her belly's like a rock. She's gonna need surgery for sure.”

“Okay, but let's do first things first,” I say.

Angry shouts have been coming from behind me. I peek around the curtain to the next bay. Patterson is there, bent over the masked drunk.

“You under control?”

He nods. He is boyishly handsome with straight black hair. The old ladies love him.

“Lemme know what the guy needs.”

I punch the intercom speaker on the wall. “Ruby, you there?”

“Yes, hon, what you want?”

“Page Neurosurgery down here STAT.”

“Okay,” Ted says, “we need blood gases, trauma labs, two units type specific now and six units crossmatched, NG and Foley.”

“Pleurivac's ready,” a nurse says, “with the cell-saver.” Around us is a quiet frenzy of nurses and techs, each doing their job.

“Okay, where's the chest tube tray?” Ted says.

“I'll do the chest tube,” I say. “You keep going.” I glance about. “Lydia, do you know how to do chest tubes?”

She frowns. “I've done a couple.”

“Well, come watch. The next one's yours. Put gloves on.”

“COVER GOWNS.” Sonya, the charge nurse, pushes the folded blue gowns into our hands.

She is right; the gowns are sterile, they protect the patient, and they protect us from the patient. We deal in blood, blood is the water we sail on, yet we dare not touch it.

The X-ray machine starts firing, a tiny beep for each exposure. First her chest, then her neck, then her pelvis.

I splash the side of her chest with brown Betadine, explaining the procedure to Lydia. “Estimate the nipple line which is about the four-five interspace, at the posterior axillary line. This is out of the way, more dependent so blood will drain, and cosmetically better if she survives. Then make a 3- inch incision between the ribs. You need to give yourself enough room to work, especially if you're in a hurry. Then dissect down with the scissors like this, pass just over the superior margin of the inferior rib. Why's that?”

“Um, because the intercostal artery and vein pass just along the inferior border of each rib. You avoid them that way, the nerve, too.”

"Good, good." My gloved fingers work in the warm wet bed of the incision, feeling her ribs, cutting the muscle between them. I reach the tough pleura beneath. "If you cut down far enough with the scissors you don't have to sweat the final penetration. Watch out now." I reach for a Kelly clamp and push its blunt tip through the thick layer covering her lungs. Dark blood spurts over my fingers and flows onto the floor. "Put your finger in quickly, make sure there's no heart sitting there, or liver or anything else. Then the tube."

I slide the clear plastic tube, as thick as my thumb, into her chest. It fills instantly with blood up to the clamp. A nurse plugs it into the cell-saver tubing and I take off the clamp. Half a liter of blood is sucked out in seconds, a steady flow follows.

I look at the respiratory therapist pumping her lungs with an Ambu bag.

"Better," she says, nodding at the bag.

I show Lydia how to sew the incision closed with black silk thread, snug around the tube.

"Whaddya got, Leon?" Tommy Kaminsky, the senior surgery resident on the other trauma team, stands by me in blue scrubs.

"Watanabe can tell you about her."

Ted runs down the case to him, his voice tense, strident. Pudgett, Kaminsky's tall, silent intern, looms awkwardly behind him. His nervous eyes dart about.

I step around the curtain to Patterson, pulling off my slimy gloves. "How ya doin', Phil?"

"Good. He's pretty stable. Got about a six centimeter wound right over the right inguinal ligament. Belly's pretty tender. I think he needs to have it explored."

"How's his urine?"

"No blood."

The man lies strapped to the bed by his wrists and ankles, head flopped to the side, snoring.

"Does he wake up?"

"You bet. He's an obnoxious son of a bitch, too."

"So what do you want to do?"

"Well, looks like team 2 is going to be tied up for a while with that girl. Ruby says team 1 is still in the O.R."

Great. How long has it been? That kid with the hole in his heart better be okay.

"So I was thinking we could call the urology resident and see if they'll do this guy."

"Good idea. Does he have a wallet? Okay, give it to the social worker and see if he can drum up some family. We ought to contact family if he's got any."

Back at the station I speak to Ruby. "Did you reach that Rothman guy, Skilkin's doctor?" The board looks bad, festooned with red tags.

"Yeah," she turns toward me. "He wasn't overly pleased. He says put the man in an ambulance and send him to St. Joseph's and he'll take care of him there."

"No way, Jose, that guy could be having a heart attack. Page him again and I'll rattle his cage a little."

"Sounds like he been sippin' a bit."

"I don't care. At least I don't have to smell his breath."

She laughs. Rohit walks up, two charts in hand.

"Hey, superdoc," I say, "how's your overdose?"

"She is okay, Leon. The medicine team put her in the ICU They are not pleased, but they came."

"I'll bet. Is she on a ventilator?"

He nods, his thick black hair falling over his eyes. He needs a haircut. He has a family and probably hasn't had time. He hands me a chart and describes an eighty-five-year-old woman with abdominal pain, then the other chart, a twenty-six-year-old woman with a headache, vomiting, and screaming in pain. She has had such furious visitations before. Her brain has been CAT scanned and electroencephalographed, treated with half a dozen different pills to stop her migraines. She still has them.

"You think it's the same old thing that she's had before?" I ask him.

"Probably."

"Probably? You think she's probably not ruptured an aneurysm in her head and about to die?"

Uncertainty crosses his face.

"Dr. Mendel," Ruby calls to me, "I got that Dr. Rothman on the phone."

I wave acknowledgment. "Okay," I turn back and grin at him. "You're probably right. What do you want to do?"

"Well, she says the DHE and Reglan usually works for her."

"You know how to give it?"

"Not really."

"Okay, the nurses know." I move toward the phone. "Order 10 milligrams of Reglan I.V., wait ten minutes, then give one milligram of the D.H.E."

I pick up the phone and plug my other ear with a finger. The noise level is rising with every bed full, kids crying, people groaning or cursing.

"Dr. Rothman?" I attempt a polite tone.

"Yes, who's this?" a tired, irritated voice replies.

"This is Leon Mendel. I'm one of the Emergency Department attendings on—"

"Will you please move my patient, Mr. Skilkin, to St. Joseph's Hospital. I will take care of him there. I don't know how he got into your E.R." Ruby is right; his speech is slurred. Oh well, it's Saturday night.

"Well, the paramedics brought him here, sir, because he was having severe chest pain which they judged to be cardiac in nature and they are required to bring such patients to the nearest hospital. I'm inclined to agree with them and—"

"Yes, I'm sure you're right. Now if you would be so kind as to put him back in an ambulance and—"

"Well, I wish I could, Dr. Rothman, but I'm not sure he's stable for transfer. He's having ongoing pain. We're pretty cautious nowadays with EMTALA and all."

"EMTALA! More government horseshit! What's his ECG show?"

"He has inverted T-waves in the anterior chest leads."

"Oh, he's had that for years, son. Just ship him on out and he'll be fine."

"Well, sir, Mr. Skilkin tells me he's never had an ECG before."

Ruby looks at me. I roll my eyes.

The phone is briefly silent, then, "Listen, son, let me speak to your attending. I admire your caution but there's no need to worry. I can't be having my patients at Municipal."

"I am the attending."

Another silence. Sonya approaches me, anxious. She has been talking on the radio.

"Just a minute, please, Dr. Rothman."

"Leon," she says, "the other girl from that accident is on the way. She's a full code. They're doing CPR"

"Terrific. Tell Kaminsky to stick around. How far out are they?"

"Five minutes."

I nod. "Dr. Rothman, I don't mean to be unreasonable about this but it would violate our standard of care as well as federal regulations if we transfer Mr. Skilkin to another facility. I would be happy to have our internal medicine team take care of him and I'm sure they would consult cardiology as well."

"I don't need a damn cardiologist to help me take care of the man."

"Well, sir, I'm afraid I don't have time to discuss this any further. Would you like to come here and care for him yourself?"

"I'm not coming down to that madhouse in the middle of the night."

That's my answer. "Okay, sir, then I'll call our internal medicine team and arrange for him to be admitted here." He starts to talk but I continue. "Would you like them to contact you after they have seen him?"

"You're stealing my patient, young fella." Anger coarsens his voice.

"I have no choice." I feel my own pulse quicken, my own anger begin. "You're welcome to come down here and care for him yourself. You are also free to contact the chief of the Internal Medicine Department if you feel that your patient's care is inappropriate. I'm sorry we can't reach agreement."

There is only silence. Fuck it. I hang up. "You lazy asshole," I mutter to no one.

"Dr. Mendel," Ruby feigns shock.

"'You're stealing my patient,' he says to me. Fuck him. Ruby, get internal medicine down here to see Skilkin, please. Tell them he's a probable MI and they need to see him within 30 minutes."

The radio sounds again; a man in a coma after being clubbed in a fight. Ten minutes out.

I start toward the trauma bays. Lydia approaches me, chart in hand.

"Okay, gimme the 25-word version. There's some bad stuff coming by ambulance."

She hesitates, then speaks. "Okay, eighteen-year-old female with crampy pelvic pain and moderate amount of vaginal bleeding. She says—"

"Is she stable?" I reach for the chart.

"Well, she looks stable to me."

"Okay. Is she pregnant?"

"Probably not. She had a period two weeks ago. And she says she has not been sexually active."

"Okay, they're all pregnant until proven otherwise. You have to—"

"Oh, c'mon." She looks insulted.

"I know it seems callous and sexist and all that. But take my word for it, you'll see why before the month is out. Every vaginal bleeder is an ectopic pregnancy until proven otherwise."

She shakes her head. "You must order dozens of pregnancy tests, hundreds."

"We do. Lydia, it saves these girls' lives. They won't tell you everything. We can talk about it more in a while. Order a CBC and pregnancy test. Ruby will show you how. Then come over to the trauma bays."

Kaminsky and Manny Altman, senior neurosurgery resident, are talking over the comatose girl. Red fluid, saline mixed with blood, is flowing from a thin tube protruding from below her navel, a peritoneal lavage catheter inserted to see if she is bleeding internally. She is. X-rays of her neck, chest, pelvis, and shattered thigh bone glow on the wall viewbox.

“Gentlemen,” I say, “what's the plan?”

“Looks like a quick trip to the CT scanner,” Kaminsky says. “See what’s going on in her head, then on to the O.R.”

“Sounds good. Her girlfriend is about two minutes out; full code with CPR in progress.”

Altman squints at me. “Same accident?” He has pale blotchy skin and his voice squeaks when he’s nervous.

“Yup, they had a hard time getting her out. I don't know any more than that.” I look back at Kaminsky. “If she had no vitals when they got her out then I'm probably going to call it, let her go.”

“Let her go?” Altman says. “You won’t crack her chest?”

“Survival from cardiac arrest from blunt trauma is virtually zero,” Kaminsky says, “maybe one in a hundred thousand cases, not worth the risk of exposure to the staff. If she’s flat line she’s dead.”

“Is your attending around?” I ask him. This will be a decision I would prefer not to make alone.

“He's on his way.”

They both gaze thoughtfully at me, through me, at nothing.

“So, Manny,” I say, “there's a guy coming in a coma after being clubbed in a fight. You need to get cooking on this girl here and get her through the scanner so we can move quickly on him.”

They turn back to the gurney.

“Leon,” Watanabe sticks a chart in my face. “This is a four year old with meningitis, I'll bet anything. Fever, lethargic, stiff neck, looks classic.”

“Okay, what do you want to do?” I hear the rumble of an ambulance outside. A nurse moves toward the doors.

“A spinal tap but you gotta see the kid first. That’s the rule.”

“Right. No, wrong; not this time.” I hand him back the chart. “Too much going on. Order his labs and page pediatrics stat. Let them do it. Then get back over here.”

He nods, snatches the chart and turns away.

“Ted,” I call after him. “Sick kids are top priority. Make sure the peds team gets down here.”

He gives me a thumbs up.

I punch the intercom switch. “Ruby.”

“Yes, hon.”

“Find Icky and get him over to trauma C right away.”

I walk out through the wide double doors. The big blue and white box of a city aid car sits in the glare of arc lights. Its engine is still on and rainwater runs down its sides. I didn't even know it was raining. The heavy summer air is mixed with exhaust.

Claudette and one of the nurses pull open the rear doors. There is shouting inside. Lee Moses, a black paramedic, jumps down and sees me, meets my gaze. He shakes his head. Another is doing chest compressions in the crowded compartment. They wear the tan canvas fireman's pants, held by suspenders over grey sweat-stained tee shirts.

A frantic voice is yelling, "Fuck the monitor. Get the oxygen bottle. All right, LET'S GO, LET'S GO!"

The stretcher slides out. It's spindly legs drop down, like an insect landing. Moses snaps them into locked position. Two other paramedics jump out.

A body lies amid the wires and tubes, skin bloodless and sallow in the glare. One eye is swollen shut, the skin purple and bulging. Her head and neck are the dull blue of cyanosis.

A feeling, something cold, sickening, starts inside me.

They move her quickly toward the open doors. One of them scurries beside the gurney, struggling to keep up the CPR, to keep blood moving through her body.

"LEON," the crew chief shouts at me, Dan Sylvester, a tall stout paramedic, usually soft-spoken. His face shines with sweat. "You gotta do her, man. You gotta crack her chest quick."

"Tell me what happened, Dan." We follow them.

"She was talking to me, Leon." He is panting, voice panicky. "It took a long time to get her out. Too long, God damn it."

"When did she stop talking?"

"I don't know. Just a few minutes ago."

They lift her onto the gurney. Nurses move in close.

"Do you want a Trauma Code, Leon?" Jenna asks me.

"Not yet."

"WHY NOT?" Dan shouts in my face.

I reach up and grab his shoulders. "Calm down, Dan. Did she have a pulse when you got her out?"

He stares, eyes wide.

"No. Doc, she didn't," Lee Moses says.

I move over to the girl. Icky appears on the other side.

"How long was she pulseless before you got her out?"

"We couldn't reach her," Dan says.

"When did she stop talking?"

“She stopped talking about ten minutes before we got her out,” Lee says.

One of the nurses is bagging her, trying to push oxygen into her lungs. Only the right side of her chest rises. The left side is hugely swollen, with the bubbly feel of air under the skin. Where ribs should be there is no resistance. The heart monitor shows a flat line. Her belly is swollen and faintly purple, full of blood.

That feeling, fear, no, worse than fear, grows stronger. Zach, what is this? I haven’t felt this before.

“When did she stop breathing?” I say.

“Couple minutes after that.”

“YOU DON'T KNOW THAT!” Dan yells at him.

“She was not breathing for ten minutes before you got her out?” I look at Lee Moses.

“YOU COULDN'T TELL,” Dan screams. “SHE WAS TALKING TO ME, LEON.”

“Are you sure, Lee?”

“NO, HE’S NOT SURE!” Dan spins me around and shakes me. “JUST DO IT, LEON. WHY CAN'T YOU JUST CRACK HER CHEST AND FIND OUT?”

Claudette's blue bulk appears. “You let go a' him, son.” Her soft voice is startling.

“I'm sure, Doc,” Lee says to me. “She was dead when we got her out.”

“YOU DON'T KNOW THAT,” Dan says, “YOU DON'T KNOW HOW LONG SHE WASN'T BREATHING.” He takes deep sobbing breaths.

“Flat line on the monitor?”

“Flat line from the start,” Lee says.

I look at Icky. “Not breathing for maybe ten minutes, lifeless on extrication. Flat line. No response to fluids and CPR.”

Another pair of paramedics rolls a stretcher by; the head-injured man.

Icky shakes his head slowly. “She’s dead. Let her go.”

“NO, NO! GOD DAMN YOU GUYS.” Dan shoves one of his crew out of the way and starts violent chest compressions. “DON'T LET HER DIE LIKE THAT. DON'T STAND THERE AND JUST TALK HER TO DEATH.” Ribs snap under his hands, the gurney shakes.

I wrap my arms around him from behind and pull him away. “Stop it, Dan. Stop it. She's dead.” I turn him around. “She's dead, Dan. We're not letting her die. She's dead already. We're not going to rip open her chest cause it won't help.”

“You could at least try,” he growls, shrugging away my arms.

“It's too late, Dan. There's no chance to save her, none, zero.”

He puts his hands to his face. “I was talking to her. She’s a nice girl. She was scared.” He looks at me again, tears starting. “I told her she wouldn't die, Leon. I told her I wouldn't let her.”

“You didn't let her die, Dan. You did all the right stuff. She’s been hurt too bad. Too bad for anybody to save.”

His crew takes his arms and walks him away.

Chapter Three

When someone dies, Zach, that's when I think of you, when a patient dies. Why is that? Kind of morbid, don't you think? There's that time, finally, that moment when everyone around the gurney knows it's coming, or that it's already come. Even the family, if they're in the room. Sometimes it's good to have them in the room. They can see the process and it's not such a shock. They can stand in there with us and feel it come, too.

It's almost a relief when it comes, when the struggle stops, the rush of putting in tubes and making decisions. Then, when we stop CPR, stop sticking in needles and—

"LEON," Wanda shouts to me as she scoots a loaded wheelchair through the department. With one hand she holds a slumped figure from falling out.

"Icky, can you do the head injury?" I yell across the station.

He nods. "I got it. Go."

"C'mon, Phil," I say to Patterson, scribbling on a chart nearby.

"He's an old lunger," Wanda says in the room. "Wife says he couldn't breathe tonight."

Bluish gray skin, flaccid jowls on an inanimate face, unconscious. Phil grasps under his arms. I take his bony legs. We heave him onto the gurney. He is mainly bones and a barrel chest.

A lunger, a man whose lungs have suffered the smoke of three or four packs of cigarettes every day for decades, whose fine spongework of tiny alveoli has been scarred and shredded into the stiff empty pockets of emphysema, always infected, barely able to take in enough oxygen to keep him alive. Now a cold or a virus has pushed him over the edge. Or perhaps his heart has given up, exhausted from years of pumping blood through those stiff lungs.

He's not really old, fifty-five, but he looks seventy with hide-like skin, tobacco-stained fingers. He lies gasping, barely moving any air. I look at Phil.

"C'mon, Leon, bag him," he says, loud, irritated that even now I'm doing the game, being the teacher. I grab the Ambu bag with its mask and start trying to push air into the man's chest.

"Crash cart," Phil says to Wanda, ripping open the man's shirt. Buttons fly. "Let's see what his heart's doing." He grabs the defibrillator paddles from the cart and holds them to the bony chest. On the heart monitor a flat green line appears with an occasional wide spike.

"He's agonal," Phil says.

Agonal, as in agony, the final agony, the last beats of a dying heart. “You’re right,” I say in a neutral tone, watching him. He’s smart, a senior resident. He can do this, make the decisions, give the commands.

His clear gray eyes flicker over mine. “You never quit, do you, Leon? Okay, hit the code switch and intubate him. Wanda, start chest compressions.”

I slide a finger beneath the metal protector on the wall and flip the little blue switch there. Again, that cold feeling rises inside me, not fear, dread maybe. You could call it dread. Not of something happening now, but of something coming. It’s been there the whole time, this feeling has, since out on the ambulance ramp. I want to walk away, to be somewhere else when this guy dies, when we give up and let him die. He’s good as dead now, look at him, nothing, truly nothing is going to stop death here.

Wanda positions her hands, one palm over the other, and pushes down. There is a loud crunch, his stiff decrepit ribs snapping under her pressure. She cringes but continues. It’s not the first time we’ve traded a few ribs for the faint chance of restarting a heart.

Someone hands me the airway box from the crash cart. Open it, find the cool steel laryngoscope blade, click it onto the handle, the tiny bulb lights up, fumble through the plastic wrappers for an 8-millimeter tube. Quickly now, this guy’s not breathing, his brain cells are dying, rank by rank, legion by legion. Open the slick wrapper, take the tube in your hand. I should have gloves on. No time. Find the syringe, fill it with air, attach it to the valve, lever open the man’s mouth, slide in the blade, hope he doesn’t vomit.

“Stop, Wanda.” The rocking of his body under her hands stops. Don’t vomit, old guy, whatever your name is. Dentures rattle loose in his mouth, pull them out, slimy disgusting things. Lift the tongue with the blade, look for the cords, lift some more, there’s the tiny slit between his vocal cords, now the tube, gently, quickly, okay, it’s in. Hold it steady, push the plunger on the syringe, inflate the balloon. “Okay, Wanda, go ahead.”

A respiratory therapist has arrived and takes the tube from my hand to start breathing for the man. I hear the switchboard operator's voice call the code through the hospital.

“Took her long enough,” Phil says, stooped over an arm. “She must have been doing her nails.” Blood drips from an IV catheter he has inserted. With a twist he attaches tubing to it.

“He needs some epi,” Phil says, taping the IV in place. I fumble again in the crash cart for an amp of epinephrine, sitting in rows of little boxes. Pop-top boxes for fast opening. Out slide the syringe and amp, now pop off their plastic tops, then fit the two together with a twist.

“Epinephrine.” I hand him the syringe to shoot into the man’s vein.

With luck his heart will start back up, if too many cells haven't died. And with more luck, much more luck, he might even wake up. If too many brain cells haven't suffocated, too many thousands of neurons with their webs of synapses, so delicate, so sensitive to a few moments of no blood, no oxygen. We are breathing for him now, forcing oxygen into his lungs, more oxygen than they've seen in years. He might survive, brain damaged, or comatose, to lie somewhere in a smelly nursing home for another year or two until he dies. But if he's really lucky he won't. What he really needs is to die here and now in whatever peace we allow him.

A tiny frightened woman appears in the doorway. "Here's the wife, Phil," I say. "I'll talk to her."

I take her arm and turn her back into the hallway, away from this scene. "Ma'am, I'm Dr. Mendel. What happened to your husband tonight?"

Her face is pinched, sallow, no doubt a longtime smoker, too. She holds a gray handkerchief up to her mouth with both hands and stares through smudged glasses, watching the code team run into the room, an ICU nurse, a pharmacist, and the internal medicine residents, Todd Pinehurst and his intern again.

This feeling, this cold dread, it's death, the feeling of death. And in that moment of her stillness I see it in her. Death slides into her unmoving eyes, turns them dull and lifeless, shouts at me for an instant until she moves.

"What did you say?"

I touch her hand. "Ma'am, we need to know some information about your husband."

"He couldn't breathe," she says. "Just like every night. He couldn't breathe, only tonight was worse. He wouldn't let me call an ambulance."

"Did he have any chest pain?"

"No, I don't think so. He never tells me..." Her voice trails off.

"Has he had any heart trouble before?"

"No, no, just his breathing, his lungs."

"What medicines does he take? Do you know?"

She opens a jumbled purse. "I used to keep a list."

It doesn't matter, I want to say, it doesn't make a molecule of difference, lady. We're just going through the motions because...because this is what we do, because this is all there is to do, all that's left to do.

Her shaking hands fumble inside the purse, then give up. "I don't know where it is." The skin of her face looks as if it might crack, the folds and wrinkles worn deep, now contorting with fear, grief. The chaplain arrives, relieving me of her.

Patterson does the Advanced Cardiac Life Support routine with Pinehurst looking on, carping at his every move. Intravenous drugs and electrical shocks to jumpstart the man's spent heart, even high dose epinephrine, 10 milligrams at once, enough to put a normal heart into seizures. Fifteen minutes work and still nothing but a flat line on the monitor.

The rest of the code team stands watching, waiting to be dismissed. If he were going to respond it would have been right away. They know it. We all know it.

"Why don't you end it, Phil," I say. "We've got other people to take care of."

"Then go do it, Leon," Pinehurst says quickly, as if he's been waiting for the chance. "Patterson and I can do this."

"Not appropriate, Todd." He's trying to irritate me. "The emergency department attending supervises all codes. You know that."

The weasel eyes in his flabby face glance upward as he makes a be-my-guest gesture with his pink hand.

"Okay, let's stop. Nice try, Phil. Would you speak to the wife? She's in the quiet room with the chaplain." I turn to Pinehurst. "Your expertise was invaluable, Dr. Pinehurst, as usual."

"Fuck you, Leon," he says.

It worked. He's made me angry. "I don't think 'Fuck you' is the appropriate response to an attending, Dr. Pinehurst, or any of your fellow physicians. And I'll be more than happy to discuss it with your chief resident. Now why don't you quietly disappear back upstairs."

I step next to the gurney.

Oh, Zach, look at this, another corpse, another dead sack of blood and muscles and guts and brains. And the man in the glass is there again, in dull green scrubs with a stethoscope hung around his neck, a solemn ghost staring back at me. Is it you, brother? What would you say to me if you could? Would you tell me to stop sending souls to you? In that place where you are, whatever place it is, where you've been for so long. How long? Thirty-three years minus eight—you were eight, right? We were both eight—twenty-five years ago.

Wanda ignores me, removing tubes and wires. She works quickly. We need the room.

Something screams from within this dead flesh, a long thin dying scream. I shiver and feel sweat start. I glance up. Wanda hasn't heard it. But I have.

* * *

Finally, around four, there is a lull. I walk out to the ambulance ramp. The rain has stopped. The dark city hums, cooling down. A cop nods to me.

Zach, brother Zach, do you see what I am, what this place is? There is death here, with its foul smell. Souls and minds packaged in flesh, that sweat and puke and bleed and gasp. Their bones break, their vessels tear, their hearts flounder, their lungs fill with fluid and pus. We try to stop it, hide it under bright lights, behind long words, fight it off with plastic tubes, complex chemicals, fence with it with tiny swords of stainless steel.

Zach, those bodies spoke to me, the old lunger, and that poor girl's corpse, before they moved her to the morgue, her organs crushed and ruptured, her brain silent, cooling and still, its maze of cells and synapses dissolving into a handful of mush. I went back and stood by her. I never do that. Her soul, something, opened a dark cavern in my mind—I saw it like a dream—and then I felt it leave and disappear howling into that darkness.

I've never felt these things before, or heard these sounds. Brother, what has happened?

Seven a.m., Peter Schulman appears, scrubbed and wary. "Well, how was the night?" He eyes his residents for the day.

"Bad," Icky says, drooped against a counter, his head on a hand. "Seven deaths and two major fuck-ups."

"Major fuck-ups? What happened?" Peter is the medical director for the department, short, balding, with tiny quick eyes.

"Matt Beauregard, the surgery R-3, and his intern," Icky says. "They stuck a chest tube into the heart of a kid with a simple gunshot wound to the belly and a pneumothorax. Hit his right coronary and they couldn't save him. Used a trocar, for God's sake. And the other was..." He glances at me.

"A girl with a ruptured tubal pregnancy that bled out into her belly," I say. "She looked stable and nobody checked on her for about an hour and then we found her dead." I shrug. "At least I assume that's what she had."

"Whose patient?" Peter says.

"Mine, my intern and technically my patient. I hadn't actually seen her. Things were crazy here for a while."

"I'd call it a systems error," Icky says. "Insufficient nurses to check on patients, insufficient rooms to put patients in. Hell, Leon hadn't even laid eyes on the poor girl when we found her dead. Improper triage, I don't know."

While Icky goes on I look for Lydia. She sits alone across the station, pale, staring away from us, at nothing. Is she the worst casualty of this night? That girl was her patient. She had examined her and, according to the unspoken rules of this game, should have figured out how serious she was, how immediate her problem. I step toward her but she stands and walks away.

I listen to Ted and Rohit and Phil hand off to the day-shift residents the five warm bodies remaining, two drunks sleeping it off, one schizophrenic awaiting a bed upstairs, a kid with abdominal pain, and a pregnant teenage girl who is bleeding, awaiting ultrasound. Yet another, maybe this one will survive.

I pour my cold coffee down a sink and move toward the locker room to change clothes.

Finally, the quiet single uninterrupted task of driving home, windows down, feel the air, put my mind in neutral. Sunday morning, six lanes of empty concrete, heating up already in the sun. The factories are quiet, Frigidaire's plant like a wall on one side, Proctor and Gamble sprawled in its valley below on the other. A simple job would be nice, running a machine, sitting at a desk.

Two deaths, Zach, two avoidable, preventable deaths. Damn, I'm going to catch a lot of grief about this night. That kid with the chest tube in the heart, can you believe he died! Beauregard came down from the operating room and told me. Finkel hit his right coronary artery with the trocar. Talk about bad luck. See, you're not supposed to use trocars anymore. They're old fashioned, barbaric. Unless you're a resident and the attending on your service is so damn old fashioned and barbaric that he still uses them. Which Chester Graffen is, so his boys, his residents, go and use a trocar to put in the chest tube because Beauregard knows that when Graffen arrives in the operating room and Finkel has to tell him what's going on and Finkel says in his quivering voice, "and then we put in a chest tube," that Graffen is going to say, "Did you use a trocar?" And Beauregard knows they'll catch holy hell if they say no.

So they did a bypass graft to try to fix the artery but by the time they realized what had happened and got him onto the heart pump and then got the graft sewed into place there was so much damage to his heart they couldn't get it started again and had to let him go.

So Beauregard tells me that Graffen wants to have a talk with me. In fact, just when I see old Graffen come stomping into the department, somebody gives a yell from Gyn 1. Lydia's vaginal bleeder was waiting for her ultrasound to see if she had a tubal pregnancy, this black girl named Katrina Morris. I run in and there's this dead girl lying on the pelvic table, her belly's huge with blood. Guess she did have a tubal pregnancy, a ruptured one and all her blood was in her belly. Damn, Zach, this kind of thing should not happen.

So we stick in a couple central lines, a femoral and a subclavian and give her about six liters of fluid, four units of blood, and do CPR for about half an hour. We turned her blood back on as fast as we could, but you could see it wasn't going to work. No response. She was dead, just died in there quietly, all by herself in that room. Nobody had checked on her for two hours. She just ruptured her tubal pregnancy and bled to death into her abdomen, not a drop on the floor.

Great couple of cases, huh, Bro. I'm going to get fried; Emergency Services Committee, Ob/Gyn Committee, Quality Assurance Committee, Risk Management Committee. Damn, I'll be explaining this night for a year. And poor Lydia; it was almost her first patient. I hope it doesn't spoil her month in the department. She's a smart girl.

What about that Rita what's-her-name and her kid with C.F., her adopted kid with C.F., for God's sake. Who in the world would intentionally adopt a kid like that? When I went back to check on her she asked me if she could cook me dinner some time. Wonder what she wanted. I guess that's an innocent enough come-on. Hard to turn down such an exquisite face. Also a little hard to trust. Too bad she drinks so much.

Home, my restful nurturing home, my depressing frightening home. Damn, Jasmine's car in the driveway, her stupid Peugeot she thinks is so sophisticated. Who cares. Okay, gird yourself. Maybe she'll just let you go to sleep.

I step inside and glimpse a white disk headed for my teeth. Duck!

Crash. Damn, a plate, she's throwing plates. I look up.

"YOU GODDAMN BASTARD, LEON. I HATE YOU." She stands across the room, by the stove, pale green panties and a tee shirt, no bra. She looks good, especially good when she's angry.

"I know that," I say, "and have known it for about three months now."

"Fuck you." She is fidgety, nervous, the way she gets when she's been doing cocaine.

"Is there a particular issue we need to discuss for me to be allowed to go to sleep for a while or may I simply go? I might lock the door, however. Don't you have rehearsal or something this afternoon?" I'll get angry soon, too. I can feel it.

"Your asshole attorney called last night to discuss our upcoming happy event."

Meaning our divorce. "He's not my attorney, Jasmine. He's our attorney. Remember, we thought we might be able to—"

"End this without strangling each other? Not a chance, asshole."

She wings another plate, which whizzes in before I can twist away. It nails my shoulder.

"Ow, shit. God damn you." I bend down and find it with my hand, watching for the next. It comes and shatters on the mantel behind me.

Anger grabs me now. "Good shot, Jas, you're starting to get your range. Here, try this one again." I spin it back at her, satisfied with the flicker of fear that crosses her face. The plate misses. "I'm touched that you're at least using our wedding china. Very symbolic and all."

She turns toward the cupboard to find more plates.

“Any chance we could cool this anger to its usual distant apathetic smolder and both live here today?” My own damn home and I can't even go to sleep here. I don’t want to argue or fight or even talk to her.

“You know...” I begin, but my voice falters. I almost want to cry. “You know I could call the police, Jas. You’re assaulting me, also destroying property that’s mine, too.” I feel stupid, struggling for words. “Community property, you stupid bitch.”

“THEN CALL ‘EM, YOU BASTARD.” She hurls another one, wide into the wall.

May as well leave. I back out the door. Another plate shatters inside, then another and another. She wins this one. I can’t deal with it.

Tears come now as I walk to the car. It’s sad, this home we had, this start of a home and a family, trashed, emotionally ransacked by that creature I married. Thank God she never got pregnant.

Driving over to Icky's, to Kentucky suburbia, far above the Ohio River on the freeway bridge. A string of barges slides along down below, the water shimmering in the morning sun. The other bridges march along upstream, stately, almost empty.

There was an AIDS patient, too. I helped Lydia with him, a cadaverous twenty-four year old in a coma. Oh, Zach, I don’t think she’d seen one like him before, end-stage, a skeleton covered with skin. He probably had cryptococcal meningitis or some other disastrous infection that only AIDS patients get. I think Lydia was shocked, but she didn’t let on.

His mother was there with him, the poor woman. She’d been caring for him at home. She fussed around the gurney, straightening sheets, helping move him so Lydia could examine him, but you could tell she was exhausted. At five in the morning, she should have been home dreaming about grandchildren.

“Look what’s happened to him,” she said, “He was such a healthy boy, a cheerful boy.” Lydia held her hand and let her talk for a while.

Death was there, too, Zach, around that bed. The air, something, was different. I had to leave them, Lydia and the woman and that awful thing on the gurney.

Ah, rich midwestern suburbia, Icky’s huge rambling lawn scattered with trees, his new house with its three-car garage. Birds, peace and quiet. I can hear Sarah's shriek through a window. She and Icky fight all the time.

I walk in through the front door and head for the noise. I almost make the fridge when Sarah sees me. “Leon, we were hoping you'd drop by. Maybe you could referee, or keep score. I mean, since you’re here anyway.” She uses sarcasm the way Jasmine uses plates.

"Thanks, sweetheart. It's so nice to feel welcome. Maybe I'll just sneak a beer and steal off to your hammock outside for a few hours. Remember the old open invitation? 'Any time things get too terrible with Jasmine, Leon, you come and stay with us. Sometimes when two people are distancing themselves...'"

But Sarah has already distanced herself from me, yelling at Icky again. She is tall, athletic, a little horse-like in her tennis clothes.

Icky shrugs at me from a barstool, leaning exhausted on the wet-bar. He nods toward the refrigerator. "Hey, open one for me, too, Leon. I always like a beer when I go to a fight."

I hand him a Pabst and head for the patio.

Sarah's shrill voice pinions me against the glass door. "Leon, will you please tell me why your partner has to come home after every shift and tell me how hard the nurses work, and how damn noble they are?"

Icky slowly shakes his head.

"I think I'll sit this one out, Sarah." I slide open the door. "We had a long night. Can I have the hammock for a couple hours?"

"Go for it," Icky says.

"Go for it," Sarah growls, "God, listen to him, Mr. Macho here. He can't just say 'Sure,' or 'Be my guest,' or something a normal person might say. No, it's gotta be something macho, as if you were Rambo or somebody."

Icky and I sneak a glance at each other.

"Rocky," I say.

"What?" She turns on me.

"You mean Rocky. It was Rocky that said that."

"Said what?" she shrieks again.

"Said 'Go for it.' Rocky Three. Never mind, nothing." I duck out onto the back lawn. Rebop, their big pointer, trots out with me.

Icky's got his creature comforts down. I slide the huge hammock on its green metal frame into the shade of two trees by the fence. The dog watches me solemnly, then trots over when I lie down. I scratch his neck, staring up at the leaves.

That girl, Zach, the one with the tubal pregnancy. I knew she was dead when I walked into the room. Not in the usual way, not because of the pallor or the stillness. You can resuscitate people out of that sometimes. No, her soul had gone, I felt it. Her poor simple soul had gone screaming away into God knows where.

Into black nothingness, death, that same place you went to, Zach, so long ago. Are you there still, in some huge black abyss, some endless place that just goes on and on?

I shiver as the feeling passes through me. Something has changed, Zach, hasn't it?

* * *

Net after net of alveoli spread around me, blood flowing, cells tumbling through the lacework of capillaries. Beyond, high above me, arch the pale beams of ribs, red muscle in between, neat bundles stretching and contracting. I know it's coming but I can only wait, watching the delicate spongework of these lungs. Whose lungs? Now a patch of muscle explodes in blood and the dull grey steel of a trocar stabs at me.

Okay, okay, I'm awake, sweating and hot. The sun has moved right over my face. I close my eyes and replay the images in my mind. Guess I don't need Freud to puzzle out this one.

Back to the house. The dog has abandoned me. I sneak open the glass door. It's quiet. I hope she let Icky get some sleep. No blood on the floor, no broken plates.

I find the phone and punch in my own number. Nine rings, where's the answering machine? Jasmine answers.

"So are you done throwing plates?"

Long silence. I hate her melodrama.

"Yes, that was stupid," she says. "I let you get the better of me."

My fault, huh. Oh, well, we're way past talking these days. "May I return peacefully to my home?"

"Your home?"

Shit. "Sorry, Jas. But saying our home sounds a little ridiculous these days, don't you think? How about 'the home in which we both currently reside?' Is that better?"

"Look, Leon, I don't give a damn. Come home if you want. I'm going out anyway."

Icky's daughter, Anna, comes roaring through the room, the dog barking behind her.

"Okay." Now I pause. Even simple things like saying goodbye get all screwed up. 'See you soon,' implies affection. 'See you later,' doesn't fit. I don't want to see her later. 'Do you want me to wait till you go out?' No, then I'm giving in, establishing a new precedent.

"So?" Jasmine says finally, hard-voiced.

"So nothing," I say, trying for a neutral tone. "Bye." I put the phone down, not wanting to hear her reply, guessing she said nothing.

"Hi, Leon. Here," Anna squeals. A tennis ball comes flying, followed by the dog.

"Hi, goofy, where are your folks?"

"In bed," she says with a significant look.

She's eleven, so I keep my face in neutral. "In bed? They must have made up."

"They always do. Throw me the ball."

"That's reassuring."

"Yeah, but Dad said we're going to the pool."

"Well, better a happy well-rested Dad to take you there than a crab."

"He'll have that F.F.G.," she says with a giggle.

"That what?"

"F.F.G."

"What's F.F.G?"

"Can't tell. Come on, Rebop." She moves toward the glass door.

"Well, I don't even want to know." This is an old game.

"FRESHLY FUCKED GLOW," she shrieks, tearing out toward the yard.

* * *

"Any low flying plates?" I try to joke as I walk in the door.

"Cute," she says coldly from the couch, still in just panties and tee shirt. Is she tantalizing me? We haven't touched in weeks.

"You look quite fetching. What's the occasion?"

A cigarette burns in her hand, its smell mingles with marijuana just smoked. "I hate this, Leon."

"Hate what?"

"What? What do you think? Living here, walking around each other, like living in the ruins of an emotional holocaust."

"The aftermath of nuclear war, perhaps? Deadly radiation poisoning the survivors."

No comment, the vacant venomous stare, the slight squint in the smoke. That mouth, I'd like to tie her up, tantalize her, torture her—

"You're a bastard, Leon. You don't care at all anymore. Emotionally you've packed up and left already."

"Speaking of packing up and leaving?"

"Four days, damn it. You know that as well as I do. I can't get into the place for four more days."

"Too bad your mother doesn't live nearby."

"Fuck you. This place is as much mine as it is yours. I'm making it easy for you by moving out myself. Even slimeball lawyer O'Connor admitted that."

"Well, do you think you can maintain a nonaggressive posture in the meantime?"

She rearranges herself on the couch, lying on her side, eyeing me. "Maybe. Wanta screw?"

"Screw? You are too weird when you get high, Jas. Especially lately."

"It might be fun in a macabre sort of way," she says, unsmiling.

Her aerobicized legs and anorexic waist are tempting as usual.

"The totally meaningless fuck, huh?" I say. "The spiteful fuck. Just take out our feelings and leave them in the other room, right?"

"Something like that. Or are you worried about your little problem?"

"My little problem?" I'm beginning to feel like I'm the cobra and she's the mongoose.

"You haven't been exactly performing on demand lately."

Lately? It's been weeks since we even considered sex. "Oh, that little problem. I see. Actually I was rather proud of my performance in that regard, or shall we say lack of performance. I think it reflects an emotional sensitivity said to be lacking among men these days. You haven't exactly been little Miss Responsiveness yourself."

"Perhaps you're reverting to your previous sexual identity? Maybe that's really you, Leon, after all. Maybe all this has been—"

"My what?"

"What was his name, your gay lover of years ago? Fritz or something?"

"His name was Fitz, and that was a long time ago. Sorry, Jas, but if you're trying to get at me you need a better angle than that. I've never been ashamed of that relationship, and you're sure as hell not going to make me now." Fitz, huh, I haven't thought about him in a while.

She crushes out the cigarette in the cluttered ashtray and stands, stretching, pulling her shirt tight over her breasts. "Well, Mr. Sensitive Heterosexual, I'm feeling very erotic right now. If you think you could surrender yourself to your purely physical urges I'll be on the bed. No commitment, no consequences, just a willing body, female body that is." She walks out of the room.

Right, just a willing body. Where has that unencumbered body been the last couple years, that same body so good at finding excuses, so good at withholding itself.

Chapter Four

"Okay, Mega-Watt, what have you got?" It's Tuesday morning.

"Mega-Watt?" Ted Watanabe says. "Leon, please." He looks still tired from the weekend.

"New nickname, I thought you might like it. It's you, Ted, with your electric personality, your lightning-fast mind."

"And of course implies no reference to my physical size."

"Physical size? Course not, never even crossed my mind."

"Right, thanks, Leon, I'm glad to see your mind is sufficiently unencumbered that you can sit around and dream up little nicknames for the residents while we're busy taking care of the sick and injured."

"It's part of my role as your attending. Okay, so...?" I nod toward the chart in his hand.

"So this mom brought her sixteen-year-old retarded son here. She says—"

"Developmentally delayed," I correct him.

"Sorry, developmentally delayed. Anyway she says—"

"Differently abled, intellectually challenged."

"Damn, Leon, do you want to hear this or should I just go find Cassidy?"

"Sorry, but if you're gonna play the game you gotta know the language."

"Well, it's bullshit language if you ask me. What's wrong with retarded? It always worked just fine before."

"You tell me," I say.

He stares down at the chart, shaking his head.

Rohit is sitting near us, listening, another chart in his hand. The board shows maybe twelve patients in the department.

"It is judgmental," Rohit says. "Such expression implies negativity, something wrong with the person."

"Well, there is something wrong with the person," Ted says. "He's retarded, his brain doesn't function like normal. Who are they trying to fool?"

"We have a case like that in New York," Rohit says, "when I was a third year student. A malpractice case, a teenager who had very bad cerebral palsy, ventilator dependent, lived in a nursing home. He came to the hospital for pneumonia, I think, and he died in the hospital. They thought he was a No-Code and didn't resuscitate him when he finally arrested. Someplace in the chart someone used the word retarded and the family said it was discrimination against a handicapped person. They sued and got a lot of money. Never use that word, Ted," Rohit says gravely.

"Sounds like a great case," Ted says, "the kind that shows the unique fairness of our legal system."

"So enough," I say, "we've got other things to do. Tell me what's wrong with this kid, Ted."

Lydia has been watching us from across the nurses station, not wanting to join in. She is quiet today, serious.

"Okay, this poor sixteen-year-old developmentally delayed male has been vomiting three or four times a day for the past five days, according to Mom. No apparent pain, but he doesn't show pain much, she says. No diarrhea, fever, or other complaints.

"She took him to the General Pediatrics Clinic three days ago and they gave her some suppositories, Compazine or something. Took him to the D.D. Clinic at Children's Hospital, where they usually go, yesterday, and they just told her to stop milk products and put the kid on Tagamet. So poor Billy is still vomiting and Mom decides to bring him here. Two opinions aren't enough, I guess."

"Mendel, may I have a word with you," an impatient growl sounds behind me.

Chester Graffen, in blue scrubs, leans on the counter. His red bullet-like face matches his personality. Terrific, just the man I've been looking forward to talking to.

"Morning, Chester. I'll need about two minutes to hear these cases and—"

"I need to talk to you right now, Mendel. I've got three operating rooms going. Your residents can manage."

Right, and so can yours. "Well, perhaps another time might be preferable when we each have more time," I say in as mild a voice as I can find, like talking calmly to a mugger.

He locks his eyes onto mine. Short gray hair frames his paper scrub hat. He's got twenty-four years here to my three, two coronary bypasses, I've been told, three former wives, and he's survived a couple big-time malpractice cases. "Okay, go ahead," he says, glancing around for a phone.

I suggest to Ted that he consider diabetes and drug toxicity from the anti-seizure medications the boy is on. He orders the appropriate blood tests.

Rohit gets thirty seconds to tell me about his eighty-four-year-old woman with belly pain.

Then Lydia waves a chart at me. “Leon, there’s an AIDS patient here who asked if you were working.” She glances at the clipboard. “Name is Fitzhugh Goddard.”

I stare at her until she says, “Do you know him? Leon?”

A horrible dark hole inside me is opening. “He has AIDS?”

“He says he does. He looks pretty thin. He has a cough and some chest pain, no fever. I thought I’d order a chest X-ray and...”

Fitz is here with AIDS, my friend Fitz. I haven’t seen him in years.

“Leon,” Lydia says, “did you hear me?”

“Yes, fine, order those things. What room is he in?”

“Okay, Mendel,” Graffen's gravel voice scrapes across my thoughts. “Now what the hell happened the other night with that Negro kid?”

My blood pounds through my chest. Fitz with AIDS. Oh, God, remember Fitz, such a wonderful guy.

I stare at Graffen’s mean, intent face. What about that kid? What does he want to hear? He is sitting there like a bull mastiff deciding where to bite me first.

“Why don't you tell me your concerns.” I manage.

“Well, now, we depend on you boys down here in the ER to handle these resuscitations ‘til we get these damn kids into the OR. Used to be we kept a couple of our own residents down here to do the job, but now you got your own specialty and all, so we got no choice but to let you boys call the shots early on.”

“Those were surgery residents who put that hole in the kid's heart.”

“I know that, but you were supposed to be supervising them. Am I right?”

“That's right. I assumed that Matt Beauregard could take over. He's a smart guy. I've worked with him a lot, and as attending on the case my decision was that he could handle it. It was a simple case.”

“Well, it sure as hell didn't end up a simple case,” Graffen says. “That boy died.”

“I know that. I’m as sorry about his death as you are. Beauregard and Finkel misread the chest X-ray because the heart was deviated to the right by the pneumothorax. They made a simple mistake which had disastrous consequences.”

I stop as Graffen glares at me. Chester, you're such an ass. I'm not scared of you. Now, for a moment, death creeps into his face, the slack aged skin, the unmoving eyes. For an instant those eyes turn dull, like someone dead, that moment when you first glance at a patient, that instant of doubt before the eyes move, or the voice sounds. Death howls like a silent beast at me, his eyes two tiny windows into a black horrible emptiness, not just Graffen dead but a world of death, there just beyond, ever present.

Now the lips move and the jaw opens like a cadaver's, mechanical.

"Okay, Mendel, we've both got things to do," he says. "But Surgery Quality Assurance is going to be all over this case. I hate to see a smart kid like Beauregard get a black mark against him for what looks to me like an honest mistake. If you're willing not to point any fingers then I'm willing to do the same." He stands, ready to leave.

I look down, running his words back in my mind, feeling my heart thump. "Right, Chester. That's fine with me." What about the chest tube, the trocar. "Except for—"

"Good, then. Too bad about the boy." He starts to leave. "He didn't look like a criminal himself. Probably a bystander. Damn Negro gangs are out of control."

"Wait a second, Chester. There's one more important point about that case."

He turns and waves a hand. "Sorry, Mendel, gotta get back in the OR. We can discuss it another time." And he's through the double doors, gone.

We will, Graffen, we will. God damn it, the little fucker won that one. He foxed me, or he thinks he did. Well, that kid's death, or rather our killing that kid, is not going to go away that easy.

Fitz, where is he? Look at the board. There, Goddard, F., Bed 9. At least he's in a private room. Are people watching me? Turn and look, two security guys glance down, drinking coffee at a counter. No, I'm imagining.

Fitzhugh Goddard, my old friend Fitz, more than a friend. When did I see him last? At Jasmine's and my wedding, in white tights and waistcoat, and jewelry, three years ago. He was exquisite, gorgeous. He danced with Jas, then with me there before all of them, bold and laughing, our secret intact. Only Jasmine and Icky knew. Did Fitz know then he was HIV positive? How long has he had it?

"What did Graffen want, Leon?" Sonja, the charge nurse, walks by.

"He wanted to compliment us on what a nice job we did with that kid Saturday night."

"Right, I'll bet."

Down the hallway, something growls at me from the doorway of Fitz's room. I stop and stand aside, in sight of the station. I don't care, let them watch. Don't they hear it?

"You okay, Leon?" Icky walks up. "Why are you standing here?"

"Icky, you remember—?" My voice locks up, I can't say the name.

"You look like you saw a ghost."

"It's Fitz," I manage finally. "You remember Fitz?"

"Fitz, yeah, who was Fitz? Oh, yeah, your old friend." His eyes meet mine. His thumb points toward the door. "Is he here? Did he get hurt or something?"

"He's got AIDS. That's what Lydia says."

Icky nods his odd-shaped head, eyes grave behind his glasses. "Have you seen him yet?"

I shake my head.

"You want me to go in with you? He'll probably remember me, too."

I shake it again.

His hand on my shoulder. "Listen, Leon, if you need to talk, I'm your man. Maybe you're trying to keep too many balls in the air."

He watches me until I nod. "Thanks, pal. You'll be the first to know."

He starts down the hall, then turns. "Leon, have you—no, never mind."

"Have I what?"

He squirms, then steps back next to me, and speaks softly. "That was a long time ago, right, Leon? You and Fitz, I mean."

"Yeah, about six years. Why?"

"You've been tested, right?"

"Tested? You mean for HIV? Yeah, I've been tested, Icky. I'm okay." I hold his gaze. "You can kiss me if you want."

"Funny guy." He trudges away.

Now, still, I hear it, something growling from the doorway, or maybe I feel it, like that feeling of death. Zach, what is this? What is happening to me? Maybe I need some time off.

Into the room and there he is, a fragile hollowed face, pale, unshaven, eyes closed, asleep. A younger man sits near the bed. I nod to him.

"Is he sleeping?" I whisper.

The man nods, with a friendly smile.

"I'm Leon Mendel."

He half rises and shakes my hand. "I'm Joel. He's told me about you."

Fitz's breathing is heavy, his nostrils flaring. I sit on a stool by the bed and take his hand. The skin is feverish. He startles and his eyes open. They settle on me.

"Hi, Fitz."

"Leon." He draws back his hand. "You shouldn't touch me."

"I'll wash my hands."

We look at each other. He was so loving then, six years ago, so ardent and honest with me. Can that have really been? I feel myself sweating, shaking inside, speechless.

"I wondered if you'd be here." His voice is hoarse. "What did you used to call it, the meat factory?"

"Right, I did." I feel awkward, unsure what to say.

He eyes the door. "Have you been tested for the virus, Leon? You must have been, right?" The hint of his southern accent remains. It stirs me to hear it, like listening to an old song.

"Yes, I'm okay, Fitz."

"Guess you switched back just in time." He starts to cough, a deep wheezing cough.

I look away. Don't be sick, I want to say, not this sick, Fitz, with this disease.

"Did you meet Joel?" he says finally, sweating now.

"We met." Joel is young, muscular, tan in white summer clothes. He smiles easily.

"Are you always so talkative around your old lovers, Leon?"

Funny, how can he be funny? "Well, they don't often visit me at work. Would you like me to show you around?"

"Right," Fitz says. "The other patients might find it a little disturbing. 'Hello, I'm Dr. Mendel and this is my old lover with AIDS. Do you mind if we take a peek in your room? I promise he won't breathe while he's here.' Or maybe you could cut open someone's chest for us. Crack a chest, isn't that what you call it?"

"Yeah, but it's not exactly a daily occurrence. I'll probably get sued for the last one." I stop. He looks exhausted. So much for banter.

"This must have come on quickly, Fitz."

"Yes, I guess I'm one of the lucky ones. No years of lingering doubt for me. No need for redefinition of identity, no career restructuring for this cowboy." He stops to catch his breath. "Oh, Leon, it's debasing what this does to you, humiliating. Don't examine me, okay? I'm awful. I don't want you to see me."

"That's fine, Fitz." Death again, I feel it, in the room, under the gurney.

"So what about you, Leon? How are you and Jas? Any kids yet?"

"No, not exactly. Things haven't been going too well for us, Fitz. We're getting a divorce. No kids, fortunately. I don't think female tympani players are supposed to have kids."

"She never seemed quite the mommy type." He turns to Joel. "Leon's wife, former wife apparently, plays percussion in the symphony, if you can imagine. But such a mouth she has. Passionate full lips with that cruel twist to them. I think that's what stole Leon here away from us, brought him back to the fold."

"Lips are important," Joel grins. "Especially for a woman. They have lips and they have lips. Oops, enough of this talk." He nods toward the door.

Lydia walks in the room. Back to business. I stand. "Do you have a doctor, Fitz?"

"An older gentlemanly sort named Herb Taft at the HIV Clinic. Do you know him?"

"Taft, yeah, he's a good guy, very sharp."

"Leon." Rohit enters the room, anxious. "There are three victims coming from a house fire. Two of them are in coma, probably they think smoke inhalation."

"Are they intubated?"

He nods.

"Okay, I'll be right there. Page the trauma team."

I turn to Lydia again. "Listen, this is a friend of mine. Just do a brief history and physical and then call Herb Taft at the HIV Clinic. Let him tell you what he wants done."

"Got it."

"Fitz," I say to him, "Taft may want you to stay in the hospital, for a day or two. You might—"

"No, Leon," he shakes his head. "I'm not that sick." He stops for a moment to breathe. "Not yet."

An infant shrieks from a nearby room. I feel my throat tighten now as I look at Fitz, the feeling that comes before tears. He is so gaunt, so ill with this relentless disease that will never go away. So spirited he was, so—

"Leon?" Lydia says.

"Right, well, okay, we can't force you, but a couple days in the hospital now may save you—"

"No, Leon," Fitz says, "don't preach to me. I'm going home. I'll take your medicine but I'm going home." His eyes have not changed, pale gray, quick, fiery still.

The three fire victims lie on gurneys in a row in the trauma bays, soot-covered paramedics coughing and trying to get out of the nurses' way. The closest is a hugely obese woman, a motionless mound of flesh in blackened clothes, her head at one end with a thick endotracheal tube in her mouth.

"Are they burned?" I step closer into the harsh smoke smell.

The paramedic crew chief turns to me, his face a circle of pink skin where his mask protected him, the rest of him black. "They didn't have any flame exposure, Leon. Just smoke, and a lot of it."

The second form is a girl, maybe twelve, also intubated but thrashing, awake, eyes wide in her blackened face. One nurse is talking to her, trying to calm her. Paramedics are tying her hands with white cotton straps to the bedrails so she won't pull out the tube. She'll need sedation quick.

Lydia is bent over the third dark form, Ted next to her. The woman is breathing on her own, not intubated, also obese and soot covered.

"Leon," Rohit calls from the first gurney, anxious, "this one, her pressure is 70 and her pupils are fixed and dilated."

"Not good." I step through the crowd around her, nurses cutting away clothes, trying to start IVs. The X-ray tube rumbles overhead. "What are you going to do?"

The walrus-size woman's skin is gray beneath the soot. At a glance she has no burns. Her pupils are wide, round black holes, unmoving, a gauge of her brain's activity and the gauge is reading zero.

Death. I stare at those holes, that feeling of dread rising in me once more. And there is a hissing sound. What is that?

"Has she got any injuries?" I hear my own voice.

"I do not find any," Rohit says, pushing his delicate hands into her flesh, examining her.

I pull my eyes away. "What's the story?"

"Well, these three were upstairs, they say." Rohit nods toward the paramedic. "Something in the kitchen caught fire. They were trapped."

Shrieks are rising from the third woman. Lydia and the nurses are struggling to keep an oxygen mask on her.

"Leon," the paramedic says, "that one said something about this one's been sick in bed. They were trying to get her out, down the stairs."

"Where'd you find them?"

"The firefighters found them at the top of the stairs. They got trapped. Bad smoke. No trauma that we know of."

The respiratory therapist, a tiny Asian woman, is pushing pure oxygen into the woman's lungs with an Ambu bag.

"Okay, Rohit. Why do you think her pressure's down?"

"It could be from trauma, bleeding inside, or it could be the carbon monoxide. Need to get—"

"Why would the carbon monoxide make you hypotensive?"

"Myocardial suppression. No oxygen is getting to the heart. All the hemoglobin is bound up by the carbon monoxide."

"Good, so you better go after both 'til you know. Send off a blood gas, carboxyhemoglobin level, give her fluids and oxygen, and get her X-rays taken. We'll tap her belly if the surgery boys don't get down here pretty quick."

I step to the girl on the second gurney. "Do we have a name?"

"Tammie," the R.T. at her head says.

I lean down to her ear. "Tammie, can you hear me?"

Her wide eyes stop, focus, and she nods. Her face is blackened, too, eyebrow hairs singed to tiny curls of ash.

I find a calm, loud voice. “Okay, good. I'm Doctor Mendel. You're in the emergency room, Tammie. You're going to be okay but you have to try to lie still so we can help you. That tube in your throat is to help you breathe. We have to leave it there for a little while. Do you understand?”

She nods but it's hard to know for sure. Her arms continue jerking at the restraints. I check her over quickly for injuries; her blood pressure is good. “Okay, Barb,” I say to the nurse, “start giving her some Ativan, one milligram at a time IV, ‘til she calms down a little. We need blood gases, carboxyhemoglobin level, chest X-ray, ECG, trauma bloods, the usual stuff. Let me know as soon as you have the level back.”

“Hi, Leon, what's up?” Matt Beauregard appears, Finkel behind him.

“Hi, Matt. Well, you're still standing. I figured Graffen would have had your butt for breakfast the other day.”

“He did, thanks, and it's not over yet.” His handsome square face looks unperturbed.

“Well, don't let him shake you up. Listen, we got these three victims of a house fire. That one's the worst, comatose, fixed and dilated, hypotensive, no actual burns but probably asphyxiated. Carboxyhemoglobin level is cooking. She needs her belly tapped real quick. Probably needs to go to the hyperbaric chamber. Looks bad. This girl here is not so bad, awake and confused, also no sign of actual—”

“Leon,” Rohit calls, waving at me. Beauregard follows me to the first gurney. “Look at this.” Rohit points to the monitor. Her heart is slowing, its tracing widening. She is dying.

“Pulse is barely palpable,” the nurse says, holding her wrist.

“Open up the fluids. Rohit, start a central line. Start some dopamine."

I look at the R.T. “She ventilating okay?”

The woman nods. I put my stethoscope on her chest. Her breath sounds are loud and clear. “Have you got an ECG?”

Someone hands me the paper. Beauregard looks over my shoulder. “Shit, look at this.” The cardiogram shows the electrical waves of a heart deprived of oxygen, of heart muscle dying.

“Massive ischemia,” Beauregard says.

“No pulse,” the nurse says.

“Okay, start CPR. Finkel, you wanta do chest compressions?”

The awkward intern moves next to her and feels for her sternum beneath the thick fat.

I hear the hiss again, like a serpent sliding around my ankles. Doesn’t anyone else hear that?

“Call a code, Leon?” a nurse asks, finger on the wall switch.

We don't need to. Everyone's here, this woman's going to die,…but..."Yeah, rules are rules. Go ahead."

Tammie in the next bed lies still now, eyes watching us over the tube rising from her mouth. Is this her mother dying here? I reach to pull the curtain across between the beds but I'm too slow. She sees Finkel start pushing down on the huge woman's chest, then eyes me after the curtain closes.

The hiss is louder now. Sweat creeps onto my skin. Does she understand? She's probably confused from the carbon monoxide. Will she remember? I look away and step back behind the curtain, my own pulse pounding.

"Dopamine's going," a nurse says. "How fast, Leon?"

A glance at the monitor. The round humps made by the chest compressions march across its screen. "Wide open." Her huge flaccid body shivers with each chest compression.

The code blue call sounds on the P.A. overhead.

A lab tech hands me a paper. "Here's her gases, Leon. Look at that carboxyhemoglobin level."

She's acidotic, to be expected. But there it is, her death knell; seventy-eight percent of this poor woman's hemoglobin is bound up by carbon monoxide. Seventy-eight percent of the oxygen-carrying molecules in her blood are out of service, non-functional.

That hiss, I close my eyes. Is it getting louder?

"Do you hear that, Matt?"

"Hear what?" Beauregard says over his shoulder. He is examining the woman, checking for trauma. "Splash some Betadine on her belly," he says, pulling on latex gloves.

"Wait, Matt, don't even bother." I wave the blood gas slip at him. "Her carboxyhemoglobin level is seventy-eight."

"What's going on, Leon?" The panting face of Elliott Greenberg appears, an internal medicine intern, responding to the code blue.

Death, I want to say, creeping death stealing another soul. Death, I want to shout.

"Leon?" Greenberg says.

Stop this, now. Be yourself. I feel the sweat now on my clothes. I don't usually sweat. "Bad carbon monoxide poisoning," I say, "Level's seventy-eight. You got that central line in, Rohit?"

"The line is in." His voice is loud with the strain of working fast.

I move close to the bed. At least I can teach him. "Her carboxyhemoglobin level is seventy-eight, pH is seven point one, chest X-ray looks good. Did you see her ECG, Rohit?"

He shakes his head. I hand it across her to him.

"Have you got her on one hundred percent oxygen?" Greenberg says. No one bothers to answer.

"Bad ischemia," Rohit says, tapping the paper.

"That's right." I hand the ECG to Greenberg. Maybe it will keep him quiet for a minute. "What do you want to do, Rohit?"

"Stop CPR," he orders.

Finkel stops. The monitor clears showing a straight line, then a wide single beat, perhaps five seconds pass, then another, the last strokes of a dying heart. The hiss is loud in my head now. What is happening to me?

"Agonal, resume CPR," Rohit says, looking at me, mind ticking fast over his options. "Asystole protocol, we can try. High dose epinephrine."

"Can't hurt," I say, "go ahead. It's your call when to end it."

I turn away. Someone bumps into me, Ralph Lyons, Greenberg's resident. "Oh, sorry, Leon. What's up?"

I point a thumb back over my shoulder. "Ask your intern. He's got it all figured out."

I move away toward the nurses station.

"Leon, where are you going?" Lyons calls after me. "You're supposed to supervise these things."

"Rohit's in charge. He knows what to do."

"He's just an R-1."

"It doesn't fucking matter, Ralph," I hear myself growl. "She's dead."

Shivering now, sweating, I sit down and close my eyes. I don't want to see it, Zach, that woman dead. I don't want to hear it, her pitiful soul's scream.

After a time Lydia shows me Fitz's chest X-ray and his blood tests. Pneumocystis pneumonia, as expected, that bizarre type of pneumonia we had hardly heard of until AIDS came along. But there is no doubt, the characteristic streaks on his X-ray. And he is anemic, leukopenic, also as expected, his white blood cells chewed to pieces by the virus, the zillions of tiny germs tumbling along in his blood.

"Go reason with him," I tell her. "He might listen better to you, might think you're more objective, more the doctor than an overly concerned friend."

But he won't stay, no matter what, and I can't really blame him. So we shoot him up with IV antibiotics and some fluid.

"When can I come see you, Fitz?" I talk to him before he leaves.

"How about tomorrow?" He eyes Joel.

"Yes, tomorrow," Joel smiles, "for dinner. I'll cook. Can you make it, Leon?"

We arrange a time and I help Fitz get ready to go. Just moving about is painful for him and makes him short of breath. Then off he goes in a wheelchair, weaving through the busy hallway.

Chapter Five

Driving home in hot glare of rush hour like a normal person, a nine-to-fiver, the flat roar of traffic all around. I need a car with air conditioning. I hope Jasmine's gone over to her little French horn player's place tonight. Some peace and quiet would be nice.

The mournful image of Fitz hangs in my mind. God, Zach, how sad this is. He's going to die soon, isn't he? Did you see him, emaciated, wasting away? Can't we do something for him? Right, what, go see him tomorrow, joke with him, make him feel good, feel like people care about him. A drop in the ocean.

Some peace and quiet would be nice, no kidding. What did Icky say, I'm keeping too many balls in the air?

And I'm hearing things, Zach. Like yesterday at the club, I'm working out on the Nautilus machines and I hear this shriek from over by the free weights, like someone just smashed a hand or dislocated a shoulder. I jump up to help but no one else has budged. Maybe ten people in the room and not one has even glanced around to see who maimed himself. This buff dude on the leg station of the universal is doing knee extensions with maybe three hundred pounds and with each rep the little wheel under the cable lets out a shriek. Needs some oil, I guess.

My heart's thumping away and I start to shake. It's calling me, that shriek, like someone getting stabbed. I lie back down and try to ignore it but every rep he does is like a cold knife in my brain. Then I look over at the one wall that's all mirror—and for a second I see this corpse, pale and flat on its back. Only it's me, moving when I do, like the guy in the glass. But it looks dead, I look dead. I have to leave that room, Zach, I can't stand it.

So I go shoot a few hoops and then hit the hot tub. I'm talking to some friendly older guy about the Reds. He's reminiscing about Pete Rose, of all people. Then he leaves and I'm lying there and I start listening to the bubbles, and the pump and all. It sounds like people whispering, or talking in low voices. So here I get the shakes again, and I start thinking about that poor girl from the car wreck, and that old lunger and I can't put a lid on it. I can't stop my mind.

Then this good-looking dude walks in with nothing on. Real lean and friendly and cool. So I start thinking about Fitz, and about what it was like with him. All this crap bouncing around in my head, I can barely keep up a conversation with this guy, and then he reaches a hand toward me, asking for the newspaper, which is in a rack on the wall behind me. I about jump out of the tub. He looks at me real odd, and then I hand him the paper, after I finally figure out that's what he wants. So I mumble something ridiculous about being under a lot of stress and get out of there.

Zach, I hope I never run into that dude again. He must think I'm nuts. But you know, he reminded me of Fitz, calm and soft-spoken, slim waisted with that line of hair from his chest down over the muscles of his belly.

Jasmine's car is gone when I pull up to the curb. But there is a woman sitting on the steps, a grocery bag at her feet. She stubs out her cigarette and stands, very slim, nice legs in a blue jumper. Wait a minute, it's that mother, the one with the adopted kid with cystic fibrosis, the "passionate redhead." What is she doing here?

She steps toward me, waving nervously. "Guess who?" she says through my open window. Her hair flames in the evening sun. "May I call you Leon, Dr. Mendel? You wouldn't mind, would you?"

She smiles now, less nervous, as if my answer hardly matters once she's broken the ice.

"Hi, I don't remember your name. I didn't expect to—"

"Rita Thal. I brought in Britnie, the girl with C.F. on Saturday night. You may not remember, you were so busy that night. I don't know how you do it, work there, I mean. It's such a madhouse."

She is carefully made up, very pretty but a bit pale.

I step out of the car. "Yeah, it does get crazy. So, what, um..."

"Yes, what am I doing here?" she says in a rush. "I'm sorry, I know it's probably dumb, but I had to talk to you. You didn't have your ring on any more, and you looked so—I don't know—so frightened the other night. I never saw you that way before. With Camille you were always so confident and sure."

Now she pauses, watching me carefully, her hands moving. At least Jasmine's not home.

"I brought some beer. It's so hot and I was thirsty." She gestures again and bounces up the two steps, agile in high-heeled sandals. She moves like someone who likes to move, to feel her body move. "I didn't know when you'd be home so I brought along a six pack. Maybe you don't drink."

"No, a beer would be good."

"Your place, by the way, if this is your place, is a mess. I hope you haven't been burglarized."

The townhouse door stands open. "You've been in? How did you get in?"

"The door was open, just like it is now. I only peeked inside."

The living room is lit by slanting streaks of sun. Again that hissing rises in my ears, or in my mind, an odd sound.

"Do you hear..." I start to say. Is it my ears, tinnitus, my hearing going bad?

Half the furniture is missing, and there are gaps in the bookshelves. Bits of string and packing tape, dustballs and trash litter the floor, a crumpled cardboard box. Again the feeling of dread, the fist clutching my gut. Dread of what? My stereo remains with Jasmine's CD player missing. The rack of discs is gone, too.

"Well, how about that," I say. "Looks like today was my dearly beloved's moving day. She didn't bother to tell me, of course, but I've always liked surprises. Thoughtful of her to lock the door." I walk over to the shelves. "Look at this. She left the walrus carving but took the geode. Well, she did pick it out herself. Used it for an ashtray in fact. Took the African fertility dolls. Thank God they didn't work for us."

Zach's picture is gone. "Where's Zach's picture?" I search the jumbled shelves, then the floor. "God damn her, where's that picture?" Are there eyes under there, in the narrow black space below the lowest shelf, eyes watching me?

"That bitch, she's just being mean, damn her." Anger growls loud in my mind. I feel it pumping in my arms.

"Who's Zach?" Rita says, standing near the door.

I look up at her from the floor. "Zach is my brother, or was, anyway."

"Was?" she says.

I nod, standing up. "Fuck it. Pardon my language. I should have known the bitch would pull something like this. I wonder what other little symbolic acts of theft or vandalism she pulled. Probably booby-trapped the toilet seat or something. Next time I lift it up to pee it'll probably explode. Another feminist statement."

Rita giggles. "Your ex-wife, is that who you're talking about?"

"Well, she's not quite ex yet. We're working on that. About a month to go. Our lawyer has to put in his hours, you know. A doctor can't just get a simple divorce. It takes months of highly skilled legal work. I mean look at the estate that has to be divided." I gesture around the room. "The accumulated wealth of a biennium."

"A biennium?" she says. "You mean two years?"

I kick the empty box into a corner. "Actually almost three, but we didn't accumulate much except bad feelings for this last year. Oh, well, at least she's gone."

"Three years and no kids? You could have done worse, you know."

"I'm sure that's true." I look at her. "So, enough about me. What brings you here, by the way?"

She laughs again and claps her hands. "Yes, well, what AM I doing here? I wondered when we'd come back to that. When we talked the other night at the hospital you looked like someone who needed some help, perhaps a sympathetic ear. So I have one, let's see..." She touches her right ear. "No, that's the snide, sarcastic one. Oh, it's this one." She touches the left ear, eyeing me nervously. "You see, I've never been one to sit waiting by the phone, and besides you live in another world from mine, or I'm sure you think you do, surrounded by your doctor friends and all those nurses. It would never even occur to you to call me up, so I thought I'd throw myself at you. Nothing ventured, nothing—"

"Gained," Jasmine's husky voice intrudes. Her silhouette appears in the doorway. "Hello, dear, how was your day at work? Brought a little friend home with you, I see."

Rita retreats a few steps into the room as Jasmine walks in. She wears a bikini bottom and tee shirt cut off above her navel. Her hair is different, gathered tight to one side, very punk. A pale skinny man follows her. He blinks at us.

"Well, Robert," Jasmine says, "I didn't anticipate you would meet Leon but here he is, the former man of my dreams, now struggling with identity, sexuality, and God knows what else."

Robert shrugs and smiles awkwardly, glancing toward my hand as if fearful I might want to shake.

The hissing seems to have followed her into the room. "Well, Jas," I say, "I can see you haven't lost your usual sense of decorum and social grace. Were you planning on staying long?"

Rita has turned away, browsing over the bookcase across the room.

"Oh, no," Jasmine says, "we'll just pick up the last boxes and be off. I see your friend can read. I'm sure the two of you want to be left alone, perhaps to discuss literature."

Without turning her head, Rita raises her hand, middle finger stuck high in the air.

Jasmine pauses, taking in the gesture. "So refined, Leon."

"You deserve it, Jas." I hear my own anger now. "Where's Zach's picture?"

"What picture?" In shadow now her head seems like a dark skull, feline and predatory. She's been doing cocaine. Her arms jerk, tense with that urgency of the drug.

"The one in the pewter frame that sat right here." I put my hand on the shelf. "That was my picture."

"Your picture but my frame, as I recall."

"Oh, I see, becoming a little petty here, aren't we? As I recall that frame was a gift to me."

"Well, sweetcakes, I ungave it." She waves toward the litter on the floor. "The picture's around here somewhere. Jesus, Leon, you've got a whole album full of pictures of Zach."

She disappears up the stairs. Robert is close at her heels, khaki shorts flapping at his bony knes.

"Should I leave?" Rita says, turning toward me.

"Oh, no, don't leave. That little gesture was quite eloquent, in fact."

Behind a pile of books on the floor I find the small photo. The hissing is loud in my head as I look at the tiny face.

"Is that a special picture?" Rita says. "May I see it?"

For a moment I don't know what to do, then I slide the photo onto its shelf. "Maybe sometime. It's a funny picture."

Rita smiles, a tiny lovely smile. "Maybe sometime."

In a few moments they are headed out the door, arms full.

"Have you got it all now, Jas, or can I look forward to seeing you again?"

"You're so sweet, Leon. Don't worry, I'll call before I come again." Then to Rita, "Well, good luck, sweetheart, I don't think Leon's had a hard-on in months. At least not around a woman."

Rita spins around. "If I was a man the only thing hard I'd get near you with is a baseball bat." The speed of her reply is astonishing. Her eyes lock on to Jasmine's, calm and confident as two cannon.

Robert glances anxiously around, then says in a surprisingly firm voice, "Jasmine, this is juvenile. Let's simply go."

Rita laughs nervously when they are gone. "Was I crude? I'm sorry."

"Hell, no. That was great. She had it coming."

"You married that woman?"

"Hard to believe, isn't it? I don't know how that happened. Obviously bad judgment."

"She's very sexy. Amazing how that can cloud a man's mind."

"True, the reality of it turned out to be something less than advertised."

"What do you mean by that?" Rita says.

"Well...say, where'd that six pack end up? I could use a beer, if you're buying." I move toward her paper bag on the kitchen counter. "What I meant was that Jasmine dresses very sexy, and acts sexy, but isn't very comfortable with the real thing. At least not with me. We did better in bed before we got married."

I pull two green bottles from the bag. Two more sit already empty. "Hudepohl?" I put the last two in the refrigerator. "Get moody with Hude."

She raises her hands to her face and giggles. "What?"

"That's what they say at the ballpark, at Riverfront Stadium, the vendors who walk through the stands. 'Get moody with Hude.' I think they're hard up for a slogan."

"Well, they've got the right crowd for that one."

"Do you want a glass? We used to have a set of seven dwarf beer mugs, if they're still here." I open the cupboard doors. "Jasmine picked them out at some schlock antique store. Sneezy's handle was missing but she even fixed it herself, made a new one in fact. She wasn't always the witch you saw today."

"Does she do something? I mean like a job, or does she just hang around in her bikini and drip all day?"

"Drip all day?"

Rita glances up and giggles again. "Did I say that? Sorry, how crude. I meant...um...dripping sarcasm and bitchiness."

"Right, I thought that's what you meant. Here they are. She left them. I'm amazed."

I rinse the dusty mugs in the sink. "Anyway, yeah, she's got a job. She's a tympani player for the symphony, if you can believe that. A percussionist."

"A tympani player?"

"You know, those big kettledrums. She puts on this elegant black gown and high heels—actually she takes off the heels when the music starts, so she doesn't slip—and bangs away on her drums all evening. That guy she was with, Robert, Mr. Macho with the skinny legs, he plays French horn or something."

"Kettle drums, not very feminine," Rita says.

"She fancies herself fiercely liberated, and being a percussionist is part of it, I think. But who cares? Fuck her, she's gone. Praise the Lord and pass the peace and quiet."

"How about you?" she says.

"How about me what?"

"Are you comfortable with the real thing?"

I look at her, uncertain what to say. "So which mug do you want? How about Bashful; he seems appropriate to the situation."

"Very funny," she says. She has a low pitched but very animated voice. It matches the laughter she seems to keep just below the surface.

We sit on the remaining couch, door open, the light fading, the hills across the river now deep blue shadows. That particular smell of alcohol mingled with cigarette smoke lies faintly about her.

"Leon," she says, a warm hand on mine. "you didn't invite me here. When you want me to leave just say so, if you've got things to do or plans or anything."

"Oh, just a couple nurses coming over later for an orgy. You know how it is with doctors and nurses."

She laughs again, watching me. She sits very straight, turned toward me, legs neatly folded, like someone who has once been taught how to sit.

"So how did you figure out where I live? The secretaries aren't supposed to give out that kind of info."

"I know. I learned about the secretaries before with Camille. I used to try to find a doctor to call at home when she was sick. I remember one night a secretary gave me Dr. Fletcher's home phone. Does she still work there?"

"Emily Fletcher, yup, she's still there."

"Well, I thought being a woman she might be more sympathetic. Boy, was I wrong. She was such a bitch on the phone when I called her. Course it was the middle of the night."

"Emily's not what you'd call warm-hearted."

"Anyway, I called that medical assistance line the hospital has, 332-MUNI, and got the names of about six doctors on the staff. I had to call several times. Of course they wouldn't give out home phones, just office numbers. So then I called the Medical Staff Office at the hospital and lied terribly. I told the lady I was calling from the Health Department and that we had to notify these doctors of tuberculosis exposure as soon as possible."

There is a hint of a southern accent to her voice.

"She said she would take care of it so I told her it was a department regulation that we notify them directly by registered mail, so she bought that and gave me home addresses. Of course, you were one of them. Wasn't that awful?" she says, lifting Bashful to her mouth.

"Another conniving female," I say. "Women these days just can't be—"

"Oh, Leon, I've seen men do the crudest, most dishonest things you can imagine. Doctors, too. In fact, especially doctors."

"Well, I'm a doctor."

She reaches for her purse. "May I smoke? Do you mind?"

I shrug, that hissing rising in my mind. I hate cigarettes. "Go ahead. Jasmine smoked. It's not like the place doesn't smell of it."

She watches me, laying her purse aside. "Good poker face, you don't like it, do you?"

"Well, not really. No, I don't, but go ahead if you need to."

"I don't need to, at least not yet." She takes my hand again. "Do you remember Camille?"

"Your daughter, the one who died?"

She nods, squeezing my fingers. "You were so kind with her, and gentle and sympathetic. No other doctor treated her that way. Really, you didn't try to manipulate her or fool her. She knew she was dying and you didn't pretend she wasn't. That's why I kept bringing her back to see you. Do you remember how you kept telling us to go to the C.F. Clinic? You got very angry about it, in fact. You told us to stop coming to the emergency room."

"Well, they're supposed to do the emotional support thing, too."

"They don't. Maybe they think they do but they don't. It's awful the way you get treated when you have an illness like that. No one will be straightforward with you. Either they treated her like a child and wouldn't tell her what was going on, or even tell me, or they put up this emotional barrier and acted like robots around her, like they're afraid to make any kind of real contact."

"So now you've adopted another child with cystic fibrosis and here you are," I say.

"No, no," she says quickly. "I mean, well, yes, that's true, but I'm not here because of Britnie." She stands, smiling conspiratorially. "I'm here cause you're not wearing a wedding ring anymore. You're fair game again, Dr. Leon Mendel. Or are you?" Her smile fades. "Am I being presumptuous? Is there some cute little nurse who's caught your eye?"

I shrug. "Not really. I haven't given it much thought."

"Ending a relationship is a difficult thing, especially a marriage. I wouldn't expect you'd be ready for another. Relationship, that is." Her quick laugh surfaces again.

I watch her, uncertain what to say. Her face is very expressive, emotions play across it in quick succession, a face that's easy to read.

"Well, it's hard to be totally spontaneous," I say, "I mean in this day and age, about a new person. Here I am, Joe ER Doc, going along doing my thing, and this very attractive redhead just drops into my lap, and on the day my wife moves out to boot."

She laughs again, then agile as a cat she lands in my lap. "Here I am, in your lap. But we're not strangers. I think I know you very well, and you know me. When you took care of Camille, I saw that you were a warm, sensitive, honest man. Or at least that you were capable of being one. And you were with me at a very hard time in my life, when Camille died. Do you remember?" Her cigarette smell mingles with a pleasant perfume. She is so thin, so light on my legs.

"Yeah, I remember. You wouldn't let us intubate her, had all the papers signed and ready. I remember that. It was a pretty unique situation, letting a child go like that. But it was the right thing to do."

"So we're not strangers. And then I saw you the other day looking like someone who could use a friend, so here I am."

She watches my face, her smile fading. "I'm being too forward, aren't I? I'm making you feel uncomfortable."

I put an awkward arm around her. "Well, I don't know. I'm not feeling very comfortable with myself these days." How dumb. "Besides...besides it's unethical for me to consort with patients, or mothers of patients."

"Consort, huh?" She rubs my chest. "Just what does consort mean? Have we started consorting yet?" She leans away and her smile vanishes again. "I am making you feel uncomfortable." She turns to get up.

"Now, wait a minute," I say, reaching for her, but she stands and picks up the mugs. "How about a refill? Looks like Dopey's empty, too."

"I'm sorry, I don't know what to say. I've been going through some difficult stuff lately. My mind is not in its usual state of constant sexual readiness."

The hissing has a beat to it now, the thump of my heart.

"Well, Leon, I only sat on your lap. It's not like I tried to drag you into the bedroom."

I watch her fill the mugs with a casual expertise.

"So I'm a good listener," she says. "Tell me about this difficult stuff you've been going through."

* * *

"Shall we have wine?" Leon says. "White wine is good with Thai food, or beer is good, too."

"Wine sounds good," I say, the monster says, my monster. Everyone has a monster, don't they? How about iced tea? Should I say that, or seltzer? He wants wine, drink wine with him. Maybe it'll loosen him up. Maybe he feels nervous with me. Besides we've already started, already had some beer.

We sit in a booth, a candle in a little house between us, like a pagoda. He orders wine from the short man, smiling and dark. Is he from Thailand? I don't even know where Thailand is.

"What is that?" I point.

"That? That's a candle," Leon says.

"Oh, I see. Thank you, Dr. Mendel, a candle. No, I mean what is it inside of? Is that a pagoda? Aren't pagoda's Chinese?"

His smile comes more easily here. I think he's relieved to be out of that awful house, all torn apart with furniture missing. And that woman. I brought the picture. I'm awful, but I slid it off the shelf and into my purse. I didn't look at it, at least. Will he be angry?

"I think it's called a wat. Thai temples are called wats. Isn't a pagoda Japanese?"

"A wat. Clever of them," I say. "Every time you say 'what' you're saying church, in Thailand I mean."

"What?"

"See, see what I mean? You said it." Where is the wine? Now is when the monster is worst, after one or two and waiting for the next.

"So where's Britnie tonight?" he says. "Does she stay by herself?"

"Yes, she seems to like being alone. No one ever trusted her alone before. Course she always lived in foster homes where there were other kids around. But she likes being alone. She turns on the TV, of course, but she usually reads a book, too. She reads a lot. She says she could never read whatever she wanted, or they never had any good books around. I think her last foster family was very religious, like Baptist or something."

"Baptists," he says, "they're always fun, easy-going, laugh-a-minute."

"Devil may care," I say.

He laughs. His face changes when he laughs, that impassive poker face goes away, that doctor face. He needs to laugh more. I'll bet he's handsome without those glasses. Will he let me take them off?

"And she talks endlessly on the phone. She made some friends in school this year and they talk for hours."

The little man brings the wine, fumbles with the cork, smiling, nodding. Here, let me do it, I want to say. Let me hold that cool smooth bottle.

"Is that a wat?" Leon asks the man.

"What?" He bobs his head again.

"A wat?" Leon speaks slowly. "Is that a wat?"

"Candle," the man says.

"See, I told you," Leon says to me, then to the man, "Candle inside a wat, right?" He taps the little house.

"Yes, oh, yes, a wat," the man laughs, "Thai temple, like church."

Just open the wine, sweetie-pie. Finally he sets it on the table and backs away nodding and smiling. I hate it when they do that, when they act like servants.

"Shall I pour?" I say, my monster says, reaching for the bottle. Too quick? Did I reach too quick? At least I didn't knock anything over. "So who's Zach? May I ask?"

"He was my brother. We were twins."

I wait, watching him. Just having the glass in my hand is better, the pale tiny ocean. I hate myself.

He nods, staring at the candle. "He died."

"Was it a long time ago?"

"We were eight."

"Twins become very close."

"Yeah, I guess so." His eyes move as if he heard something, then they go far away.

"What are you thinking of?" I ask.

"Oh, I'm sorry. I was remembering, we had this backyard where we played that was like..."

"Like what?"

"Well, the house sat on a hill, like a ridge really. All the houses on our side of the block were on it, and then you went down the slope to the backyard. Then there was an alley. But there were some very tall trees that made it almost like a tunnel, the backyard. In the summer the trees would shade the yard, and all the other yards along the alley.

"It was this little world where we played. I don't know, it's hard to describe. Where did you grow up?"

"Me? Are you changing the subject? I wanted to hear—"

"Yes, I am," he says, grinning. "You seem like a southerner. And every now and then I hear a little bit of an accent."

"I am sort of a southerner. Is that good or bad?"

"Good or bad? Neither really, you just seem to have the mannerisms, a graciousness or something."

"Well, thank you, if I was standing I'd curtsy."

Now the man and a graceful, black-haired girl put plates in front of us. Then they give a little bow, palms together.

"I hate it when they do that," I whisper to him.

"Do what?" Leon says, arranging the plates.

"When they bow like that and do that little thing with their hands. Like servants or something. I mean, what would you do if you were eating dinner at Denny's or someplace and the waitress bowed when she served the food?"

"Well, maybe they mean it. They do stuff like that in Thailand. I went there once. That little hand gesture is sort of a greeting and a prayer all rolled into one. It's like saying 'Bon appetit.'"

The food is good, spicy. The wine is fair; at least it's cold.

"You went to Thailand?" I say.

"Yup, couple years ago. Jasmine's in the symphony—I told you that, didn't I—and they went to Bangkok to perform. So I got to tag along. It's a pretty cool place, Thailand."

"Where is it? It's near Vietnam, isn't it?"

He nods. "Just down the block. It's a beautiful country, every village has got one of these." He taps the wat with a chopstick.

"You went with that woman?"

"That woman. We used to have fun together, believe it or not. She likes exotic stuff."

He eats slowly as we talk. I don't think he's hungry. He tells me about working in the emergency room, and how the old people are sometimes the hardest to figure out, how teaching the residents can be difficult at times.

He has a very expressive face once he relaxes, quick to smile and laugh. But when it settles, his face, when he looks away, down at his food, or watches me talk, it is an anxious face, pale, worried.

The waiter appears. "You wan' more wine?"

The bottle is empty. Leon eyes me. I hate this moment. Of course I want more wine, two or three bottles more, and a smoke would be nice, too.

"I could drink another glass," my monster says. I imagine my hands choking its bull neck, tiny hands helpless against its laughing strength.

"Me, too," he says, then to the waiter. "Sure, we'll have another bottle."

"I don't usually drink this much," he says to me. "Do you?"

I want to giggle, or scream maybe. "I drink more than I should sometimes."

After a time I say, "Would you tell me more about Zach?"

"More about Zach. Like what?"

"It's hard for an eight-year-old to understand when someone dies."

He gazes at me, mystified for a moment. He's a little drunk. "Oh, you mean me, when I was eight."

"You said you were eight when Zach died."

"Right. Well, he got hit by a car. He was riding his bike and a car hit him."

"Were you with him when it happened?"

He nods, lost in his memories. "Yup, I saw it all."

"Did he die right away?"

"No. No, he didn't. He should have." He speaks very slowly now. "It would have been better but..."

Now he shakes his head, leaving the words hanging.

"You were close, weren't you?"

"Well, we were only eight when he died. How close can eight year olds be?"

"Leon, children become very close, closer than most adults. So close you're like part of each other, you live and breathe together, you know what each other is thinking and feeling. I have a sister—we aren't twins, but we're only about a year apart—and we did everything together. Our father called us his two-headed demon."

"Okay, so what?" he says, angry and a little loud.

Oops, I did it, didn't I, me and the wine. He's obviously not a drinker. I watch him until he settles.

"So we were close," he says. "I guess we were close. I don't remember it all very well."

The picture, take out the picture. Is this the time? Do you want to know him better, see what he's really like?

"I brought this." I slide the picture across the table, face down. "I didn't look at it."

He picks it up and flinches as he looks, as he realizes what it is. Fear and something else cross his pale face. He slaps it down on the tablecloth again, covering it with his palm. He saw something.

"What did you see?"

He shakes his head as if shaking off a fly, and hands the picture to me. It is a little boy in a cowboy suit, squinting in the sun and waving, a healthy little boy.

"Childhood is important, Leon. You shouldn't pretend it's not."

"I'm sure you're right." He nods, glancing around the room. "Do you—you don't hear anything, do you?"

* * *

In the car on the way home, I'm trying to drive. She tells me about the business she used to have, sort of a franchised daycare business she tried to get started, only it fizzled out because one of the staff slapped a kid and the parents threatened a lawsuit.

Childhood is important, she says. You shouldn't pretend it's not. Who's pretending? I know it's important. We knew, didn't we, Zach? Didn't we know that! More than anyone, more than Mother and Father and those doctors and everybody?

Who is this woman who wants to get into my life all of a sudden? And why? Should I trust her? Zach, I don't really trust anybody right now. Maybe Icky, but I can't think of anyone else. She seems honest enough, straightforward, sincere, but it's too simple, and she's too pretty.

"So why in the world would anybody intentionally adopt a kid with cystic fibrosis?" I blurt out. "Seems like you're just asking for a broken heart. You know what's gonna happen to her, right?"

A long silence.

"Mind if I smoke?" she says.

"Sure, go ahead." I'm wondering if she even heard my question, or if I insulted her or something.

She takes a couple slow puffs on the cigarette, then, "Well, everybody dies, Leon. It's just a question of when. Let's talk about Britnie some other time."

She should be driving, I realize. She is handling her wine much better than I am. Then she reaches over and rubs my arm. "May I spend the night, Leon? That is, if you still have a bed left."

I cover her hand with mine. Do I need this, want this, someone new to complicate my life?

"Well, that's certainly a tempting offer. You know, Rita, there's a lot going on in my life right now. Some of it's kind of weird, stuff I don't understand." I'm so articulate when I'm drunk.

"I know, Leon. I can tell. Maybe I can help you. I'm pretty good at that sort of thing, helping people understand themselves."

"Well, what about Britnie?"

"She's okay by herself. She's old enough. I'll call her."

"What about the safe sex stuff? We hardly know each other."

"The last time I slept with a man was about two years ago. My ex, I have an ex, too. I had an AIDS test done about six months ago, and it was okay."

"Why'd you have an AIDS test done? Sorry, that sounds awfully suspicious, doesn't it?"

Cigarette smoke, lit by oncoming headlights, wreathes her face. She turns and clutches my arm. "I used to be a dope fiend." Then she laughs and says, "No, I'm just kidding. Warren, my ex, was a bit of a jerk. Don't you love that name, Warren. And who knows who he slept with before we split up. So when I started thinking about adopting a child I thought I should find out for sure first. What about you?"

The hissing returns, rhythmic again, but different now, or more distinct, almost like someone whispering to me. I shake my head, wishing I could shake it off. The image of Fitz's diseased body comes to me in the dark. I feel myself shudder.

"What is it, Leon? Do you have AIDS? Is that what's disturbing you?"

"No, no, I got tested about three months ago myself, when I found out Jasmine was fooling around with that French horn worm, you know, the one with the muscular legs."

Rita laughs. "The tan, muscular legs."

"Right, well, he doesn't seem like the type to be HIV positive, but you never know. So I wanted to be prepared in case some little vixen like yourself should show up on my doorstep."

It's louder now. I feel my heart pound.

"Little vixen, huh. So what else?" she says. "Something else is bothering you."

I watch the street ahead. Again, what to say, where to start, how much to reveal?

"You don't trust me, do you?" she says. "Or you don't know if you can trust me."

I park the car. "Well, you don't know if you can trust me either, do you?"

"We can use condoms." she says. "Or we can just snuggle up together, not have sex."

* * *

Well, Zach, Jasmine was right, the bitch. I'm naked in bed with this woman who's willing to do anything I want. And old Leon can't get it up. The whispering sound is loud in my head now, no words but a voice, anxious, urgent, someone whispering in my ear while this lovely creature is trying to make love to me.

She is lovely in her way. Slim, graceful, with the delicate curves of a woman, just enough to the eye, and to the hand. Her scent, her bouquet of something toward peach, mixed with the wine.

I want to make love with her, not just touch her and kiss her, but slide deep inside her, feel her writhe to my stroke. But I can't.

"Not so much wine for this little fellow next time," she says finally, patting me, then kissing my cheek.

"I'm sorry. It's not you, Rita. You're very sexy." I search for something more to say.

"It's okay, Leon."

"I hope you'll give me another chance."

Lying now with her back against me she rubs my leg in response. We lie still on the bed, a candle for light, humid air close around us, crickets outside in the shrubbery.

"When I was a third-year med student I had a patient with cystic fibrosis. I was doing pediatrics and we had cystics all the time but there was this one little girl who had terrible C.F. She was only three years old, only she was about the size of a one year old because she was sick all the time. And she was constantly in the hospital with infections. Her stupid mother was about seventeen, and on welfare of course, and unmarried and didn't know how to take care of her, and didn't really want to. She wanted the kid to be a little toy or a doll or something she could put away when she was tired of playing with it, or if she met some guy and wanted to go out or something.

"And I think she'd figured out it was only a matter of time 'til the kid died anyway, so maybe she didn't want to be around, or didn't want to get attached. So she hardly ever came to visit this poor little girl, and the nurses would park her in a room way down at the end of the hall in one of those big steel cribs. I think the nurses used to avoid her, too, it was so depressing.

"Can you imagine having your three-year-old kid in the hospital and not spending all the time you could with that kid, helping them not to be scared and not to think you weren't going to come back again and all that? You know those little kids have got all kinds of fears when you stick them in the hospital."

Rita is quiet, probably asleep.

"So this little girl—I think her name was Angel or some dumb name only a fifteen year old would think up for her kid—she was really cute and really needed someone to spend time with her. I used to go down there late at night when I was on call or after I got everything done and was ready to go home, and play with her for a while. She was really a little sweetheart. I can't imagine how that mother could never come visit her.

"She'd wake up with just the sound of a footstep and jump up when she saw me. Then I'd take her out and sit on the floor with her and we'd play these little games. She was so tiny, and didn't talk very well, so we'd practice talking, saying different words. She didn't even really walk very well either, so we'd do that stuff, too. I'd hold her hand and she'd toddle down the hall.

"But you know what she really wanted to do. She just wanted to be held. She just wanted contact with another human being, hugging and sitting on my lap and being carried around. It would break your heart.

"I even thought about adopting her. Can you believe that? Here I am, like twenty-four years old and I thought about adopting this little girl. Her mother didn't want her. I used to imagine the conversation with the dean of the medical school. I figured somebody would think I was up to something bad, something sexual or something, a single guy adopting a baby girl. But I wouldn't have had the time for childcare and all that. My classmates would have thought I was nuts.

"That poor kid, I'm sure she died years ago. Great story, huh."

But Rita is asleep.

I lie listening to the whispers in my mind, like a child's voice speaking to me from somewhere, an urgent message said over and over, words I cannot make out. Whose voice is it, Zach? But I know whose voice, I remember that voice, like I remember my own.

Chapter Six

Rita is dressing when I wake up. She looks scrubbed, fresh.

"Did you shower?" I say.

"Yes, you don't mind, do you? I felt so good, I had to get up."

My body aches from the wine as I roll over. My mouth feels awful.

"It was so nice to snuggle with you, Leon. It's been a long time for me since I had someone to curl up with." She bounces around the bedroom, smoking a cigarette.

"Do you drink like that often? We put down a lot of wine."

"I like to drink," she says, looking out the window. "Too much. It's a problem for me." She looks boyish from this angle, in the sunlight with her hair so short. As a girl, a teen, she must have been beautiful, delicate, graceful.

"I'll cook you dinner tonight," she says. "I live over in Mount Adams." She looks at me uncertainly. "If you want to, that is."

"Dinner, huh. You sure you want to give it another try? That was a pretty sad performance last night, I mean by me."

"All I said was dinner, Leon. I'm not in it for the sex."

"What are you in it for?" I say, meeting her eye as she sits by me, then I add quickly, "Never mind, that's a bad question. No answer needed."

She pokes me with a finger. "What are YOU in it for, Dr. Mendel?"

I raise my hands, thinking. "I don't know. I don't know what I'm in anything for right now. Probably for the sex," I joke. "I like sex...normally."

"Normally?"

"Dinner, wait a minute. I'm supposed to go over to a friend's tonight for dinner."

Her expression clouds. "A friend?"

"It's an old friend, a guy. He has AIDS and he showed up at the hospital yesterday. I hadn't seen him in a long time and I didn't know he was sick. He's gay and lives with this guy named Joel and they invited me over."

"He has AIDS?" she says.

I nod, thinking of Fitz's gaunt face, how changed it was. "It's a really bad thing. I had no idea he had it." I look at her. "Do you want to come? It might be kind of interesting. He's a very sharp guy, or at least he used to be."

"Is it safe?"

"Of course it's safe. You don't get AIDS from just being around someone."

"Oh, you don't need me along. I'm sure you have lots to talk about. It might seem odd, I mean, you're still married aren't you, technically, legally, or whatever." She laughs once more.

But I want her to come, I want to see her again. With a clear head I want to talk with her and explore her thoughts. And more, I want to touch her skin, her gentle curves, and hear her sighs, watch the play of expression on her face.

"Leon?" She pokes me again. "Are you there?"

"Yes, yes, no, I'd like you to come. I mean I'd like to see you tonight. You're very refreshing like...like, um, I don't know. But it'd be fun. Fitz used to be a very funny guy, quick-witted. You'd enjoy him."

Then she is gone. I find some orange juice, coffee, and aspirin to stop the hangover. What am I doing today? I've got that stupid Quality Assurance meeting this morning. That'll be fun.

In an hour I'm there, the meeting. I sit with Icky, Lydia, and Peter Schulman, a necktie on for my own hanging. There are a dozen of us around a big table. One of the hospital administrative types is talking, Cornelius Ponty, a fat, fiftyish, Vice President in Charge of Major Fuck-Ups or something like that.

There's this thing in me now, this sense of my blood flowing, my heart pumping, my nerves firing. I hold up my hand, expecting it to shake, but it doesn't. I feel under my arms, expecting my shirt to be wet, but it's dry. I look at peoples' heads, feeling them staring, but they're not. Even the bran muffin on my plate, somewhere in my mind, some part of my brain expects it to hop like a toad or show fangs and strike, but it doesn't even quiver.

"This is not intended to be a fault-finding meeting," Ponty says. "We do not want to point fingers today but simply to establish what actually happened. Perhaps then we can begin to plan management of the problem. First, let me go quickly around the table so everyone knows who everyone else is."

Beyond him, out the wide window, is the harsh glare of the city, a jumble of rooftops and ugly old skyscrapers along the river.

The hiss is here all the time now. People's voices are a part of it, whispering. I turn to see but they stop.

"To my left is Gunther Eberhart, from the law firm which represents the hospital, then Rose Reilly, director of nursing, then Phyllis Sizemore, from risk management, then Dr. Marianne Collier, chairperson of the Obstetrics and Gynecology Department. Then would you help me, Rose?"

"Yes." Rose smiles her quivery little smile. She's maybe sixty and petite, grandmotherly with a shaky old lady's voice, but tenacious like a pit bull, I've been told. "This is Dawn Appleton, Emergency Department head nurse, then Sonya Broderick, night charge nurse, then Dr. Schulman, medical director of the

Emergency Department, Dr. Polyzarin, Dr. Mendel, and then I'm sorry, Doctor, but I don't know your name."

"I'm Dr. Neumann," Lydia says next to me, her voice calm and strong. That's good. When the wolf pack gathers, act like a wolf.

"Thank you, Rose," Ponty says. "And of course then we have Madeleine Hamel from quality improvement."

She nods, a sleek snake, with impeccable auburn hair.

"Now, Mr. Eberhart, would you care to take the reins at this point?"

Speaking of wolves, the lawyer stands, slender in a tailored dark suit. "Okay, good morning. I appreciate all of you showing up. I know you are all busy people and have better things to do. I hope we can keep this fairly short.

"From a legal standpoint this is a privileged meeting, which means it is completely confidential, between attorney and client. If a lawsuit should ever arise from this tragedy, and we have no reason to believe at this time that one will, then nothing said at this meeting could ever be used against any of us, or in fact even subpoenaed into court. So feel free to speak openly, please.

"The patient's name is Katrina Morris, I believe. Now, Dr. Schulman, would you review the case for us?"

Peter leans forward and looks at me. "Well, I think Dr. Mendel might be able to do a better job. Leon, would you mind?"

Thanks, Peter. "Sure, I'd be happy to," I hear my voice say. I finger the chart copy in front of me. Okay, be cool, this is the last group in the world you want to lose it in front of. "This occurred last Saturday night. Approximately one-thirty a.m. we received a radio call from a city paramedic rig, ambulance that is, that they were bringing in an eighteen-year-old female with pelvic pain, vaginal bleeding, and stable vital signs. At that time the department was extremely busy, with approximately twenty-five patients and several of them critical.

"The ambulance arrived, the patient was placed in one of the gynecology rooms and triaged by one of the nurses upon arrival. She had stable vital signs at that point."

"And triaged means what? Just so we're all clear on this, myself included," Eberhart says with his disarming smile. He has small eyes, their steady gaze detached from his expression.

"Triage means an initial rapid evaluation to determine what level of urgency is needed for that patient's care. Are they in danger of dying right now, some time soon, or not at all and therefore can wait while patients with more urgent problems are cared for?"

"And this is routine?"

"Every patient in the E.D. gets triaged."

"The E.D?" he says.

"The Emergency Department." Why do I dislike this guy, even though he's on my side?

"This is a routine duty of the nurses?"

I nod.

"When you say stable vital signs, Dr. Mendel, what does that mean?"

He must know this stuff, a hospital attorney. "It means that her pulse, blood pressure, temperature, and respiratory rate are all normal. The implication of this is that she has no immediate potentially life-threatening problem."

"Thank you, what happened next?"

"She was triaged to the urgent level, which is the second category. It means the patient should be seen by a physician within twenty minutes of arrival."

"The urgent level," Ponty speaks up now. "So the nurse must have thought she was seriously ill."

"Well, it was the nature of the complaint, vaginal bleeding in a possibly pregnant woman. The patient herself was quite stable and gave no actual signs of having anything seriously wrong. She could have simply had menstrual cramps. The vast majority of women who come in with vaginal bleeding are not pregnant and go home in a couple hours. The concern was that she could have had exactly what she did have, an ectopic pregnancy."

All these eyes are on me; I feel warmth rise in my face. That hiss is under the table now. Why would—

"Would you go on, Dr. Mendel?"

"So at that point, Dr. Neumann went to see the patient and evaluated her as a possible ruptured ectopic pregnancy as well. A blood count and a pregnancy test were ordered."

"Okay, now Dr. Neumann, you're a first-year resident?" Eberhart says.

"That's right," Lydia says.

"In what specialty?"

"Family practice."

"But you were in the Emergency Room in the middle of the night?"

"All family practice residents rotate through the Emergency Department."

"I see. And why is that?"

"It's part of our training. As family physicians we are expected to care for our patients when emergencies arise."

"Forgive my naiveté," Eberhart says, his mouth twitching into something like a smile.

Sorry, pal, I'll forgive it, but I don't believe it. You're testing her to see what kind of client she's going to be.

"So what did you think after you examined Miss Morris?" he says.

"She was upset and anxious," Lydia says, "but appeared to be in no distress. She was only bleeding a very small amount. I made a brief presentation of the case to Dr. Mendel and ordered—"

"So Dr. Mendel was your attending on the case?"

"That's right."

They're watching me, I know. There, see how they look away.

"Okay, so Dr. Mendel, do you recall that presentation?"

"Yes." It's louder under the table. Doesn't anyone else hear that?

"Could you review what Dr. Neumann told you for us?"

Ignore it. Talk. "A stable eighteen-year-old female with a small amount of vaginal bleeding. She ordered a blood count and a pregnancy test."

"Did she say anything to make you concerned that the patient might be seriously ill?"

"No, but again, it was the nature of the complaint. Every female of child-bearing age who is bleeding or having lower abdominal pain is treated as if she has an ectopic pregnancy until we can show that she doesn't."

"Every female, Dr. Mendel? How can that be?"

"That's right. Just like everyone with chest pain is having an M.I., a heart attack, until we can show that they're not."

"I see. So this is sort of a mind set you all take."

I feel anger rising in me. I glance at Peter who raises his eyebrows and shrugs. Be cool, don't let it show. Neutral tone. "That's right."

"Did the patient know she was pregnant?" Eberhart says.

"No, in fact she denied having had sexual intercourse for at least six months." I glance at Lydia who nods.

"She denied it?" Eberhart says.

"That's right."

"Why would she be dishonest with you?"

Oh, c'mon. "It's not unusual. She probably didn't want to be pregnant, didn't think she was, didn't want anyone else to know. Emergency Department patients are dishonest all the time, about all sorts of things."

"I see why you are so cautious," Eberhart says. "Please go on."

"Well, this girl had the misfortune of coming in at a time when we were all extremely busy taking care of severely injured trauma victims. Her pregnancy test came back positive. This took perhaps forty-five minutes from the time Dr. Neumann examined her. Then an ultrasound was ordered to determine if she had a normal pregnancy or not and she lay in bed for about another hour waiting for that to get done. During that time—"

"Why did it take another hour before the ultrasound could be done?"

"Well, the ultrasound technician had to be called in from home and then prepare the machine. I don't know what always takes so long, but at night and on the weekends it always takes a long time." I stare at the darkness between my feet. Is there something down there?

"Okay, so is there a policy regarding how often a patient such as this is rechecked to make sure she has not gotten worse?"

I nod at Peter. He can handle this one.

"Yes, we do have policies for such situations which are meant to serve as guidelines subject to the judgment of the nurse and doctor," Peter says in his director's voice.

"Okay," Eberhart says, "now please keep in mind that I am on your side. These things are difficult to discuss sometimes but we are not adversaries here."

Peter shrugs again. "Fine, I'm not sure what the exact policy states. Do you know, Dawn?"

With her Georgia lilt, Dawn, the E.D. head nurse, says, "The Policy and Procedure Manual states that pulse and blood pressure should be rechecked every twenty minutes in female patients with vaginal bleeding." She looks wide-eyed at Peter, as if she might cry.

For a moment Eberhart is silent.

"There are other safeguards here which also failed," Peter says. "There's a call button in every room for the patient to call for help if she needs it. I don't know why this patient didn't—"

"The call button wasn't there," Dawn says. "Someone had stolen it earlier in the evening, as best we can tell. There was none in the room."

"Stolen the call button?" Eberhart says.

"The button is on the end of an electrical cord which plugs in to the wall," Peter says. "You can hand it to the patient or attach it to the rail of the bed so they can reach it easily. Equipment is stolen from the department daily. You would be amazed what patients will walk away with."

Eberhart shakes his head. "Didn't the patient have anyone with her? A husband or family member?"

A husband? Get real. I glance at Sonya who rolls her eyes.

"Um, these patients are rarely married," Peter says. "They frequently do have boyfriends or mothers or friends who come in with them. And we do encourage having someone with the patients when they have to wait long periods of time. That might well have saved her life in this case."

"Couldn't she have simply walked out of the room and called for help?" Eberhart says. "It seems to me someone bleeding to death would be alarmed by so much blood and try to get help."

"She was bleeding internally, into her abdomen," Peter says. "There was only a small amount of vaginal bleeding. She didn't know she was bleeding internally. She undoubtedly fell asleep, or let herself go to sleep, as patients frequently do, and then died."

"Okay," Eberhart says, struggling to maintain a positive tone. "Did anyone at all look at her during that time?"

Sonya speaks now, "The only person who went in the room was the unit secretary who had the patient sign a permit for the ultrasound. That was about an hour before we found her dead."

"The unit secretary. Okay, so this patient was triaged to the urgent level, then examined by a first-year resident in family practice, and then lay in bed alone for almost two hours except for the secretary coming into the room for her to sign a permit. Is that correct?"

Is there a body under the table? Zach, there's something down there, moving around. Why doesn't anyone else—

"Dr. Mendel, is that correct?"

"As far as I know that's true. I have not spoken with all the nurses who were on that night."

"It appears to be true," Dawn says. "All the nurses have been questioned. The nurse assigned to that room was also assigned to the trauma bays and was too busy there. She did ask one of the other nurses to look in on the patient, however that nurse then became occupied with yet another critical patient."

"Sounds like you needed more staff," Eberhart says sympathetically.

"We always need more staff," Dawn says, glancing at Rose Reilly.

The discussion drags on. I run through the failed resuscitation.

Finally Eberhart says, "Well, no matter how you slice it, this case—I'm sorry, let me rephrase that—no matter how you look at it, this poor girl's death is a tragedy. It occurred in the same way that many mishaps occur in health care, as the result of a chain of events, each of which by itself would be harmless, but combined together produce a human tragedy."

There's something under there, hissing at me, a snake uncoiling, about to engulf my legs.

"Wouldn't you agree, Dr. Mendel? You were the attending physician here. It would be difficult to find fault with any single individual in this situation, don't you think?"

I feel the rush of blood in my head. "Yes, finding fault here is difficult. I don't think it was any one person's fault." Something big down there, a python. C'mon, Leon, keep talking. "I was the attending physician so I suppose in the eyes of society if you have to find fault, then I'm the lucky guy. But you could assign blame to the nurse who didn't recheck vital signs."

"Leon," Sonya squeals, "that's not fair and you—"

"Wait a minute, Sonya." I hold up a hand. "Let me finish. Or to the charge nurse who should be aware of such patients in the department and the need to keep careful track of them." Sonya's face turns crimson. "Or to Dr. Neumann who should have been aware of the gravity of the patient's problem, or to myself for the same reason. That is the first level of blame.

"Or you can blame the hospital for running an emergency department which is chronically understaffed, where chaos is the rule, not the exception, where disasters like this could happen any night, or any day—" There IS something under the table. I feel it moving. "—where lots of patients sit for hours all the time. Right now there's probably someone in that waiting room downstairs with abdominal pain who could have a rupturing aneurysm, or a kid with a fever who really has meningitis.

"Or you could blame the health care system for creating such a terrible setting for poor people to get their health care, where it's really the judgment of a group of nurses and physicians who have time only for a glance at a patient—"

I stand up quickly, throwing my chair back. It wavers but doesn't fall, thank God. "Is there something—" Stop, don't say it. Now you're on your feet. Act like it's intentional. All these eyes watching. "—a glance at a patient to decide who needs immediate treatment and who can wait, in a place where there are forty or fifty or sixty patients at a time, with some of them drunk and screaming and combative, strapped down on gurneys in the halls, with ambulances coming and going and a bunch of underpaid overstressed nurses trying to help a few doctors sort out the bullshit from the truth. But where for once that judgment failed, where one patient fell through the cracks."

Enough. I look around, raise my hands in a shrug. "Sorry, I guess I am emotionally involved."

"Yes," Eberhart says, "I'm sure this has been a trying—"

"I don't think finding fault here does any good," I interrupt him, but don't know what to say next.

"Why don't you sit down, Leon," Icky says under his breath. "It's okay."

Chapter Seven

"You were gone last night with him!" Britnie yells from inside. I sit smoking on the marble bench out front, waiting for Leon. These little benches are so elegant, one in front of each house, cool in the summer heat.

"You're right, I was," I call back through the screen door.

"Are you gonna to stay all night tonight, too?"

"Come to the door, will you."

"Why do I have to come to the door?" Britnie says, glaring through the screen at me. She holds my eyeliner pencil in her hand.

"The neighbors don't need to hear this conversation, my dear. What are you doing?"

"I'm just practicing." She nods at the pencil. "Besides the Sanderbergs are deaf anyway. So you gonna sleep with him tonight, too? Maybe you should stop smoking. It makes your lungs like my lungs. I read that in a book about C.F."

"Thank you, I appreciate your concern. If we spend the night together we'll come back here. Will that be okay?"

"Back here?" She makes a face. "You mean he might be here in the morning?"

"He might."

"I hope your bed doesn't creak," she says, giggling. "I think I'll put cotton in my ears."

"Please." Where is Leon? He's late.

"Rita, how much wine did you drink?" she says. "That bottle in the fridge is almost empty."

"Who's the adult in this house anyway, Britnie? I don't need you monitoring how much wine I drink."

"But you drank a lot. It's not good for you."

"I'm a little bit nervous, okay? We're going to some friend's of his and it helps me be relaxed. And besides that, it's none of your business."

Through the screen she nods superiorly at me.

"Don't you think you're a little heavy with that stuff?" I say. "You missed a couple spots on your cheeks."

"Very funny. Is that him?" She points toward the street.

His boxy old BMW, a classic he calls it, rumbles up the street.

God, I feel nervous as a teenager getting into the car. He smiles. I lean over and kiss his cheek. "Hi, doc. Is this okay?" I'm wearing a skirt and blouse. "I had no idea what to wear. I don't go out much lately."

"You look fine, great in fact. Nice neighborhood you live in."

I wave to Britnie. "Yes, Warren is to thank for this. My ex, have I told you about Warren? Remind me not to if I ever do. But I did get the house."

"How's Britnie doing? She feeling better?"

"Yes, much. She's not coughing nearly so much, and she slept the whole night last night. Thank you so much for taking care of her, Leon. Do you mind if I smoke? I'll blow it out the window. How did your meeting go? Didn't you have an important meeting today?" Talk much? I start to giggle.

"What's funny?"

"Oh, I'm sorry. I'm just so nervous. Can you tell? I mean I talk this way when I get nervous. I just go on and on, like I'm seventeen again."

He glances at me. "Have you been drinking?"

Ugh, there it is. Did he have to say that? "Yes, I had a glass of wine. Can you tell?"

"I noticed the smell. Sorry, I get so exposed to it at work."

"Well, it is six-thirty, and I only had a glass." God, I feel anger rising in me like a volcano. "Look, Leon—"

"Fine," he says quickly, "fine, Rita. No problem, I'm sorry I mentioned it. It's none of my business. If I was facing an evening with me I'd probably need a drink, too. In fact I would have had a beer myself if I had anything besides Hudepohl in the fridge." Now he grins at me.

His curly hair is wild sometimes. I reach to smooth it, to touch him and make peace, peace with myself, I think. "The Hudepohl was fine with you last night, or were you just being polite?" God, how can I wait until later, until I've got him naked in bed with me again! He's so good with his hands.

I fumble for a cigarette. "So how was your meeting? Doesn't your cigarette lighter work?" The little knob won't stay pushed in.

"Sorry, I think Jasmine throttled it in a fit of anger one day. The meeting was okay. We were rehashing a small disaster from the other night, Saturday night in fact, the night you brought Britnie in."

"Oh, my. Did something bad happen? Are you in trouble?"

"We were a little overwhelmed for a while. Too many sick people, so one of them died who didn't need to, or who shouldn't have, I should say. In fact two died."

"Two people died? Saturday night? While we were there?"

"Well, I'm not sure if you were there or not when they died. One of them died in the operating room."

He's so matter-of-fact about it.

"People die there," he says quietly. "That's what it's all about."

"Well, don't think about it, Leon," I say, touching his arm. I want to have fun tonight, to feel good together. "Don't think about it now, anyway."

We drive into Clifton, the lawns of the university outside.

"Where does your friend live? What's he like? I haven't been around men who are gay, Leon. What should I do?"

Act normal, he tells me, be myself. What is normal? I'm not sure anymore. Who is this self I'm supposed to act like? How does she act?

We stop on a quiet, tree-lined street, old houses cool and dark in the shade.

"I used to live about two blocks from here when I was a resident," Leon says. "I shared a house with some friends. Love this neighborhood. Fitz lives on the second floor."

We walk up a half-dozen steps to the front porch.

"A university prof used to live downstairs. A zoologist, I think. Maybe he still does."

A smiling man dressed in white meets us at the door. Joel, Leon introduces us. He takes my hand with a gentle grip. Young and handsome, is he gay, too? Must be. He leads us up to the second floor and outside to a sunny porch suspended in the green of the trees.

"Hey, old man," Leon says, "here we are. Is this the Jimmy Buffet look?"

He speaks to a gaunt, pale man in Hawaiian shirt and straw hat, sitting carefully in the shade.

"I like Jimmy Buffet, Leon. You got a problem?" His voice is a hoarse whisper, so quiet you have to listen closely. "Who's your lovely friend? We have not met, have we, my dear?"

"No, no, I'm Rita, Leon's latest...um, latest what? Friend, maybe?" Oh, please, can I start over.

"Friend, huh," Fitz says, "friend is safe. Good friend, I'll bet, knowing Leon, very good friend." I think it hurts him to talk.

"Should I shake your hand?" I say. "I really don't know what the proper thing is."

"No, no," Fitz says, "no need. It's quite safe, in fact, but it causes such anxiety. You'll only want to wash it afterward, and then you won't be able to relax 'til you do. Very nice of you to ask, though. Some people back up against the wall as if I were spewing forth lethal projectiles."

"Just your jokes," Leon says, "but I'll shake your hand." He takes Fitz's hand, carefully, as if holding a bird's wing. Then he leans down and hugs him.

"Oh, Leon, don't do that," Fitz says. "You wouldn't do that if I wasn't dying."

"I would, Fitz, I would. You're my favorite faggot in the whole world."

"Ah, I'd forgotten your quick wit and tasteless sense of humor. It's such a relief to see you haven't lost it working in that place."

He is panting, working to breathe as he talks. An inhaler appears in his hand. "Pardon me," he says, taking two puffs from the tiny container. "My breathing is not going well, Leon."

"Sangria, anyone?" Joel appears with a pitcher and glasses. "It's a good summertime drink, don't you think?" He has thin sensual lips, very expressive.

He passes around glasses of wine, deep purple in the light. I watch Leon as he takes one. Is it okay to drink now, doc?

"You've got another twenty minutes out here, Fitz," Joel says, and then to us, "He's not supposed to be in the sun. The medicines make his skin so sensitive."

"Yes, thank you, Joel," Fitz says, eyeing the glass in his hand. "You take such good care of me. Look how my hand shakes, Leon. What does Taft call it? Tremor, right? Not shivers or shakes but tremor. Ah, the lexicon of medicine, such an array of words to describe the sufferings of your fellow man. Anyway, lovely Rita, tell me what you know of this young man so that we can converse from a common ground."

"I know a lot about Leon." Like what? Like I know he can't get it up if he drinks too much of this. "We're sort of new to each other as far as relationships go, but I know he can be kind and warm-hearted and sensitive with his patients. And I know he's divorcing a woman who shouldn't be allowed out of doors without a leash, and maybe a muzzle. Is that awful? And I know he's feeling more stress in his life right now than he's willing to admit to."

Fitz nods, tiny beads of sweat gleaming on his face. "A leash and a muzzle, huh. What happened to her, Leon, to Jasmine? She seemed quite the catch at the time, intellectual, provocative, adoring."

Leon looks up. His mind has been somewhere else. "What? Yes, she did, didn't she," he says. "I don't know, Fitz. I don't have a pat answer for Jasmine."

"Honest answers are good," Fitz says quietly. It's an odd thing for a man to say, a surprising thing.

Joel lies in a hammock, hands behind his head. There are birds in the branches nearby.

"It didn't work out," Leon says. He looks uncomfortable. Maybe he doesn't want to talk about her in front of me. "I don't know, Fitz. I was dumb. We didn't know each other very well, I guess. She's not nice, not a nice person. She's cold and distant and selfish."

"Did you guys try to get help, counseling or something?" Then to me, "You don't mind us discussing this, do you? I mean I can understand it if you did, but if it's all said and done, their divorce that is, then I suppose—"

"I don't mind," I say. "It's interesting in fact, very informative." I smile at Leon, but he is deep in thought.

"Yeah, we got help," Leon says. "We bought a couple of books on how to save your marriage, with these exercises you do, like writing down what you love about the other person and then reading it to them, or taking five minutes to tell the other person what makes you angry at them, and they're not allowed to interrupt. Jasmine liked that one. She does anger well."

"Did you love her?" I say. Bits of orange float on the surface of my wine. Don't suppose I could smoke out here with Fitz and that cough.

Leon is glancing around again. What is he looking at? "Love Jas?" he says. "That's the question, isn't it. I don't know. I'm not sure what the word means anymore. I thought I loved her, when we were married anyway. I thought I was 'in love.' She was sexy, smart, unusual, independent, had a mind of her own."

But did you love her, I want to say. I watch him as they talk. He looks distracted, anxious, nodding his head at times.

"Where'd all that feeling go?" Fitz says.

"Hah, all that feeling got slain, massacred, mowed down by a hail of selfishness, bitchiness, spoiledness, whatever the word is. But it doesn't matter anymore, Fitz. It's over, gone, dead and buried."

"You're a warm, gentle person, Leon," Fitz says. "I remember. Maybe she couldn't deal with that. Maybe you overwhelmed her with niceness, she probably never had anyone as nice to her as you. Couldn't deal with it."

"Well, thanks, Fitz, but I don't know. She could set me off pretty well, too. She knew how to pull my string."

"You guys saw a counselor? What did the counselor say?"

"The counselor finally told Jas to get some individual help, told her she had some issues of her own she needed help with. Then asked me out."

"She asked you out?" Fitz says. "The counselor asked you out?"

"Yes, but it wasn't a she."

Fitz slowly smiles, then a hoarse laugh which he stifles quickly, hunching his shoulders in pain. "God, it hurts to laugh. My throat is full of thrush. It even hurts to swallow." He sits panting. "What is thrush, a fungus or something? The counselor was a guy and he asked you out?"

"Well, it was at the end," Leon says, "after we'd decided to split up. He couldn't help us, we were both so angry with each other."

"So you must have told him about me," Fitz says, "about us."

What am I hearing?

"Jasmine did. Very accusatory, like she was damning me to hell. Pretty funny, in retrospect, although we didn't know he was gay at the time."

Leon looks at me now. What is going on here? Is this a joke? Am I the joke?

"Did you go out with him?" Fitz says. "No, you wouldn't have."

"Not my type," Leon says.

What is your type? "Leon," I say, standing. I don't like this. "Is there something I should know here? Or did I hear wrong?"

"Oh, my," Fitz says, "did I say the wrong thing? You haven't told her, Leon?"

"Told her what?" Leon says.

"Yes, what?" I say. Are you gay, Leon? Is that your problem? Should I leave? Will I have to leave?

Leon steps towards me.

"Are you gay, Leon?" I feel that same volcano once again. Has this been some kind of joke, some misguided sexual—

"I'm not gay," Leon says, taking my hand.

"He's not," Fitz says, his voice is more hoarse, almost a whisper. "Leon and I..." He stops to catch his breath, dosing himself from the inhaler again.

Leon takes both my hands now. "I'm not gay, Rita. There was a time, about six years ago, when Fitz and I were very close. We became close friends, and for a brief time we were lovers."

Fitz nods his head for emphasis, whispering, "Leon's a wonderful lover. I envy you, girl."

"Fitz helped me a lot at a time when I needed help," Leon says. "And he helped me realize that I'm really not gay. I'm just another straight horny guy who likes naked girls just as much as anybody."

"Sad but true," Fitz says.

I start to laugh again. "You two guys are weird together. Did you know about all this, Joel?"

Joel rolls toward us in the hammock, raising a fist. "May there be lead in your pencil, whatever direction it may point. Help yourself to more sangria, by the way." He waves toward my empty glass.

"Really, Joel," Fitz says, "so juvenile, but apt, I suppose."

Joel tries to move us inside for supper but Fitz shoos him away. "I don't care about the stupid sun. I'll survive. Let's eat out here. It's too lovely an evening to coop ourselves up inside."

"You'll have a rash in the morning," Joel says.

"A rash, I can deal with a rash," Fitz says, "a mere blemish on my physical presence." But he isn't smiling. He sounds a little angry, maybe desperate. He color is worse and he is working harder to breathe.

"Fitz," Leon says, "you're not doing well. You look worse than you did yesterday at the hospital."

"Maybe the medicine needs some time to work," Fitz says, looking away.

"Have you talked to Taft?" Leon says.

"I'll call him tomorrow. Can we talk about something other than my health?"

Joel brings out a cold soup, cream of leeks, as we gather around a small glass table. We maneuver a chair for Fitz so he is sitting in shade. A refilled pitcher of wine appears also.

"You like my sangria?" Joel says to me.

How much have I had? "Yes, too much, I'm sure. I haven't had it in a long time." Leon's had his share, too. Don't drink too much there, mister horny straight guy.

I watch him as he sits in the fading sunlight. He keeps looking around the porch, in the corners and under the chairs. He looks worried about something.

"So, Fitzhugh," he says suddenly, "how long have you and Joel been together?"

Fitz is toying with his soup. He doesn't look hungry.

"Joel and I, we are not what we seem. Joel is my caretaker. We have been—"

"Caregiver, not caretaker," Joel interrupts. "I don't weed the garden and put up the storms."

"Yes, yes, aren't we touchy," Fitz says. "Joel is my caregiver, God forbid. He's part of the AIDS Cooperative, as am I. It is a very well-conceived organization in which those of us who have the misfortune to be HIV positive care for those of us actually dying of the disease, in return for the promise of similar care when their time comes. Many of us in the community are left with no one to care for us when we become ill. It's the misfortune of—"

Now Fitz starts coughing. It hurts him, you can tell, the way he hunches over. He turns away from the table and Joel moves to help him. He looks so skinny and frail, just bones beneath that crazy shirt. Joel helps him puff on his inhaler. How many times is he going to use that thing?

I touch Leon's arm, and he nods. He sees it, too. Fitz looks awful.

The coughing stops and he turns back to us, sweating, panting, pale. He takes several swallows of the wine.

"I'm sorry," he says. "I know I create a repulsive presence. You don't need to stay." He breathes carefully, afraid of more coughing.

"It's okay, Fitz," Leon says.

"Illness is part of living, Fitz" I say, "part of all our lives."

"This is more than an illness." His voice is angry. "It's a curse."

"And you're not repulsive," I say. "You're sick, Fitz, and you're suffering. A suffering person needs loved ones around. People aren't meant to suffer alone."

As he struggles for air he eyes me, listening, thinking. What is he thinking? I glance at Leon.

"That's right, Fitz," Leon says. "I had no idea you were sick. I'm glad we made contact again. You could have called me any time."

Fitz nods, speaking slowly, "I know that, Leon. And I have other people. I have friends." His breathing slows.

"Friends," Joel pipes up, "yes, I daresay. Fitz has lots of friends." He pauses, pouring us more wine. "A gaggle, a coterie of extremely eccentric individuals."

I think Joel likes his wine, too. He goes on, "Some well educated, some well off, some gay, some straight, artists, professors, musicians, but all of them eccentric. And I think—" He pauses, raising a finger. "---I think that maintaining one's level of eccentricity, if it is high, requires much time and energy, leaving most of your friends with little time and energy to help ease your suffering."

"Rats from a sinking ship," Fitz mutters.

"They're busy people, Fitz," Joel says. "And they do come around. Andrew and Raoul were here Sunday, if you'll recall. And even your sister called, n'est-ce pas? She's coming to see you."

"Yes, dear sweet Becca," Fitz says, "I can't wait to see her smiling face."

"So you didn't know about Leon and Fitz?" Joel turns to me now, suddenly bright, airy.

"Um, no, I didn't. In fact I don't think I ever met a man whose had a thing with another guy before. A guy who's gay, I mean, obviously." Do I sound dumb? I don't want to sound dumb to Leon.

"Or who would admit to it," Fitz says.

"Yes, I suppose." Can we change the subject? "This is yummy, Joel, cold soup. I don't ever have cold soup, unless the microwave's broken."

They laugh, thank God.

"But still, I don't know, where I grew up and the kind of guys I met...I can't imagine any of them ever did anything with another guy."

"Really," Joel says, a little loud. I think he's getting drunk. "No gay guys around, huh. Where was this?"

"Well, I was an army brat, or a marine brat really. We lived at Camp Lejeune. It's in North Carolina."

"Ah, the marines," Joel says. "A few good men."

"Be nice," Fitz says. "You know not to whom you speak."

"You're right," Joel says, pausing to drink some soup. He turns to Fitz. "You haven't touched my soup, Fitzhugh. I slaved all day and you haven't touched it."

A smile flickers on Fitz's gaunt face. "I took some. It's very good, a masterpiece even, an objet d'art. But my appetite is vanished. I'm sorry, Joel." He still sweats. He must be feverish.

"But Rita," Joel says in a patient teacher's voice, "there are gay men everywhere, and lesbians, too, lest we be sexist here. Even the military, in fact especially the military, has its share of us. Despite their clumsy discrimination, their stupid policies."

Intellectual conversation, hang out with a doctor and this is what you get. So big deal, I can talk, too. "In the marines?" I say. "You think there are homos in—I'm sorry, I mean gay men—in the marines?"

Now Leon is laughing. "Yeah, Joel, how about it, homos in the marines?"

"Call us what you will, we are there. There is no doubt." He stands. "Excuse me, I must get the salad."

"Well, maybe they were there," I say, "but I never knew it."

Leon is looking down at his feet. Now he leans slightly to look under the table where he sits. He shakes his head as if there is a mosquito near his ear. What does he hear?

I watch Joel reappear with a wooden salad bowl. The funny little way he walks, is he doing that for me, or is it the sangria?

"It seems so odd to me." I'm talking again. What am I saying? "I mean, I don't care who does what with who. Or is it whom? But I don't see how you could want to. I mean the way a guy likes a woman, you know, the way he's attracted sexually. It's so different. I just don't understand it, is all."

There are little flowers on top of Joel's salad, of course.

"Maybe Leon could explain that," Fitz says. "He's been there and back, maybe he can bridge the impasse for you."

"You're asking me?" Leon says. He looks embarrassed.

"Not what goes where," Fitz says. "She's not asking that. But what is the physical attraction? What makes some men want to touch each other?" Fitz is still breathing fast, almost panting. He should be in the hospital, like Leon said.

"Perhaps you'd like a moment to gather your thoughts," Fitz says. "Lovely salad, Joel."

"I'm not sure what thoughts to gather," Leon says.

"Do you remember when you first started looking at boys, Rita," Joel says. "You were probably in junior high or so."

"I don't remember ever not looking at boys," I say, giggling again. This is embarrassing to talk about, but if it doesn't bother them then what the hell. "But, yes, go on."

"You might stare at a boy's arm and imagine yourself touching the muscles there, or watch his hips as he walks down the hall."

"Mm, hmm." Like Leon's, when he wears those scrub clothes.

"And there were certain boys you just wanted to be near, to stand near and feel the heat of their skin."

I nod. I must be blushing. This talk is turning me on, the wine and this talk and these three men. God, poor Fitz.

"Well, I felt the same way," Joel goes on. "When I was thirteen I would daydream in class about the boys, wake up in a sweat at night. It wasn't anything weird or sick. It wasn't my father who rejected me or abandoned me. I had a great family, my parents loved me, took good care of me. I was a healthy, normal kid."

"And now look at you," Fitz says, "serving us radiccio with little flower petals on top. Expecting us to eat it. How sick, you homo."

Leon is laughing hard now.

"And you never felt that way about a woman?" I say. "Never wanted to touch a woman, never noticed a woman's legs, or a woman's breasts?" Now Joel looks embarrassed. "Well, not really. I mean I went out on a few dates in high school. I wanted to be straight like everybody else, for a while. But it just wasn't there."

You've never been in bed with a woman, I want to ask. Ooh, could I give it a try, just once?

"But that's my point," he goes on. "It's a natural thing that a person is born with. Just like some people have red hair." He nods toward me.

"But what about the way you act?" I say. Oh, God, why did I say that? "I don't mean you in particular, or Fitz, but some gay guys act so weird. I mean I think it's cute sometimes, but it seems so put on."

"Effeminate, you mean?" Joel says, the humor leaving his face. "Like sissies. There probably weren't many sissies around Camp Lejeune."

"Some of us are a bit affectatious," Fitz says.

Leon moves suddenly, kicking his feet beneath the table. "Sorry," he says, "my feet are acting weird." He looks frightened.

"Well, we all have mannerisms," Joel says. There is an edge to his voice. "But look at the mannerisms of straight men. They can be just as affected, swaggering around, slapping each other's hands. Everyone has mannerisms. You have mannerisms, Rita."

Why is he angry? What did I say?

"Yes, I'm sure I do."

"The way you hold your wine glass, for example, and the way you drink?"

"Yes?"

"Joel," Fitz says, "didn't I smell some delicious fish thing in the kitchen?"

"What about the way I drink?" Suddenly this isn't fun anymore.

Joel looks at me but Fitz starts coughing again, turning away from us. Joel helps him with his inhaler but he keeps on, that awful cough. It makes me cringe. Joel moves him inside, steadying him.

I stare into the dark greenery around us. What about the way I drink, and who gives a fuck about it anyway? I want to cry and I hate it. It's a weak feeling and I hate feeling weak.

"Why did he say that?" I turn to Leon.

"Say what?"

"About my drinking."

Leon studies me as if I just appeared. "He was talking about mannerisms. What did he say about you?" He missed it. Maybe that's good. But I didn't miss it.

The sun is gone. We sit in cool twilight. Inside the coughing goes on.

"Can't you do anything for him, Leon?" I reach for his hand. "Can't anyone do anything?"

"Not really." He shakes his head. "Nothing that will really help. You've been through this before."

I have, with Camille. I rest my head on my arms. I had too much to drink. I don't want to be here anymore, with Fitz and his sickness. But obviously we can't just leave. I said it before, my own words, people shouldn't suffer alone.

"Leon," Joel calls from inside, "would you come here?"

I follow him. Fitz lies pale, ashen, on his bed. His cough has stopped. "Something's different, Leon," he says. "Something feels different."

"Are you having pain?"

"No, no pain. I'm very lightheaded."

"Coughing can make you that way," Leon says in that calmest of voices. He sits and takes Fitz's wrist. "Your heart's beating very fast, Fitz. Too fast. Has it ever done this before?"

"I don't know," Fitz says, angry, frustrated. "How should I know?"

"No," Joel says, "no, it hasn't. What's it doing?"

Leon sits silent, two fingers resting on the bony wrist. "It feels like you're in atrial fib, Fitz, probably from using that inhaler so much, or it could be from—"

"What did you call it?" Joel is upset, almost panicky. "What does it mean, Leon?"

The room is draped in printed cloths with unlit candles about, the sixties harem den. Where's the hookah?

"Atrial fib," Leon says. "It just means his heart is beating too fast. Lots of things can cause it."

Joel helps him raise Fitz's legs onto pillows. Then Leon massages his neck, first one side, then the other.

"What are you doing, Leon?" Fitz whispers.

"Sometimes this stops it. There's a reflex that you can trigger by rubbing this artery in your neck. Sometimes it'll slow down your heart."

"Sometimes?" Joel says.

Leon eyes him. "Sometimes. Usually not, in fact, but it's worth a try. Fitz, when your heart is beating so fast it drops your blood pressure. That's why you feel like you do."

"You mean like I'm going to die?" Fitz says.

"You're not going to die," Leon says.

"I am, Leon."

Leon is silent, feeling his pulse again. "We should take you to the hospital, Fitz."

"No." Fitz shakes his head. He is so white, like wax stretched over bone. "I'll stay here. I am going to die, Leon. Why not tonight? There's not much time left anyway."

Leon shakes his head. "This is not the way to die, Fitz. All you need is some medicine to make you sleepy and little jolt to the chest."

Not the way to die, he said. Such words, and he said them so easily.

Fitz shakes his head.

Leon rises and walks silently back out to the porch. He stands with arms folded gazing into the near dark. Is he trembling? I move beside him. I don't know what to do.

"He won't die," he says. "He'll just be miserable. He needs to be in the hospital anyway." Now he clutches his hands flat over his ears. "God, I wish this would stop. I don't need this right now."

"What is it, Leon?" I put a hand on his arm.

"I don't know what it is. I'm hearing things." He acts scared. "I don't know."

Now he walks back to Fitz with a careful controlled step.

"Fitz, you won't die from this. You'll just lie here miserable and weak until your heart goes back to a normal rhythm. But it could be hours. It could be all night. Besides, you need to be in the hospital for your breathing, Fitz, for your lungs. You're not getting better here at home. You don't want to die this way, Fitz, from pneumonia. It's a long, terrible death."

He sits on the bed, removing the pillows beneath Fitz's legs. "C'mon, Fitz." His voice breaks as he starts to cry. "Please let me take you there. This is not the way to let your life end. It's not time yet."

Chapter Eight

Bombing bad, bombing bad, Zach, your voice, why do you keep whispering that? What does it mean? You're driving me crazy, yes, crazy, the operative word here. I feel every heartbeat, every breath, the hair on the back of my neck.

Why hasn't anyone said anything? I know they can tell. The nurses are watching me. They've been talking about me, pointing at me.

Okay, four p.m., two more hours and I'm out of here. Maybe I'll miss the knife and gun stuff if I'm lucky. I have to go see Fitz upstairs. Fitz, God, he looked so awful last night, until Lyle finally shocked him, got him back into a rhythm. Maybe I should have left him at home like he wanted.

Joshua Lowenthal appears in front of me, a second year res from the other team, tall, husky, with dark hair and a heavy beard, one of those guys who looks like he has a five o'clock shadow all day long. He's smart, good in a crunch, but not known for his interpersonal skills.

He shoves a chart into my hand, shaking his head in disgust. "Jesus, Leon, this guy...this guy comes in here saying he's got a kidney stone, that he's had 'em before and all. And of course he's allergic to Toradol, or he says he is, so of course we've got to give him a narcotic. And he looks like he's got a stone, and he's got blood in his urine.

"So I check his fingers to make sure he's not pulling a fast one on us, and sure enough, he pricked his finger for the blood in the urine."

I hear whispers and glance around to see who, but no one is there.

"Leon?" Lydia sits waiting, chart in hand. "What's the Toradol got to do with it?"

I look back at Josh.

"Well, you give Toradol for kidney stones, right?" he says, slightly irritated.

"You do?" she says, exposing her ignorance. Good for her. That takes guts.

"Of course."

"Maybe your colleague hasn't dealt with kidney stones much, Josh," I add. "Perhaps you could enlighten her."

"Okay," he says, struggling to calm his voice. "Toradol is an injectable anti-inflammatory, right? Generic name is ketoralac."

Lydia nods politely.

"So anti-inflammatories are prostaglandin inhibitors which act to relax spasm of the ureter caused by stones, right?"

"Okay," she says. "I didn't know that."

"Also works for gallstones, relaxes the cystic duct from the gallbladder." Then, turning back to me, "So this dude says he's got a kidney stone but he's allergic to Toradol, so our only option to give him pain relief is a narcotic, right? Then he fakes the blood in his urine by pricking his finger and putting the blood in his urine specimen."

"A standard ploy," I say. "He's looking for narcotics. So just discharge him and he can take a hike."

"Well, that's what I was going to do," Josh says, "but then he starts giving me this song and dance about how he has this chronic back problem from an old injury and he can't get any help for it because he has no insurance. He can't work because of his back, and he had surgery for it a couple years ago but that didn't work and he's trying to get on disability but he's been waiting months for the labor disability board to evaluate him. But, you know, Leon, the guy really does look like he's in a lot of pain. I mean maybe it's an act but he can barely move on the bed. Triage had to bring him back in a wheelchair."

I watch his face move as he talks, serious, intent, the heavy beard. Your hair keeps growing after death, I've read, for several hours. His lifeless face on a steel table being shaved by a dark-suited man appears in my mind. "Doesn't he have a doctor of his own?" I say. "The guy who did the surgery or somebody?"

"No, he says he can't afford it. He doesn't have any money because he can't work, and so nobody will see him in their office to help him. He says the surgeon who operated on his back told him there wasn't anything more he could do for him. Some guy named Stambaugh. He prescribed physical therapy but the guy can't afford to go and do it. That was months ago."

"Leon," someone calls. Who—no, don't look. Just a sound, just a voice. It sounded like Fitz. No, he wouldn't come down here. He was so weak last night, even after he got shocked. It drained him. He couldn't even walk when we got him up to his bed.

And then afterward, at Rita's place, what a mess that was. She was so angry, at Joel and then at me. This alcohol thing, I need to convince her—

"Leon," Josh says, "Are you here?"

"I'm here. Sorry, I've got a lot on my mind. Okay, so what do you want to do?" The radio is going off and now Ted is waiting, too.

"I don't know," Josh says, shaking his head. "Either the guy is a drug addict and knows all the right things to say, or he's telling the truth and he's a pathetic guy in a bad situation."

"Or both," Lydia says. "Maybe he's had chronic pain for a long time and become addicted to narcotics because that's the only way he can get any relief."

"Oh, please," Ted says, slumped against a counter, "The voice of humanity, mercy, and benevolence. Did you look for needle tracks on his arms?"

"Yeah, yeah," Josh says, "no tracks."

"Well, Lydia might be right, Josh," I say. "The world won't end if you give the guy a shot of morphine. My own feeling is it's better to give pain relief to the people who need it and not worry so much about the addicts who might be putting on an act."

He nods, writing the order on the chart. "You know, Leon, sometimes the easy shit is harder than the bad stuff. The patients that are really sick are easier to take care of than the ones with nothing seriously wrong, like this guy."

"Emotional objectivity, my boy. Do not let yourself get emotionally involved. Right, Megawatt?"

"Right, Leon, anything you say." He waves a chart. "When you're finished being sensitive to drug addicts I've got this totally flipped out psychotic dude that Cincinnati's finest just brought in. They found him dancing in the middle of the Fifth Street Bridge, playing matador with the cars. Looks like a schizophrenic break to me. I think I've seen him before. We need to restrain him and get some Haldol into him."

"Yeah, go ahead. Then page the psychiatry resident to come see him."

Lydia's patient is a workman from downtown with a cut finger. I show her how to inject anesthetic at the base of his finger, a digital block, to put the whole finger to sleep.

Bombing bad and bombing bad. Zach, you sound hoarse, angry, urgent as if you want me to listen.

Ted's psychotic guy, Claudette and Roxanne are wrestling with him, restraining him to a gurney with padded leather cuffs on his wrists and ankles. This is routine, they talk about their work schedule over his skinny flopping body.

I move beside the bed. The possessed face is young, with several days stubble and tangled damp hair. He is panting, straining against demons he doesn't understand. His eyes slant down to meet mine.

"Hi," I attempt a friendly tone. "I'm Doctor Mendel. What's your name?"

"THERE ARE SPIES," he shouts. "THERE ARE SPIES. STOP THEM!"

"Do you know his name, Claudette?"

"Dennis something."

"Dennis," I pat him on the shoulder. "Dennis, we're trying to help you if you can just relax a little."

"That's no use, Dr. Mendel," Claudette says, "we been trying to calm this boy down but he don't calm."

"RANCID," he shouts, "IT'S RANCID. LET ME GO."

"Rancid, huh?" I glance over him, his pupils, his skin, his breath. Is he drunk, overdosed, hypoglycemic? Has he got meningitis or seizures? Did Ted miss something or is he really just crazy? Just crazy like I'm becoming. When will they have to strap me down?

Has an aneurysm burst in his brain, or did someone hit him in the head with a baseball bat? Or a stroke from shooting up cocaine, or maybe organophosphate poisoning from spraying weed killer, or botulism or any of the other hundred or so illnesses that might first make someone act crazy and then kill him if we, if I, make him lie strapped to a gurney for the hour or two it will take until the psychiatrist gets down here.

It's my decision, not Ted's, not Claudette's, my responsibility if we're wrong. Zach, you could have done this stuff, slid through these decisions, confident, never a second thought. A glance at the patient, a word or two, then out the door, next case. But you're not here, are you?

So what's the call? He's just crazy, a sad decompensated schizophrenic. I might do a blood test or two, but he looks crazy to me, sounds crazy, acts crazy. You never know for sure, or at least not until you walk back into the room an hour later and there he is, snoozed out from the Haldol, but still alive and still just crazy. We could even put him on a monitor to tell us if he starts to die. But no, I've seen this guy. He's been crazy before. On another day I might sit and try to talk to him, try to calm him amidst the storm in his brain, let him open up the world of his delusions, turn over the stone of his mind and watch what crawls beneath, try to imagine what he feels—

"Dr. Mendel." Claudette says. "How long you gonna stand there starin' at this boy?" She and Roxanne are watching me, waiting.

"You're right. I'm in a daze." I shake my head and smile like it's nothing. There's a haze around me, Zach's whispers like a roar.

At the station Lowenthal is pacing, two charts in his hand.

All right, be cool, be calm. "Whatcha got, Josh?" I say to him. My voice sounds like someone else's.

"This guy won't go away, Leon, the guy with the fake kidney stone. I gave him 10 milligrams of morphine and he's some better, but he really can't move. Hurts too much. He says he's been living in his car and can't even drive it."

"Lives in his car? No wonder his back hurts. Well, I don't know, Josh. What do you think you should do with him?" I watch his face to be sure I'm making sense. "Maybe one of the social workers ought to talk to him, find him a place to stay."

"Why you talking so loud, Leon?" Lowenthal says.

Everyone at the station is watching me. I'm the one who needs a social worker, or maybe a shrink.

"Was I talking loud? Sorry."

"Maybe he needs to be admitted," Josh says. "Pain management, physical therapy and all that."

"Admit him? For back pain? The orthopedics guys will never go for that." I glance at the clock. This is almost over. I need to leave. "Well, who knows, go ahead and page them, tell them to come evaluate the guy for admission. They'll hate you forever, but if he can't move he can't move."

"Leon," I hear Fitz call me. I turn. Is he down here? How did he get down— No, it's just Rohit waiting for me, chart in hand.

"Are you okay, Leon?" Rohit says, his wide dark eyes watching me. What does he see? We're training these guys to recognize illness, physical and mental, to make judgments at a glance. Can he tell I'm losing it, really losing it?

"I'm okay, just not feeling too good today. What have you got?"

"You want me to go tell this case to Icky?"

"No, no, that's okay. Go ahead."

We look at X-rays of an eighty-eight-year-old man with a fractured hip. I send Rohit off to arrange his admission.

Finally Lyle Cassidy appears, my replacement.

"How's your friend doing?" he says, "That Fitzhugh guy?"

"He's okay. I'm gonna run up and see him as soon as I'm off. Thanks for taking care of him last night."

I move to leave and Lyle watches me. What is he thinking? Is he wondering about me, wondering why I'm getting divorced, and why I happened to show up last night with a gay friend with AIDS?

A hand rests on my arm. "Dr. Mendel, I'm Kelly Woods, from utilization services." A woman in business clothes smiles at me, carefully groomed, clipboard in hand. "Do you have a moment?"

"Okay."

"I believe you're admitting a patient named Ricky Donnelly for back pain. Is that correct?"

"Back pain? Yeah, that must be Lowenthal's patient. The orthopedic guys were supposed to come down and take a look at him?"

"Yes, he's being admitted to the orthopedic service."

"LEON!" I hear a shriek from across the department. Ted's crazy guy. No, not my name, just a shriek.

"Dr. Mendel?"

I turn back to her. "Yes, I'm sorry. Go on."

"Dr. Mendel, the diagnosis of back pain does not meet admission criteria for Medicaid reimbursement. The hospital won't be reimbursed for his admission." She pauses, watching me.

"Okay," I say, "What do you need?"

"Does the patient truly require hospitalization? Would an extended care facility be more appropriate?"

"An extended care facility? You mean a nursing home?"

She nods with a practiced smile.

"You think we could get this guy into a nursing home at—" I look at my watch, "at 6 p.m. on a Thursday afternoon?"

"Well, you're right. That might be difficult. But with this diagnosis—"

The light pops on in my head. "Ah, you just need a better admission diagnosis, don't you? How about incapacitating pain? Would that help?"

"Yes, that would be helpful, of course only if it's appropriate."

"Appropriate? You mean if it's true? You mean if the guy really has bad back pain so that he can't move."

"Well, that's certainly your judgment." The fake smile again, she glances around, looking now to leave. "Shall we add that to his diagnosis?"

"How about excruciating, or disabling, or agonizing? Which would be best?"

"Incapacitating pain is just fine," she says, edging toward the exit.

"How about paralyzing, torturous, or unendurable? Would that squeeze a few more dollars out of the state? Crippling, that's a good one, or all-consuming."

"Thank you, Dr. Mendel. I can see you're busy." She turns and walks off.

* * *

An awkward teenage couple step into the hospital elevator with me. She is pale, heavy, perhaps post-partum, maybe going to the nursery see their new baby. They whisper and giggle, uncertain what to do with their hands. A tall senior resident in a white coat over blue scrubs ignores us all. He's a Vascular Surgery Fellow and doesn't recognize me out of the department and out of scrubs.

Fitz, how could he get AIDS, one of the smartest guys around. Software whiz who sat at home and designed desktop art and publishing programs, who could zoom around the country with his keyboard and modem, or even around the world, snatching a couple of megabytes from his company's Chicago branch, chatting onscreen to some paint program nut in Taiwan, clicking on a music program to run in his headphones. Fitz who filled up the here and now, jammed it full of friends and parties and work and fitness and sex, so he could squeeze out a past full of family who died and a father who wouldn't speak to him, an old-fashioned New Orleans patrician who kicked him out, his only son, excommunicated him when he found out Fitz was gay.

Fitz, maybe he can help me. I need help after last night with Rita. She said it doesn't matter, sex between us doesn't matter. But it does, of course it does. And she's wondering now if I really am gay. I'm not gay, but I need to show her I'm not. No amount of talk is going to matter in the end.

Six north is a general medicine floor. The wide hallway bustles with nurses, housekeepers with linen carts, and transport techs pushing bored gloomy patients in wheelchairs. A ghastly pale old lady slides by asleep on a gurney, a naso-gastric tube dangling from her nose.

Leon, Leon, dying people murmur at me from open doors.

I hardly ever come up to these floors, only for Code Blues, which the ED attending is supposed to supervise, plunging off the elevator, hoping someone can point me the way to the room where a patient just died. Running into a crowded room where an ancient carcass lies on the bed, bloodless skin yellow under the lights, arms bruised from innumerable blood tests and IVs, some poor octogenarian whose organs have failed one by one until finally the heart goes, too. A frightened nurse doing CPR, residents milling around shouting orders, then we poke tubes into its flesh, squirt medicine into a bloodstream that doesn't flow, shock a heart that doesn't want to pump, try to salvage a couple of more days of misery, try to delay the surrender in a battle that's already been lost.

The unit secretary looks up at me, a bored girl with too much mascara.

"I'm Doctor Mendel. There's a patient named Goddard, Fitzhugh Goddard."

She runs a cherry-colored nail over a rack of white plastic cards, then points out my way.

The door is shut but I knock and push it open.

"Just a minute," calls out a nurse's voice, "Who is it?" I peek around the curtain and see Fitz's gaunt form, naked except for a diaper, getting a bath from a gloved student nurse.

"Hah, look at you."

A startled glance, then slow recognition from eyes still lively, the hint of a grin. He looks exhausted.

"Talk about pearls before swine," I say, "this pretty young lady giving you a bath. Better than you deserve."

The poor girl looks hurriedly between us, sponging Fitz's fingers as he lies on towels. "We're almost done," she says, struggling to smile.

"Hi, Leon." His voice is feeble. "Need a bath? Maybe we could get two for one."

She reddens. She is perhaps nineteen with no idea who I am.

"It's okay," I say to her. "I'm Doctor Mendel from the Emergency Department. Fitz here is a friend of mine."

She nods, gathering up towels and basin. She straightens Fitz's sheets, tries to arrange the IV tubes running into his arm, and makes a rapid escape.

"Thanks, you're an angel," Fitz calls hoarsely after her, then begins to cough.

I step to the window and wait for it to pass. On the wide sill there is a stack of magazines and some unusual flowers, purple petals forming deep cups. Against the sunshine the cups are so dark they are like holes, and again I feel it, death lurking in those holes, staring out at me, waiting. Like a world behind this world, burning through here and there, in dark places, people's eyes.

"Don't say it, Leon," Fitz rasps, struggling to stop coughing.

"Say what?"

"I hate it when people ask me how I'm doing. It doesn't seem like a polite thing to ask in my situation. It's like they're saying 'How are you dying?'"

Bombing bad, bombing bad, your whispers are different now, Zach, closer.

"Okay, I won't. Besides, it's pretty obvious, Fitz. You look awful, like a reject from Somalia."

"Thanks, I try to stay slim." The shape of his skull shows through the thin blond hair, still damp from the bath, pale scalp under the spikes of hair. "Sit over here, Leon. The light is hard on my eyes."

"So what's old Herb say?"

"Who?"

"Herb Taft, your doctor."

He nods, barely moving on the bed. An oxygen cannula hisses next to the bed. He lets me slide it beneath his nose. The image of his gaunt face with an endotracheal tube jammed into the mouth comes to me, a ventilator huffing and sighing, keeping him alive.

"I like him. He's like talking to your father," Fitz says. "And he talks to me like he's talking to a child, well, maybe a teenager. But I think he's being straight with me. I've got bad pneumonia, Leon."

He fingers the plastic oxygen tube. "It's scary not being able to catch your breath all the time. And my kidneys are shot from one of those medicines. At least that's what he says. I don't know, but they hurt." He rubs his flank. "And I'm so skinny, Leon. Jesus, I didn't imagine how skinny I could get. Look at this."

He holds up an arm, the contours of bone obvious beneath the skin.

I look away, just my eyes so he won't notice. There it is, the feeling of death, my insides tightening, the adrenaline seeping into my blood. But there must be something more, not just adrenaline, releasing into my blood, some other hormone, some kind of evil complex lipid that eats at your soul, a fear hormone, that seeps into the blood and then into the muscles and the nerves and the brain. Fitz must feel it now, all the time—

"So what about you, superhero?" he says. "You seem a bit edgy lately, distracted, not the old easy-going Leon."

I shiver and look at him. "I'm becoming psychotic, Fitz." Why not tell him?

"Strong word. Is work getting to you?"

"No, really, Fitz." I edge my chair closer, checking to see that the door is shut. "I'm going nuts, certifiably psychotic. Hallucinations, distortions of reality, voices, intrusive thoughts, uncontrollable emotions."

He watches me, gray eyes sunken in a bristled face. "Seriously, Leon?"

"Seriously. It's frightening, Fitz. I'm losing control and I can't do anything about it."

"You always were wound a little tight, Leon. Maybe you should just sort of let it happen, let your mind go for a while."

I look across his bed, out at the feverish blue sky. "That's novel advice."

"So why is this happening to you?" he says. "Stress? You're obviously dealing with a lot of stress. Stress is your life, Leon. You used to thrive on it. How about drugs? As I recall you and Jas used to do a little coke now and then."

"No, she still does but I stopped a long time ago, Fitz. Not my thing."

"Okay, what's left? Sexual identity, how about that? You and Jas, was that an issue?"

I feel myself sigh. Is there something under his bed? I hear something moving down there.

"What are you listening to, Leon? Are they paging you?"

"No, sorry. I think my own mind is paging me. I'm hearing things, Fitz, imagining things."

"Well, is it sex?" he says and I remember why I loved him once.

"I don't know, Fitz. I was fine with Jasmine, 'til the very end, anyway. She got so mean I think I was afraid to put myself inside her. Thought I might not get it back."

I watch the drops fall in the drip chamber of his IV, some nasty yellow poison, clear and almost pretty, jewel-like with the sun on it.

"But now I'm having problems with Rita. Damn, Fitz, I really like Rita." Anger at myself makes me stand and move to the window. "I'm not gay, damn it." I turn and face him.

"It's not a curse, Leon."

"I know, Fitz. But I'm not gay, that's not the problem." Now the words come slowly. "I'm not having problems with Rita because I'm gay. I'm having problems with Rita because...because I'm becoming psychotic." An urge to smash the glass in front of me makes me raise my fist, but I stop, giving the window a gentle thump.

Now I spin and face him. "Right? Remember, Fitz? You said so yourself. You said I should go back, that I wasn't really gay."

He nods. "I've been wrong before."

"I don't think so, Fitz. I do better with a woman. I just think Jasmine was the wrong woman. She turned mean and petty and selfish."

He holds my gaze. "Why?"

Why. There it is, there Fitz is, cutting through all the bull, cutting right to the big question. "Good question. I don't know why, Fitz. The counselor didn't know why. But it wasn't the sex. We had good sex. She was the one who was uncomfortable with sex, afraid of it, used it to manipulate me."

"Would a man do that?"

I gaze back at him, thinking. "I don't know, Fitz. I don't know if a man would do that. Does it matter?" The dark places in the flowers seem to grasp at my gaze. "I think a man might do that, just as much as a woman. I think some of your friends are just as capable of bitchiness and manipulation. Damn, Fitz, this is not what I need, you trying to convince me I'm really gay after all." I feel desperate, like crying. "You told me I wasn't gay, damn it."

He pushes at the pillow. He is tired. "I'm sorry, Leon. You're right, and I still think it's true. But it's a tough thing, and I've seen people agonize over which way to go, and come out for a while and then go back." He lies panting. "But you were such a lover, Leon." He looks at me like no other man has.

I reach for his hand. "God, Fitz, I'm sorry this has happened to you."

He squirms on the bed, trying to change position. It hurts him to move.

"Hasn't any of your family come to see you? I thought your sister was coming."

He shakes his head. "Becca, she doesn't know me anymore," he rasps, then shrugs under the pale gown. "I hope she doesn't come, to tell the truth. It would be meaningless."

Fitz's mother died, I remember him telling me, when he was young. He and two sisters grew up in a huge empty plantation house outside New Orleans, raised by maids and nannies and a father who was rarely home and whom he avoided when he was. Then the father and one sister died, too. He has told me how but I don't recall.

On his side, breathing fast from the exertion of moving, he eyes me. "When am I going to die, Leon?"

I hold his hand.

"That's the thing I want to know," he says. "Taft won't tell me, the nurses won't tell me. Will you tell me, Leon?"

"They don't know, Fitz, and I don't know either. It's hard to say. Maybe you'll be okay for a while. Maybe they'll get you better and you can go home for a while."

He waves a bony hand, dismissing my words. He shakes his head, eyes heavy, exhausted. I want to say more, something more than what he's already heard. When do you want to die, Fitz, I want to say. When will you be ready? Are you ready now? Can I help you get ready? But his eyes are closed. I sit with him till he sleeps.

Death is here, in the flowers, in the shadows, waiting for Fitz. I want to grab those flowers and crush them in my hands, get down on the floor and kick at the dark place under the bed, jerk open the closet door and grab it, strangle it, pound it against the wall.

Bombing bad, bombing bad. I walk down the hall and stand trembling at the nurses station, the words roaring in my ears. Don't they hear that? Are they watching me? I find Fitz's chart, a blue binder in a rack under a marker board, and there next to his name on the board is the round orange tag that marks him a No Code. Without even looking at the chart I can see that Taft has given the order, has filled out the advance directive, which Fitz must have signed as well, authorizing the hospital to let him die in peace when the time comes. When the time comes, as he dwindles and dwindles and finally dies.

A No Code, so that when some poor timid nursing student, tiptoeing into his room to take his blood pressure or make his bed, finds him eyes closed and limp, and she realizes that he is more than asleep, that he is not breathing at all, that he might be dead and she stands for a moment panicked, uncertain, who perhaps if she is brave will touch that cold wrist to take his pulse and not find it and be further panicked because she isn't sure if she felt in the right place, but who one way or another will rapidly realize that he is dead and maybe shout for help down the hall or maybe hit the code switch on the wall, so that when she does, the alarm won't sound, the P.A. system won't rouse residents making rounds or sleeping to rush into Fitz's room and start CPR and do all the silly things we do to try to bring back someone from the dead, so that instead he will be allowed to die. Allowed to die, what an expression.

"Do you need some help, doctor?" an older nurse asks me, smiling above half-glasses.

I have been standing, staring at the closed chart. "No, sorry." I slide the binder back into its slot, unopened. I know what it contains. "Fitz is a friend of mine," I say, gesturing toward the orange tag on the board.

She nods, holding my gaze. "I'm sorry. He seems like a very nice man."

Chapter Nine

Okay, now the mirror. I haven't worn this skirt in so long. It's good for my legs. The tank top, hmm, sexy. Too sexy? Britnie will make a crack. I don't care. Maybe no bra, he might like that. No, then you can see my nipples. Britnie will have a fit. God, I'm so flat. But he knows, he's seen me, touched me.

I need a glass of wine. Is it time? No, I'll wait 'til he comes, if I can, if he comes soon. What time is it? He said he had to go see Fitz.

I'll be good, no wine 'til he comes, just like he wants it. Just like a normal person. Like I'm not a normal person. I'm a normal alcoholic and normally I would have had a couple glasses by now and normally I wouldn't feel like my skin is inside out and my insides are a bunch of angry snakes. Shit, I hate this.

Down the stairs, into the living room.

"Rita, what are you wearing?" Britnie says. She hasn't moved in an hour.

"I thought you were going to pick up this room, young lady," I say.

"I am, I am. Don't have a cow." She rolls off the couch. "But why are you wearing that skirt?"

"Because I feel like it. Why are you wearing those jeans? Would you like to put on some music, by the way, while you're picking up those CDs?"

"You want to look nice for Leon, don't you? Sweet and feminine in a skirt, and that sexy little top."

"SO WHAT!" Oops, way too loud, damn it. This living room is hopeless, laundry, her doll stuff, books in piles, at least she's reading.

"What's your problem?" she says.

Go into the kitchen. Have a glass. I don't want to tear his head off when he walks in the door, or Britnie's if he doesn't come soon. Have a glass. No, don't, he'll smell it. So he smells it, big deal. It's been all day. I've been good all day, and what does it get me? A cigarette, have a cigarette instead. No, then I'll want the wine even more. How about a Valium? I wish I had some.

Okay, the salad, does he like salad? He said he does. He likes to be healthy. Tomatoes, does he like tomatoes? Britnie hates tomatoes. Should I put them in or not, or make a separate salad for her? Look at my hands. God, what if he sees me shaking? I can't cut anything like this.

Okay, stop, think. Look at yourself, all in a tizzy. Over what, over a guy, for the first time in how long? A guy, finally, in your life. And the monster, my MONSTER! I wasn't ready for this. Great, so now I'm crying, staring over the sink, out the window, crying. The classic pose, roll the cameras.

So have a glass and calm yourself and be like a normal person, or wait and go nuts and scream at Britnie and say God knows what to Leon when he walks in and maybe he'll see my hands shaking and hear the shake in my voice and see the anxiety on my face. Or maybe he won't.

"Rita."

"What?" I spin around to her.

She stares. "You're crying."

"I know I am. Sorry."

"Why?" She steps toward me. "Why are you crying?" Now she hugs me, a surprising gesture. She usually keeps to herself.

Now the doorbell, of course.

"Great timing, huh," Britnie says, smiling up at me. "I'll get it. You go in the bathroom and fix your face."

Now we stand in the living room, glasses in hand, my monster back in its cage. He hasn't noticed, or hasn't let on if he did.

"That's Britnie's," I say. "Hasn't she done a nice job?"

He's admiring the fish tank. He looks pale, tired. Nice Hawaiian shirt, though.

The shell on the gravel bottom opens, letting out its bubble of air and showing its pearl.

"Looks great," he says. "Looks like you take good care of it. You've even got one of those little clamshells that open every—"

"It's an oyster," Britnie says. "Only oysters make pearls."

"Well, excuse me. I stand—"

"See, you're not so smart," she says. "Well, you might be smart, probably are I guess, but you don't know everything."

"Never claimed to," he says. "How about you?"

"Yeah, right." That stops her, for the moment.

We move to the kitchen where the water is boiling. I drop in the pasta.

"This is nice," he says, standing in the open back door. "Good view of the city. I didn't know it just drops off like that back here. I mean I've driven by here before but you can't see this from the street."

"It's like a cliff," Britnie says. "But there's a path that goes down over there."

"So how's Fitz doing?" I say.

"Well, he's still alive. In good spirits, I guess you could say."

"Is he going to be all right? Will he be able to go home again?"

Leon's eyes are red. Has he been crying? "I don't know," he says. "He's got pneumonia, and probably not much of an immune system left to fight if off. I didn't look through his chart for details."

Now he gives me a scared look. “It’s like I don’t want to be a doctor with him, and know all the details. Sometimes I think—”

“How’d he get AIDS?” Britnie says.

“Well,” Leon glances at me again.

Go ahead, I gesture to him. She needs to know this stuff.

“Well, he’s gay. He’s probably had the virus for several years.”

“So he got it from having sex with another guy who had it?” Britnie says. She is very matter-of-fact.

“Yup,” Leon says, “that about sums it up.”

“Would you like to put the bread on the table?” I hand her the basket.

“Why do men want to have sex with each other?” she says from the dining room. “That’s weird.”

“Good question,” Leon says, “one that people have pondered for centuries. Quite a controversial question these days, in fact. Some women have sex with each other, too.”

Britnie makes a face. “Lesbians,” she says. “How can women have sex with each other?”

Leon points a thumb toward me. “A good mother-daughter question.”

What does Britnie know? We haven’t talked about this. “Well,” I say, “women can give each other pleasure, physical pleasure, in different ways. It’s not sex for making babies. It’s to make each other feel good.” Is that enough for now, I hope?

“Good answer,” Leon says, raising his glass.

“Wimpy answer, if you ask me,” Britnie says.

“We can go into the details later, if you’re still so interested, young lady. I’m sure Leon doesn’t want to listen to us have a sex education talk.”

“Wimp,” she says, tossing the salad. She has that same fine hair that Camille had. “You just don’t want to talk about it.”

“You’re right,” I say. “I don’t.”

“Did you ever have sex with another man?” Britnie says to Leon, grinning like it’s a big joke. “Like with that man in the hospital? You said he was your friend.”

Did she really say that? “That is none of your business,” I say, then to Leon, “You don’t have to answer that.”

“Kids say the darndest things,” Leon says, unphased. Thank God. He eyes me as he says, “No, I have friends who are gay but I’m not.”

“Well, Miss Curiosity, don’t you need a nebulizer treatment before dinner?”

And I need a cigarette. Outside the kitchen door I lean back on the rusty iron fence railing. Leon stands opposite.

“Do you mind?” I say. “I know you hate it.”

He shrugs.

"I hope you don't mind Britnie. She's never been around adults who would talk to her before, or treat her as if she had any brains."

"She seemed shy at the hospital. Guess she feels more comfortable here."

"I guess so. I had no idea, to tell you the truth."

"How long have you two been together?" he says.

"Oh, we met in the winter, January I think. The adoption process took a ridiculously long time. It's still not finalized. We're still in the trial period, or evaluative phase, they call it. I wish they spent as much time taking care of the kids as they do making up terms for it."

"Who's they?"

"Oh, Juvenile Protective Services. Britnie was in foster care. Just another kid, bounced around from one home to another. They're such squalid places, Leon. I mean I guess the people who take in foster kids are good people, saints in fact, but it seems like such a sordid business. They get paid a certain amount each month for each kid, and then they have to be like parents, but they aren't anything like real parents because the kids get moved around so much. At least from what I saw."

"Hey, Leon," Britnie calls. "Help me set the table."

Leon and Britnie conspire to light candles and darken the room. The aquarium shines from its shelf. And so here we are, dinner, candles, music, the three of us. And wine, red wine, the dark glass glowing by my hand. Just having it there, sometimes, is all I need.

"This is cool," Britnie says, flailing at her pasta.

"Look at your fish tank in the dark," Leon says. "It looks nice."

Britnie nods, noodles dangling from her lips.

"What kind of fish have you got? I can see a couple black moons and an angel."

"There's six guppies, two angelfish, and two black moons." She lists them with pride. "And a creepy snail."

"I had a tank when I was a kid," Leon says. "It's fun, but you gotta take care of it. You know what helps a lot is a sucker catfish."

"A what?"

"It's a bottom fish. It cruises around on the gravel and up the sides and keeps things clean. Kind of like the snail. It's ugly as sin, got these little things like tentacles sticking out of its head. You know what a catfish looks like?"

"Sort of the janitor of tropical fish," I say.

Britnie giggles. "Don't say janitor, say custodian," she says, mimicking someone. "That's what our teacher always says. Maybe we could get one and make him a little brown uniform to wear with his name embroidered on the shirt."

"What would you name him?" Leon says.

"How about Janet, short for janitor?" I say.

"Or just Larry," Britnie says. "That's the name of the janitor at school. He always walks around like a zombie in those ugly clothes with his name on the shirt. It says Larry." She giggles again.

"I'll bet he's a very nice man," I say.

"No, he's not. He's always peeking in the girls' restroom or in the locker room."

"Have you seen him do that yourself?"

"Well, no, but that's what the other girls say."

"Britnie was new at her school this past year," I explain.

"I bet he's a nice guy," Leon says. "Probably a simple, hard-working, lonely guy."

"Right," Britnie says. "He limps."

"He limps?"

She nods.

"You mean when he walks?"

"No, when he does push-ups. Of course I mean when he walks. That's the only time you can limp, isn't it?" She glares at him gleefully.

Leon looks at me.

"Britnie doesn't warm up to everyone," I say. "You should be flattered."

"So he limps," Leon says. "What's wrong with limping?"

"Well, he's weird. He never says anything and just limps around watching us all the time."

"He's probably imagining tying you up in the broom closet and tickling you with a feather duster, or drowning you in the mop bucket."

Britnie almost chokes on her food, laughing.

"God, don't give her any more ideas," I say. "Her own imagination is bad enough."

"Does he drool, too?" Leon says.

She slaps her hands over her ears, closes her eyes, and struggles to swallow her food.

* * *

After dinner Rita and I sit in the dark outside the kitchen door. We swing gently in a decrepit porch swing hung from the tree. She holds her cigarette and wineglass with one practiced hand.

"So did you have a bad day, I mean with Fitz and all?" she says.

Her profile is lit for a moment by the glowing cigarette at her lips. I barely know this woman. How much can I trust her?

"I don't know. Something's going on with me and I don't know what it is. It's frightening."

"Was it upsetting to see him?"

"Fitz? Yeah, it's upsetting. He's gonna die soon. He's younger than me. Used to be a real whiz with a computer, software designer. Used to do all this amazing stuff, graphics, paint programs, and desktop publishing. He's really an artist, too."

"You still love him, don't you?"

Love Fitz? Do I? "Yeah, I guess you're right. I mean not in a sexual way, but he was a terrific guy. Is a terrific guy."

Now she turns to me. "Maybe you are gay, Leon." She is calm, very serious.

"No, I'm not gay, Rita. I know I'm not, and I know you won't believe it until we make love, but I'm not. Fitz is the only man I ever touched and I've had plenty of...well, let's say my share of girlfriends."

"Not to mention a wife."

"A wife, yes. Funny, for a minute I had almost forgotten her. A good sign, don't you think?"

"You said you were tested for AIDS, didn't you?"

I nod in the dark. "Fitz must have got it since he and I were together. It was six years ago. And he was not promiscuous. Is not, I should say." Damn, I keep doing that.

"What did you find upsetting today?" she says.

"Well, he's dying. Isn't that upsetting enough?"

She says nothing.

"And what? I don't know..." I try to replay the feelings of the afternoon. Zach's whispers are far away now. "I think that I remembered how close we were, how warm he was toward me. I was a resident back then, pretty insecure, lots of anxiety about taking care of patients, lots of responsibility I never had before, long hours, tired all the time. He used to listen to me talk about all this stuff, difficult patients and attendings who were bastards."

"How did you meet?"

"Um, let's see. We met at a party. There was always lots of partying going on around the medical center. Still is, in the bars in Clifton, and around the university. You'd meet all kinds of people. He was friendly and we started playing racquetball together, going out for beer after, that kind of stuff."

"Did you ever have a thing with a man before?"

I shake my head. “No, it never even crossed my mind. Never had the urge. Never felt that close to another man before.”

She sits silent, and I think back to that time, to the state of mind that left me open to a male lover, a couple of nasty experiences with a nurse and then a law student named Celia who had lied to me, left me bitter and angry. What a lawyer she must be now.

“Fitz was a different kind of guy than I’d ever met. There was no masculine competitive thing with him. And there was the novelty of it, making it with a man. Does that seem odd?”

She laughs. “Odd? Well, yeah, I’d say, getting it on with another guy just to try something new. I’d say that’s a pretty rare one, Dr. Mendel. Most men have such a phobia about even touching another man, such a—”

“There was more to it than that. Fitz helped me a lot. I went through a time when I began to realize how much people suffer. I’d see all these people passing through the ER, people with chronic diseases, disabled people, and people who have had strokes and are trying to get along. Or they have M.S. or diabetes and it’s made them blind or they have kidney failure or something. They lead awful lives, and most of them end up in poverty because our totally fucked health care system doesn’t take care of them. So not only do they lead miserable lives of physical suffering and pain, but they have to live in poverty as well.”

She squeezes my hand. “I’ve seen that suffering, Leon, with Camille. I sat in waiting rooms with her, and clinics, and I talked to people like that. I used to feel like I was one of those people.”

“It’s a terrible thing. But nobody much wants to hear about it, or talk about it. Most people ignore it, in fact, medical people, the people I knew. But Fitz, he would listen to me, and he understood, and he would talk to me about it.”

I stop and sit, listening to the crickets. Somewhere a bird whistles, a single bird in the dark, as if calling out from a dream.

“So do you think it’s Fitz being so sick that’s making you feel the way you do?” Rita says.

“I don’t know.” How can I tell her what is going on in my head, what words can I use? “I’ve been having this preoccupation with death. This feeling that death is close to me, that it’s in the background all the time. As if we live in this place, this world that is very fragile, like a shell surrounded by death, and the shell keeps cracking, or I keep seeing holes in the shell, places that are dark or indefinite, like sometimes when I look in someone’s eyes, or...I don’t know.”

Talking about it I feel it, as if the air has turned cold. The feeling of dread, I glance around at the darkest places, up in the leaves, or just over the bluff where it drops away.

"But I started having this before Fitz showed up. The other night, Saturday night, when you and Britnie were there. That's when I first noticed it. But I don't know why those deaths bothered me in particular. I've seen people die before, people whose deaths have bothered me a lot more."

Faces drift to the fore in my memory, people I've tried to resuscitate, people I've watched die. "I've had children die in front of me, and people I've been talking to. That's the worst thing, I think, or at least the worst thing for me, when you've been talking to them, trying to distract them or reassure them or make them feel better. Then they die and you feel like you knew them a little."

Now I squeeze her hand. "You must know about that yourself. You must know about that a thousand times more strongly than I do."

She looks at me in the dim light. Her face is tranquil as she nods. "Once," she says evenly, noncommittally, "but you've seen a lot of people die."

"But no one really close, no one like your own child, like Camille."

Voices come to us from an open window a couple houses down, someone yelling, then laughter.

"What about Zach?" Rita says.

Zach, what about Zach? Something, the barest flicker of a shadow, swoops beneath the tree branches in front of us, then another right behind, silent.

"Was that...did you see something?"

"Bats," Rita says, "just bats. Someone told me they live over the cliff there. They come out at night. They're harmless."

I've seen bats before, but I feel myself cringe.

"What about Zach?" she says. "That must have been a terrible thing to have happen to you as a child."

The swing has stopped. I lean back with my hands behind my head. "I guess it was. I don't remember it very well."

"What was he like? Do you remember him?"

"Well, yeah, I sort of remember him. We used to laugh a lot, get in trouble a lot. We spent all our time together. In fact our parents used to try to get us apart to do things separately, but we didn't like to."

In the dark it seems easy to think back. "I remember we had this story that we used to tell each other. We made it up and it took place in our neighborhood and all the people who lived around us were part of it, all the neighbors. I guess we had seen this movie or something where everybody either lived above ground, like us, or underground. Those were the bad guys, the people who lived underground. Anyway, it was kind of funny."

"Tell me more," she says.

"Oh, it was just a kids' thing. I don't remember it very well."

"How did all the neighbors fit in?"

"Well, let's see, the people we liked were the people who lived above ground. They were called Toppers, because they lived on top of the ground, and the people who lived below were called, um,...it was a funny word, they were, oh, yeah, Subbers, which was short for subterranean. We must have got that from the movie. Toppers and Subbers, that's right."

The memory seems to fill my mind with a cool glow, again the image of kids playing beneath a tall canopy of leaves.

"So, all the neighbors we didn't like were Subbers and they had entrances to the underground world hidden in their houses, in the fireplaces. Their houses were just a cover-up. They would come and go through their houses and no one would know. And there were a couple other entrances outside as well. There was this old culvert pipe with a little stream that came out by the alley. We used to dare each other to go inside. It took a turn about ten feet in and was very scary, at least to seven year olds. And of course our parents wouldn't let us go in there, which made it all the more intriguing, as you can imagine.

"So the main plot was that the Subbers were trying to take over and dig tunnels into everyones' houses. They would come at night while you were sleeping, dig a tunnel up to your house, and sneak in and take over your brain or something. I don't remember exactly. If you had a dog then they couldn't come because the dog would hear them and bark. I remember if we heard a dog barking at night in the neighborhood we knew it was the Subbers trying to get into someone's house."

"Sounds pretty elaborate," Rita says. "Were the other kids in the neighborhood in on this?"

"Well, yeah, I think we did try to get some of the other kids involved. I remember trying to persuade the Getz kids to get a dog. They lived across the alley and I remember explaining to them, or Zach explaining it to them, but I think it was lost on their parents. Their mom was a nut about keeping the house clean and didn't want an animal around. They liked to come over to our house cause they could make a mess without getting in trouble."

Rita's questions open a flood of memory, a hidden volume of my mind whose pages have not seen the light of conscious thought in how long, a decade, two decades? Zach explaining, persuading, running from house to house with me right behind, peeking in windows, hiding in bushes. The sleepy block of houses in a Cleveland neighborhood called Roosevelt Heights, spacious old houses with screened-in porches, wide lawns under oaks and willows and birches. Hedges and bushes and gardens and garages and an alley down the middle of it all, ideal terrain for a seven year old whose imagination never quit, and his twin brother who happily tagged along.

Zach, she wants to know about you, to know you. How fearless you were, and how brash, a giggling boy standing on the old Peerless's porch, reaching up to the doorbell. Mrs. Peerless, you said, I really have to go to the bathroom and I can't make it home. And you danced from one foot to the other as if it were true. And Leon has to go, too. That poor sweet old lady, florid faced, flustered but kindly, let us into a silent somber home, steered us away from a man's white hair, bright above the back of an ancient rattan wheelchair, to the tiny medicine-smelling bathroom. Then she offered us cookies and milk, and we sat in a silent linoleumed kitchen. Only you didn't sit for long but jumped up and started exploring, a slide-open breadbox, leaded-glass cupboard doors revealing ancient crockery, but no fireplace. And so I sat, munching happily on homemade butter crescents, waiting to see how you were going to pull it off.

May we say hi to Mr. Peerless? you said.

Well, now, Mr. Peerless is blind, boys, and he doesn't hear very well. But I suppose so, if you speak very loud to him.

Then the moments of confusion as the poor old man tried to comprehend this sudden invasion of his world by Topper spies. We knew he was a Subber. And there was the fireplace, just as you guessed, cold, dark, screened, well-disguised. So while she and I shouted nonsense at the old man—THESE ARE DAVID MENDEL'S LITTLE BOYS, MARTIN. THE TWINS, YOU REMEMBER THE MENDELS ACROSS THE ALLEY, DON'T YOU, DEAR?— you whispered our secret spell that closed off the fireplace, that magically crumbled the unseen Subber tunnel.

Mission accomplished. We left finally, left them in their peace, and ran across the lawns, triumphant, gleeful, while I wondered at the tiny universe we had invaded, the two people living that silent austere life, every day just a wall away from our sunny adventures. And I ran fast to keep up, to stay close to the glow of energy, wildness, and imagination that was you.

Before Rita asks it, that next inevitable question, I step off the porch swing into the dark. I move behind the tree where she can't see me and cover my ears. He got hurt, I want to shout, got hurt and died, so just leave it, let it go. I want to run through the narrow space between the houses and jump in my car and go, or off the edge of the bluff and take flight.

But then Rita is there, gently pulling one hand away from my ear.

"It's okay, Leon. I'm sorry. Let's do something else," she says. "I didn't mean to make you upset. Let's go inside and see what's on TV."

* * *

What is it? Oh, Leon is up. Going to the bathroom? Can he find it in the dark, not wake Britnie? What time is it anyway? Five-fifteen. No, he's going down the stairs. He's not leaving. He wouldn't leave now, would he? Not now, after such sex. God, I've never felt that way before. Fitz was right. He is a good lover.

So get up, go downstairs, don't let him leave. Out of bed, put something on. Ooh, I feel good. God, what he did to my nipples! He wouldn't leave, would he? Down the stairs, into the kitchen. The back door is open. Oh, he's just sitting there, in the doorway.

"Hi, having trouble sleeping?" I say. "It's warm tonight. What have you got? Is that orange juice?"

"Yeah, I guess I was hot," he says.

"Join you?" The refrigerator light is blinding. I find my wine and pour a glass. "Are you okay?" I sit beside him, kiss his cheek.

"I'm fine. It's nice out right now."

"I should have opened more windows." I rub his bare back. "For a guy worried about his sexual identity, you make a lovely straight guy, Leon."

"I think you're the one worried about my sexual identity." He rubs my thigh.

"Okay, so I'm not worried anymore. Does it make you feel better? I mean, I know it's not that simple, but such lovemaking must make you feel good."

I need a cigarette. Will he mind?

He leans back against the doorframe and looks at me in the dark. "That was the first time in a while for me. And the first time in a long time with someone new. Yes, it makes me feel good. Of course it does." Now he takes my hand. "How do you know it's not so simple? Maybe you're just what my brain needs right now."

"Well, thanks, Leon, that's a nice thing to say. Um, would you have a fit if I smoke right now?" I set down the glass and stand up. "I mean I don't want to be unromantic or anything but I'm dying. It's terrible, I know."

Bad habits, I'm just a huge bad habit. The pack is by the phone. "So you think a few good screws is all you need? Typical male attitude." I sit by him again.

The light from the match is so stark on his unhappy face it makes me freeze. "Oh, Leon, what is it? Are you sad?"

"Oh, I had a bad dream. It scared me, I guess."

What should I say? What's the right thing? "It scared you?"

"It was about Zach, about how he got hurt. Stuff I hadn't thought about in a while."

"What kind of stuff?" I say.

"He got hit by a car." The words tumble out of him and then he is silent.

The dumb birds are rattling away already up in the tree. Somebody shuts a car door.

"Zach did?"

"Yup, just like that. One second he's just a goofy kid. The next, wham, he gets clobbered. We used to ride our bikes all over the neighborhood, a couple seven year olds, you can imagine. That neighborhood was like our giant playground, full of kids and dogs, and our parents just let us go. No helmets, people hadn't even thought of bike helmets then."

He stops and I don't know what to do. Should I say—

"About a block away there was this kid named Skippy Bennett and his front yard was a hill down to the street, just grass and no trees. We rigged up this jump for our bikes with a sheet of plywood over a box, like a little ski jump. We were nuts. But not really, we were just kids. I remember this policeman asking me how we made it, like it was some criminal thing, like asking me how I got a rope over a branch to hang someone.

"It was kind of a rainy day and the grass was slick and we'd push our bikes up the hill and then ride down and go over the jump and fly up in the air. Dangerous as hell when you think about it. Mostly we would just land and slide on the grass and fall and laugh. But not old Zach…"

He sits thinking, remembering.

"No, not old Zach." He says it slowly, in a whisper, as if he might cry. "He was like my idol, that guy. My whole goal in life was to be Zach. I looked like him and talked like him anyway. We were twins, identical twins. I've told you that, haven't I? And everything I did then was to be just like him. That guy was brilliant."

He looks distracted, listening.

"Did you hear something?" I say.

He shakes his head as if shaking off an insect.

"So this one time, the last time, he zooms down the hill and flies over the jump and lands upright, didn't fall. Meanwhile this kid named Willie, somebody's big brother who had a Chevy that he fixed up. You know, typical teenage thing, this pimply kid who could barely talk cause he was so awkward and shy, but he's got this car and he knew every part in that car. So he came around the corner and he headed down the street.

"Damn, I remember it so clearly now, like somebody branded it into my mind. Zach landed right about where the sidewalk was and he tried to stop. But his tires just skidded because it was wet, and then he went over the curb and into the street. Willie hit the brakes. You could hear the car tires slide on the wet pavement. And then there was the crunch of Zach's bike going under the car, and this thud when he hit the pavement. This thud."

Leon stops and sits, trembling, his hands to his face. I think he is crying. God, what should I do?

"You haven't thought about this in a long time, have you?" I say.

He shakes his head.

"It could have been a movie," he says suddenly. "It all happened so matter-of-fact. I remember standing up there watching and thinking how quiet everything was, Zach just lying there. He didn't scream or cry or anything. He just lay there, no blood, quiet as could be.

"I remember wishing it was me. Hard to believe a kid would think that, but I did. I stood and looked down at Zach lying there in that one moment of quiet, that little kid lying in the street, and I wished I had been hit instead of him. It was almost like he was the best part of me and somehow it would have been better…"

He is silent again.

"So he died?"

"Yup, Zach died." He is angry all of a sudden. "Right then, in an instant, with that thud of skull against concrete my brother Zach was dead. He never said another word, never had another normal thought, never made another purposeful movement. Course he didn't really die, his body didn't die.

"Skippy went inside his house and got his mom and there were a couple moms up the street who heard it happen. You know how somehow people know, or the word spreads, when something bad is going on. It's like in the ER, you hear a word or a sound, or you see someone rush into a room, and you know something's going on."

He pauses. It's getting light, the sun coming, our side of the earth turning to face it.

"Anyway, so there were all these moms yelling and pointing, and finally this ambulance pulls up. And these two ambulance guys are looking at Zach. Remember what ambulances used to be like, these big station wagons, Cadillacs or something? They were more like hearses than ambulances. I remember these two guys were both smoking cigarettes. These two dumb guys who probably couldn't make it as taxi drivers or security guards so they let them drive an ambulance. They weren't trained how to take care of people. They didn't have a clue. Primitive compared to now.

"The one smacks Zach on the cheek a couple of times to see if he'll wake up. Can you believe that! They didn't worry about his neck or anything. Someone had gotten our mother and she was there watching all this. She pushed that guy back so hard he fell over. He was crouching down and she gave him a shove, screaming at him in Latvian. Our parents were from Latvia. He just tumbled over backward, lost his cigarette.

"So those two goons loaded him onto a stretcher and shoved him into the back of their ambulance. Mother grabbed me and we climbed in, too. Those guys hardly said a thing to us. They sat in the front and just talked about baseball and made jokes. Here's my mother crying and holding Zach's head, which is all bruised, one side of his face was swollen and purple, and three feet away those two guys were sitting there telling jokes."

He stops again.

"Well, that kind of stuff still goes on," I say. "I mean that kind of insensitivity."

He nods and looks at me as if he forgot I was here, relieved to see me.

"I know it does. It happens a lot. At work we joke around all the time, but at least not right in front of people."

I wait again but he says nothing. "Do you want to tell me more?" I say.

"It's so depressing. Aren't you tired of this?"

"Tired of this? Tired of one of the most important events in your life?"

Again he listens for a moment, turns his head.

"What do you hear?" I say.

He shakes his head. "Well, I don't know how important it was, but it was definitely bad news for us. Here we had this happy little family and all of a sudden someone drops a nuclear bomb on it.

"The whole hospital thing was a mess. There were doctors coming and going, and each one telling us something different. I don't know, I guess I was sort of kept out of the way, which of course made it all worse. I was just seven and didn't have a clue what was going on. But I remember my folks all upset and angry, yelling at each other all the time, yelling at me.

"And being home without Zach there, it was so quiet, I remember that, quiet and depressing. They were at the hospital all the time. I had this old aunt who came and stayed with me, but she couldn't hear very well so you couldn't really even talk to her. Aunt Rachel, and Zach had named her Aunt Whatchel cause she was always saying 'what,' whenever you spoke to her."

"So he didn't die right away?" I say.

"I don't know," he says, looking under the steps suddenly. What is he looking for?

"We brought his body home, but he wasn't in it. We brought it home. A nurse helped lift him into the car and Mother sat in the back seat with him and held him up so he wouldn't slump over while we drove home. He already smelled that way."

He shivers and pauses, remembering. "And then we got him home and some of the neighbors were there to welcome him. They had flowers and toys for him and they were going to sing songs and stuff, but they just stood and watched when Father carried him inside. His head hung back with his mouth open and bobbed back and forth. He was limp except for his arms, which kept twisting the way they did. Father shouted at them to go on home, that it wasn't any of their business. And these were our friends and some cousins, too. Mother tried to apologize to them. It was such a horrible time."

Now Leon stands and steps down to the grass. He walks over to the edge of the bluff, turns and comes back. In a tired angry voice he says, "So there it is, now you know all about Zach. Big deal, that was a long time ago, long ago and far away."

"I'm sure it was a big deal for you at the time. I think it's still a big deal, Leon, for you. And for me if you want it to be. It's important to talk about things."

"How can you drink wine so early in the morning?" he says suddenly.

Oh, please, not now. "Sorry."

"Doesn't it turn your stomach? It would mine."

I raise my glass toward him. "I'm an alcoholic, Leon. This is what alcoholics do. We drink." I'm not going to apologize any more. "It calms my stomach, makes me feel good. It's a disease, Leon, you know that. You see alcoholics all the time in the emergency room, don't you?"

"That's what they say, it's a disease." He sits down again.

"An incurable disease," I say. "You're born with it and it never goes away. My mother had it and nothing she did ever got rid of it. She went to treatment programs, Alcoholics Anonymous, even went in the hospital once she was so sick. She got better and didn't drink so much afterward, but she was still an alcoholic. Still is. I had two grandparents who were alcoholics. One of them didn't drink, didn't take one sip of alcohol for fifty years. The other one died from it."

"Your mother, huh. She was an alcoholic?"

"Still is. She lives in Charleston. She taught me a lot about it, too, how to cope with it, not to be ashamed of it. Not to let it ruin my self-esteem, so it wouldn't ruin the rest of my life."

"Didn't she teach you not to drink?" Now he grabs my hand. "I'm sorry. That's a stupid thing to say. I know it's a hard thing to deal with."

"Yes, she taught me not to drink. Yes, yes, yes, but it's not that easy, Leon. It's hard not to drink in a world where everyone drinks, where your friends drink when they're having fun, or relaxing, or socializing. Where you meet a new guy you like—," I punch his arm, "—and want to have fun with. Try going to a party—no, never mind, I'm not going to give you that speech. You probably hear it a dozen times a day at the hospital."

"Well, I hear it enough that I believe it."

"I was sober for a couple of years after my divorce. I was so glad to be rid of that jerk I would have happily lived in a convent. But then Camille died and I started up again. Typical, huh, typical alcoholic story. Something bad happens so you hit the bottle again. Oh, well, that's me, Leon. I'll stop again soon."

I look at his face, that face I was kissing a few hours ago, this guy who was kissing me and fucking me, who I would have begged to fuck me, who fucked me like I don't think anyone ever did before.

"I really will, Leon." I grab his leg. I have to touch him. "Please, Leon, don't think of me the way you think of all the drunks you see at the hospital. I have been sober for most of my life, and I will be again." Now I feel tears coming. Damn it, I hate to cry. "Please let me be different in your mind from those people. I know you never really will until I prove it to you. There are lots of alcoholics who lead normal lives."

He pries my hand off his thigh. "Okay, okay, I will, I mean I already do, Rita."

I was digging my nails into him. "Oh, God, I'm sorry. Did I hurt you?" Now I start to giggle.

"It's okay." He squeezes my hand and then reaches for me. "Listen, Rita, I'm not exactly the picture of normality myself right now. But I don't think your drinking is that big a problem for me." Now he smiles. "As long as it doesn't affect your libido, um, your sex drive."

"Thanks," I say. "I know what the word means. And it won't." I lean forward to kiss him. "And I can prove that to you now, can't I?"

Chapter Ten

Home again, what's left of it. Like a bomb crater. Oh, well, better this than having Jasmine around. At least it's quiet. Jasmine, I haven't even thought about her since she left. Good luck, mister Robert-the-French-horn-player, I don't envy you. She'll chew you up and spit you out.

I'm working night shift tonight. I'll need more sleep sometime today. Rita is a demon in bed, once she gets going. Once I get going. I told Britnie I'd take her to the zoo this afternoon. I'll sleep after that.

I watch the coffee dripping into the pot, your whispers barely there. I told Rita a lot about you, Zach, didn't I, last night and this morning, things I had forgotten, haven't thought of in a long time. That was such a terrible time, wasn't it. You coming home from the hospital like that, being like that. Lying there in our room in your bed. I start to sweat, thinking of it. It went on for so long, you lying there, staring, never speaking, and your arms...

I can't think of it. It sickens me, frightens me, that same feeling of dread rises inside me. God, I can't think of it. Do something else, go for a run.

I grab my Nikes and lace them on. Better run now before it gets too hot. Off down the hill toward the park, my thighs and shoulders stiff and protesting. The concrete and even the dirt are still warm from yesterday, just waiting for today's long blast.

Can we trust Rita with that kind of stuff, brother? She's a good person, isn't she? She seems like someone to trust. But maybe I'm just grasping for anyone, the first woman to come along after Jasmine. A pretty face, a good screw, an ear to pour myself out to. Look at her, divorced, unemployed, alcoholic, not exactly the kind of girl you'd take home to meet mom and dad.

What if things don't work out between us and she gets angry and goes to somebody at the hospital, an administrator, and tells them what's going on with me? Did you know Dr. Mendel who works in your emergency room used to be gay and now he's hallucinating and hearing voices? He's mentally ill. You shouldn't let him take care of patients. He's not safe.

And what about me, Zach? What is happening to me, to my mind? A thirty-three-year-old white male physician with thought disturbance, hallucinations, both visual and auditory. What else? Pressured thoughts, intrusive thoughts, paranoia. Reality dissociation? Not really, not yet. Well, maybe a little.

Onset of symptoms has occurred at a time of emotional stress. He is able to continue to function at his work, at least so far. Has good insight into his situation, no denial. Has not yet sought professional help.

Am I becoming schizophrenic? Thirty-three is a little old for onset, no family history. Was there, Zach? Mom and Dad were weird but they weren't crazy. Uptight, neurotic maybe, but not schizophrenic. And you never had the chance to be. No, I'm not schizophrenic. How about functional psychosis, in response to multiple new stressors? Pretty rare disease. Possibly, hopefully. That means it'll go away when the stress goes away. But it never showed up before, all through med school and residency, all those nights with no sleep, long days, all those exams.

Intermittent impotence, perhaps associated with alcohol intoxication. At least that's better as of last night, and this morning. I wonder if Britnie heard us. History of one homosexual affair six years ago. God, I can't imagine telling that to anyone. Uncertain sexual identity, homosexual panic perhaps? What about the other day with that guy in the hot tub? No, that's usually a symptom of some other disorder.

Fitz was the only time. What about all the rest of the last fifteen years of heterosexuality? High school, college, I never even thought about guys, was happily heterosexual. I like to look at women, fantasize about women. Remember those books Fitz gave me, when he was trying to persuade me. That's what convinced me I wasn't gay. Said your fantasies were what counted, what you thought about when you masturbate, when you dream. No, I'm not gay, it's not that.

Fitz, I gotta go see him again today, maybe before I start work. I hope he's better. AIDS, what an awful thing, relentless, unstoppable. The first arrival in a new age of disease. We're going to see more viruses like it, I'll bet.

The running, the physical effort feels good. Little helicopter seeds from a group of tall maples litter the path. So peaceful, these trees, imperturbable, the park nearly empty.

What if I don't get better? What if I keep getting worse? What about work? Gotta have a clear head at work. Everybody's already watching me. They probably figure I'm on drugs or something. Course they know about the divorce, probably blame it on that. Gotta be careful though. What if I really screw up, make a judgment error, something obviously wrong. I'll be making the rounds of the community hospitals looking for work, the walk-in clinics.

There's brief reactive psychosis, comes on suddenly at a time of major stress, lasts a couple weeks, sometimes months, then goes away just as quickly. Rarer still, but maybe. This can go away any time as far as I'm concerned.

So what about help? I should get help. Will this go away on its own? Maybe now that Jasmine's out of my hair, and if things mellow out at work. That madhouse will never mellow out. Maybe then this will go away, like a bad case of gonorrhea. Or is it going to be like herpes, just keeps coming back whenever things get a little rough. If Icky came to me and said he was hallucinating I'd tell him to go see somebody. So who? Gotta be careful. Nobody on the medical staff, gotta keep things very confidential.

A psychiatrist or a psychologist? Someone who is hallucinating should see a shrink, a psychiatrist.

At home, an hour later, Peter Schulman calls, my fearless leader.

"How are you feeling, Leon?"

Zach whispers something behind me. I start to turn but stop myself. "I'm okay. How are you?"

"Listen, Leon, a couple people in the department have expressed concern to me. Said you seem to be upset, stressed out."

"Oh, yeah? Who?" I don't really care who.

"Well, I can't really say who, Leon, being director and all. You know that. But they're genuinely concerned about you, old man. Nobody's out to get you. These are people who care about you."

"Yeah, yeah, it's hard to say—"

"I know you've been through a lot lately, with Jasmine and all, and someone said a good friend of yours showed up the other day with AIDS. They said it seemed like quite a shock to you."

"Well, it was a surprise. I had no idea he was sick, hadn't seen him in a long time."

"These things can be upsetting. Sometimes you aren't even aware how they affect you. Plus you caught all that flack about the other night."

There's something inside the phone handset. I hear tiny claws against the plastic, a nasty little reptile inches from my mouth. I hold it away from my skin. It seems to vibrate in my hand as he squirms. I want to drop it, hang it up and run.

"Maybe you ought to take a little time off, Leon. We can drop you from the lineup for a week or two." Peter's always using baseball jargon, especially in the summer. "Everybody's in town, we can pinch hit for you for a while 'til you get yourself together. You can do a couple resident talks at the Friday conferences and we've got A.C.L.S. recertification coming up. You can run that if you want."

He's right. I should do it. But that's giving in, admitting there really is a monster in the phone, admitting I'm going nuts. I want to shout back at him, at the tiny holes in the phone where this demon is drooling and hissing.

"Well, Peter, I think I'll be all right." I struggle to find a calm voice. "I'm feeling better today, got a good night's sleep and all. I think it was a temporary thing. I appreciate your concern, but I'll be fine."

"You know, Leon, the nurses and residents really look to us for leadership." I imagine his pointy face jabbering. "I mean, whoever is on duty has to be able to make clear decisions, good judgment is key."

"I know, Peter, I've been there." I feel myself getting angry. Angry at whom, at myself, at the situation. "I'll be fine. I've been under emotional stress before. Besides, Jasmine moved out yesterday and things are calming down."

He rattles on in his rapid-fire way about having an open ear if I need someone to talk to, about seeking emotional support if I need it, even invites me to drop in for dinner with his family if I'm feeling lonely or want a home-cooked meal. His kids are maniacs, as I recall, little dervishes who bounce from wall to wall around their chaotic house, while his wife Esther smiles proudly.

"Thanks, Peter, maybe I'll take you up on that," I lie. "You sure Esther wouldn't mind?"

"No, no, not at all, Leon. She'd welcome another adult at the table."

I'll bet she would.

* * *

"They're lucky," Britnie says. "They don't have to worry about clothes and makeup and all that dumb stuff."

We stand watching the baboons at the zoo, gruff, angry-looking fellows, some ambling, some rushing about on their island, a miniature mountain with haggard trees clinging to the dirt.

"My teacher said their brains are a lot like ours. They have the same emotions and feelings and stuff like that."

"Think it's true?"

She turns her gaze at me. A smile from her lean, angular face always seems a surprise. "I guess so. They do stuff like hug each other and get angry sometimes. I've seen them laugh and even kind of tickle each other."

"Then how come they don't worry about clothes and makeup and all that, like you said?"

"It'd be hard to put on makeup when your face is covered with fur, Leon. Besides they don't have stuff like that. They don't need clothes. They've got fur."

Mom and dad and mom and dad, Zach says to me in an urgent monotone.

"They could wrap themselves with jungle leaves," I say, "smear clay on their faces, make hats out of banana peels and feathers, or something like that."

Britnie rolls her eyes. "Right, Leon, hats out of banana peels?" Then she giggles. "How about this? We could do an experiment. Go to the Salvation Army store and get a bunch of old clothes, like from the bum boxes. You know those big boxes at the front where they put the really beat up stuff that they give away for free?"

She looks at me. "No, you probably don't, do you? I had this one foster mom who called them the bum boxes. Anyway, we could sneak down here at night and throw a bunch of clothes in there for them, and then watch what happens. It'd probably be pretty funny."

"They wouldn't know how to put them on. And they wouldn'tknow the men's clothes from the women's."

"Well, we could help them."

"Help them? You mean jump in there and help them dress? Show them how to do the buttons and zippers?"

"Sure," she giggles, "they have fingers just like ours. They could learn to do stuff like that. I've seen monkeys dressed in clothes on TV."

"Show them how to put on underwear? How about bras, you think that big female over there would go for a bra? She's about a C cup, don't you think?"

"Right, Leon, I'm sure." She laughs as if it's a relief to laugh, to know she can do it. Or is it just me imagining it?

"Are you coming over tonight, Leon?"

"No, I'm working night shift tonight. Won't be able to make it."

"You like working there?" Britnie says.

"Well, that's a tough question. I think I like it. It's difficult sometimes, stressful, but I can help people there, relieve their suffering, sometimes even keep them from..." I stop, not wanting to say the word.

"From dying?" Britnie says.

"That's right."

She takes my hand, her face serious, eyes still on the baboons. "Do you think they know they're going to die?"

And there it is, death roaring in her eyes, twin dark beams firing from her face, sweeping across the air as her eyes move. An old gray baboon across the way watches her solemnly. Does he see it, too?

I want to duck as those eyes turn toward me. Zach is loud in my ears. I look away.

"What do you think?" I say. "How do people learn about death?"

"We read about it, or we tell each other about it," she says, her face a narrow mask again. "Same as we learn about anything. In church they talk about death all the time."

"Have you been to church much?"

The old baboon makes a hooting noise deep in his throat.

"Ugh, I've been to all kinds of churches. I hate church. My foster parents were always dragging us off to church on Sundays. There's always some old man up there carrying on about sin and eternity. So boring."

We walk on in the morning sunshine. I'm flattered by her hand still in mine. And scared by it, scared by something, for my pulse is pounding, my skin damp. Run and hide, run and hide, Zach is droning now.

"Do you believe that stuff," I say, "about sin and eternity?"

"I don't know. Rita says I should believe in God, but she says God's not mean and cruel, like the preachers in church say. What do you think?"

God, another dusty old place in my mind where I haven't been for a long time. "God's a tough one. I never know what to say about God. I think it's a concept, an idea, and each person has to decide for himself what to make of it. But a lot of people..." I wonder if I should go on.

Half a dozen hippo eyes stare at us from the surface of a pond, black bubbles fixed in pairs on the water, their bodies submerged.

"Look at these guys," I say. "They look comfortable."

"A lot of people what, Leon?" She jiggles my hand.

"Well, a lot of people turn to God when they think about death. I mean if you believe in God and believe that God does good things, or has good reasons for the way things happen on earth..." I stop again. This sounds stupid.

Somewhere an elephant cuts loose with his morning bellow.

"Rita says I should talk to God sometimes when I feel like it. She says that's the best way to pray."

"That's probably good advice."

"I went to a funeral once," she says suddenly. "There was this kid with diabetes at this foster home where I lived. He was sick all the time and finally he died. And then they had a funeral for him. I didn't like it. All of us in the home had to go and see him lying there with all that dumb makeup on his face. Ugh, it was awful, Leon. And then his dumb real mom came, with some guy. I'm sure it wasn't his father. And they were drunk and acting like idiots. His real mom, it was so sick, she was a drug addict and had been in prison and stuff. Never came to visit him or anything, never tried to help him when he was sick, and all of a sudden here she is at his funeral. She had this old purple dress on with frills around the neck that went down in this big cleavage. Talk about tacky."

A small black bird lands casually on a hippo's nose, the eyes don't even blink. "Have you seen people die, Leon?"

"LEON!" I jump at my name in a tiger's roar from somewhere behind.

"It's okay, Leon," Britnie laughs. "They're in cages."

"Sorry, guess I'm a little jittery today. Never did like cats much." That feeling of dread, that's what it is, that's what I feel. Why now, why here?

"So have you?"

"Have I what?"

"Seen people die?"

Her delicate features are serious now, her eyes steady on mine. Now suddenly those eyes become yours, Zach, lying in bed, arms twisting. The memory of you seems to barge into my mind. It makes me turn away from her, makes me look away into the trees beyond the walkway. I can't think about that, Zach. I can't think about you like that, like you were.

"What is it, Leon?" Britnie says. "What's the matter?"

"It's nothing, I'm sorry. What were we talking about?"

She is quiet, watching me, waiting.

"People dying," I say. "Yes, I've seen people die. It's part of my job. People die in the emergency room sometimes."

"What's it like?" Her voice is soft. "I mean for the person who's dying?"

"Well, what's it like? That's a tough question to answer. People die in many different ways." I should be careful what I say, shouldn't I, or should I be frank, truthful? "Death itself is peaceful, like falling asleep, or at least that's what it looks like. It's hard to say what it's like for the person who is dying, hard to know what happens inside their head."

How much does she want to hear? Again she waits, watching me. She is an interesting girl. Few people can do this, can say nothing.

"Oh, I don't know, Britnie. I'm not sure I know any more about death than anyone else. But it looks to me when people die that it's like they fall asleep, they lose consciousness, their mind stops working and just never starts again."

I glance around, hoping no one else is hearing this. "Beyond that I don't know. You just can't say beyond that."

"What about all that stuff about out-of-body experiences, you know like when your heart stops for a little while and then somebody starts it up for you again, where you're like dead for a few minutes and then you come alive again. I read about that once, people see themselves rising up out of their bodies toward some kind of light, or they see the doctors working on their body after they've left it. There was this book."

"I know. Those things may be true. I couldn't really say."

Now suddenly she is avid. "But you save people, right? You bring people back after their hearts have stopped and stuff like that. Don't you?"

"Yeah, we do. That does happen from time to time." I lean against the rail, feeling the sun on my face. "But usually those people are in no shape to talk right away. They stay unconscious for a while. In fact they're lucky if they wake up, if their brain still works when they wake up. I don't know. I've never had the chance to talk to someone who's had that happen. I think there was a movie about this, about some med students who—"

"Yeah, I saw it, Flatliners, it was dumb."

She moves off along the rail beside the hippo pond, sliding her hand along the warm metal, then pauses and returns. She gestures toward the hippos. "It still seems like you'd be better off if you didn't know you were going to die, like them. My English teacher called it self-awareness. She said that's when you know you're alive and you know that you're gonna die sometime, too. She said only humans have it. She said it's what makes people do art and sculpture and stuff like that, because everybody knows their life will end and they want to leave something behind that will always be there, like for people to remember them by.

"But it seems like if you didn't have self-awareness then you'd be happier, cause then you wouldn't know you were going to die and you wouldn't worry about it."

"Well, you might be right. But I think we're sort of stuck with it, part of being human." Mom and dad and mom and dad, Zach is yelling from far away.

"I wish I didn't know about death, Leon." She turns to me and takes my hands. "I wish I didn't know I'm going to die."

I hold her hands and stand facing her, cowardly avoiding her eyes, wondering desperately what to say.

* * *

At the hospital, an hour before my shift, I stand in the back of a crowded elevator. A long howl sounds somewhere in the building, getting louder as we rise. Doesn't anyone else hear that? I imagine stacks of corpses on every floor, each room full of all the people who have ever died there. When the doors open I cringe, but there are no bodies. I look at the heads around me, people talking about the heat outside, baseball, the usual stuff. I check each face for signs of life, expressions, eye movements. I'm getting worse.

On Fitz's floor dietary workers are pushing their tall meal carts, tall enough to hold a body upright. Down the corridor each doorway breathes death at me as I pass.

In the room Joel sits on the floor beneath the window reading a magazine. There is a woman in the chair by Fitz. She has a severe, almost pretty face. Fitz's sister, the thought comes to me, although I've never seen her before.

Joel raises a hand to me, some kind of warning in his eyes.

Fitz stirs on the bed, a corpse moving. It sickens me to see him, so pale and thin, wasted.

"Leon, you're here," his mouth moves, his voice hoarser than yesterday.

"I'm Rebecca, Fitz's sister," the woman says with an irritated smile. "You're a friend?" There is no question of shaking hands. Her bony fingers stay locked in her lap.

"Yes, I'm Leon Mendel." I want to look beneath the bed, in the corners of the room. I can hear it.

"Leon's one of the heroes of the emergency room," Fitz rasps, "the man you need when your head gets knocked off, or you get disemboweled by a Rottweiler. Becca has a Rottweiler."

"He's a perfectly normal dog. The children love him."

She wears black, something like a leotard and shorts, sort of a thirty-something Joan Jett crossed with an angry urban mom. She'd probably claw you to death when she has an orgasm, if she has orgasms.

"Hi, Joel," I say.

Joel nods, engrossed in the Atlantic Monthly.

"We were rehashing our childhood," Fitz says, "dredging up all sorts of psychopathology. Becca's trying to discover why I'm a queer and I'm trying to learn why she's such an overbearing controlling bitch."

"Oh, fuck you, Fitz," she says, freeing her hands in a gesture of anger. But she recovers quickly. "Is he always so candid?"

"That's Fitz for you," I say. "Never one to mince words."

"Nothing like one's own imminent death to enable one to be frank," Fitz says. He is breathing hard now with the effort of conversation. Sweat gleams on his forehead.

She eyes him awkwardly, then turns to me. "You're a doctor?" she says.

"Yup, I work in the Emergency Department downstairs."

"Do you know the doctor who's taking care of Fitz?"

"Herb Taft, yes, he's a good guy, very knowledgeable."

"Is he a specialist?" There is underlying hostility here.

"Yes, he's an infectious disease specialist."

"Is there anyone better," she says, "an AIDS specialist or something?"

It doesn't matter who Fitz's doctor is now, I want to say. "That's what Taft is. He runs the HIV Clinic."

"What about at the university? Wouldn't Fitz be better off there, at the university hospital?"

She has a harsh voice for a woman. I look at her. Has she been crying? No. Sad even? No, she doesn't look like the type to be sad. Angry, bored, guilty maybe? What she is asking is what guilty relatives ask. I turn to Fitz but he shakes his head, looking away out the window.

"No," I say, "he's fine right here." But I regret the words as they come out.

"Fine?" she hisses. "This is fine? Does he look fine to you? Look at him."

Why did I come up here? I could have come later on. Now Fitz turns to her again. "I am fine right here, Becca. I'm dying and this is where I'll die. I might even go home to die."

"Well, at least they could give you something to help you with your breathing," she says, and then to me. "Look how he's struggling to breathe."

I nod. "He is."

She stares at me. "Well, can't you give him anything to help his breathing?"

"He's getting it. He's getting everything we can give to help his breathing, except one thing."

"What's that?" She is suspicious.

"A ventilator," I say as calmly as I can. I shouldn't have even brought it up. "The only thing more we could do for Fitz is put a tube down his throat and put him on a breathing machine."

She glares at me now, but I turn to Fitz. He lies looking out the window again, tears in his eyes. I sit by him on the bed and take his hand.

"I'll come back," she says suddenly and leaves the room.

"So that's her, huh?"

"That's her," Fitz says. "She'll go have a cigarette now. She's been going out about every half hour. But she's not so bad, Leon. She doesn't have a clue about AIDS, or being gay, or anything else."

"That's charitable of you. I thought you didn't want to see her."

He shakes his head. "Everything changes, Leon. Everything." Now he points to a pitcher by the bed. "Would you pour me some more ice, please? My hands shake so much I can't do it."

He takes some chips of ice into his mouth now, his whole body moving with the effort of breathing.

"She's not so bad," he says again. "We were close as kids. We had fun together. It was a difficult family to have fun in. She's been through a lot herself, divorced, working, a single mom." Again he pauses to breathe. "The American dream, isn't it?"

I look at his skull so prominent beneath his skin, his eyes twitching in their sockets. I hate this, the feeling of death creeping around my feet. How can Joel sit there so calmly?

"Leon," Fitz's jaw moves, "you're staring at me."

I shake my head. "Sorry. Sorry, Fitz, I'm all screwed up." I stand, feeling helpless. Now what? "I don't know. Listen, what can I do for you?" I feel desperate. "There must be something?" I say it a little too loud. What can I do to put life back into your body! There must be something. Even Joel is watching me now.

"It's okay, Leon," Fitz says. He is very calm, holding my gaze. "I'll be okay."

I want to run, or strike out, hit something, push something away, tackle something and throw it to the floor. I want to grab this thing that's destroying him and wrestle it down, twist its arms behind its back until I hear the shoulders pop and tear, twist its head till the vertebra crunch and it screams and goes limp in my arms.

"Leon," Joel says, "Leon, are you okay?"

Again I shake my head, shake my mind free. "Yeah, I'm okay. Listen, I guess I should go downstairs and go to work." I turn to Fitz. I don't want to leave. "Maybe I could sit here and read to you or something. I'd really like to if you—no, never mind. I guess I can't. I've got to go downstairs. Damn, Fitz, I'm sorry."

I'm going to cry in a minute. Why didn't I come earlier? I could have spent the afternoon. "I'll come tomorrow, okay. Tomorrow afternoon I'll come and sit with you for a while."

Fitz nods. "That would be nice, hot shot. Are you going to be okay yourself? You look a little out of sorts."

"I know. I'll be okay," I say. I don't have a choice, do I?

* * *

Night shift, Friday night shift no less. The department is busy, crowded, and hot. Nurses in their green scrubs move quickly from bed to bed. There are residents from upstairs admitting new patients, disgruntled because we're making their night longer with each admit, wheeling them off into the elevators. New interns I don't recognize follow at their heels, wide-eyed, listening, watching.

How am I going to do this? I should have called in sick. Emily Fletcher is the other attending. Just-the-Facts-Fletcher she is called, serious, humorless, aggressive in treating patients, tolerates no nonsense from the residents. Or from anyone else, her fellow faculty as well.

Zach, your voice is here all the time now, sometimes garbled, sometimes clear. Can't you go away, leave me alone. Let me think clearly tonight. I strain to make out your words.

Phil Patterson leads me into Room 6, where a tiny aged lady lies beneath a pile of blankets.

"Mrs. Glemenac," he shouts in her ear, then to me, "I don't even know how to pronounce her name. She came in by ambulance. Apparently she fell, then made it to the phone to call 911, and the medics found her lying on the floor.

She must have scooted herself across the floor to the phone." Then shouting to her again, "This is Dr. Mendel, he's my attending."

"Yes, I fell down," the scratchy voice replies.

"It's okay, Phil," I say. "I doubt she knows an attending from an orderly."

I start peeling away the blankets to get at her hip. "Damn, how could anyone be cold on a summer night like this?"

"Yeah, well, wait till you're eighty-six with diabetes and Parkinson's and what else?" He holds up her chart, looking at his notes. "And chronic atrial fib with aortic stenosis and hypothyroidism and—"

"Okay, okay, how do you know all that?"

"This is the stuff from her old records. She was here last year in heart failure."

I look at the peculiar deformity of her upper leg. "It's not her hip, it's her femur."

What else is wrong with this lady? Why did she fall? What is that haggard face hiding, those scared, confused eyes? She is oblivious of us. "So what are you going to do, Phil?"

"Well, I already ordered her X-rays and lab work, then I figured I'd go ahead and call the orthopedic guys to come and admit her."

A sixtyish man enters the room. He wears worn dark clothing and walks with a shuffling gate.

"Hi," Phil says. "Are you a relative?"

"She's my mother," he says numbly, a vacant voice.

I try to smile, watching his eyes. "Looks like your mother took a nasty spill."

"She hurt bad?"

"Looks like she broke her leg," Phil says to him, "the big bone in the thigh. It's called the femur."

"I knew it was sumpthin'," he says, "the way she couldn't git up an' all."

"Were you with her when she fell?"

"Naw, I was at home, just up the street. Them ambulance guys called me on the phone."

"Your mother lives alone?" I say.

He nods. "She do. She got a chore worker comes in now and then to help her out."

"So she's normally able to be up and around, fixing her own food and dressing herself?"

"I git her groceries for her, but she do for herself mostly. We talked about puttin' her in a home, but she wouldn't have none of it. Couldn't pay for it anyways. She falls down all the time. Just the other day, in fact, I come in an' there she was jus' layin' on the floor in the kitchen. Had to shake her to wake her up."

"Has she been taking her medicine?" Phil says, looking at the chart. "Looks like she's on about six different kinds of pills."

"She s'posed to be on them pills but she can't pay for 'em. I take her to some doctor an' he give her all them prescriptions but she can't buy 'em. That one pill cost eighty-five bucks just for one month's worth. Hell, she hardly got enough social security for her rent and some food."

"Better figure out if she has any other problems, Phil," I say, moving toward the door. "At her age she could have most anything wrong, infection, stroke, metabolic stuff."

"Right, Leon, I already ordered labs on her."

"You'll need to check her ECG, urine, chest X-ray, thyroid function tests, liver function, ammonia level, might try some Narcan on her, too. Check a blood alcohol, find out if she drinks." I nod toward the son.

Phil looks at me, irritated. "Leon, I've already examined her. She's wide awake, afebrile, no focal neurologic deficit, doesn't smell of alcohol. Are you serious about all that?"

Zach is loud in my mind, the feeling of death rising again as I glance at the mound of blankets covering the stick figure of a person, one stick broken. He's right, I'm being ridiculous.

"Your judgment, Phil. But you might consider admitting her to a monitored bed. Sounds like she's having syncope." I gesture toward the son, the information he gave us, and walk out of the room. I feel Phil's eyes following me, doubting me.

Ted and Lydia are waiting at the nurses station, laughing about something. Their smiles vanish as I approach.

"What's so funny?"

"Nothing," Ted says, a counter edge denting his wide rump. "I got a three for one here, Leon. Mom brought all three kids in. Only one is really sick at all—"

"What were you guys joking about?" I hear my voice say. Was it me?

They glance at each other. "Um, it was really nothing, Leon. Just joking about this drunk patient yesterday who tried to make a pass at Lydia, said he wanted to take her to Mexico with him."

Is he lying to me? Were they talking about me? "Okay, so you got three kids there?" I wave at the charts in his hand.

"The reason they came in is cause of the five year old who has a bad cough, but he's got no fever and looks fine. He vomited a couple times, too. Needs some cough medicine and that's about all."

"Five year old coughing and vomiting. Is he coughing up blood, any TB exposure?"

Ted eyes me doubtfully. "TB exposure? In a five year old?"

"Well, there's a lot of it going around now, particularly in the inner city."

"Yes, I know, Leon. I'll ask the mother before I let them go home."

The image of a coughing child in a dirty bed in a dark tenement room rises in my mind, cigarette smoke clouding the air, rats on the floor. "Does the mom smoke?"

"Course," Ted says, "isn't that what welfare checks are for, cigarettes and malt liquor?"

"What about the other two kids?"

"They don't smoke," Lydia jokes. "Not yet, couple more years."

I feel myself getting angry as Ted grins. They're baiting me, leading me on.

"Ages three and two," Ted says, "both afebrile with runny noses. They both look fine."

"Sounds good. What room are they in?"

Ted points. "Room 12."

"Do you think the five year old needs a chest X-ray?" Death again, I feel it from Room 12's doorway, across the department.

Again Ted eyes me. "Leon, it's just a kid with a cough. He's fine."

Lydia presents a twenty-four-year-old woman with a toothache. "She can't find a dentist that will take her, Leon. And there's a three-month wait at the dental clinic." Her calm hazel eyes watch me.

I take the chart from her hand and glance at the demographic information on the back. "She's on welfare. No private dentist will take welfare patients. It's not worth it to them."

"You mean they just turn them away?"

"Yup, unless they can pay up front, fifty dollars or so, which of course they never can."

"But she's got three kids. She can't work."

"And of course she's not married, and each kid's probably got a different father."

"Well, she is unmarried. I didn't ask about the father of the children. What difference does that make?"

All these women, teenage girls really, having kids, unmarried, on welfare, spending their checks on cigarettes, junk food, and alcohol. And the fathers, teenagers also, macho assholes looking for a quick screw, then moving on, no thought to the consequences. I think of the blocks and blocks of slums surrounding us, teeming with these people, ignorant, helpless people who—

"Leon?"

"Sorry, my mind was wandering. Well, go ahead and—I mean, what do you want to do?" I coach her through the routine of penicillin and pain medicine for the toothache.

"I can't believe how much of this kind of thing we see here, Leon. So many patients with minor problems, kids with colds, rashes, little cuts and bruises. Why don't these people go to the clinics?"

Behind me someone is talking in a low voice, saying my name. I turn to look but no one is there, of course.

"The clinics are full," I say, turning back to her, "or they have to sit and wait for two or three hours there. They know if they're lucky they can get in and out of the ED fast, especially during the day when it's not so busy."

"But they can make appointments at the clinics."

"That's true, but that takes foresight, planning, organization. Plus it takes a telephone and a telephone book. And even if they do call they usually get put off for a month or so 'til the next opening. You've rotated through the clinics, haven't you?"

"It's July, Leon. This is my first month here," she says.

"Oh, yeah. Well, there are two public hospitals in Cincinnati, University Hospital and us. There are God knows how many thousands of people in this city on welfare. If you're on welfare then the clinics and the emergency departments are free. You don't have to pay a nickel. Just walk in the door and flash your welfare card. Our tax dollars at work, yours and mine, paying for the health and welfare of these people.

"And Municipal's right in the middle of it, deep in the heart of the welfare state, a nation within a nation of people who go from one generation to the next living off the taxes and benevolence of the rest of the people. Their parents are on welfare, they grow up on welfare, and they stay on welfare. A newborn baby is every sixteen-year-old girl's ticket to financial independence. You don't need an education, you don't need a job, all you need is a child and those checks start rolling in. You can sign up for low-income housing, food stamps, the WIC program which gives you free formula for your baby.

"Did you ever notice how these mothers hardly ever breastfeed their kids? If there was ever a group of mothers that should breastfeed their kids, for all the benefits of breastfeeding, not to mention the economic advantages. But just try asking a few of them. They stare at you like you're nuts, like it's dirty or something. It's the same stare you get if you ask them if they're married. Married? What's that mean? I done forgot. Why would I want to get married? I might accidentally marry someone with a job, God forbid, and then I couldn't stay on welfare. Course I wouldn't ever tell them down at the welfare office, even if I did. But then I'd have to ask some man for my cigarette money, and money to get my hair done, or get my ears pierced. Did you ever notice how many of these babies have their ears pierced? They can't breastfeed their kids but they can damn well get their little ears pierced."

Emily Fletcher steps in front of me. "Thank you, Leon. We all enjoyed your discourse, and I'm sure the dozen or so patients within hearing did as well. Now perhaps we should go and take care of them."

Her face is skin stretched over bone, a skull wrapped in its covering, swiveling on the hidden vertebra of its neck, its jaw clacking.

"Sorry, Emily." I struggle to refocus my mind, my heart thumping. Zach is calling me in unformed words. I look around at them, Fletcher, Lydia, and Rohit, more skulls, their eyes twitching in their sockets, watching me lose it, watching me going nuts.

"At least talk a little more quietly, Leon," Fletcher says. "I could hear you clearly over in Room 6. Are you all right?"

All right by Emily's definition means at least a hundred and sixty points of I.Q. ready to fly like a missile at the next patient's problem, whether it's a hangnail or a trauma code.

I nod at her, trying to form an answer. "Yeah, Emily, I'm fine." Her eyes seem to dull as death flickers through them. I look away. "Yeah, yeah, I'm fine. Sorry if I got a little too loud."

Chapter Eleven

I glance at the patient control board. It's filling fast, a half dozen red tags, each a patient waiting to be seen.

"Okay, Rohit, what have you got?"

"This is an eighteen-year-old female who is pregnant, approximately five months, with right lower quadrant abdominal pain which began yesterday. She has vomited twice. She has no urinary symptoms, no vaginal bleeding, no past GI problems. Her exam, she is moderately intoxicated, no fever, she has great tenderness in the right lower quadrant with rebound, uterus is nontender, fetal heart tones are 148." He pauses, watching me with his dark, candid eyes.

"She's intoxicated? You mean she's drunk?"

He nods. "Yes, she is drunk."

"Pregnant and drunk with belly pain." Run away, run away, Zach is saying to me in a shrill irritating voice. God, can't you give it a rest, brother. "Okay, pelvic exam?"

"She does not want pelvic exam," Rohit says.

"You mean she refuses?"

He nods.

"Dr. Mendel," Ruby calls to me from behind her computer. "They need a doc in Room 4, a child with difficulty breathing."

I feel my adrenaline start. "Okay, Ruby, would you find Phil Patterson and tell him to head that way?" Then to Rohit, "What's her white count?"

"Fifteen thousand, urinalysis normal."

"Fifteen thousand, could be up just from being pregnant, or it could be what?"

"Appendicitis."

"Right, a difficult diagnosis to make in a pregnant woman. Okay, what do you want to do?"

"I thought maybe ultrasound. They could look at her appendix, also show severe constipation."

"Good thought," I start to move toward Room 4. "You'll need the surgery resident to see her before radiology will do an ultrasound. So page them to come down here and then keep moving." I wave at the board.

"The surgeon won't come 'til the pelvic exam is done," Rohit says.

Run away, run away, Zach's shrill voice.

"Don't mention it unless he does, then tell him I said this is a special case, and if that doesn't fly tell him I'll talk to his attending. That'll get him down here." I see now why I'm talking loud, to drown out my own mind.

"Okay, Leon." Finally a smile crosses his handsome face.

Room 4, a child with difficulty breathing, could be anything from a stuffy nose to epiglottitis, about to swell her airway shut and stop her breathing altogether.

Phil Patterson meets me outside the door. "What's up?"

"Let's find out." I follow him through the doorway.

Inside a four-year-old girl sits on the gurney, breathing hard, retracting, the skin between her ribs pulling in tight with each breath, but not in trouble yet. She is tiny, with black hair and fine pale skin. A Hispanic mother stands behind her, watching the nurse struggle with an oximeter transducer, trying to attach it to the child's finger.

"What's up?" Phil says again.

"This is Angela," Lynne, the nurse, says, "and she's been coughing and having trouble breathing since early this morning. Is that right?" She turns to the mom.

"Yes, right," the woman says. "She have this terrible cough. I never heard it before." She is worried but not frightened.

Asthma, croup, or epiglottitis. Kids with epiglottitis don't cough, or so the textbook says.

"Has she ever had a problem like this before?" Phil says.

"Oh, no," the woman shakes her head.

"Has she ever had asthma?"

The woman shakes her head.

"Is she on any medicine, for her breathing or for her lungs?" The woman may not understand the word asthma.

"No medicine. I give her some cough syrup but that is all."

"Has she ever had croup?" Phil says.

"What is this?"

Phil repeats the question but the answer is no. I want to jump in and take over but Phil is doing fine. The oximeter registers finally on the monitor screen above, 94%, not normal for a child but not terrible. There is time. I could leave, go see some other patient. There are so many.

"Her cough," Phil says, "is it like a seal barking?"

"Like what?" the mother says.

"Have you heard her cough?" he says to Lynne.

She shakes her head.

"Like a seal," Phil says, turning back to the mom. "You know what a seal is? Like at the zoo, swims around and claps its flippers?" Phil claps his hands in front of him. This is important to know and he is serious.

The woman watches him, mystified by this intense young doctor imitating a seal. It must be some other word she hasn't learned yet. "I do not know."

Phil turns to the girl, taking her hand. "Hi, Angela, how are you feeling?"

The girl pulls back, toward her mother.

"Sweetie, can you talk to me just for a minute?" But she ignores him. He leans over and listens to her lungs with his stethoscope.

Asthma we can deal with, we do it all the time. Croup we can deal with, too. Epiglottitis can kill, it's rare but it can put a normal, healthy child into respiratory arrest in a couple hours, with three docs thrashing and yelling and sweating to get a tiny tube through swollen vocal cords that have no visible opening, seconds ticking, oxygen level dropping, neurons dying, parents cringing to see their own child handled so—

Then she coughs and there it is, the hoarse, unmistakable bark of croup. Phil eyes me and I nod.

"How about a round of racemic?" he says to Lynne.

"You got it." She moves away to get the medicine, racemic epinephrine, nebulized into a mist to be breathed and shrink the swelling in the child's trachea. We'll watch her for a couple of hours, start her on prednisone, then send her home with Mom if she stays clear.

Another one bites the dust. I turn back toward the station, the thump of my own heart calming. There is laughter somewhere, frantic laughter. I feel someone pointing at me, but a glance across the department reveals only busy staff moving about, patients on gurneys behind curtains. Who was it, who was laughing at me?

Again I think of Zach, of you, brother, in that long ago bed in that long ago house, lying there, your arms jerking at nothing, endlessly jerking. Again the dread rises in me, twists me inside like a fist clutching my guts. No, don't think of it, put it away, out of your head, far away.

I shuffle through the charts of patients waiting in the waiting room, not yet on the board. They've been triaged, checked in, and asked to take a seat. The urgent ones are brought right back, the rest have to wait their turn.

Damn, there are a lot. The waiting room must be packed. The ancient wooden chairs and dirty linoleum floor, kids coughing and vomiting, exhausted parents, people bleeding and in pain. There's a TV that rarely works, and a pop machine that's usually empty. The people spill into the halls and out the doors. All these people, this endless stream of poor and sick, from the blocks and blocks of tenements and rundown houses surrounding us, from the hundreds of thousands who live in the city, all funneling through our doors. How can we do it? There are more and more, always more, more this week than last, more this month than last. I feel a twinge of panic, fear that seems to open up and have no bounds, a dry feeling in the back of my mouth, something numb—

"Busy night," Fletcher's voice behind me. "Are you okay, Leon? There's talk, you know."

I turn and look at her square, grim face. "Talk?"

"I don't give it much credence, but yes, there is talk about you, Leon."

"Groundless," I say, turning toward the charts, "hardly worth mentioning."

Hands trembling, I thumb through the clipboards until she walks off. Okay, pick out three quick ones, leaving the abdominal pains, the chest pains, the vaginal bleeders, the psychiatric cases, leaving them for the residents so they can learn.

A black seventeen year old who punched a door last night. His X-ray shows a fifth metacarpal fracture. He sits sullen in untied high-tops, knee-length shorts and baseball cap on backward.

"Hi, Daryl, I'm Dr. Mendel."

"Fix my hand, man." He shoves it forward as if punching me.

"What did you do to it?"

"I hit a damn door."

"Angry at the door?"

"You ain't funny. No, I weren't angry at the door, but you don't get arrested for punchin' the door."

You do for punching your girlfriend, or your mother, or your child.

"I looked at your X-rays. You've got a bone broken right here." I take his hand. "It's called a metacarpal bone."

"Yeah, I know'd it was broke."

"So, we'll put you in a splint and then you need to go to the Orthopedic Clinic tomorrow to get the bone pushed back into place. The nurse will make an appointment for you."

"I don't need no appointment shit, man. Why can't you fix it right here?"

"I can try but it might not stay in place. It might even need a pin to hold the bones together properly." My words are flying right by his ears. And I won't even try to explain our rule that the orthopedists set bones, that we refer such patients to the clinic so their residents can get the experience, so their malpractice coverage takes the heat for a bad result, as if this kid would ever call a lawyer for anything.

"There ain't no end to the bullshit around here, every time I come in here."

"You're right," I say, "and I'm sorry, but that's the way it is." And you'll never pay a nickel for it, I want to say, bullshit or not.

"Work on that anger thing, Daryl," I say leaving. "It might save your life."

Next is a fifty-five-year-old woman with hives, an allergic reaction. She is kindly, scared. I try to be nice, reassure her, hold her hand for a moment. I order shots of Benadryl and epinephrine for her.

Then a two year old with burns across his chest from pulling a hot coffee cup down upon himself. They are superficial, he will heal. The father is angry at himself, awkward at comforting the child. Do the burns match the story? A burned child is always a subject of suspicion, the possibility of abuse. But this unlucky kid passes the test. I reassure the father, try to soothe his guilt with an accidents-will-happen comment, then order a shot of Demerol to relieve the child's pain and the nurses can do the rest, cleanse the peeling skin and show the father how to care for it.

Run away, run away. Across the department I see an older man walking by in tailored beige pants and suspenders over a white shirt, his suit jacket draped over an arm. One of the private attendings, there is an entrance here from the physician's parking outside. I know him, Herb Taft.

"Dr. Taft," I call after him. But suddenly I fear seeing his face. Death roars in my mind.

He turns and smiles at me, eyes friendly behind round wire-rims, friendly and alive. I am, no doubt, one of the many physician faces he has seen around here before but whose name he does not recall.

"Leon Mendel," I say quickly, "I'm one of the emergency physicians."

"Thank you, Leon, how are you?" He wears a bow tie, dapper, impeccable, the old-school intellectual look.

"I'm sorry to bother you but one of your patients is a friend of mine. Fitz Goddard, up on the sixth floor?"

He nods, smiling still. "Yes, Fitz. A very likeable fellow."

"I just wondered how he's doing."

"You're his friend?" Taft says. Confidentiality is always a touchy issue with an AIDS patient.

"Yes, we're good friends. I've been visiting him each day and trying to help him out." This puts my own sexuality on the line, but I trust that for Taft this won't be an issue.

"Well, Fitz isn't doing very well, Leon, as you can probably tell. He's got bad Pneumocystis pneumonia, and his immune system can't put up much of a fight. His CD 4 count is very low."

I nod, watching his face.

"You were a resident here, weren't you?" he says.

"Yes, sir. You were one of my attendings on the medicine rotations, about five years ago. We've spoken on the phone about a few of your patients in the

Emergency Department, but it's usually in the middle of the night and I wouldn't expect you'd remember."

He nods again, calm as can be.

"So do you think Fitz will survive?" A stupid question, no AIDS patient survives.

"Survive? You mean this episode?" He searches my eyes. I'm putting him on the spot. "I doubt it, to be honest. He has refused hyperalimentation and a ventilator, which is probably appropriate in his case. It's a shame, this disease is so relentless."

"A ventilator, do you think—" but I can't say any more. I am about to cry and my voice locks up. I stand mute, then shake my head and can only manage a thank you. There is more, much more I need to say to this man. Fitz is a special person, I need to say. He's a good person, kind and warm and loving and what? And someone I love. But I can't say any of it.

"I'm sorry, Leon," he says, touching my shoulder before he leaves.

Lydia waves a chart at me. I find a counter to sit on. Death shrieks and screams at me from above, the whole building seems to throb with it, as if the twelve floors over my head were teeming with corpses.

"A forty-seven-year-old male with chest pain," Lydia says, "dull, aching substernal pain radiating to left shoulder, no nausea or shortness of breath. Did break out in a sweat. Onset while driving in his car, lasted about twenty minutes, and he feels better now. Oh, yeah, got very lightheaded and had to pull over to the side of the road. He felt like he was going to pass out."

"Okay." Leon, Leon, Leon, now Jasmine's voice hisses at me.

"No past history of heart disease, smokes about one pack a day, positive family history but no other risk factors that he knows of."

The radio sounds its tone across the station. A nurse moves to answer.

"Regular exercise?" I ask.

"What do you mean?" Lydia says.

"Well, sometimes these patients do some kind of exercise, although not usually smokers, but if the guy told you he runs three miles a day or swims fifty laps each morning before work you might not be as concerned about his heart. Right?"

"I'll ask him but I doubt it. He's pretty fat."

"Fat people are allowed to exercise," Ted's voice sounds behind me. "There's no law against it."

"Ted plays racquetball," I say, "or so rumor has it."

"Sorry, Ted," Lydia says, "nothing personal."

"Only obnoxious fat people exercise," I say, "insipid, sarcastic, self-important fat people."

Ted staggers backward. “Whew, Leon, I’m stunned, outgunned.”

“Okay, so what do you want to do?” I say to Lydia.

“Leon,” Rhonda, the charge nurse, waves the radio report form at me. “There’s a couple of shooting victims coming. Medic 2, sounds like a gang fight or something. One in the chest, one in the leg. Lines are in, vitals are stable. They said there were two dead at the scene.”

“Okay, call the O.R. and the supervisor and page the trauma team.”

“I know, Leon, I know.” She turns away. She’s tired and has been working hard.

Death, more death, not just upstairs but out there, tearing holes in the hot dark streets, emptiness punching through.

Lydia finishes her presentation. The man has a normal cardiogram, the usual case. Chest pain, probably angina, possibly a man about to have a heart attack, even about to die.

“So what do you want to do?” I say.

“You say that all the time, don’t you?” she says.

“I do. I’m supposed to be your teacher while you’re here, and this is how I teach. Would you like me to hand it to you on a platter?”

The radio sounds again.

“Well,” she stares down at the chart, “new onset chest pain, probably cardiac. Needs to be admitted.”

“Right, and we’re not going to have time to mess with him. So page the internal medicine resident and tell him we’ve got a patient with unstable angina who needs to be admitted.” Rhonda is waving at me from the radio. “If he gives you any grief about CPKs or treadmills or any other nonsense you tell him the E.D. attending said he needs to admit the patient and he can discuss it with me after he’s examined him.”

“Medic 3,” Rhonda says. “They’ve got a policeman that’s been shot, too. Same fight. In the abdomen and his pressure’s dropping.”

So we wait the few minutes, put on the cover gowns with their slick film of waterproofing, bloodproofing really, the gloves, the paper masks over our noses and mouths, and goggles, wide plastic glasses with side pieces. Like soldiers awaiting the charge, hearing the hoofbeats coming but not knowing who’s going to top that rise, how many, how well armed, how angry.

Pretend to keep busy. Rohit tells me about a depressed woman whose husband brought her in because she had been scratching her wrists with a knife, threatening to do more. Both forearms are covered with scars from years of similar behavior. She has been here many times, a chronically depressed woman, difficult to help, impossible to cure. I tell him to put her on the social worker’s list and sometime tonight someone will sit and talk with her, try to figure out what mental Band-Aid she needs to get her through the weekend. That's all we can do.

Claudette stops me. "'What's going on out there, Dr. Mendel? They got some stuff coming at us?"

"Yup. Three gunshot wounds, maybe a gang fight."

"Three victims?" Roxanne says behind her.

I nod. "One's a cop."

The ambulance entrance doors swing open and there are shouts, red and white flashes bounce off the walls. The first gurney rolls in, a black kid, a teenager, growling and cursing, the paramedics talking to him, cajoling him. IV bags swing from the poles and he has a bandage on his flank.

"How's he doing?" Rhonda says.

"Good. His pressure's holding steady. His belly hurts though."

"Trauma C," Rhonda waves them to the far trauma bay.

Another gurney, another angry black face slides in the door, silent, staring at the ceiling.

"Is this the leg wound?"

"Yup. This is Lamont," says the paramedic. "Lamont, this is Municipal Emergency Department, where every—"

"Is he stable?" Rhonda cuts him off.

The paramedic's grin fades. He nods. "Lamont is stable."

"Okay, Trauma B."

"Leon, do you need help with these traumas?" It's Emily Fletcher, deadpan, steely-eyed, taking in the situation, ready to pounce.

You asshole, asshole, asshole, Jasmine is shouting at me.

"I'm okay, Emily. They look pretty straightforward." I try for a businesslike voice. "Why don't you keep the rest of the department going and I'll let you know if I need any help." She nods and moves away. Thanks, sweetie.

I have little to do. Both trauma teams are here, Matt Beauregard and Tony Kaminsky, calmly going through the motions, asking the questions. Even Finkel, poor skinny Finkel, looks like he'll make it 'til the next bathroom break.

The ambulance entrance doors stay open with people coming and going, paramedics, police. More sirens wail. There are three loud cracks, gunshots, outside somewhere, not far away. Everyone pauses, looks toward the entrance.

Jagged holes tearing open in the street, death, the image jumps into my mind.

One siren's scream keeps rising until the department is filled with it, then it cuts out as they stop outside. I walk out into the heavy air, the acrid exhaust. The back doors open and three very serious paramedics crouch over a gurney.

"Move the IV bags over," one of them shouts, "Jimmy, jump down. All right, watch the monitor. Switch the oxygen over. All right, let's go, c'mon, c'mon."

The stretcher slides out, its legs drop.

"How's he doing?" I say.

"He got two bullets," the lead paramedic says without looking up. "One in the belly and one in the leg. We've given him 3 liters and—hi, Dr. Mendel—3 liters and he's holding his pressure around 90. Gonna need the operating room for sure."

I follow them inside. A police cruiser roars around the turn and squeals to a stop, lights flashing.

Trauma A, ten feet from the door. Phil Patterson steps over, eyes traveling quickly, words flowing. "What kind of weapon was it?"

"Don't know, probably a large caliber revolver, maybe a thirty-eight. Something serious."

To the lab tech, Phil says, "Type and cross 6 units, 2 units type specific, a.s.a.p." To the paramedic again, "How much blood at the scene?"

"Um...maybe three, four hundred cc's on the street."

"What was the lowest his pressure got?"

"We got 60 the first time, maybe twelve minutes after the shooting."

The officer is awake, moaning, an older Hispanic face I've seen here often, joked with, drunk coffee with in the middle of the night. A couple of X-rays to make sure his chest is okay, to make sure the bullet stopped in his belly, and then Matt Beauregard will roll him off to the operating room and fix him, stop the puddle of death growing in his abdomen, the maroon puddle leaking from his intestines or his spleen or his liver.

Beauregard with Chester Graffen snorting at him, Graffen walking in, an hour into the operation, after Matt's opened his belly and found the tears in his viscera, found which artery is blasted open and flowing free, tied it off with skilled hands, tiny sure movements of gloved fingers, and found the next, and the next, until the entire O.R. crew pauses and waits and watches the inside of this man's belly, waits and watches for the next rising puddle of blood, and there is none.

Then Graffen will walk in, smelling of scotch, and growl at poor Matt about something, chromic sutures instead of vicryl, or a different retractor to hold the liver, some ridiculous idiosyncrasy just so he can growl.

I stand close to the frenzy around the man's gurney, watching the details, the monitor, the oximeter, watching Patterson and now Beauregard going over him. The details, the resuscitation, this police officer's life, my responsibility right now, until he enters the operating room.

Beyond, through the open doors, a figure appears, a black teenager. He moves quickly inside, an Oakland Raiders jacket on and dark kerchief tight on his head, he steps along the far wall, looking, an arm inside the coat. His half-closed eyes glow with death.

"Hey, buddy," a nurse shouts, "you're not supposed to be in here!"

He grins, writhing, the other hand pointing down. "My brother been shot. I jus' wanna see my brother." He keeps moving, stepping, looking around a curtain.

"Police!" the nurse yells out the open doors. "Get out. You gotta get out."

"I be all right." He glides away from her. "Where's my brother, Lamont?"

Two paramedics move toward him. As the thought comes to my mind a weapon appears from under the coat, a short rifle, dark, blunt. "Now don't you mess, boys. You see what I got?"

The nurse screams. There are shouts. Shit, where's Claudette?

A cop runs in from outside, fumbling at his holster. "Everybody down," he shouts.

The boy turns and points his weapon. "Don't touch that gun, Mr. Man."

The policeman stops his hands and shouts again. "Everybody down. He's got a gun."

The twenty or so people in the trauma bays crouch down or move away. More screams.

"Hey, pal," the cop says, angry, unafraid, "you got a big question to answer right now. Gonna mean whether you spend the rest of your life in prison or not. You ever been to prison?"

"Shut up, pig." His face gleams with sweat, his arms and legs twitching. Is he high, cocaine, speed? He moves toward us. I watch him over the stained pantlegs of the shot policeman. The weapon looks almost frail, the delicate barrel pointing from the military-looking stock, no wood, all flat black metal.

"In about one minute you're going to have six or eight other officers all around you," the cop says. "You're not leaving here, pal. That's for sure."

He's here to finish somebody off. Lamont? The other kid maybe? The cop here on the gurney? Someone is sobbing.

"Now, you can walk outta here with me and my friends nice and peaceful and you'll do maybe two, three years." The cop is talking fast. "Should be more but that's all you'll get. Or you use that thing and you're gone for life. Aggravated first degree, you'll be an old man in prison, boy, fifty, sixty years, no pussy, nothin', for the rest of your life."

"I said shut the fuck up, asshole," the boy yells.

"Hey, Doc," the policeman on the gurney in front of me whispers urgently, twisting his face toward me. "I can't move, take these damn things off my legs."

I reach for the straps that hold down his legs. But he's shot in the leg. He can't stand. I don't know what to do.

"HEY, DUMBFUCK," somebody shouts from across the department. There is movement. "PUT IT DOWN RIGHT NOW, BOY." It's Claudette.

He sees the man in front of me. "Der he is," he hisses, "der's the fucker."

Claudette appears around a corner, weapon drawn. "I gotcha, son. Drop it now. I don't want to—"

The boy spins and there are three fast slaps of sound from his weapon, and in the same instant a thump from behind me, Claudette's gun firing, then another and another.

He falls, stumbling, firing again. Lights shatter above. He's next to me, twisting like a snake. Someone, a nurse, bumps against me. I push her away. There is blood, screams. I see that thin barrel coming around, blunt, black, ugly, the dark hands holding it bloody. I can get it. I grab the hot steel and point it up. It jerks in my hand, firing again, like a hammer at my head. Glass falling everywhere, on my face. Don't let go. I need to get a knee into him.

Now more hands jerk the gun, a burly blue shape knocks me backward.

"I got it, Dr. Mendel. I got it." Roxanne's voice. "Let go, hon. Let go, now." More blue shirts behind her, thumping the boy, shouting, slamming him onto his stomach.

I lie on my side, against a cabinet, the cover gown tangled round my legs. Death shrieks all around me, tearing through here and here and here, surrounding me. I want to curl up and hide, cover my eyes.

"Claudette's bleeding bad," someone shouts.

"It's okay, people," the cop from the entrance shouts. "It's okay, now. We got him. You're safe now."

People start to move, voices everywhere. Someone helps me sit up. I want to laugh. Someone talking in my face, a nurse, pointing. Now I stand. She keeps jabbing at the air with her finger.

There on the floor is Claudette, squirming, coughing blood, blood all over her. Nurses move around her, Beauregard and Patterson, lift her onto a gurney. There's Fletcher's face, pale, grim, giving orders.

"Leon, Leon..." Two or three people are talking at me. How about the boy? I look down. He lies still in a pool of blood, hands cuffed behind his back.

I glance at the officer on the gurney. He's awake, looking about.

Someone pulls my hand. Rhonda, kneeling beside the boy.

"What about him, Leon?"

"Is he alive?" Do we need to save him, now that we've shot him?

"I don't think so," she says. She has a gloved hand on his neck. Death, he is death, a demon, punching holes with his gun. I don't want to touch him.

"Damn it," I hear Emily shout from the crowd around Claudette. "Get the suction going. Get a line in her right now. Page anesthesia and ENT stat and tell 'em we need 'em five minutes ago."

"Roll him over." I kneel by Rhonda and we pull him over.

Roxanne squats next to us. "Don't save his sorry ass, Dr. Mendel." There is venom in her voice. "He needs to die."

There is a wound in his head, two in his chest. They have stopped bleeding. His blood is no longer flowing. Not breathing, no pulse in the neck, no pulse in his groin. He's dead. I look at his slack grey face, a tattoo by the angle of his jaw, a scar across the eyebrow. Death is here in his flaccid lips and those horrible eyes, death looking out, staring flat, unmoved, at me.

Rhonda touches my arm. "Are we gonna let him go, Leon?"

We could crack his chest and give it a try, flop him onto a gurney and spend twenty minutes of furious activity, putting in IVs and cutting him open to see if there was a chance to sew up his aorta or the holes in his heart or his pulmonary arteries or whatever. We might, if he were a cop, or a nurse, or almost anybody else.

"Leon?" Rhonda knows it, too, but it's my call.

My hand shakes as I slide the eyelids closed. "He's dead. We've got other things to do." I stand. "Get someone to move his body out of the way."

Are there more? I glance toward the doors. Are there more gangbangers slinking through the streets with their guns, creeping toward the hospital, running through alleys, hiding behind dumpsters, closing in on us with death in their hands? I feel the same dread rising. No, there are many cops here now.

And Claudette, what about Claudette? She lies behind a cluster of docs and nurses. I've seen her take down an angry biker, crazed on PCP, a huge muscular guy, quick as a cat she had him on his belly and cuffed. Another time, a shouting drunk came through the door waving a pistol to finish off someone he'd wounded. Claudette gave him the end of her baton in his ribs and broke his arm before he'd even seen her. I look toward her but she is hidden by the crowd.

I close my eyes, listening to Zach calling. My heart jumps like a quaking animal. I feel the air move in and out of my lungs, my frail ribs that wrap around it all, the thin cover of my skin.

Chapter Twelve

Ted grabs my arm. "Leon, Fletcher needs help. Claudette's bleeding like crazy. She got hit in the neck."

I peel off my slimy gloves and look around for more. The bloody cover gown, too. I don't want to expose Claudette to that kid's blood. God knows what he had.

"Can't you get a line in her!" Emily shouts, fear in her voice. "Somebody, Phil, do a subclavian. We've got to get her paralyzed."

Emily stands by Claudette's thrashing head, bright blood all over them both. Claudette is coughing, retching, gasping. Blood pours from her mouth and every cough sends a spray of red.

"Leon, she's been hit in the trachea and the carotid. I can't see to intubate her. She's aspirating with every breath."

Claudette writhes on the gurney, eyes wide. She reaches a frantic, dripping hand out to me. Phil has the catheter but he needs a nonmoving target.

"It's all right, Claudette," I say loud, taking her hand, loud so she'll hear it in her haze of pain and panic. "You need to lie still and not move for a minute. We're going to put you to sleep, take you away from all this."

I grab her shoulders and pin them onto the gurney. "Hold her elbows down and her knees." People move close around her.

Around us, under the gurney, death is creeping. Leave her alone, it moans, you can't help her, she's dying and you can't stop it.

"Cut her shirt right here," my voice says. Someone cuts her shirt between my hands, exposing her shoulder.

"I can't breathe!" she rasps, gagging, twisting beneath our hands. She is very strong. And with her cough warm blood sprays me, too, my cheeks and my face. It drips from my goggles.

"Okay, just a minute, Claudette. Now turn your head to the side. Suction her mouth. Now Phil's gonna give you a little poke here."

Then to Patterson, "C'mon, Phil, do it. No betadyne, just get the needle in."

To the nurse, "We need twenty of Valium and a hundred of succinylcholine."

She holds up the syringes, already filled and ready.

Phil slides a long needle through the skin below Claudette's clavicle. Dark blood appears in the attached syringe.

Now Claudette starts to shake. Her back arches.

"Shit, she's seizing," Emily says. "Not enough oxygen, she's having a hypoxic seizure."

It's around my legs now, this dark fog, reaching for my arms. It's there, just outside my field of view. If I turn my head quickly—I can't see from the blood on my goggles. I pull them off. Someone hands me another pair. There is blood in my hair. My mask is wet with it. A hypoxic seizure, not enough blood going to her brain, not enough oxygen. We need to fix her right now.

"Hold the needle, Phil." My own voice again. "Where's the Valium?" I take the syringe and struggle with Phil to attach it to the shaking needle. "Don't let go."

This needle might save her life, this needle with its razor tip in the stream of a vein perhaps a centimeter in diameter, if the tip stays in that stream, despite her shaking, if it doesn't poke out through the thin wall of that vein.

I draw back on the plunger and blood appears in the barrel. Still in the vein. Now I push the plunger and squirt the Valium into her. It will stop the seizure and put her to sleep.

"Now the sucs." Again we struggle to detach one syringe and attach another. Her seizure is resolving, the shakes lessening.

The succinylcholine is in. In one minute she will be paralyzed, all muscles flaccid. But her brain can't wait one minute.

The fog wraps tighter on my legs, like some huge snake, growing beneath the gurney, reaching to drag at my arms, at Phil's arms, waiting to burst up and cover Claudette. She's dying, it wails, not words but something else. She's dying and you can't stop it.

"YES, WE CAN!" someone shouts. I wrench my arms up, out of its grasp. "Okay, Phil, do the guidewire and put in the line."

Now her body grows still, her head tilts limp, her gasps cease. Her neck is swollen and bleeding, a terrible hole below her chin. The stream of blood continues, pulsing out of her neck and from her mouth. Is she dead already, a bleeding corpse, a dead thing with blood flowing like a river out of it. Hot blood pumping through tubes in dead tissue. It seems so odd to think of it—

"LEON," Emily shouts at me, "grab the damn suction. Hold her cricoid." She steps close, laryngoscope in hand.

I feel for Claudette's trachea. "It's there, Emily. I can feel it. You just have to find it. Suction."

I stick one suction tube in the hole. Emily needs a moment of clear vision, no blood, to find Claudette's vocal cords, to slide the E.T. tube into her trachea so we can breathe for her, so we can stop her from filling her lungs with blood, and keep her alive long enough to stop the bleeding, too. Another suction tube goes into her mouth.

"Leon, what the hell is going on?" Larry Heilprin, the ENT senior resident appears, eyeing me. "You're covered."

"Gunshot wound to the neck," I say, "through the trachea and left carotid. One of our security guards. You might want to ask the vascular guys to join you."

The dark fog is spreading. Doesn't anyone else see it! She's dying, it shouts to me, dying, dying, dying.

"NO, SHE'S NOT!" someone shouts back.

"Why are you shouting, Leon?" Emily slides the silver blade into Claudette's mouth and peers through the blood and distorted tissues. "Jesus, I can't see a thing."

"Here, look for bubbles." I push down on Claudette's belly, just below the ribs, a slow Heimlich. Is it me that's shouting? It is me, isn't it.

"Okay, there, there it is," Emily says. She wrestles with the suction and the laryngoscope, muttering to herself. She, too, is drenched in blood.

"Got it." She straightens up and hands off the tube to the respiratory therapist.

I grab a handful of wet gauze sponges and hold them over the hole in Claudette's neck. Now we can stop the bleeding and get her ready to go to surgery.

Heilprin finds a pair of gloves and starts giving orders. Claudette might live, if she hasn't lost too much blood, if her brain wasn't without oxygen for too long, if bubbles of air didn't get into the open artery and go up into her brain. She might walk and talk again, if too many neurons haven't swollen and burst, if too many synapses haven't melted away from lack of oxygen. She might.

In moments she is gone, off to surgery, off to reconstruct her carotid artery, if they can, and then her trachea. To perform some wizardry and make Claudette whole again, if they can.

I lean against a counter and stare at the bloody arms that seem to twist about my chest, from that fog of death scarlet fingers creep toward my face.

"STOP IT!" someone shouts. "STOP IT!" The hands are getting closer.

Now Lydia is there in front of me, her gloved hands holding the bloody ones.

"DON'T TOUCH IT," the voice shouts.

"You're okay, Leon. Don't shout anymore. Here, let's take off your mask and goggles."

The red screen in front of me rises away. The air is cool.

"Now walk with me to the locker room," Lydia says, leading me. "You'll be okay."

"WHERE IS IT! DON'T TOUCH IT!"

"It's okay, Leon. You don't need to shout. You're safe now." She pulls me with her away from the gurneys, and down the hall. "TED," she calls out, "COME AND HELP ME."

In the quiet locker room Ted shakes me. "Leon, you're okay, man. It's us, Ted and Lydia. You're all covered with blood. Calm down, Leon. You're okay. Now let's get this scrub shirt off and get you into the shower. These are your own hands, Leon. They're just all bloody."

They wrestle me out of my shirt and my shoes and steer me into the shower. It's there in those lockers, growling.

"WHERE IS IT! GET AWAY!"

"C'mon, Leon, be cool," Ted says, manhandling me. "You're gonna need some Haldol in a minute if you don't calm down. Now we're gonna turn on the water. You ready? It's going to be cold. Cold water coming, wildman. Let's get all this blood off and you'll feel better."

It covers me, cold and clean, a welcome shock, it takes me away and the bloody hands swirl and swirl and are gone. Ted and Lydia, watching me, what are they doing? My scrub pants are still on, blood swirling around my feet.

"What are you guys doing?" I say.

"Let it run through your hair, Leon," Lydia says. "You've still got blood in your hair."

I bend my head into the clean water, hide beneath it as it pours down. What happened? Why am I standing here? Leon, Zach is calling me, Leon, come get me. Where, Zach, where are you?

Hands turn me beneath the water, rinse my hair.

"C'mon, Leon, let's get with the program."

The water stops and now a towel appears in my hand.

"Which one is your locker, Leon?" Lydia says.

"I just need some scrubs. They're on the shelf over there."

They exchange a glance. "Listen, Leon," Ted says, "maybe you ought to go on home or something. I don't think you ought to go back out there. We'll manage without you."

"We'll call Lyle in early," Lydia says. "He starts at seven anyway."

Come get me, Leon, please. Where are you?

"Where is he?" I say.

"Where's who?" Ted says. "Leon, which locker is yours?"

I stare at the silent lockers. Is Zach here, in one of them? In those rows of dark dead places, like cells in a dungeon.

"Leon," Ted looks pained, frustrated.

"This one." I fumble with the key, then hand it to Ted. "What about the others? They're all locked, too. I need to get him."

"Get who, Leon?"

Lydia steps out as Ted pushes me through the motions of dressing.

"Sorry, um, am I okay, Ted? God, what am I gonna do?"

"That's okay, man. It was pretty hairy out there for a few minutes. You could have been shot. And then you had to deal with Claudette and all that blood. How about we call somebody for you, Leon. Like your wife, or—no, I guess you guys aren't a thing anymore, are you. How about your new lady-friend? What's her name?"

I follow Ted back through the department to the lounge. There are strange faces now, people taking pictures, detectives in blue jackets with orange letters on the back. By the monitors a nurse is sobbing, a chaplain bends over her.

Lydia sits with me in the lounge. She calls Rita to come and take me home.

"Leon," she says finally, "there are still patients waiting to be seen. I have to go out there. Will you be okay? Just sit here until she comes, okay?"

I nod and watch her leave.

There is a news commentator on the TV, the sound turned down, calling me in Zach's voice. It's here again, the dark fog just beyond my vision, vanishing when I look, wrapping around my legs. Is this where he is, amidst the death, here, in this underworld that is creeping through everywhere now? What if I let it cover me, let myself sink into it? Will Zach be there? He needs me to come get him. Until it smothers me, too.

No, no, I can't. I stand and move toward the door. Go outside, get away from it. I move quickly down a hallway.

"Leon," someone calls me, the corpse of that kid. "LEON," it shouts.

No, no, go outside. Maybe Zach is there.

"Headin' home, Dr. Mendel?" a voice says, a housekeeper I think.

I nod, pushing open the door, stumbling into the parking lot. There is some light, dawn, cars like gray boulders, the fog swirling beneath them, between them. It can't hurt them, can it, just lumps of metal anyway, dead lumps of steel.

Leon, Leon, come help me, he says over and over. Where are you, Zach? There, by the dumpster, where it's still dark. Are you there? The fog, the dead concrete, the space between the huge dumpster and the wall.

"Zach," I shout at the high steel wall, the trailer-size container of death, bandages, dressings, all the dead refuse of this place where people die, organs and parts and bodies all wrapped, limp and twisted, blood clotted like clay. There, see the wisps of fog from its cracks.

"ZACH, ZACH!" It opens at the top. Can I climb it? I hear him struggling among the bodies. "ZACH!" The metal is cold, slick, wet with dew.

"Leon," a different voice calls me now.

What if I can't get him out? They take it away in the morning, I've seen them.

"Leon, what are you doing?"

They take it away, an angry truck pulls up and ratchets the monstrous thing up onto the trailer. Then where do they go?

Someone is here, touching me. "Leon, are you deaf?"

"Rita." Her face smiles, her eyes smile. Why is she here? Did she talk to you, Zach? Did you tell her to come?

"Hi, Leon," she says, laughing, uncertain. "So...what are you doing out here? Why are you climbing up on the dumpster?"

I don't know what to say. Zach, what should I say? "I don't think he's gone, do you?"

"What?" she says.

"Zach says I don't think he's gone." I point up. "I mean..." I don't know what I mean. I try to climb but my feet slip. I hang by my hands. Something hurts my arm. Damn it. I kick for a foothold but there is none. Zach! I kick again and my hand slips. I drop back down to the concrete, staggering.

She grabs my wrists. "Leon, they called me, some woman named Lydia. She said you were terribly frightened, someone came in with a gun? Is that why there are all the police cars?"

"Zach is here, inside here. He needs help."

"Zach? Oh, Leon." She takes my hands, watching my face. "How could he be in there? This is a dumpster, Leon. Zach wouldn't be in a dumpster."

"It's full of dead people. He's calling me."

There are tears on her face. "You're not thinking right, Leon. You're confused."

We stand staring at each other.

"Maybe we should go," she says. "Will you come with me?"

"What about Zach?"

"What about Zach," she says slowly. "Well, Leon, Zach will be at home, too. He'll be wherever you go."

"No, he's here." I pull against her.

"Leon, this is a dumpster. It's just full of trash. They don't put dead people in here. Remember, they bury dead people, in the cemetery. Zach will be at home when we get there and he'll be with you wherever you go. Zach is here because you're here. If you leave he will leave, too."

"I can't leave him here."

"Leon," she steps close to me. "Leon, you're acting a little crazy right now. Do you understand that? If you stay here and someone else finds you they'll take you back inside and call a psychiatrist. They'll put you in the hospital and call you insane. You don't want that to happen, do you?"

She leads me to my car. "Here, let's drive your car so everyone doesn't wonder why it's still here. Do people know your car?"

She watches me, waiting for an answer. "Okay, how about we go home and relax for a while. You've been up all night. You could go to sleep for a while, Leon."

Inside the car she holds out her hand, smiling. "How about keys?" She urges my hand to my pocket. "So does that sound nice, Leon, going home? Or do we need to talk? Why's your hair wet? Did you take a shower or something?"

She drives out of the lot onto the street. "You can talk to me, Leon. It's good to talk when you feel this way."

"I can't stop thinking about Zach, and hearing him calling me."

"Whew, this is a funny car," she says, "the way it drives."

"Thinking about Zach, and listening to Zach, and talking to Zach in my mind." Where are you? I twist in the seat, looking out the rear window. "Where is he?"

"Zach's coming, too. He's in the back, in the trunk."

"You're just saying that. Why would you say that?"

"Well, you said he was in the dumpster. That doesn't make much sense either." I watch her drive. She glances at me, then begins to giggle, her eyes anxious. "Well, you did."

"He talks to me, calls me to come help him."

"Why does he need help?"

"Because he's there, on that side, in the..." In the what? Words fail me, but I see you, Zach, sitting in the bed, waiting for me, waving at me to come. "See, if I could just get there, then I could go get him." Get where, where are you, Zach? How do I get there? I watch buildings go by in the gray light, the awful fog is all around. Is the whole city covered in it? "It's everywhere, isn't it?"

"What did you say?" She touches my arm. "You're sort of talking to yourself."

"Death, the city's covered with it."

At home Rita helps me undress. I am tired. Maybe sleep would be good. She lies with me, saying little.

I lie still, frozen, eyes closed, no movement. Am I breathing, is my heart beating? If I don't move, if I'm just a mind, just thoughts suspended in time, no substance, then I can let it all go, can't I? Not worry about eating, drinking, body functions, time passing, sleeping, waking. Just thoughts suspended in space, not worry about going crazy and losing my mind. Just thoughts so it wouldn't matter, right? The logic of it—is it logic?—seems to bounce around in my brain, in a circle going faster and faster until I can't remember where it started or what it means.

What happened to me there in the department? What did I do, what horrible side of my mind did I show to the world? I won't think of it any more. I need to sleep.

Chapter Thirteen

Leon's fridge is almost empty, a carton of milk that smells okay, some dubious fruit, and a half-full jar of sun-dried tomatoes. No wine, of course. But there's some coffee on a shelf and the coffeemaker looks like it works. Maybe I should go out and get something, doughnuts or eggs to cook. I don't know what he likes.

Should I stay? Will he want me here when he wakes up? He needs somebody around. What if he acts crazy again, tries to climb another dumpster or jump off the roof and fly? God, what is he going to do? He needs a psychiatrist or something. He said this never happened to him before.

Talk about a restless sleeper, he was kicking like a dog having a bad dream, and jabbering away about blood and ventilators, a lot of medical stuff.

No wine, shit. I'll be crawling in a while. I could run out and get some, use doughnuts as an excuse. No, I hate that. I checked all the shelves, the closets. Like a thief, I hate that, too. Why doesn't he just have an old bottle of bourbon or something stashed somewhere? Well, maybe I can start cutting back. I've got to do it soon. I've got to show him I can do it, show myself again, and Britnie. Shit, shit, shit, I hate this part.

Maybe he could prescribe me some Libriums or something for a few days. God, can I ask him that? Will that freak him out? Are there some in the medicine cabinet? Anything, a Xanax, or a Dalmane? That bitch was really into her drugs, he said.

The bathroom is pretty clean, especially for a guy. No, nothing, some Benadryl and Advil. Looks like she cleaned the place out pretty well. What are these? Diet pills, God, she was really into it. They can't be for Leon.

There's the phone again. Should I answer it? There's no answering machine. I guess the wicked witch of the north took it, too. What if it's somebody from the hospital, or his mother or something. I could pretend I was an answering service, find out who it is, anyway. No, I'd start laughing. Better let it ring.

Around noon he wakes up, a blank stare on his face until he sees me, then a smile, a good smile.

"You're still here," he says. "I'm glad."

"How do you feel?"

"Better. Damn, I was a mess, wasn't I." He sits on a stool by the counter, staring at nothing. "It was such an awful night. Poor Claudette." He cringes at the thought. "I should call and find out how she is."

"Who's Claudette?" I say, but he just shakes his head. "Somebody's trying to call you. The phone rang again about an hour ago but I didn't answer it. I was afraid it might be your mother or somebody. You need an answering machine."

"It was probably Peter calling to tell me to go see a shrink." Now he looks at me, frightened, almost in tears. "I can't go back to work, Rita. Not 'til I do something."

I hug him from behind. "What do you need to do?"

"I don't know. Go see a shrink, I guess. Damn, people at work won't ever trust me again. They'll always be wondering when I'll lose it, when I'll start shouting again right in the middle of a big crunch." Now he turns to face me. "It's not the crunches that bother me. I can handle the crunches. It's Zach screaming in my head and this feeling of death creeping around me." He shivers, putting his arms around me.

Then, that fear vanishes from his voice. "Hey, there's something familiar about this bathrobe," he says, untying the belt. "Did I say you could wear my bathrobe?" That was quick. I guess your not so worried about going nuts afterall. Now his hands touch me beneath the robe.

"I thought you were so scared, worried about going crazy, like 15 seconds ago. What happened there last night anyway?" God, he's so good with his hands.

"Kiss me," he says, "help me to forget, drown my sorrow with your body."

"Well, okay, whatever it takes, Doctor. I'm sure you know best, Doctor."

So we end up in the shower together, and then the bathroom floor. At least he's fixed his other little problem. Men are like animals sometimes, once they've got a hard-on. And it's so intense when I haven't been drinking. I'd forgotten about that, the way my mind has an orgasm, too, little pleasure-bombs that go off in my brain.

Afterward I lay naked on the bathroom rug and watch him shave, cool tile under my shoulders. That was a lot better than a Librium, but it won't last as long. He's pale for the middle of summer, and thin. I bet he hasn't been eating.

He says there's a deli down the hill. We dress and walk out in the sun. It's muggy and still, like it gets before a storm.

"I've got to go see Fitz today," he says.

"How's he doing? Did you see him yesterday?"

Leon nods. "Yup, I guess it was yesterday, wasn't it. It seems like about a week ago." Then he is silent.

"Is he awful?" I say. That poor man, he seemed so brave the other night, making jokes when it hurt to talk, struggling to be charming when he couldn't catch his breath.

Leon nods again. “Yup, he’s awful. He’s going to die soon. But I don’t know, it was funny, his sister was there. She was something, talk about a stressed out, angry woman. But Fitz was very philosophical about it. He was glad to see her. She’s the only family he’s got, and I guess they sort of made peace with each other.”

“So what will happen to him, Leon?”

“He’ll get worse and worse and then die.”

“Won’t his doctor help him? Don’t they give tranquilizers or narcotics to help people like that?”

“Yeah, they do,” he says. “At the very end you can do that, but it’s not a simple thing. It’s not like Fitz or Taft—that’s his doctor—can just pick a day and say, ‘Okay, today is the day.’ You have to let nature take its course, or at least that’s the concept. Nature…AIDS hardly seems like a natural thing, does it? Anyway, at the very end you can pretend you’re giving pain medicine to ease the patient’s suffering. You may spare them a day or two, or maybe a few hours. But Fitz might linger on for days. He’s just lying there, not eating, and he’s so depressed. When people lose hope they get very depressed.”

“I know. What about Hospice? I thought they sent people like Fitz home these days, so they could die at home. Or Joel, he seemed to take pretty good care of him.”

“Yeah, Fitz mentioned going back home. I think maybe Taft hasn’t given up yet. Maybe he thinks he can get him well again for a few more weeks. I don’t know.” He shakes his head as we walk. “I need to go see him again today.”

It’s a Jewish deli. A chubby European-looking girl with long black hair makes us bagel sandwiches, probably the owner’s daughter. She wraps them in waxed paper and hands us huge pickles. A shelf of wine coolers smiles at me from the fridge. Three or four would be nice but I grab only one for each of us. Leon doesn’t seem to notice.

We cross the street to a park and find some grass beneath a tree. There is a broad layer of clouds sliding in and the smell of rain coming. Leon is very quiet. I bring up last night and the ER again but he shakes his head.

“It’s too nice a day, being out here with you. I don’t want to think about it.”

We unwrap our sandwiches in silence. I open the wine cooler. God, I’m shaking. Now, don’t gulp.

“Tell me about Camille,” he says finally.

I look up. “I don’t do very well talking about her,” I say like a reflex, “and besides, she’s gone.”

He nods slowly, avoiding my eye, squirting mustard onto his bread.

She's not gone, she'll never be gone, but do I want to share her with him? Do I want to tell it at all, feel it again. Do I want to burden him, burden us, with this shadow. No I don't want that shadow over us.

"She was very different from Britnie," I say finally. "That surprised me for a while, but now I realize—I mean I don't know what I expected. Maybe I thought I'd just get another Camille. Is that selfish? Do you think that sounds selfish?"

"Well, it depends how you—"

"Britnie is much more talkative, and she's wants to know about things. She's curious about adults, relationships, how people—well, you saw the other night. She's obviously not afraid to talk to adults, once she feels like she knows you a little. Camille was more withdrawn, very quiet. I don't know if you remember her at all."

"I just remember her face and her being in the E.D. I never got a chance to talk to her or anything. It was always too busy."

"I learned a lot from Camille. She made me be a grown-up. It was like I had to learn what it meant to die so I could help her. I had to get through the denial and the anger and finally accept it myself so I could help her do those things. And she was a child. A child's mind isn't ready for those things, Leon. She never really accepted that she was going to die. She never became philosophical about it, abstract and calm about it.

"They had this counselor—that was one of the things I hated about the Cystic Fibrosis Clinic over at Children's Hospital—this counselor who tried to work with Camille. The Wooden Man, she called him. He kept talking to her about dying, about accepting dying and getting ready for dying. He was so depressing, and Camille hated him. He had this sort of wooden face, with no expression at all. He would sit there and talk to us and just his mouth would move. Camille said one time she wanted to sneak a look behind him to see if he was plugged into a wall outlet.

"But you were really good with her, Leon." Now I can't stop myself. "I used to call the emergency room to ask if you were working. The secretary would always say, 'I'm sorry, but we're not permitted to say which doctors are working.' So then a couple times I said I was your sister and wanted to talk to you. Then they'd go to get you, if you were there, and I'd hang up. But at least I knew you were there, so then I'd bring Camille in to see you."

God, how can I eat when I feel this way, with my stomach in a knot. Shit, what'll he say if I go get another one? I'll ignore it. I'll sit here calmly and ignore my skin crawling and the reptile gnawing on my guts. Zen and the art of alcohol withdrawal.

"So now you're going to put yourself through it all again?" Leon says, but in a kind way.

So that's it, that's how it seems. Put myself through it all again. Yes, I guess it must look that way. But not for Britnie.

"I don't think of Britnie like that," I say. "She's not like Camille, Leon. She's got a very different personality and hasn't been nearly as sick as Camille was by the same age. She might live a long time." It makes me mad, him putting Britnie in a box like that. She's a different person.

"People with C.F. are living much longer than they used to, Leon. You know that. The medications are better and doctors know more. She'll live a long time.

"Damn it, Leon, how could you say that? You sound just like a doctor, just like you've got it all figured out and know everything that's going to happen to everybody."

"Okay, okay, sorry, I'm oversimplifying. Britnie is a different person."

I'm going to cry. I grab his hand. "I know I'm crazy, Leon. I know that Britnie will die sometime. She'll get sick time after time, and she'll cough and cough and get skinnier and skinnier and hate me and hate herself and hate the world. But you know..." I have to stop now and breathe. It's hard to talk. "...you know what she'll have that not very many people have? She'll have somebody who will love her and be with her and care about her for her whole life."

Thunder growls at us from somewhere.

"However long that is," I add. "Seems stupid, doesn't it? It still seems stupid."

He squeezes my hand. "It doesn't, Rita. It really doesn't. It's a good thing, a good thing that you're doing. You're going to give Britnie a lot of love and happiness."

I watch his face, but he is sincere. He's not just humoring me. I can't sit still anymore. "Leon, I need to go to the bathroom. I'm gonna run over there and use their bathroom."

I stand and run across the grass. Slow down, just a jog, like a jogger just jogging across the grass. Is he watching? Just a little jog for Rita the jogger. Right, that's me. It feels good to run, to let all my twitching muscles do something. I should run, be a runner, run every day until I'm too exhausted to lift a glass. They say exercise helps.

The chubby girl looks surprised. I put two coolers on the counter. "It's so hot out," I say, opening one. "I'll just drink this one here so I can leave the bottle." I turn away to browse the salamis. No smoking, of course. There's a newspaper box. I stoop to glance at the headlines. Okay, done, not too obvious.

"Here's the bottle," I mumble, leaving it on the counter. But she has disappeared into the back.

Thunder booms loud as I step out the door. I can see rain sweeping across the park. Good, I love storms. Now run back. Rita the runner again. Don't drop the other cooler. Beat the rain to the tree. Leon hasn't moved.

"I got another cooler. It's so hot. You want some?" Please, no disapproving looks. I hate lying.

We sit close as the rain comes, turning the air beyond the branches into a rushing gray curtain. It's warm, what gets through the leaves to us. "Okay, your turn," I say.

"My turn for what?"

"To bare your soul, to speak to me of your innermost thoughts and feelings. Or memories, memories would be good."

"How about sexual fantasies? What I always wanted to do but never had the right equipment for."

"Right," I say, "maybe you could show me later. Are you into leather or latex? No, really, Leon, it might help you work things out in your mind. Talking is very therapeutic."

"Okay, Sigmund, go for it. What do you want to hear?"

"Well, tell me about last night, and why you got so upset." To put it mildly. I can't say raving mad. I watch his face.

"Oh, just another night in the old ER." He tells me about Claudette getting shot and the blood everywhere, about the feeling of death around him and fighting it off.

And about Zach, Zach calling to him, Zach lost in some black void of death. Talking about it makes him nervous and his eyes begin to wander again, anxious glances over his shoulders as if something were there. I don't think he's even aware of it.

"Why do you think he's calling you, Leon?"

He shakes his head, leaning back against the tree trunk. He stares into the rain now for a long time. "I don't know. It's like Zach's there, somewhere, really there, needing me to come help him. It's stupid. He's been dead for twenty-six years. But I can't stop thinking about him."

"Why does he need you?"

"I DON'T KNOW!" he says very loud, angry now, fists clenched. "I don't know why he needs me. There is no he! He's dead. There's no Zach. I keep telling myself that. There's just me!" He looks desperate. "There's just me. Zach's gone, long gone."

I hold his hands and wait until he can listen. "He's not gone from your heart."

"I've been thinking about him a lot," he says. "I mean, remembering things I haven't thought of for a long time."

His fists relax in my hands. "I used to have this dream that he'd call me to read to him. Over and over he'd call me. And I wouldn't do it, or I couldn't or something. But I had to stand there in the doorway of our room, in the dream, and listen to him call and call. It seemed like it would go on for hours. I hated that dream, and I must have dreamed it a hundred times. I had to sleep in the same room with him. It was our room and we didn't have any other rooms where I could sleep, or my parents wouldn't let me, or something, I don't remember."

The rain is slackening now.

"He didn't die for a long time," Leon goes on. "He just lay there in that bed. You know, I started hating him. I used to get angry at him, angry at this poor kid who lay there always twisting, his head always turned to one side, and no life in those eyes, no awareness. Even at night he'd be doing it, in the dark until he fell asleep.

"I hated him for being that way. I remember shouting at him to stop, when our parents weren't around. I think I probably even slapped him a couple times. I could have slapped the wall for all the difference it made. There was no awareness there at all, or at least none you could see. I even went back and apologized to him, shouted at him that I was sorry, that I was sorry I hated him.

"'Stop twisting,' I remember saying to him, 'stop twisting, Zach,' a hundred times, a thousand times. 'Lie still, damn it. Look at me, won't you.' I grabbed his head, and I wanted to grab his eyes, to point them at me to make him listen. I screamed at him, like I was screaming at myself, like it was part of me that was out of control."

He stops, frightened at his own memories.

Lightning flashes above us, very close, with a huge bang.

We sit in silence as the noise dies away. Then he stands suddenly, as if he's angry. "So there it is, now you know all about Zach." He is angry. "Big deal, that was a long time ago, long ago and far away."

"I'm sure it was a big deal for you at the time," I say.

"Fuck it. C'mon, let's go back. Don't you need another wine cooler or something? Or a cigarette? Can't smoke in the rain, I guess, can you?"

Oh, how sweet. Why is he doing this? "Why don't you let me worry about my drinking, Leon, and my cigarettes."

"Right, sorry. I don't know, Rita. I just can't deal with all this. Are you coming?"

Deal with all what? All Zach, all me, all my bad habits. You didn't seem to mind a little while ago on the bathroom floor.

"Go ahead," I say, "I'll be along. I like it here."

"Oh, c'mon, Rita, I can't leave you here alone. This isn't that great a neighborhood."

Fuck you, Dr. Mendel. Why do you care? Suddenly I feel sad. "It is a problem, isn't it?"

"Isn't what?"

"My drinking, and my smoking." I stand. "Just me being me." Maybe I'll go home. I don't want to.

"Damn, I don't know, Rita. I don't know if it's a problem. We hardly know each other."

"We've had a lot of sex for hardly knowing each other."

"Well, who ever said that was a good indicator that you knew someone? Look at all the—"

"Leon!" Don't be an asshole, Leon, please.

"Well, it's true, isn't it. It takes nothing to get in bed with someone. Strangers sleep together all the time, no one gives it a thought."

"I do." Damn it, I don't want to cry again, not now. "I don't sleep with strangers."

* * *

Back to the hospital again to see Fitz. I'm starting to hate this place. I'll go in the front, avoid the ED. I don't want to talk to anybody about last night. I don't even want to think about it.

At least I'm off for a couple days. Supposed to ride with my paramedic crew tomorrow. That should be easy. Sundays are always good, lots of action.

Fitz is sleeping when I enter, bed tilted up to an untouched meal tray. But he's slumped to the side, breathing hard, his face gleaming with sweat. Again his skull seems to leer at me beneath the sunken contours of his face. The curtains are drawn and the lights are off, casting the room in shadows. There is an ugly smell.

He is dying, this withered sack of tissues and blood, rancid with the millions of viral particles overwhelming it. Rancid, that word again. And this is Fitz—my hands come up to my face—this monstrosity is my friend Fitz. I feel tears start in my eyes, and I stand by the bed crying. I loved him, still love him, will always love him. But there's nothing left to love, look at him.

Death is here in this room, not just in the dark places, but everywhere. I feel that same fog but it vanishes when I look. I want to run, get away. I could leave, not wake him—he'd never know—go away and not come back here.

Jump up, jump down, Zach's childish voice is singing over and over, like a nursery rhyme.

"STOP IT," I hear myself shout.

The slumped figure stirs.

"Fitz." I push him gently upright.

He rouses and looks at me. "Leon," he whispers, and clutches my wrist.

"How are you doing, Fitz?" I don't know what else to say.

He pulls himself erect and glances down at the tray. "I can't eat," he rasps. "It hurts too much to swallow."

"How about something cool," I say. "This pudding might feel good."

He waves me off and lies back, panting. "Are you working downstairs?"

"No, not today, I'm off. Fitz, you ought to eat something. How about if I help you?" I reach for a spoon but his bony hand stops me. He shakes his head.

I sit down, holding the wasted hand between mine. "Is your sister still around?"

He stares. "I don't know. I forgot what she said. What time is it?"

"It's about six."

"It was good to see her," he says vacantly. "How are your voices?"

"Still there, here, I guess," pointing at my head. "I don't know what to do about it."

"Why don't you go see somebody?"

"I should. You're right. I should, but think of the—" implications, I am about to say, but he is beyond burdening with such talk.

Now Fitz starts to shake and his mouth contorts, eyes clinging to mine. I realize he's crying. "Damn, Fitz." I move to hug him but he pushes me off, shaking his head. For two or three minutes he cries, until he is breathless and gasping. I set his oxygen tubing straight beneath his nose and move to the valve to turn it up.

"I was really hoping you'd come, Leon. It's pretty lonely here." He pants, struggling, restless from his hunger for oxygen. "What am I going to do, Leon?" There is fear in his eyes, panic.

I hold his trembling hand, waiting for his breath to return. Run and hide, Zach is shouting at me, run and hide.

"You'll be okay, Fitz. You'll get better soon."

"No, I won't, Leon." He is angry now. "You of all people, you know that's crap. You know I'm dying."

"You're right, Fitz. I won't lie to you."

He starts to cry again, then mouths the words, barely audible, "I wish my mother was still alive. I would have liked to see Mom."

I need something to do so I move his bed table away, covering the untouched dishes with their lids.

When he is calm again I say, "Maybe you will see her, Fitz."

He watches me and then smirks. "Right, the old heaven thing. Do queers go to heaven, Leon?"

"They go to queer heaven. There's lots of hair salons and clothing stores, nice baths, and the leather bars are free, no cover."

He struggles to smile at the joke.

"What about your friends, Fitz? You always had a ton of friends."

"Yeah, they come," he whispers. "They laugh and dance around the room and try to cheer me up. They bring me stuff. It's scary for them, Leon. A couple of them are HIV positive, too." He stops to catch his breath. "It's not fair, Leon. We weren't bad people, you know. We didn't hurt anyone. Yeah, we fooled around a lot but nobody got hurt. We took care of each other, a lot more than straights do. 'Til this." He motions toward himself.

"We didn't know about it, Leon, 'til it was too late. We didn't know how many people had it. Nobody figured here in Cincinnati it would be that big a deal."

He pushes the button to flatten the bed, then motions me back to the chair. "Leon, will you help me?"

"Sure, Fitz, what do you want me to do?"

He looks at me for a long time, the wheeze of his breathing audible in the silence. "Will you...will you help me die, Leon?"

"What do you mean, Fitz?" Jump up, jump down, I wish you would stop, brother.

"You know what I mean," he whispers. "This is misery, Leon. Some chaplain came by today, and the nurses have stopped joking around. They're so serious. They're waiting for me to die. Help me end it, Leon, please. You can do it, get some medicine, morphine or something and just put me to sleep. It's a simple thing, isn't it?"

A simple thing. A simple thing to kill someone. I sit back in the chair and look about the room, the plain walls with a painting of flowers, probably a hundred copies around the hospital. I have stared at it before, in other rooms during codes. The little closet, the sink with its oversized handles for the clumsy hands of the sick. These spaces we have created for ourselves to heal in, and die in.

"Leon," Fitz says, lying on his side toward me, eyes intent.

"Damn, Fitz, what a thing to ask." I watch his heavy breathing. "Are you ready to die?"

"Course I'm not ready to die. Do I look like I have a lot of choice? Taft himself said that I could ask for pain medicine any time I wanted. I'm not in pain, Leon, except my throat. Why would he say that?"

I want to fight the death I feel here, fight it or run away from it. "Okay, Fitz, you're right, I guess. But what about your...your affairs and all that?"

"It's okay. I took care of all that. The Gay Coalition has got lawyers and accountants who help you with all that. We take care of ourselves, Leon."

"Yes, I believe it."

Again silence, as he lies panting, watching me.

There is a knock at the door and a dietary worker comes in to take away the tray, her hair in a net. "Don't you want to eat nothing?" she says. She is short, heavyset, flushed as if working hard.

"I don't think he's hungry, thanks," I say.

"Lemme get you something else, hon," she says to Fitz.

He shakes his head.

"His throat hurts and it's hard for him to swallow."

"How 'bout some sherbet," she says. "It goes down real easy."

I glance at Fitz but he has turned away. "That's okay," I say. "Thanks anyway."

"Well, you gots to eat something, sometime," she says leaving the room.

I make sure the door is closed and return to his bedside. He lies facing away, toward the curtained window.

"Fitz, are you serious about this?"

He nods.

"It's not that easy. I'll have to be careful."

He nods again.

"Fitz." Zach is roaring in my head. My mind feels like it's being tightened with a crank, tightened and tightened. I put a hand on his arm. "What can I do for you? Can I read to you, or turn on the TV or something? I'll sit with you for a while." I feel desperate.

He covers my hand with his. "It's okay, Leon," he whispers. "Thanks, thanks for coming. I'll just go to sleep."

"I'll help you, Fitz. I will. But it's not an easy thing." I stand staring, no idea what to say. I hate to leave him here, like this.

"Listen, if you wake up maybe you ought to ask for some of that pain medicine. It's to make you feel better, Fitz, to help you sleep and not suffer. It's okay to take it." I want to say more but I don't know what. Again he nods.

I find a magazine. "Listen, I'll just sit here with you until you're asleep. I'm not in any hurry."

But quickly he is asleep again, exhausted, panting still. I adjust his oxygen once more before I leave.

Now, in my car, in the parking lot, I'm paralyzed, in the glare of the afternoon sun, the hot stifling air here in this little space, the metal handles too hot to touch. Open the windows, start the car. But I can't. I sit thinking of Fitz, trapped inside a dying body, nowhere to go, no way out. I want to cry for him but it won't help, I want to cry for his hopelessness, for such a smart guy now leaving a world he loved so much, alone, no one to go with him, no idea where he will go.

I'd better move, I guess, before someone comes along. I saw Dr. Mendel just sittin' there in his car, just starin', not doin' nothin', just starin'. I hope he goes and gits him some help. He's a good doctor when his mind's right.

I start up the car and open the windows. I watch the sea of concrete and asphalt and brick that moves in front of me. You pave paradise, put up a parking lot, the words from that old song come to me. Our minds aren't designed for this, or our bodies. We didn't evolve to live on flat floors, with walls everywhere, and whole days spent under fluorescent light, and constant encounters with strangers. We're supposed to live in small bands, outside in the quiet of vast wilderness, with green all around, and quiet.

And incurable diseases, everything was incurable then. You either died or you didn't. Just like Fitz, only he's going to die for sure. He looked so miserable, so depressed and lonely. He knows what's going to happen, and he's right.

So what should I do? I can't talk to anyone about it. Not even Rita. She knows way too much about me already. No one. If I'm going to do it for Fitz I can never tell a soul.

What would the normal person do? The normal rational person who has the means to put an end to someone's life, who happens to be a doctor in the same hospital and could probably get away with it. How would I do it? Potassium, digoxin, morphine? No, not morphine, if I got caught stealing morphine I could never explain it. People would think it was for myself, they'd never believe me. Insulin, no, he'd have seizures before he died. Paralyze him in his sleep with Anectine so he stops breathing. No, I'd have to sedate him first so he wouldn't wake up, which means I'd have to steal some Valium or Versed. Same problem as the morphine.

Inderal would probably do it. Ten milligrams of IV Inderal all at once would stop his heart. He wouldn't feel a thing if he were asleep.

I shiver thinking of Fitz's room, the darkness there, the feel of death lingering, that fog, silent, imperceptible.

Maybe tomorrow night after riding with the paramedics. I'll get off at eight, I can come home and fool around for a while until it's late, then drop by the E.D., grab some potassium, or the Inderal's not a bad idea, maybe both. Then put on some scrubs and a white coat, go up on the elevator. The night nurses will think I'm just a new resident or an anesthesiologist, someone they don't recognize.

What if I get caught? What if a nurse recognizes me coming out of the room and then goes in and finds Fitz dead? That would be just dandy, an incident report, an investigation. Dr. Mendel from the Emergency Department was seen leaving the room of his former homosexual lover who was found dead moments afterward. What if somebody calls the police? Kiss one medical license goodbye. I'd end up juggling petrie dishes in some lab, if I didn't end up in prison.

I could report it myself, pretend I found him dead when I went into the room. Pretend I was making a late-night visit after getting off work to see how he was doing, and I found him dead.

Can I do it? I told him I would.

At home, as the door swings open I don't want to go in, into this space that is just mine now, just a space where nothing moves unless I move it, where only the light changes, sunlight that creeps across the room all day long and then vanishes. I could die here and lie for days, the sun crawling over my skin, dust settling on me.

No, Rita would come, wouldn't she? I'd better call her, make peace. I was a fool at the park. Why did I say those things, lash out at her like that? Stupid. My soul stirs at the thought of her, her warmth and spirit. I could love her if I let myself.

Chapter Fourteen

In the car again, Sunday noon, to Station 3 to ride with my paramedic squad, make sure they're doing a good job. Sundays are usually busy, a good time to ride.

God, I'll need some coffee. Rita would hardly let me sleep. I guess it's been a while for her. There haven't been many men she could relax with, she said, who were gentle with her. Gentle? I guess I was gentle, like being gentle with a tiger.

Okay, ride with the squad today, then what? Go see Fitz again. Poor Fitz, I hate to even think about him. I need to go see him again, make sure he really meant it yesterday. How am I going to do it, how can I do it? I told him I would. And he needs someone to do it for him. Talk about playing God.

Here it is, Station 3, Cincinnati Fire Department, stately, graceful, ivy-covered brick with white trim, built in the days of fire horses and Dalmatians. Its tall arched doors are swung open and there are neat squares of grass in front, the only grass for blocks. The building is surrounded by run down stores and tenements, glaring concrete. Two project high-rises face each other down the street, shimmering in the noonday heat.

A dozen kids, maybe a Sunday school class, stand crowded around one of the engines as a uniformed firefighter talks to them. Two boys in the back are karate kicking each other.

The big box-like ambulance, my home for the afternoon, parked in its bay.

Little girls have pretty curls but I like Oreos, Zach's voice is singing to me. That old jingle, he used to love to sing them. We used to.

Inside the glass-walled office sits another fireman. I don't know his name. "Hi, Dr. Mendel," he says, "gonna check out life on the streets with us again today?"

"I guess so. It's a hot day for it."

"Hot fun in the summertime," he says. "I think the Thud and Nan are upstairs somewhere. They've had a couple runs this morning."

"Well, I hope I didn't miss anything good." From a row of hooks I take down a red nylon jacket with the fire department symbol on the front and the word OBSERVER in big white letters across the back.

The squad room upstairs is cool and dark compared to the glare of the streets. Two rows of people sit eating at the long table.

"Hey, Leon," Klaus hails me as I enter, "the hero of Municipal Hospital, wrestled the mad gunman to the floor, disarmed him." Klaus, the Thud, former

F-105 mechanic in Vietnam, hence the nickname, after the planes which were called Thuds because of the heavy bombs they carried or something.

The deep shadows of the room make me nervous. I move to the wide bank of windows that looks down on the concrete apron, and the city wasteland beyond. I feel the fear of Friday night, the thin black gun barrel rising from the floor, the hot explosion of it in my hands.

"Must have been pretty scary, Leon." I hear Nan Flanagan's voice now, the other paramedic, filling in for my silence.

Say something. "Well, I didn't exactly wrestle him to the floor. He had three bullets in him already and fell in front of me. I just grabbed his gun."

"Modesty, modesty," Klaus says. "Riley was there. He said it was a very ballsy move. Leon, you want some lunch?"

"Very funny, and what gourmet specialty are you guys having for lunch today?"

"We've got some pretty good chicken salad," one of them says.

"Yeah, it's probably even healthy," another voice. "Got these little green things in it. What do you call them? Oh, yeah, vegetables. Got vegetables in it."

"All right, in a minute," I say. I move down a hallway to the paramedic office and find the logbook, a bulging binder full of pink run reports, barely legible carbon copies of the scribbled reports the paramedics make after each run. They are stained with sweat, coffee, sometimes blood, written while screaming through the streets with sirens on, or while flirting with the nurses in the ED. As medical supervisor of this paramedic crew I'm supposed to review these reports, look for errors in treatment, give training sessions, and ride as observer every three months.

I find a chair and sit at the end of the lunch table. I feel their eyes on me. Do they know what's going on? Rumors travel fast among the ED's and the medics. Little girls have pretty curls...

The chicken salad bowl lands before me. I look up at the group of faces all intent on their food. Only Nan is looking at me, her pleasant squarish face smiling. She has curly blond hair and glasses that give her almost a studious look at times.

"I'll just have some of that iced tea, thanks," I say. Then hefting the logbook, "Looks like you guys have been busy."

"Nothing like a nice hot summer to bring out the best in everyone's disposition, lots of beer drinking, lots of fights, lots of accidents," Nan says.

"Accidents and fights together," Klaus says. "Seems like most of the time now when we get called to an accident the drivers are going at it by the time we get there, everybody's punching each other out, or worse. Leon, the other day we get this call to an MVA with possible injuries, and we get there and this one guy has a baseball bat and the other guy is a city worker and he pulls a shovel out of his truck and they're going at it. They didn't get hurt in the accident but by the time the police got 'em apart the one guy had a bunch of broken ribs and the other had a bad neck injury, big gash from the shovel. He ended up in surgery. We had to take him in with handcuffs on, if you can believe that."

I begin leafing through the reports, looking for vital signs properly recorded, IVs and medications, reasonable legibility. Here is a teenage girl who overdosed on Benadryl, a fifty-five-year-old man who had a seizure and a badly bitten tongue, an eighty-three-year-old woman who passed out at the wheel and ran into the rear of a city bus.

I feel them watching me. They know what's going on, they've heard. Dr. Mendel's cracking up. Sure, he grabbed that guy's shotgun, but the nurses told us he's been getting weird lately, started shouting or something right in the middle of a resuscitation. Again I look up, but all the faces are eating, talking baseball now. They're quick, these guys.

Within minutes the two-note tone sounds on the speaker overhead that signals a medic response, then the disembodied female voice of the 911 dispatcher, "Engine 5, Medic 3, medical response needed at five eight two Central Avenue, second floor, domestic violence, fifty-four-year-old male with stab wound to the abdomen. Police are present. Cross street is Twelfth Street. Code 3." The message repeats as we head down the stairs.

Nan is large, perhaps burly is the word, but quick on her feet, fast like a bowling ball thrown hard. "You ride up front with me, Leon," she calls to me. "Thud has to check the kits."

She turns the key with one hand and flips the siren switch and the lights with the other. The ambulance comes alive and in seconds we are rolling down the apron. A few dark faces along the street turn as if in slow motion to watch us go. Somewhere, a few blocks closer to the scene, Engine 5 is rolling as well. All the firefighters are trained as EMTs, first responders who can control bleeding or start CPR, or even defibrillate if need be, shaving a minute or two off the response time until paramedics arrive.

I hear Klaus rummaging with gear in the back.

"Thud," Nan calls over her shoulder. "Help me with the streets."

His face appears between us, leaning forward from the rear compartment. He has thick features, a heavy nose and jaw, small light-colored friendly eyes. He is usually thoughtful, slow to speak.

"Central and Twelfth is going to be near the park, on the river side. Go past the overpass and turn down Tenth."

"My favorite neighborhood," Nan says.

Heads turn and cars move to the side as we roar down the street, flying through intersections far too fast, but the path opens before us. My arm aches and I realize my hand is clamped hard on the armrest, knuckles white. I feel it again, out there, death, its shadow dodging down the street ahead of us, out of sight, crouching between cars, hurrying around corners.

The revolving lights of two police cars show us where to stop. Engine 5 is there, too. Twenty or so people crowd the street, laughing and shouting at us.

Klaus lifts out two orange cases, the carry-in kits, then closes the rear door. Nan touches the automatic lock switch as we step out. In this neighborhood half the equipment would be gone when we returned.

Up the stairs of a tired old tenement with windows broken and blotches of gray wood showing through the old paint. Run and hide, run and hide. There is shouting upstairs, a woman shrieks. The smell of mold, spoiled food, and people long in need of baths. I hate these places.

In the room there are police and a grotesquely fat black woman in handcuffs sitting on a bed, yelling angrily at no one in particular with slurred drunken speech.

Two Engine 5 firefighters crouch next to a middle-aged man, holding a bandage over his obese belly. He is awake and does not look in immediate danger. There is blood on the floor but not a lot.

Calmly the EMTs watch us enter, part of the routine. "This is Albert," one of them says. "He has a single stab wound to the abdomen." He tells Nan the man's vital signs as she crouches, clipboard on her knee.

"Hello, Albert," Nan says, then asks more questions as Klaus opens one of the kits and sets up to start an IV.

The police are writing their reports, asking questions, talking to the neighbors.

Albert is drunk too. He turns his head and shouts, "She done this to me. That fat bitch done this. She stabbed me in the belly. She had no call. I ain't done a thing an' she pulled out that knife and tried to kill me. Damn bitch."

The woman starts howling incomprehensible curses. The nearest officer tries to shut her up.

Klaus glances at me and I shake my head in agreement with his disgust for the place and the people, these good citizens of Cincinnati who live off our tax dollars, who bought the beer or whatever it was that made them drunk today with money from welfare checks, this man who will now receive thousands of dollars of medical care for free, ambulance transport to the hospital, an Emergency Department evaluation, then surgery and recovery, maybe four days in the hospital, and then back home, never having to spend a cent, who if they hadn't been drunk in the first place wouldn't have argued, wouldn't have fought, and wouldn't need us or a surgeon or a hospital at all.

Upstairs there is shouting and a child shrieks. The police glance at each other. There is a filthy sink jumbled with dishes and beer cans, a hallway to another room where I hear more voices. The walls are stained, with dark holes here and there. I hate the holes, I can't look at them.

I feel it here, too, in this place, behind the walls and in the floor, in the rusted pipes and wires, death creeping up from deep in the ground below. Mad, sad, glad, Zach's voice says, mad, sad, glad.

With the IV started and flowing into the man's arm, Klaus uncovers the wound. "What do you think, Leon?" he says. It is a three-inch laceration in the man's left lower abdomen, away from the spleen and any large vessels. Blood oozes slowly from it.

I'm an observer today, not supposed to help in the decision-making unless there is a dire situation. I shrug. "Where's the weapon?" I ask the policeman.

He points to a Formica table where a large kitchen knife lies, perhaps nine inches of blade, smeared about halfway up with blood. A deep cut, could have hit anything.

"What kind of vitals have you got?" I ask.

"Pressure's 150 over 96, pulse 98," Nan says.

I nod. "Hard to say for sure. He'll need to be explored, see what got cut." He'll make it to the hospital, need to have his abdomen explored by the surgeons, a good resident case, make sure his intestines aren't cut and leaking into his belly, or his ureter, his iliac arteries. With all that fat to protect him chances are good everything is intact inside.

The EMTs have wrestled our gurney up the stairs. Now they lift Albert onto it and strap him down. He continues cursing the woman until Nan asks him politely to stop.

There is a new voice now, a man's deep voice, angry, yelling at me although the words are garbled. It makes me think of that hospital long ago and us waiting with you, Zach. Mother, Father and I, we didn't even know what we were waiting for. It's Father's voice, with his heavy accent, wearing his suit coat with no tie, like he always did, and plain white shirt. His foreign refugee's face, scarred from acne as a teen, a teen in prewar Latvia, jaw too big, a little crooked, and his lumpy nose in that skinny face. Cursing in his incomprehensible tongue as he saw you lying there, your bruised and swollen head.

You boys and those bicycles, he muttered at me, so angry he had to talk slowly, remembering to speak English.

"Leon, would you bring the kits," Klaus yells at me. "Save us a trip." They are moving down the stairs. Albert says nothing as Klaus and Nan and the two

EMTs struggle with him down the narrow stairs. He lies calmly, eyes open, as if used to being carried, royalty on his sedan-chair, no words of thanks or sympathy as they struggle down. He could have walked down, I'm sure.

He waves at the crowd in the street. Whenever there are flashing lights there is always a crowd.

"Whassa matter, Albert?" someone yells. "Did Gert try to get on top?"

His smile vanishes. "That ain't funny. That damn bitch stabbed me with the damn kitchen knife. I'm hurt," he says, drunkenly indignant.

"Maybe now you quit beatin' that poor girl," a woman's voice yells.

I sit in the back with Klaus and Albert, his foul breath filling the space.

"Where we going, Klaus?" Nan calls back to us.

"All right, Albert," Klaus says to him, "this being America and you being an American you are entitled to decide which hospital you want to go and get fixed at. Course your choice is somewhat limited by the severity of your condition and the current financial situation of our city's fine hospitals." As he talks he pastes monitor leads on Albert's chest and the green waves of his heartbeat start marching across the tiny screen.

Albert starts to speak but Klaus continues. "You are entitled to decide whether the fine health care providers of University Hospital or Municipal Hospital shall have the privilege of ministering—"

"You take me to University," Albert blurts. "I ain't going back dere to dat Municipal Hospital. They 'bout killed me there last time."

Klaus grins at me now. "University Hospital. Are you sure that's where you want to go?"

"Dat's what I said, ain't it?" Albert nods importantly.

On another day and in another mood I might have inquired how we almost killed him at Muni, but not today.

So Nan drives us to University Hospital, with its fancy new E.D. and worse chaos than ours sometimes. Inside Klaus gives his report to two scared third-year medical students and a bored nurse. "This is Albert," he says as they swing him over onto one of the trauma gurneys. "Albert is fifty-three years old and was involved in a domestic dispute with an intoxicated female about an hour ago. He was stabbed once in the abdomen—"

I see Willy Lammers, the attending, across the way helping another student with some X-rays. We were residents together. He is sharp, quick-witted, but prone to panic and shouting when things get tight. He flutters a hand at me and walks over.

"Leon, you're alive. Damn, I heard what happened yesterday over at your place." He has a thin, nervous voice, always urgent. "You could have been shot."

I nod.

"Must make you think twice about coming to work, I'll bet, huh?"

"Well, Willy, I haven't had time to give it much—"

"I think twice about coming to work these days, I'll tell ya. Have you heard what's going on over here, these malpractice cases?"

It is here, too, in the voices behind curtains, the people moving. Close by someone is moaning, someone else who feels it, feels death seeping into his body.

"No, I haven't heard about—"

"Leon!" a man's voice shouts. I turn, my heart thumping. "Leon!" from a curtained bed. A cry of pain, wasn't it? Not my name. How can that man know I'm here? No, I'm imagining it, hallucinating.

"Oh, that's just some guy getting his shoulder put back in," Willy says. "Listen to this, Leon. Consuela's getting sued for a missed meningitis, a little nine month old who came in with a fever and went home and came back two weeks later with meningitis. Two weeks later! Can you believe that? It could have been an entirely different organism in two weeks."

Now a shriek from across the department, Jasmine's angry voice, an image of her bleeding terribly, dying. No, it can't be. Get out of here. Go outside.

"—a wrongful discharge against us and the Surgery Department, abandonment they're calling it." Willy is talking about another case now. "The kid did fine, actually, no perforation or anything when they finally got the appendix out. They're just trying to get some money out of the hospital. Found some asshole lawyer who's hot on EMTALA violations. They claim if he'd had insurance we wouldn't have sent him home. Can you believe that?"

"Sounds like you're getting screwed. Listen, Willy, I've got to go. My medic crew is pretty busy today." I move toward the doors. "Take care, man."

We stop for some pop at a 7-11 on the way back to the station. It's a hot sweaty day.

Five minutes back at the station and the tone sounds again. I come out of the bathroom and scramble down the stairs behind them.

"What do we got?"

"Pretty exciting stuff," Klaus says. "Eighty-four-year-old male at a nursing home having trouble breathing."

"Oh, well, at least he'll be sober."

Nan moves the rig into the street, flashing lights but no siren. "I had an old nursing home guy take after me with a shoe about a week ago," she says. "We had to restrain him to get him to the hospital."

The afternoon air blows hot through the window. We drive up to a hotel-like building called the Autumn Leaves Home. How poetic. An older man in a velour athletic suit, the manager, leads us onto the elevator and up.

The place is decent, clean with only the vague smell of urine. Grey and white heads over bathrobes watch our progress down the hall. In a room there is a pale ancient figure propped up on a hospital bed, breathing hard, clutching an oxygen mask to his face.

"This is Mr. Lauderblad," says a surly middle-aged nurse standing by him. "He started getting short of breath earlier today. I gave him some Lasix but it hasn't done much. His doctor said to send him to emergency."

The man is emaciated, bony, the withered muscles in his neck tensing like wires under the skin with each breath. His eyes stare at nothing. More death, a soul inside a corpse that should have been allowed to escape long ago, but no, kept caged for who knows how long, kept caged by a misguided family or an apathetic physician in an ill-conceived health care system that won't allow people to die.

Nan asks a few questions. The man is eighty-four with dementia and chronic congestive heart failure and diabetes and prostate cancer. The nurse recites the list of his diagnoses from a clipboard she carries.

Klaus asks the important one, "What's his code status?"

The nurse and manager look at each other, uncertain. "'What difference does that make?" the manager says. "You just need to take him to the hospital,"

"What if he stops breathing on the way?" the Thud says. "What if his heart stops?" Klaus looks tired, disgusted.

"I'll go get his chart," the nurse says.

"How about a transfer form," Klaus calls after her, "a list of meds, allergies, medical history." He raises his hands in a gesture of uselessness.

"Don't they have those things on file at the hospital?" the manager says.

Nan is listening to the man's lungs, pasting on the monitor leads.

"Transfer form is required by law," Klaus says. "The rest depends on which hospital we go to, whether he's been there before, how long ago, and whether the medical records people can find his chart and how long it takes. You been down to Muni Emergency recently, or University? It could be chaos this time of day."

"How do you feel, Mr. Lauderblad?" Nan shouts in his ear.

"Yah," the man says, nodding, "Yah, daht's right." His voice is muffled under the mask.

"Do you feel sick?" Nan shouts.

"Yah, yah."

"Can you tell me how old you are?"

"Yah, daht's right."

"That's about all he ever says," the nurse says, returning with chart in hand. "He is a Do Not Resuscitate," she points to the page. "'Do not resuscitate,'" she reads, "'do not intubate, do not transport to hospital except by physician order.'" She throws a hard look at Klaus. "Well, we got the physician order."

Klaus shakes his head and shrugs.

"Who's his physician?" I say. I'm only supposed to observe, but I can't help myself. This poor man should be allowed to die in peace.

"Dr. Benning is the doctor," the nurse says. "He cares for many of our patients."

"Was that who you spoke to?"

"No, it was another doctor, Linrud I think. Benning's off today. They cover for each other."

"Did that doctor know this poor man is a Do Not Resuscitate?"

The nurse glares at me. She doesn't need this. "I really don't know. Who are you anyway?"

I tell her.

"Well, look at him," she says. "He can't go on like this much longer."

I smile at her, reaching for a friendly voice. "Would you mind calling that doctor again? Maybe we could reason with him. It seems a shame—"

"Forget it, Leon," Nan says. "Let's just take him in. It'll take too long to reach the doc. What if we get another call while we're waiting?"

"Yah, daht's right," the old man chimes in.

She's right, I suppose. She's been in this situation many times.

A quick trip to unload the old man at Christ Hospital, a community hospital nearby, and then we head back to the station once again.

Before we reach it there is another radio call, "Engine 3, Medic 3, medical response needed at four eight four zero Fifth Street, floor number thirty-four, office number three-four-zero-zero, forty-eight-year-old man having chest pain. Cross street is Sycamore Avenue. Code 3."

Nan switches on the siren and lights as we speed up. "That's downtown," she says, "an office building."

Again through the streets, dodging and weaving much too fast. The shape of a bus starts to move across an intersection and Nan lurches us slower.

"Jesus, Nan, you always drive like this?" The words are out before I can stop them.

She glances at me. "Sorry, Leon, I'm not going that fast."

"Never mind," I mumble, "I'm just not used to it."

Father's angry voice comes to me again. Curse you boys and your damn bikes. He shook you, Zach, couldn't believe you were truly unconscious, shouted in your ear, might have slapped you if Mother hadn't pulled him back. He hated the hospital, hated the helplessness, the waiting, the not understanding.

The siren seems to scorch my brain, as if a bare wire has been threaded through my ears.

"Medic 3 at the scene," Nan speaks quickly into the radio as we arrive. We beat Engine 3. Dispatch will cancel them, the chicken salad boys, although they may show up to see if they can help, out of curiosity, boredom. Their own medic crew, the Thud and Nan, and besides Dr. Mendel's on board and rumor is he's hit the wall, losing it, over the edge.

We park in the Loading Only Zone, in front of a nameless wall of tinted glass that rises and rises into the sun. An odd call for a Sunday, usually these buildings are empty on the weekend.

This time the gurney goes with us, kits on top beside a portable monitor/defibrillator. There are few people on the street. A young security guard motions us to an elevator, then slides an odd-shaped key into the control panel and rises up with us, uninterrupted by the intervening floors. He is calm, efficient.

Hit in the head, now you're dead, hit in the head, Zach's voice again. At the hospital Mother held the door open for the two men carrying you. He'll be all right, lady, one of them said, talking around the cigarette held in his lips, eyes narrow in the smoke. I seen a lot of kids get thumped on the head like this, an' most of the time they come around pretty quick.

Mother looked at the man as if he were speaking an unknown language, as if she had no idea how to answer.

I don't like to think of you then, Zach, these memories frighten me.

A heavyset nurse in white pointed the way to the men. She wore a cap like a white flag rising from her hair, a dark stripe across it and a tiny insignia. The Emergency Room, for that's what it was, smelled that old antiseptic smell of hospitals, alcohol or formaldehyde or mercurochome. There didn't seem to be anyone there other than her and some voices behind a curtain.

"So did that guy just walk in off the street Friday night, Leon?" Nan says.

My thoughts swing back like a rusty hinge. "What guy?"

"That guy that shot up your E.D. Your hero act."

"Right, yeah, I guess he did. We, um, we'd just got all these gunshot wounds, including one of the police and people were coming in and out of the ambulance doors, a lot of people. So he just walked on in. He had his gun under his jacket."

"A shotgun?"

"No, I guess it was an assault rifle, skinny little barrel." My voice is loud, strained. I try to control it.

"Probably a modified AK-47," the Thud says. "Seems to be a popular weapon these days. So what happened then?"

The black face comes to me, the dead eyes, the body writhing as it moved, wired, crazed. "I think he was high. He looked pretty high, probably doin' crack." Or death, wired on death, death incarnate, creeping.

"Claudette was the hero. She's the one who yelled at him and—" I can't say anything more. The thought of her takes my voice away, makes me want to cry.

"Drew his fire," Klaus says solemnly.

The elevator doors slide open and now no one is listening. A plush carpeted foyer and a man in shorts and sport shirt motions us into a suite of offices. "Thank God you're here," he says. "He must be having a heart attack. He looks awful."

I feel it here, too, but there is only wood paneling, tall windows, computer screens, and coordinated colors.

On a leather couch lies a very pale middle-aged man, similarly dressed. There is the death. His jowly face is damp with sweat, tense with pain. He is heavyset, probably a smoker.

The Thud starts in with questions as they ease him out of his shirt. His name is Carl and he's had terrible pressure in his chest for about an hour. Nan works on starting an IV.

"I don't need all this," he says. "My wife will be here soon and she'll drive me to the hospital."

"Carl, let us do a few things first," Klaus says, "and see if we can't get you feeling better. Have you ever had any kind of heart disease?"

"No, never had a problem with my heart."

Klaus pastes monitor leads on his chest, but the round patches don't want to stick on the wet skin.

"Have you ever had this kind of pain before?"

"No, never like this. Well, actually I do get pains from time to time but I just figured it was my stomach. I usually take some Rolaids and it goes away. It's just my stomach."

"Well, maybe that's true, but those things can fool you. Do you smoke cigarettes?"

Of course he smokes and of course he doesn't exercise and of course he eats a high fat diet and so on, although Klaus asks only about the smoking. He sprays some nitroglycerin into the man's mouth.

The other man, a business partner perhaps, stands close by, uncertain what to do. "We were just doing a little contract work, trying to catch up before the week starts. Is that an ECG? Is he having heart trouble?"

"It's a monitor," I say, "not an ECG. He is quite likely having heart trouble but we can't tell for sure. We have to assume he is."

"I better go make a couple calls," the man says. "Where are you going to take him?"

"We'll take him to Municipal," Klaus says. "It's closest."

"My wife can take me there," Carl says. "This isn't necessary. Bob overreacted. I told him not to call 911."

"He might have saved your life, Carl," Klaus says. "How are you feeling now? Are you still having pain?"

Hit in the head, now you're dead. First they did nothing with you, Zach. A doctor came by, unshaven, very tired, and opened your eyes, peered at them, then examined you very carefully, moving your arms and legs. He and a nurse undressed you and covered you with a gown. He spoke to Mother, but I didn't hear what he said.

Then we sat and waited, Mother nervous as a cat, rearranging your covers, mumbling in Latvian at you, touching your cheek, praying. Until Father arrived and then she began to cry.

Stop, Zach, stop making me remember that day. It happened a long time ago and I put it away.

Where is the doctor? Father said, his accent heavy. What are they doing for this boy?

The doctor came, Papa, Mother said. He looked at him. He said we have to wait and see when he wakes up.

Was it Dr. Lester? They have to call Dr. Lester. I don't trust any of these other people. How do they know this boy is not seriously hurt?

"I don't feel very good," Carl says, and his eyes roll upward.

"Shit, there he goes," says Nan, watching the monitor. "Give him a thump, Klaus." Her own hands are busy taping the IV catheter in place.

The Thud's big fist lands hard on the man's chest. I move forward to help. The monitor shows the rapid zigzag of fibrillation. Yup, it's the real thing, a blood clot is blocking one of Carl's coronary arteries, part of his heart is dying and those dying cells are having seizures, putting his whole heart into a seizure.

The thump does nothing. Klaus's hands move to open a set of defibrillator pads, flat squares of moist conductive material.

Bob, the partner, reappears. "What happened? What are you doing?"

I grab the Ambu bag and mask from the open kit and move to the man's head. "Get that IV taped," I say. Shocking him may dislodge it and then we're in bigger trouble, he's in bigger trouble.

Nan moves fast, the tape slipping from the sweaty skin. I settle the plastic mask over the man's face and squeeze the bag to push air into the man's lungs.

Death has been waiting, lurking. Now it screams at us, defiant. I feel myself shudder.

Klaus slaps one pad over the sternum, the other over the ribs on the left, then reaches for the paddles. He presses the Charge button and the tone sounds.

Nan pulls back to avoid the shock.

"Wait," I say. "Get it taped."

"I've got to shock him, Leon."

"You'll need the IV. There's time." Death mocks us from the dull half-closed eyes, the limp muscles.

Hands flying, Nan winds the tape around the man's arm a couple of turns, tears it off, and backs away.

"Do it." I raise the mask away from his face.

Klaus fires the paddles. The unconscious man's body jerks. We watch the tiny monitor, as if this life itself were hidden in the little window. When the tracing settles down again it is unchanged.

"V-fib," Nan says. "Hit him again, three hundred." She reaches over to the machine and turns up the wattage.

"Oh, God," Bob says, "is he dying?"

Klaus pauses until the tone sounds then jolts the man again. Again no change.

"Number three at three-sixty," Nan says, turning it up now to the maximum.

The pause, the tone, the machine clicks and the Carl's body shakes. But this time there is a rhythm, this time the tracing settles down to a clean line with complexes marching across the screen. I bag him again.

Klaus reaches a hand to the man's groin. "Good femoral pulse."

"Time for Lidocaine," Nan says, turning to the other kit.

As she squirts the medication into the IV—an anesthetic to numb the conduction system of the man's heart, to keep it from seizing again—I watch him for movement. Death howls in frustration, withdrawing a step or two. I squeeze air into him, watching the slight rise of his chest. Will we have to intubate him? Will he wake back up enough to breathe for himself? He should, his brain was without blood for only seconds. A hair's breadth from dying, right to the edge of the cliff and falling over when we grabbed an arm and hauled him back.

"Is he okay?" Bob says, frantic. "What happened?"

"His heart fibrillated," I say. "He is having a heart attack. He's okay for the moment but it might happen again."

Yes, it might, and again and again, as the damage to his heart muscle spreads, and as it spreads he might not respond to shocks or Lidocaine or CPR or anything else we can do. Death is close by, leering, licking its lips. He could still die, in a minute, an hour, a day.

But now he breathes, a deep rattling breath. An arm flails.

"Let's move," Klaus says.

With quick practiced hands they pack up the kits, then collapse the gurney down close to the floor and we swing Carl onto it, alive, breathing, for the moment. Now they raise the gurney again, clicking the legs back into place, and we head for the door.

"Has his wife been called?" Nan says.

"Yes, she's supposed to be coming here," Bob says.

"Okay, you wait here 'til she comes and then come to Municipal Hospital Emergency."

"But he said his doctor is at Christ Hospital," Bob says.

"He needs the nearest hospital with a cath lab, and Municipal is it. They'll take good care of him there."

Bob opens and closes his mouth, not used to being told what to do. "Will he be all right?"

Nan and Klaus look at me.

"We don't know," I say. "We'll do everything we can for him. He'll get the best care available. It depends on how much of his heart has been damaged."

Onto the elevator again.

Hit in the head, now you're dead. Is Zach dead, my voice asked. In that bewildering place I watched our parents closely, afraid to move, to speak.

Father turned angrily on me. He's not dead. He's breathing, isn't he?

An older man appeared. He limped and avoided our eyes. He trundled you off for X-rays of your head. Father quizzed him on where he was going and why, then went along, anger tightening his movements.

Dr. Lester arrived, in green scrubs and surgical hat. Father grabbed his shoulders. He examined you and then talked for a long time. Mother cried, Father muttered and cursed. Then someone rolled you away again. We sat for hours on stained chairs. A black and white TV blared from the wall.

"Leon." Nan shakes my arm. She has been speaking to me. "I said you ride in the back with Klaus. I'll drive."

I nod.

"We're going to start bagging you in a minute."

"Sorry."

Out into the heat again, the glaring glass-walled canyon of the street, and into the rig.

Now we sway through the empty downtown streets, siren on, wailing at no one. Carl is awake and talkative, but still pale. Maybe the defibrillator shocks broke up the clot blocking his artery.

We roll into the drive at Municipal and Nan spins us round expertly into the ambulance bay. I open the doors and step out, the concrete and steel monolith rising above us, a warren of people dying, all lying in rows, in beds, in rooms. Fitz is up there somewhere, one of those windows, one of those rooms, a single skinny body in a simple bed, a speck, but with all the suffering, all the pain of the whole world, panting, exhausted, overwhelmed. There is a huge hollowness in me at the thought of going to see him. I have to.

"What are you looking at, Leon?" Nan nudges me out of the way as she pulls out the gurney, clicking the legs into place.

"Hey, Nan, listen, I've got a friend up there who's really sick. I need to go see him for about five minutes."

She watches me, nodding. Does she know, somehow?

"Okay, here, take my radio in case we get a call."

I nod, taking the black instrument. "I'll just be a few minutes. I'll come back down to the ED and meet you inside."

She nods, busy with the gurney. "You come down quick if we get a call. We can't wait around." They vanish inside.

I turn, avoiding the E.D. I don't want to talk to anyone.

Again an elevator full of strangers. I study each face—death feels so strong here—I glance from one pair of eyes to the next, but they are all alive. I cringe inside each time the doors slide open, waiting for the fog to creep in, surround us, smother us.

Now, walk down the hall. Why? Why am I going to see him? To make sure he still wants to die? To make sure he's really desperate enough, miserable enough, exhausted enough, in enough pain, nauseated enough, depressed enough, and, most important, convinced enough that none of it will ever get better. Hopeless enough, that's what it really means. Hopeless enough that he wants to die.

So then what will I say? Catch ya later, Fitz. See ya round. Or a real goodbye, an aware goodbye, can I do that? Both of us aware that this is it, our final goodbye. I might cry.

But he is asleep when I go in. So gaunt, so pale, on his side in an awkward pose, asleep or comatose. His gown is stained with sweat, his breath rasps across cracked lips. There is a terrible smell here, a smell I have smelled before.

Oh, God, Fitz. Should I wake you? I need to talk to you, need to make sure. I watch his body struggling to breathe, each breath like a spasm, the shriveled muscles in his neck, the hollows between his ribs. No, I guess I don't. Look at you. It's so obvious.

But I want to say goodbye. I want to hear your voice one more time and hear your wisdom again, the wonderful things you say and the way you say them. And tell you things, tell you that I love you and that lots of people love you, everyone who ever knew you. I won't be able to, will I? I should have said them all before.

Now I feel my own tears. I won't wake you. I don't want to stir your mind and make you feel yourself dying any more.

I've got to do it, don't I. I've got to do it today, tonight. Take you away from this suffering. Set you free from this miserable end to your life. Tonight, Fitz, I'll come and do it for you tonight.

But what about now, Fitz? You need some water, and a bath and a clean gown and someone to fluff your pillows and sit you up straight, hold your hand and make you feel like you're not alone.

I stand still, letting the tears drip from my cheeks. But most of all you need to die, you need to pass quietly and quickly away, out of this life.

Downstairs again I walk into the ED. Nurses say hi and I nod, smiling, trying to act normal.

"Riding with your squad today, Leon?" I hear Peter's nasal voice.

"Yup, today's the day. How are things going here?" Peter, you're the last person I want to see. Have you heard about Friday night? You must have heard.

"Good, good. Not much excitement, but we're moving down the stretch and doing fine. Gotta good team today," he says in his medical director voice, for whomever is in earshot.

We move to a quiet corner. "Heard you had a rough night Friday night, with Claudette and all."

I nod. "How's she doing?"

"Well, she's alive, still in a coma upstairs. Sounds like she'll be on a vent for a while." He looks me in the eye. "I don't think anyone knows how she'll come out of it, Leon."

I nod again, avoiding his gaze. I don't want to think about Claudette and all that blood.

"We should talk, Leon," Peter says.

"Okay."

"I'll be home tomorrow. Will you call me?"

"Okay."

"You're one of our heavy hitters, Leon. We want to keep you in the lineup."

Again I want to cry. It's a nice thing to say. "Thanks. I'll call you."

Peter turns away. I move to the med room, a tiny space just off the nurses station. Glass-doored shelves of medications line the walls, pills and IV preparations. There are the Pixis machines, squat cabinets for dispensing narcotics with a computerized locking system for which each nurse has a code. People are watching me, they must be. A glance out the door but no one is in sight. My pulse thumps in my neck. I pretend to be getting a couple of aspirin. I scan the cardiac medications and find the Inderal. A quick glance about, no one near, I slide open the drawer and retrieve a vial. Now the digoxin. There's the drawer.

"Hi, Leon, what are you up to today? " A nurse, Lynne, comes around the corner.

"Oh, nothing much," I mumble, "just getting a couple aspirin."

"I mean why the observer jacket?" She busies herself drawing up something into a syringe.

"Oh, I'm the medical supervisor for Medic 3, so I have to ride with them now and then, make sure they're taking proper care of the citizenry of our fine city."

"Right. Oh, well, at least it's something different." She turns and walks quickly away, syringe in hand.

I pocket the digoxin, then find some Kleenex to keep the glass vials from breaking against each other.

"LEON, LEON," Jasmine's shrill voice screeches across the department. No, it can't be her. I look over to where some poor teenage girl in restraints is getting an IV started, probably an overdose patient. "LEAVE ME ALONE," she shrieks again.

We ride back to the fire station, windows down.

"So Leon," Nan says, "you all right or what?" She sits sweating in the heat, elbow resting on the window.

I glance at her. "I'm all right."

She grins. "It'd scare the piss outta me, a gangbanger walkin' up to me with an assault rifle, a gunfight right in front of me, bullets flying."

I nod, not sure what to say. Klaus is busy in the back. I shrug. "What can I say. It was scary."

"Did you get any kind of debriefing? You know, like critical incident debriefing. Like they're supposed to do with us after a bad run, when a kid dies or something."

I shake my head. "Critical incident debriefing? When's the last time you actually had one? I've always wondered who is supposed to do them."

"We had one once, after that apartment house fire couple years ago. Remember that one in Riverview where all those kids were trapped upstairs?"

"That was years ago. You guys deal with major trauma almost every shift. You have critical incidents all the time."

"Yeah, no shit. So do you. Plus you said you got that friend back at Muni who's dying." She looks me hard in the eye for an instant. Does she know? Can she see what's going on with me?

I watch the buildings going by, thinking of Rita. "I'll be okay, Nan. I've got somebody to talk to."

Alone in the tiny paramedic office I sit staring at the logbook. They're playing Ping-Pong down the hall, Nan and the Thud and the other firemen. I can hear them laughing, making jokes about me.

An avalanche of memory seems to press upon my mind, frightening memories that I want to put away, out of my head. But I can't, I sit horrified, fascinated, sweating and scared, at these shiny new pictures I don't recall ever having looked at before, but I know they are mine, ours.

They operated on you, Zach, operated on your head, your brain. Mother took me home and I didn't see you for days. Mother and Father took turns at the hospital, neither of them talking much at home. It was a solemn lonely place.

Then one day they took me to see you. He won't know who you are, Leon, Mother said.

Who will he think I am?

Well, he doesn't really understand who anybody is right now. His brain has been damaged and it has to get better. He doesn't act like himself, but he'll get better.

Who does he act like?

You lay there, a skinny, pale child in a helmet of bandages, a yellow tube in your nose. You stared off to one side, stared and stared, while your arms moved, twisted slowly above the blanket. Was this you, Zach, this creature with eyes like an animal, lifeless, vacant eyes?

Mother leaned down and kissed your cheek, holding the tube out of the way. Zach, look who's come to see you. It's your brother, Leon.

No, don't think of it. Here, do these reports, there is still a pile that need to be looked at. Here, a forty-four-year-old male who slipped on a wet floor at Taco Bell, the manager of the place, and dislocated his shoulder, vitals signs recorded, no level of consciousness noted—Your blank face didn't move, Zach, your eyes didn't flicker.

Say hi, Leon, Mother said. Give Zach a hug.

Hi, Zach. How could I hug this creature they said was you, how could I touch you? I moved close where I could smell you, a frightening smell.

Hug him, Father said, tense, angry. He's your brother.

Is he dead?

Father's hand stung the back of my head. He's not dead, damn you, so stop saying that. Look at him, he's breathing, isn't he, moving.

Part of him is dead, Leon, Dr. Lester told me one day. He was squat, grey-haired, older than our parents. We walked in the hospital hallway and he held my hand.

The part of his brain that he thinks with and talks with got hurt and doesn't work anymore, he said. Some of it is dead and some of it is bruised. The bruised part might get better when the bruising goes away. And the rest of his brain might be able to take over for the part that's dead. But that takes a long time to happen.

Why didn't you fix his brain when you did the operation?

I only helped with the operation. There was a very special doctor called a neurosurgeon who did the surgery. Leon, you can't always fix someone's brain once it's been hurt. The operation was to stop the bleeding inside Zach's head. Zach's brain won't ever heal completely but it will heal somewhat. We just have to wait and see how much it will heal.

How much it will heal. It didn't heal at all, did it? I finger the grit of dried blood on one of the run reports. Death, a speck of it, clotted, congealed, dried into dust. I can feel it in here, under the desk, behind the shelves, in the dark hallway outside the office, watching me, listening to my thoughts. I turn and look behind me, then under the metal desk.

It's here, behind everything, underneath everything. It's out on the streets, in the glare, in a car somewhere or a dozen cars, or sliding along the sidewalk with a gun under its jacket.

The tone sounds, the dispatcher's voice with words I can't make out.

And somewhere in that black abyss behind everything is you, Zach, your soul down there miles below in the dark. And that girl with the tubal pregnancy, Katrina something, and that huge fat woman from the fire, and that kid that got the trocar in his heart.

Nan's face in the doorway. "You coming, Doc?" Her smile fades. "You all right, Leon? Look a little pale. You want to sit this one out?"

"Let's go." I grab my red jacket.

Into the rig, siren on, down the apron, onto the street.

"What's the call? I couldn't hear it."

"Two-year-old kid had a seizure at the Coolidge pool. Don't know if it was a near-drowning or what." Nan reaches for the radio microphone. "Medic 3, rolling to Coolidge pool. Do you have more info?"

At an intersection a couple of teenage boys dance out in the street in front of us. No weapons. Nan hits the horn and speeds up. They dance away, yelling at us.

"Sorry, Three, don't know any more. Does not sound water-related."

It's not far, a community pool near the projects, a crowd of people. Out of the rig we move over hot concrete amid dozens of black children in swimsuits to a wailing mother, only a teen herself, and two lifeguards bent over a child on a folded towel. The baby is crying, thrashing its legs.

Nan touches the woman. "Okay, tell me what happened."

The wide-eyed girl points to another. "You talk to the lady, Shantrelle. I cain't explain it."

Klaus examines the child.

"She was jus' layin' there," says Shantrelle, "then she made this funny sound like a hiccup or somethin' and then she went all stiff all over. She was in the shade, laying there under the chair. We put her in the shade an' she was sleepin'."

The girl's anxious eyes move over the crowd around us. Her face twists into a self-conscious smile at a muscular boy nearby, then her eyes return to Nan.

"What happened next?" Nan says.

"Well, then she went all stiff, like I said, and all this drool came out of her mouth, and she wasn't breathing none. We thought she had a heart attack. And then she stopped and started breathing again. And then...I don't know. You talk to the lady, Trina. It's your damn chil'."

There are maybe thirty people crowded around us. I know it's here. I feel it. My eyes scan the figures for weapons, a hand hidden under a shirt. Two police stand talking outside the fence. I want to get out there with them, get away from this crowd, this heat. The sun flashes off the water into my eyes.

"I know'd she was sick," Trina, the mother, says. "She throw'd up this morning."

"Has she had a fever?" Nan says.

"Don't ask me," the girl says, "We ain't got no thermometer."

"Did she ever have a seizure before?" Nan says.

The girl looks at her.

"Or a fit or a spell?" Nan goes on.

The girl shakes her head. "Not as I knows of, nothin' like this anyway."

Klaus takes the child's temperature. She has a fever but is fine otherwise, a febrile seizure, not a serious thing.

A couple of adolescents are trying to get into Klaus's kit. He shoos them off.

"Whassa matter, man? We just wanna see what you got in there. Bet you got some good stuff. Bet you got some money-makin' stuff."

"You need to take her to the emergency room," Nan says to the girl. "She needs to be checked to make sure she doesn't have meningitis or something serious like that."

"Now how'm I gonna do that?" the girl says. "I thought that's what you guys were for. You got an ambulance."

"She doesn't have to go in the ambulance," Nan says, glancing at me. "She's doing fine. You can take her in your car."

"My car, like I got a car. I ain't got no car. Why cain't you take us to emergency?"

The crowd is starting to drift off, kids splashing in the pool again. An older woman appears, a scarf on her head, the child's grandmother or an aunt perhaps. "That's all right, girl. Don't be taking up these people's time. They got other things to do." Then to Nan, "We'll get her there. We'll get her to the doctor."

I follow Nan and Klaus through the crowd toward the gate. There are hundreds of people here, the pool packed with children shouting and splashing, groups of teens all around. How many weapons are here hidden in bags and clothes. How many bullets wait in dark steel chambers, waiting to explode and tear through skin into muscle and artery and nerve. I glance at the cops. They know what bullets do, aren't they worried?

"Medic 3 back in service," Nan says into the radio. "No transport required."

Chapter Fifteen

I began to hate you, Zach, not really you but the speechless, twisting creature that lived in your bed, the horrid feeding tube in its nose, the diapers it wore, the smell of it. I hated the way its eyes never wavered, staring to the side, never looked at me, never looked at anything. So that even when I walked around the bed and stood in front of them, stood in front of their gaze, they didn't see me. I hated its skin that paled and paled, its muscles that shriveled.

Read to him, Father would bawl at me, angry. He was angry all the time, angry at Mother, angry at the Rabbi, even at Dr. Lester.

Dr. Lester brought a stack of comic books one day. Here, he said, these might be good, lots of color and action. Zach needs lots of stimulation. He didn't believe it, I could tell. Did he? Did he expect one day something in your head would go click and you would be back?

Green Lantern, Flash, Batman, I acted them out, jumping and prancing around the room, imaginary cape whipping in the breeze. But you never saw, never looked, never listened, your crawling arms never paused, your staring eyes never flickered.

Mother exercised you, moving your arms and legs, stretching the muscles. Twice a day, she was very good. She carried you into the living room and put some nice music on the record player. Sometimes Dr. Lester helped her, showed her how to stretch your different muscles, how to move the joints.

I helped her, too. I remember the feel of you, the moist slack skin and the cords beneath, the feel of your joints as they grew stiffer no matter what we did. And your face that never changed, your eyes that never met ours.

Father hated to touch you.

Would you feed Zach, please, dear, Mother would say. She began to hate the task herself. Nutriment, the stuff was called, squat cans of it in chocolate, strawberry, eggnog, and vanilla. Like bad-tasting milkshakes, I tried it a few times. But you never tasted it. You couldn't swallow, you would choke.

Pour it into the rubber bag, add a half cup of water to keep it from clogging the tube, shake it up and hang it on the pole Father made from an old broomstick. Then plug it into the tube and here's dinner, Zach, your favorite, eggnog with water, down your nose. Then I sat and guarded the tube from your wandering hands, your bony fingers twisted in spasm.

Died, died, you tried and tried, Zach's voice again, as I sit in the tiny paramedic office. Do I have to do this, Zach? I can't stop it, can I. I can't stop you from levering open my mind, like a can opener opens a can, cleaves the metal and bends it back. Is this what psychosis means, this compulsion of thought and memory that I can't stop.

Father brought home a little TV from the store one day to put in our room. The sound of it seemed to slow you down, but your eyes never looked, never moved from their blind sideways gaze.

At night you stopped, sleep was the only thing that stilled the creep of your arms, your hands mittened with white thumbless covers that Dr. Lester had brought, with ties to keep them on, to keep you from snagging your tube and pulling it out. We kept them on you most of the time, except when Mother would massage your hands, rubbing your fingers, stretching them one by one. I wished she would do that to me.

She sang to you, Latvian children's songs in her surprising voice, like a girl's. But Father hated the songs, scolded her in the old language when he heard them. The old language, they called it that.

Laughter in the squad room down the hall, a shout, jokes about me. They're watching a movie, Nan and Klaus and the firefighters, waiting for their dinner.

They know I'm losing it. Nan knows for sure, and rumors move fast among these guys. Soon the whole fire department will know and pretty soon Peter will be on my case. The paramedics are losing confidence in you, Leon. They're worried you might throw them a wild pitch in a clutch situation.

More laughter, I want to run out there. Quit laughing at me, I want to yell, I can't help it. I sit in the cool little office sweating, listening to your words forming in my mind. Died, died, you tried and tried.

There it is again, that moaning. How can it be here? No, no, it's the tone, the dispatch tone. Time to go. Stand up, close the book, put on the jacket, go out the door, act normal. What about these bottles in my pocket? I should leave them in the car, if I can get to it. Maybe when we come back.

Mocking words die on the firemen's lips when I enter. They turn away, back to the TV, tiny movements they think I don't see.

I follow Nan and Klaus down the stairs.

"Okay, what have we got?" I close the ambulance door as we begin to roll.

"Boating accident on the river, possible drowning," Klaus says, leaning over the seat from the rear compartment. "Damn, we're gonna miss dinner."

"Medic 3 rolling," Nan says into the radio mike. "Have you got any more info?"

"Negative, Three. Police at scene. I will try to find out."

Down Maple, sirens on, an old street on the edge of downtown, still treelined, sloping down to the river. A stylish neighborhood once, rows of trim townhouses, wrought iron rails and gates, now slum, tenements, with a tangle of freeway ramps overhead.

A ladder truck lumbers into view, its harsh horn blaring, turning onto the street a block ahead.

“There’s Six,” Nan says. “That means Campbell will be in command if there’s a situation.”

We follow the red truck to the flashing lights of two police cruisers parked by a wide public boat ramp. A police boat sits tied up, its blue light revolving as well. There is a small park here, its parking lot full of cars and empty boat-trailers. The wide river stretches away, sliding by flat and brown. Two fire department boats are being readied to go.

Help, Leon, help, Leon, I hear from out on the water. I watch to see if anyone else hears it.

We walk over to a group of police and firefighters talking to three teens in swimsuits, two girls and a guy. Campbell, a lieutenant in dark gray shirtsleeves, steps over to us.

“Afternoon,” he says. “We just wanted you guys on standby, in case we get lucky.”

“What’s up?” Klaus says.

“Well, these poor idiots were out there drinking beer and trying to water-ski, it sounds like.” He has a clean boyish face, his serious voice almost surprising. “I guess one of the guys fell out, leaned too far back to finish his beer or God knows what. No one saw him fall out. They say they turned around and he was gone. They think they might have hit someone’s wake or something, and out he went.

“Anyway, by the time they noticed he was gone and came back around to get him he was nowhere to be seen. Course they’re not sure if they came back to the right spot or where that spot was or if somebody else picked him up. They’re so damn drunk, Jesus.”

“They’re sure that somebody’s missing though?” Nan says.

“Oh, yeah, the one girl says it’s her fiancé.”

“How long’s it been?”

“Oh, maybe a half hour, forty-five minutes by now I guess.”

“So you guys are going to do a search?”

“Yup, all three boats, police chopper, radio hails to the other boats out there, course most of them don’t have radios.”

There are half a dozen boats in sight, skiers, pleasure boats. As they talk I scan the surface for a pale shapeless floating mound. Somehow I want to see it, find it, be able to say, yup, that’s him, that’s the guy, and know that he has been pulled out, put in a bag and carried away. I hear Father's voice growling at me now, old country words that make no sense. They never wanted us to learn the language.

"Don't suppose he had a life jacket on," Klaus says.

"Nope, they weren't wearing them," Campbell says. "I guess anything could have happened to him, could have got a mouthful of water or hit his head on some junk in the water."

"Or maybe he swam to shore like a normal person. Or he could be laughing it up on somebody else's boat right now," Klaus says, "drinking their beer and flirting with some other girl."

"You got it," Campbell says. "Anyway, why don't you guys make yourselves comfortable and we'll let you know if anything comes up."

"Or anyone," Nan says.

Campbell ignores the joke, walking back to the main group.

The two fire department boats rumble away, small open boats with outboard engines, two men in each. They'll search the shores, around the bridge pilings, talk to people in other boats.

I sit under a tree, watching the broad plain of moving water. Nan and Klaus putter around the rig.

The river is ugly, fearsome, as if I sit at the edge of one dimension looking at another moving slowly by. Death again, half a mile wide and a couple of hundred feet deep. Imagine tumbling slowly down into that foul water, bumping along through the trash and junk on the bottom, the car bodies buried in slime, the old refrigerators, God knows what junk from the century or so this city has straddled it. How many bodies lie forgotten down there, bones covered in mud, twisted in piles, snails sliding down ribs, skulls hung with green muck. There must be hundreds.

Down river a ways the bridges arch high above, their huge feet planted in the water. A line of barges moves among them.

Ugh, what a job, looking for that flash of white bloodless flesh, an arm or a leg flung up on a rock or log, a corpse twisted in some inhuman position, so obviously dead.

Leon! I hear my name in a high-pitched scream from out on the water. No, I'm imagining. It is a child's shout, or a girl's laugh, from one of the boats. The sound of the city is loud if you listen, the low roar always there, cars on the freeways, boat engines.

You damn kids, Father said it so many times. He carried anger with him all the time then, Zach. Do you remember? His growling words distorted more, the grammar worse. His homely face, pocked, with its nose that led him around the house, that nose so obviously foreign, crooked, lumpy. I hid from him, stayed outside to play when he was home, cringed through meals.

He and Mother settled into a sullen war, she hating him for avoiding you, he hating to be with you, to be in our room, to wash you or feed you or read to you.

Did he hate me, too? Did he blame me for you, Zach? He played with me, read to me, took me places with him, but it was never fun, never relaxed and friendly.

Talk to Zach, Dr. Lester said, talk to him like part of the family. And so I did. I talked to you lots, what was going on at school, what our friends were doing. I'd tell you jokes and act things out for you, events from school. Maybe somewhere in there, inside your head, you were listening, hearing, understanding. You became my silent confidant.

I prayed for you, sincere prayers that you would come back, that your brain would heal and you would return to me, but I hated the thing that remained of you.

Gnats whine at my ears, nearly invisible. I bat at them helplessly.

What if Fitz wakes up? What if I walk into his room and he's lying there watching TV. Maybe I need some morphine, or Versed, or something to put him out. So how am I going to get it? It's all in those Pixis machines, with entry codes. If someone even sees me fooling around with one of them I'll be in trouble. Drugs, Leon's on drugs. That's why he's acting weird. We saw him trying to get into one of the machines. He was watching me when I entered my code.

People came to visit, Zach, family to see you. Father hated them to see you, but if they came during the day, when he was at the store, Mother would walk up the stairs with them, take them to our room. They brought toys, and stood awkwardly watching as I unwrapped them for you, realizing how ridiculous the game or puzzle was for this creature twisting before them.

It's lovely, Mother would say. Leon will help him with it. Leon's very good with Zach.

I remember Aunt Lillian. She was young with a fragile prettiness that needed protection. She snatched back the package before I took the wrapping off, rushing down the stairs in tears.

Mother called after her, followed her downstairs, and they talked outside on the grass, in a light rain, then hugged and she went away, giving the toy to mother for me to play with. I hated those toys, Zach, those toys meant for you. I ignored them, wanted to burn them, throw them out the window.

Flop, something lands next to me on the grass, leathery, shriveled. A head, God, someone's head, flattened as if the skull has been removed, tiny shining eyes. I hear myself shout, roll away, jump up. Zach's head, damn, what in the world! I'm about to run when it focuses in my mind to a baseball mitt. I stop myself and stand, shaking.

Nan and Klaus watch me, each with a glove on. "Thought you might want to play catch," Klaus says. "Didn't mean to scare you."

I pick up the glove. What to say now? "Sounds good. Sorry, thought it was a grenade. Vietnam was rough on me." I walk toward them.

"I didn't know you were in 'Nam," Klaus says.

"That's just the problem, I wasn't." I try to grin.

Nan giggles. "That's good, Leon, quick. Did you just make that up?"

We talk and joke as we toss the ball. What do they think? What will they tell their buddies? I tossed Leon a glove and he 'bout had a fit, jumped away like he'd seen a ghost.

Radio chatter, Nan lifts the receiver from her hip and pauses to listen. "Sounds like shots fired in the projects, Wilmont field."

"So what else is new?" Klaus says. "Hell, we'll never get dinner." He tosses me a pop fly.

One of the police cruisers screams away up the street. A few minutes pass. More chatter. "Two people down," Nan says, the receiver to her ear. "They're going to call us off here, to go up there. Dispatch is talking to Campbell right now." She jerks a thumb toward the other vehicles.

Listening, she shakes her head. "Campbell's such an idiot. 'Await BLS report,' he says. Two people shot and he wants to wait for the EMTs to scope it out. Here we are, paramedics, ten blocks away, waiting for some drunk fool that's either drowned or on some other boat by now and he wants EMTs first. What are they going to do, apply pressure to stop the bleeding?"

The late afternoon sun has dropped behind a bridge, turning the haze over the river a smog brown.

You're darn tootin', I like Fig Newtons, Zach's voice now.

"Okay, there it is," she says, turning toward the ambulance. "Let's roll."

We climb on board. Campbell steps around the fire engine and waves at us as we back up.

"You idiot," Nan mutters, waving back to him and spinning the steering wheel. "EMTs to a shooting." She flips the siren on as we roar out onto the street.

Leon, Leon, Leon, it shrieks at me, a banshee on the roof. I move to cover my ears, then stop my hands. I hope they don't notice.

In less than a minute we are there, a brown stubble playfield behind the Wilmont projects, a crowd of blacks, three police cruisers, two fire trucks. People move away from our bumper as we roll onto the dirt, shouting, pushing each other.

"This shit I hate," Nan yells, "angry people with guns."

"And cocaine," Klaus says, reaching across the seat for the box of latex gloves on the dash. "Think they're invincible, can't be hurt." He drops a pair in my lap.

Plastic goggles appear on their faces. "You need a pair, Leon, over your glasses?"

"My glasses'll do."

We scramble out, the uproar loud suddenly with the siren off, the air humid, heavy. Another Medic rig is pulling up. A cop waves urgently.

The EMTs crouch around two bloody bodies. They chatter at us, helpless, frustrated, afraid. Death is here, in this crowd.

A man, maybe forty, lies on dirt dark with blood. His face is gray, mouth slack, an EMT bagging him. Blood oozes from the side of his head.

Klaus pushes the bag away, feeling the neck for a pulse. "Is he alive?" His other hand opens the latches on the kit. "Gotta pulse. Okay, go on bagging him while I find a tube."

Nan has moved past to the other body, a skinny girl, moaning and twisting.

"How long they been down?" Klaus shouts. "Here, Leon, you wanna do this and I'll get a line going?"

"Maybe fifteen minutes," an EMT says, looking at his watch. "Call came in at five eighteen. We were here at five twenty-three."

Angry voices sound close by, a knot of people pushing. Two police move to break it up.

"LEON," a woman screams, no, not my name, just a scream. I kneel by the bloody head. It has a mean face, a hard skinny face, smeared with blood on the brown skin, the wide pupils stare at nothing. Death staring at me, a dead brain inside this head, a bullet full of death fired into this skull, a jumble of mush where a brain used to be.

My gloved hands move in front of me, clicking the laryngoscope together, grasping the tube. Blood, Leon, be careful, death spilled all around, blood, feel it soaking your pants under your knee.

Leon, a cop shouts nearby. No, not you, ignore it. Someone, a woman, is sobbing, Leon, Leon, Leon.

The hands open the mouth, slide the scope in, move the tongue out of the way, look for the cords. There, the thin dark slit, death in there, beyond those cords, the horrible cave of his trachea, death waiting.

"Is that his only wound?" Klaus says.

"Only one we found."

"Who's the shooter?"

"Don't know. The cops are trying to figure that out. Might not be far away."

The tube slides in. I inflate the balloon. "Here, don't let go of this." I yell at the EMT, handing him the tube. "Klaus, I need a tube strap. You sure this dude's alive?"

Klaus is taping an IV to the man's arm. "He's got a pulse."

The hands take the plastic strap, my hands, and pass it under the neck wet with blood, back to the mouth and snap it around the tube.

Klaus fits a neck collar around him. "We gotta roll," he says. "Where's Nan?"

I move through the crowd to where she kneels with the crew from the other rig. An older grim-faced policeman stands by them. The girl squirms on the dirt beneath them.

"She says she's pregnant," Nan says as I squat by them.

"Hi, Dr. Mendel," a nervous paramedic from the other crew says.

His partner wrestles a lowered gurney into place by the woman. She is young, maybe sixteen, shot in the left side of her chest. Her belly is flat, skinny. If she's pregnant, it's early. She is frail, sickly, a neglected-looking child, and now shot. Her mouth twists, a gold front tooth glimmers, her eyes gaze unfocused, dazed, from pain, fear, drugs perhaps. She ignores Nan, or has no awareness of her.

"Carlotta," Nan says to her, patting her shoulder with a bloody glove, "Carlotta, we're going to move you onto the gurney now. You just lay still, sweetheart. You're gonna be just fine."

They have bandaged her, started an IV in each arm. Now she needs a fast ride to the hospital.

"My baby," she rouses suddenly. "What about my baby!" she shrieks, pushing away their hands.

They struggle with her onto the gurney, close the strap buckles to hold her down, then raise her up until the legs click into place.

"Let's roll," the paramedic says. "See you guys at Muni."

The policeman tries to clear a path for them over the dirt, through the crowd. There is more shouting, more angry voices.

Run to the alley, run to the alley, Zach yells at me, an angry voice.

Klaus and the EMTs have moved the man to our rig. Nan and I help get him inside, then I climb in back with Klaus.

"Scene time eight minutes," Nan yells back to us as the engine starts. "Not bad, eh, Leon?"

LEON, LEON, LEON, the siren starts up before I can answer. I close my eyes.

"Leon, Leon," now Klaus is tugging my arm, yelling. He meets my gaze for an instant, pokerfaced, serious. "Can you bag him?" Klaus has a streak of blood on his cheek.

My hands take the Ambu bag and I begin pushing oxygen into the man, down the tube into this gray mean face, into the mask of a brain now probably destroyed.

Klaus connects the monitor and the man's heart rhythm appears, widely spaced blips crawling across the screen. "Bradycardic, better hyperventilate him."

I nod and reach with one hand for a towel from the stack on a shelf. "Here, you've got blood on your face."

"What?" Klaus looks at the towel, mystified.

I reach up and wipe his cheek. "You've got blood on your face," I yell.

"Oh, thanks." He glances at the cloth and grins at the unexpected gesture.

At the hospital I watch them disappear with the gurney through the double doors. The other rig that brought the pregnant girl stands empty, doors still open. In the sudden calm I close the doors of both ambulances.

I step around a corner to the staff entrance, avoiding the ED. There is a wide hallway and the staff locker room. No one inside, I take off my pants and turn on the cold water at the sink to wash the bloodstain from the knee. The silent boring room is a relief. I squeeze the water from my pants and step back into them. At least the wide wet patch will dry, won't freak out the patients, and doesn't carry a zillion lethal viral particles like the stain might have. AIDS, the new twist to modern medicine, every drop of blood potentially lethal, every bleeding patient a pariah.

Outside again, there is a patch of grass in the curve of the driveway, empty for now of winos or street people. Around me the city seethes, heat rising from the acres of hot asphalt streets, hot concrete walls, hot steel cars blowing hot exhaust.

You died, too, you died, too, cries the music booming from a rusty Cadillac driving past, its windows open, dark inside, deadly.

You grew thinner and thinner, no matter how much we fed you. The smell of you filled our bedroom until I hated going into it. I fought with Mother to keep the window open. The draft will make him ill, she would say.

The creature living in our bedroom. Sometimes I grabbed your hand, catching it from its endless loops, squeezed it, pinched the fingers, watching your face for any change at all, once I fished an ice cube from a cup of pop and wrapped it with your hand, held your fingers closed for minutes while it dripped, but there was no change in that face, that blank expression, that mask you wore.

No, God, I hate this. I roll over on the grass and look toward the door. C'mon, you guys, lets get back in the rig and go. I can't stop it, can I, Zach, these thoughts of you lying there, dead on the inside and live on the outside, haunting me.

I slapped your hand with a ruler, a wooden ruler from your schoolbag that hung for months on its nail in the closet, slapped you hard, again and again. The white skin flushed red, seemed to glow. I covered it with the mitten. But you felt nothing, Zach.

We were like the Peerless's across the alley, that old couple so alone, just a wall away from the rest of the neighborhood, the carefree kids who skipped through their days. A prison with sickness and odor and sadness our cellmates.

At bedtime I lay watching you in the dark, your shadow moving, twisting endlessly, the sheets moving, until you fell asleep. It wasn't you anymore, Zach, it wasn't my best friend, my playmate, my brother. You had gone away, vanished. Instead I had this creature that did nothing, said nothing, that took my room from me, this partly dead inside creature. I hated it. I lay in the bed staring at it, hating it.

Fitz at the Ritz, Fitz at the Ritz, a strange voice now, little more than a whisper. Fitz, what about Fitz, up there in his room, I hope he's still asleep, full of morphine and asleep. Should I run up one more time and see if he's awake, say goodbye to him. I never said goodbye. Should I tell him what I'm going to do, tell him when—

"Aye, Leon, let's go," Nan's voice behind me, across the drive. "If we're lucky we'll get back in time for spaghetti."

"What's happening with our little buddy?" I ask Klaus inside the rig.

"Well, they were gonna ship him off to the CAT scanner but he started having runs of complete heart block. They even put an external pacemaker on him. Didn't look good."

"Bet he deserved it," Nan says. "Bet he was dealing drugs or a pimp or something. He looked like the type."

She drives for a few minutes. "I don't know, I don't know about this shit."

I watch her damp chubby face, a friendly pleasant face that laughs easily.

"Which shit is that?"

She glances across the seat, shakes her head. "You ever get tired of busting your butt to save criminals and bums, Leon? Going into the projects like that, knowing there's folks there with guns that would be happy to blow you away. Course you don't have to actually go there, go out and get 'em, but we do. You gotta work on them at the hospital, though. You ever get tired of it?"

I glance back at Klaus leaning through the opening. He meets my eye and shakes his head. "You just need some dinner, girl. A little firehouse cooking and you'll be smiling again. Holmes was cooking tonight. He's always good for something hot and spicy."

I skip the spaghetti—I'll be leaving soon—and retreat to the office again, the fat book of trip reports as my excuse, the barren little office with a single window looking out at a dirty gray wall across an alley, the light finally fading.

The flood of memory continues. I can't stop it. I sit stunned, paralyzed, staring at nothing out the window. Where will this end? Will I be strapped down on a gurney in a few hours, this miserable dream replaying in my head 'til I'm part of it again, 'til it is me and I am it and the welcome chaos of this real world shrinks to nothing?

Dr. Lester came each week. He sat and talked to Mother, sat holding her hand while she cried. He had thin silvery hair combed straight back, his cheeks drooped in jowls that he frequently rubbed.

He visited Father at the store. On a day off school I stood forgotten behind a row of shelves, sorting pipe fittings into their bins. They talked, Dr. Lester on a stool, Father pacing behind the counter.

The Sinai Home is a good place, David. There are good people there, nurses and aids who are trained to take care of—

He's a child, Father broke in, angry the way he was all the time. He is seven years old. You don't send a seven-year-old child to a nursing home. How would he understand? We take care of him just fine.

David, I visit your home every week and you know what I see? I see a family that used to be very happy, that has become very unhappy. Rachel is a different—

What do you expect? One day we have twin boys riding their damn bikes around the neighborhood, going to first grade, doing good in school, smart boys, lots of friends. Next day what? One boy is an invalid, brain damage, can't eat, laying in bed all the time, making a mess. And you're worried we are not happy? Of course we are not happy. But we don't send Zach to a nursing home because we are not happy. We take care of him.

I hear laughter from the squad room down the hall. I want to walk out there and yell at them, tell them to give it a rest, that I can't help what is happening to me, that it's none of their business anyway. I can hear their voices but not the words. Even Nan is laughing at me. I'll go out there, speak to them. They need to see, understand that I'm okay.

I stand and quietly open the door, listening down the dark hallway. There are empty sleeping cubicles to either side. They are playing a game, a boardgame or something.

No, don't do it, they're not talking about you. You'll just make it worse. I sit back down but I know, I know they're laughing at me. I hate them for it.

You went back to the hospital. You became feverish, began vomiting even the tube feedings, some kind of infection. But for a few days I had our room to myself. I almost got rid of the smell, Mother took me to a movie, and the twisting creature in the twilight, rustling the sheets as I tried to sleep, was not there, only a lovely silence, stillness. That was when I cried, that was when I remembered my best friend Zach, my playmate and block-cruising partner. I remembered the Toppers and Subbers, your wild ideas and endless games. That Zach had died, that Zach whom I happily followed from morning until bed, without whom I had never imagined my life, that Zach had died and left me. That quiet bedroom suddenly became a very lonely room.

Sitting here, thinking of it, I find myself crying now, too. I cry for a long time, feeling helpless and pathetic, watching the door.

Velma, the name comes to me, she was a nurse or an aid or something. Older than Mother, skinny and mean, Dr. Lester had sent her to help out with you. Not her, he wouldn't have sent her, but he must have called an agency to send someone. Velma who smoked all day long, who lit each cigarette from the ugly lipsticked stub of the one before, smelled of burnt tobacco from the moment she walked in, and left the house smelling of it when she left. Mother couldn't ask her to smoke outside, too polite or too intimidated. This was 1968, times were different, and Mother a foreigner, an immigrant, never sure what was polite, appropriate.

Just keep away now, you, I remember that hoarse voice saying, just keep away and lemme take care a your brother. I can't do for him with you underfoot. She'd turn up the country music on the radio in our room and bathe you and change your bed, rolling you around like a side of meat, your head flopping and arms flailing, thumping the wall or nearly coming off the bed. Her stained uniform would have suited a truck-stop waitress just as well.

Please, you must be more gentle with him, Mother said to her once.

Velma eyed her, squinting in her cigarette smoke, bathing Zach in the tub. It don't make no difference to him, she said, he don't know no different, this boy.

Mother gazed at her, her mouth working, searching for the right English. He does feel things, she said, you can't tell me he doesn't.

Well, maybe I cain't tell you he don't but it's fact.

Mother turned away, mumbling in the old language.

Sometime later, perhaps a month, we sat in our room, Mother on your bed reading to us.

You're wasting your time, reading to that boy, Velma said, walking into the room. Ain'tcha figured that out by now?

The doctor said it's good for him.

Velma leaned over, looking down at the book, and laughed that mean laugh of hers. Good for him, that's a laugh. Good for you, maybe, but it don't do nothing for him.

Mother's voice grew small. The doctor said it will help him get better.

Velma coughed her raw cough, shaking her head. Get better, he ain't gettin' no better. He's got brain damage, that boy does. He ain't gettin' no better.

She started to walk away when Mother, moving fast as a cat, spun her around and slapped her hard, yelling, probably cursing, in Latvian, pointing her down the stairs and pushing her toward them.

I scrambled to pick up the fallen cigarette but Velma's stained claws beat me to it, and then she was gone, cursing, down the stairs.

Mother cried for a few minutes, standing looking down the stairs, her hands to her face. Then after the door had slammed, after that witch was gone, she turned and looked around our bedroom, at you and at me, and then she opened the window wide and turned laughing to us, a carefree powerful laugh. I don't recall her laughing like that any other time.

The tone once more, loud, as if it were in my head. It's late, I've been here a long time.

Nan's head in the door. "We're outta here, Leon. You comin'? It's twenty after eight. Did you fall asleep or something?"

"Yeah, I guess I did. You go ahead. I'm gonna head home. Thanks for taking me along today. You guys are doing a hell of a job."

"Right, see ya round. Get some sleep, Leon, I think you need it." And she is gone.

Right, sleep, I wish that were all it was, all I need, just sleep. Okay, so now what? You told Rita you'd come over. But what about Fitz? When are you going to go back to him? You could go now and get it over with. And then what, go have a lighthearted evening with Rita? Right. It's not even dark out. Maybe just go home for a while and then back to Muni around midnight, after the nurses change shift at eleven.

I feel the dull ache of fear inside me, fear of sneaking around the hospital, of taking someone's life. But most of all, I see now, it is the fear of doing the wrong thing for Fitz. Why do I have to do this, why do I have to be the one?

I haven't moved. I should call Rita, decide what to do. What if I tell her, what if it slips out. I can't tell her. No matter what, I can't tell her. That's the one thing. I don't know her that well. Maybe it would be better just to go home.

But it's not the wrong thing, it's so obviously the right thing. You saw how Fitz looked today. Someone, Taft, should have done it days ago. Well, maybe a day or two, at least he got to make peace with his sister. I should feel glad that I can help him like this, do the final doctor thing for him, the final relief of suffering.

God, pick up the phone. I dial Rita's number.

"Leon, it's you," Britnie says, excited, then yells, "RITA, IT'S HIM. God, Leon, you're making her nuts," she jabbers on. "She's acting like a teenager waiting for you to call, a teenager with a wine bottle anyway. God, Leon, you've got to get her to stop drinking. When are you coming over? I got a new CD. Actually it's an old CD, or an old group anyway. They're called the Supremes, this black women's group. They're really hot. Did you ever hear of them? On the picture on the front they're all dressed up—"

There is a click. "Leon, where are you?" Rita says.

"Oops," Britnie says, "gotta go. Are you coming over?"

"I'm not sure, sweetheart. Why don't you let me talk to Rita."

"You're not coming?" Rita says quietly. "I thought you were. I thought we'd be together tonight."

"I know, I did, too." I don't know what to say. I keep seeing Fitz lying in his bed. "It's been a bad day. I've got to go back and see Fitz again tonight."

"Tonight? Didn't you get to see him? Were you too busy?"

"No, well, I did but he was asleep. It's hard to explain, Rita. I just have to go back over there later tonight." I hear myself breathing. "I think I need a couple hours to myself, Rita."

"You're not okay, are you?" she says. "Maybe you shouldn't be alone, Leon. What if I just come and meet you at your place and we can just sit and talk if you want. Besides," she laughs, "I'm a little sore after last night."

Last night, when was last night, and what did we do?

"Please, Leon," she says. "You shouldn't be alone when you feel like this. We could go for a walk. Or a swim, how about a swim? I know some people who are away and they let me use their pool whenever I want. There wouldn't be anyone else there. It's really a nice pool."

I agree to come by and pick her up and go for a swim. I don't want to be alone with the stew of my mind. It frightens me. But no matter what I'm not going to tell her about Fitz.

I gather the half dozen reports I've pulled with deficiencies, all of them minor, and place them in the captain's box for review. How can you be hard on these guys, Nan, the Thud, and the other paramedics stationed here? They're on the same pay scale as the rest of the city workers, trash collectors, sewage department guys. What a comparison. They're out saving lives, making life or death decisions daily, putting themselves in danger, and what do we pay them, the same as some guy who rides around on the back of a garbage truck. Oh, well, nothing new here, it's the same with the police, the same with the nurses at Muni.

Going down the stairs, red jacket in hand, I remember the bottles in the pocket, the bottles of poison. I fumble for them but no one is about, just the lone soul in the glass office downstairs, bored, feet up, reading.

I mumble an awkward goodbye, the glass vials hot in my hand, my eyes on his. Does he know, does his casual glance down mean anything, did he see them, the weapons in my hand? Why was Dr. Mendel carrying a couple bottles of medicine in his hand? Will he ask Nan and will she search the extra kits to see if I've stolen the morphine or the Valium?

* * *

"YOU AND LEON ARE GOING SWIMMING AND I CAN'T COME?" Britnie shrieks.

"You don't know how to swim," I say, pawing through my drawers for a swimsuit. Do I even have one?

"So what! I never get to go swimming. Why don't you take ME swimming sometime!" She is very upset.

"Listen to me for a minute, Britnie. Leon is going through some very difficult times right now. He's having an emotional crisis and he needs—"

"It didn't sound like he was having a crisis last night when you guys were fucking all night." She covers her mouth and starts to giggle.

I stare at her. What do I say? "Well, I suppose..." Now I start to laugh with her. "So you could hear us?"

"Mm, hmm," she nods behind her hand, eyes wide.

"Okay, well, you're growing up, and you know what? Leon's the first man I've been to bed with since my divorce three years ago. And he might be the first man I've ever really loved." So what, why am I saying this to her? "So if you heard us fucking, as you put it, then...then you heard two loving adults making love. And maybe that's not such a bad thing. Making love is a wonderful thing if you're with the right person."

"Okay, okay," she says, "but I want to go swimming with you guys."

"Do you have a swimsuit?"

Now she looks close to tears. I move to hug her. "Britnie, here's a promise. Tomorrow, you and I will go to the store and find you a nice swimsuit, and then we'll go to the pool, the Lerner's pool. They said I can use it whenever I want. Besides I have to water their plants. And we'll spend the afternoon. Maybe work on teaching you to swim. It's really easy once you get the hang of it."

"What about Leon?"

"Well, maybe he can come, too, if he's not busy. That would be fun, wouldn't it?"

"What about his emotional crisis?" Now she looks impish, about to giggle again.

"I don't know. Maybe two pretty girls in new swimsuits will help him get over it."

The doorbell chimes. Damn, it's him. I need some mouthwash. "Will you answer it, please? I'll be down in a minute."

But she has already vanished. She's crazy about Leon. I think he's the first man who ever spoke to her like a person.

I fumble with the Listerine, nasty stuff. I wanted another cigarette before he arrived. I thought he'd be longer. And I've had way too much wine. I hope he can't tell. I'll bring some along. That'll be nice in the pool. Maybe help him relax. I don't have a suit. I guess I'll be naked. God, I can't wait. I hope he's not too depressed. I might attack him. Grab a towel anyway, two towels.

Okay, down the stairs, easy light step. Don't walk like a drunk. Britnie stands close to him, blushing, chattering.

He smiles, a distracted smile. His eyes are sunken, dark. Is he sick? Hold your breath, kiss him.

I separate him from Britnie and we escape into the muggy evening. In his car I give him a real kiss. Do I smell okay? I'm sure I don't, but he kisses back. I love his chin.

"Well, how were the mean streets of Cincinnati today?"

"Mainly they were hot, too hot." He is tired, struggling to be cheerful. "Sorry I'm so late. It was a busy day."

"No problem, you were probably saving some poor soul's life, right?"

"Just watching," he says slowly, thinking about each word. "But they did defibrillate one guy. Saved his life. So where's this pool? I don't have a suit."

"Me neither," I giggle again and rub his thigh. God, I'm acting like a teenager in heat. "I don't think I've been swimming in a couple years and I have no idea where my swimsuit is. Warren probably took it and throws darts at it. He was weird about sex, and he was so damn jealous about me."

I point us toward Avondale. "You're gonna love this house, Leon, and the pool is sort of nestled into this little grove of trees. I'm supposed to be housesitting for them while they're off in Spain or Taiwan or someplace. I mean...Does that sound stupid? I mean Taiwan is over by China or Singapore, isn't it?"

Leon's eyes wander anxiously. Now he glances at me and nods. "Near China," he says.

"Spain or Taiwan," I babble on. "It does sound stupid. So, I think they went to Spain, or Europe anyway."

"You're supposed to be housesitting?"

"Well, I am, really. I mean they want me to come by every day and diddle around with the plants and bring in the mail and stuff. I don't quite make it every day though."

He is lost in thought, eyes roving. He always looks like he's watching out for something. "What are you looking for?"

"What?"

"You look like you're looking for something."

He shrugs and shakes his head. "I don't know."

It's a tall, beautiful old house with huge trees all around. Must be nice to be rich. I unlock the door and switch off the alarm. "It's always so quiet here, compared with the city. Don't you think it's quiet?"

Leon stands peering inside. Is he afraid? "Well, come on in," I say. "I'll turn on some lights."

Wrapped in towels we creep across the back yard, a twisty path through shrubs and under trees, like walking into some tiny ancient forest.

"Are you okay, Leon?" He is hanging back, in the light.

"I'm having trouble with darkness these days. I don't know why."

I go back and take his hand. "C'mon, it's just their back yard. There's no one here besides us."

He lets me pull him along. There is a light in the little pool that bounces off the tree trunks around us. Branches hang down over the water.

We slide naked into the water. God, this is so sexy. I move close to him. I've got to touch him.

"So, how are you feeling?"

"I'm okay," he says too quickly.

"What did Britnie have to say?" Try to keep it light for a while.

"Oh, not much, something about a new CD you got her. The Supremes, she said."

"I always loved the Supremes. I thought she might like it. Do you remember that greatest hits album with a deep blue cover?"

He nods with a slow smile. "She asked me if I'd ever heard of them."

"I know. Well, she's just a kid and she's led a pretty weird life so far, pretty isolated in a lot of ways."

He nods again, holding me, but he is restless and far away.

"What can I do for you, Leon?"

He breathes slowly. “I don’t know. Nothing, everything, something, help me restart my brain, reinitialize my hard drive or something. I need Norton Utilities for my mind.”

Now he touches me, strokes my hips. “All I could do today was think about Zach and remember all about him and me. I couldn’t turn it off. I mean the crew I was with, we went on all these runs, a stabbing, and a guy who went into v-fib, and a shooting, for God’s sake. A real shooting at the projects with angry people running around and cops and the whole bit. And all I could do was keep thinking about Zach and the way he used to lay in his bed and how he got worse and worse and finally—”

Now he shivers, pushing away from me and moving into the water. He ducks under the surface and glides across the pool. Zach, why is he so fixed on Zach? What happened with Zach? They were seven years old.

Now he comes back to me, walking in the waist-deep water, a slim shadow.

“What finally happened to Zach, Leon? Do you remember?”

He is breathing hard and as he turns his face back to the light I see that he is crying. He lets me hold him, unable to speak, shaking his head slowly.

Finally, in a hoarse whisper, he says, “He died.”

“I know that. You’ve told me. But how did he die, I mean finally?” Will he hate me for this? Will he get angry again?

His face hardens again as the tears stop. “I’ve got to go,” he says. “I’ve got to go back to the hospital and see Fitz.”

“How did Zach die, Leon? Do you remember?” This is where he needs to go, isn’t it?

“I don’t want to talk about it,” he says, almost in a mumble, then louder, “I can’t talk about it. I...I can’t remember that!”

He is silent, restless in my arms. Damn, it’s not going to happen, is it? We’re not going to make love in this romantic place. He’s going to leave, and me like a cat in heat.

“Won’t Fitz be asleep?” I say. “You said all he does is sleep all the time.”

“I know. But I have to go anyway. I’m sorry, Rita. I’ll come back, if you want. I’ll come back and spend the night with you.” He climbs out of the water.

“Can’t you just go in the morning?”

“He’s dying.”

He’s dying. I know that, too. So if he’s dying what good...the only thing you could do for him...the only thing...oh, now it comes to me, now I see. You would know how to do it, wouldn’t you.

“Okay,” I say finally. “Okay, maybe I could...maybe do you want me to come with you, Leon? Maybe you need someone with you, maybe you need me with you." Please let me come, Leon. Let me help you do that. You shouldn't have to do it alone.

We stand toweling ourselves dry.

"No, I'll just go by myself," he says. His voice is flat, distant, the voice he might use to tell a patient something awful.

"Please, Leon." I move to him, touch the damp hair on his chest. "Let me help you." Is it because I've been drinking? Is that it?

He stops my hand and holds it, looking off into the dark. "No, Rita, I have to go back there alone. I'm sorry."

Chapter Sixteen

You're darn tootin', I like Fig Newtons, Zach is singing in my head. Give it a rest, brother, can't you just give it a rest. I repeat it to Rita sitting by me in the car. "Do you remember that jingle? I hear Zach singing stupid commercials, in my head."

She sits smoking, very quiet. "Leon, maybe I understand you better than you think, or what you're going through. Why don't you let me come with you. I can help you."

"I know," I say, "but I can't. If you really understand me..." I pause. Then what? I don't like even talking about it. I just have to go do it. "I'll come back. If you want to help me then let me come back here and be with you." I stop in front of her house.

She flicks the cigarette butt out the window then turns to me. Her expression moves quickly to laughter. "Britnie heard us last night."

Heard us what? Oh. "We can go back to my place."

"No, no, it's fine, it's okay. We can close the other door in the hall. She's heard it before. I mean not from me but from her foster homes." She takes my hands, then becomes still in the dark. "Be careful." She kisses me and steps out.

The drive to Muni, windows open, streetlights on, headlights, stoplights. And in between darkness. Is death out here, in the dark? There are people still out, music thumping from open tavern doors, from boomboxes, folks sitting on front steps, shouts, laughter. Death, where are you? C'mon, death, c'mon out and show yourself. Again, let me see you again. I've seen you a lot lately, held you in my hands, felt you flow red across my fingers, slid shut your eyelids. So c'mon, my windows are open, slide in here with me if you're out here.

"Leon," comes a yell, "hey, Leon, my man." No, not me, someone else, Jean or John or Ron or Tom, some other name.

Something, a kid on a bike, there, in front of me. Hard brakes, shit, tires screeching on dry pavement, slamming to a stop, eyes closed waiting for the crunch, the thump of his body against my bumper. But it doesn't come. Another screech from behind, the car following, but now in front nothing, nobody, no boy, no bike.

"WHAT THE FUCK ARE YOU DOIN'!" comes from the driver behind.

I stare at empty pavement, no bike, no kid. Great, just great. I start moving again. There was a kid there, on a bike, rode out from behind that damn car. My pulse is pounding as the fear subsides.

People stare at me, see me driving by, see my face in the car. There's that crazy doctor from Muni Emergency, you know the one? Look at him driving 'round here, screechin' his brakes. What's he doin'?

I hope Fitz is asleep. The thought of him makes my adrenaline start again, squeezes me deep inside. What if he's awake? What will you say to him? It's midnight, he won't be awake.

You can't do it, you can't do it, Jasmine's husky voice comes to me.

Fuck you, Jas. Where should I park? What if someone sees the car? Should I try to park far away and walk? What if someone sees me, some resident walking home, some nurse waiting to catch her bus? No, the doctor's lot, the usual spot.

What door should I go in? No, no, wrong attitude. I'm going to visit my friend who's sick, big deal. It's late, but so what? Us ER docs, we keep weird hours.

Suddenly, again, I want to cry. Why do I have to do this, why do I have to live this day, this night, wouldn't someone else like to live it for me, trade me lives for a night, take a shot at mine, just for a challenge maybe. I'd even pay someone to trade. Course whose life would I get in return, probably Fletcher or Peter. Imagine sleeping the night in his head, imagine his dreams, probably all baseball or something painfully dull. Dull wouldn't be so bad right now.

The physician's parking is quiet, dark, a scattering of cars.

I sit for a moment in the silence, the hum of the hospital, the city, voices around a corner. Did Zach know all along, within that head, within that mind? Was he aware of us, of himself? Now in the dark I see him, his eyes staring off to the side. Mother even had Father move his bed by the window so those eyes could stare outside, those constant twin beams of what? Blindness, nothingness? Could he see anything, did anything register inside that head?

When I read to him I held the pictures up for those eyes, up to meet that slanting gaze, pictures of Flash and Green Lantern, of Sinbad and Robinson Crusoe. For a long time I thought he would get better, thought that brain would heal and one day something would indeed go click and that pair of eyes would light up and swing round and those lips smile and that mouth make words, or at least sounds. Maybe we'd have to teach him to make words again. And that face would come alive once more, that face that could have been his elbow or his navel, for all the emotion it ever showed.

Enough. I step out and walk toward the door. Damn, there's someone, who is that, a housekeeper, I think.

"Wa's happenin', Doc?" a flash of teeth, off work, feeling good.

"Hey," I nod to him.

Slip inside, an empty hallway, act casual. Leon, Leon, there are whispers behind me. No, no one there. I hear voices from the E.D. round the corner.

To the locker room, also empty. Find some scrubs, put them on.

What if Fitz is awake, seriously, what will you do? Tell him you're going to do it? Talk to him, talk to him as his heart stops and his consciousness fades?

I go through the automatic movements of changing clothes, putting on the scrubs. My mouth is dry, my blood pounding, and now, just now, I feel very scared.

Wombi, wombi, wombi, Zach is shouting at me, something incomprehensible.

I find my white coat, transfer the glass vials. A syringe, I need a syringe. Shit, I didn't think of that, a couple syringes really. I can't walk out into the department. I sit for a moment on the bench in this silent place. Right, nothing is silent anymore. Syringes, why didn't I grab a couple in the med room, stupid, stupid. I'm breathing hard. Why? I'm scared.

All right, calm down, be cool, you'll find a syringe up on the floor, on a med cart or something. Now get out of here, what if someone walks in, what will you tell them?

If I had my street clothes on I could just say I came to see Fitz, tell the truth even. I could walk right through the department and tell them I came to see my friend, even walk into the med room to get some aspirin, and pocket a couple syringes, like I should have done before. I could do it again. All right, so do it.

I change back quickly, into my pants and shirt, could have even put them on over the scrubs, if I'd thought of it. Oh, well.

Okay, stand up, leave the scrubs, walk out there.

Into the mayhem, it doesn't look too bad, nurses moving about, Ruby at the desk, her back to me. At least Peter should be gone, it's night shift now. I don't need him seeing me here at odd hours, wondering, monitoring me. There's Lyle Cassidy, talking with an elderly man, a husband or a father, and there's Josh Mendenhal.

Into the med room again, no one there. Whispers behind me from the Pixis machines, ignore them, the narcotics calling me, right, the morphine, the Valium. I could use a Valium myself right about now. The rack of syringes, grab a couple, please no one see this, put them in a pocket, quickly, good, now the aspirin, now a cup of water from the sink. Turn and go out intothe station, let people see you swallow the aspirin.

"Dr. Mendel, you been out cattin' around?" Ruby says to me. "It's past midnight."

I walk over to her. "Just can't get enough, Ruby. So many women and so little time."

She laughs her carefree laugh, like cool water to my mind. “That’s a dangerous hobby these days.”

“No kidding. No, I was riding with my medic crew. Today was my observer day. Just wanted to get a couple aspirin.” I toss the paper cup at the trashcan. “How’s the night shaping up?”

We talk for a moment and then I leave. I don’t want to talk to Cassidy or Mendenhal or anyone else. Lyle sees me and waves as I walk out. I return the wave and pretend not to notice his questioning look.

Back to the locker room, now back on with the scrubs. Do you need to? Yes, what if one of the nurses upstairs sees you in street clothes. In the scrubs you can be right out front, they won’t wonder what you’re doing. There are always residents wandering by, and the E.D. docs show up any time, coming back from a code on the floor somewhere, intubating somebody if anesthesia is tied up.

Or just tell them you’re going to visit Fitz. In the middle of the night? They know he’s gay. Well, fuck’em, I don’t care what they think about me. By morning it won’t matter, by morning Fitz will be gone, just a cold body in a bag in the morgue.

The thought makes me pause, sad, scared, not at the risk to me but at the death swirling around me, following me, invading me. I gaze at the shadows of the locker room, the rows of dark empty boxes of death, hungry death eyeing me from the vent slots in the doors.

Okay, scrubs and white coat, clothes in your locker, now get out of here. What if Mendenhall or somebody walks in? You’re not working tonight, it will look very strange. I touch the bottles of death in my coat pocket.

Now where, up the stairs, not the elevator, the elevators come out next to the nurses station. You could ride to the floor below and then walk, no, then the nurses on that floor will see you. Just walk up the stairs, the north stairs, they come out near Fitz’s room.

Past the dark gift shop with its flowers and little knit doodads in the window, made by the volunteers.

Fitz, I can’t believe I didn’t see him for so long, three years since the wedding. Jasmine didn’t like him, maybe felt threatened, a former lover and all, different sex. I could have talked to him at least, phoned him, kept in touch.

I watch the stairs pass under my feet. He used to be a Buddhist, wonder if he still is. I haven’t asked him. He used to talk about following the Middle Way. As a Buddhist he’ll be reborn, or he must think that. I should have asked him, now I’ll never be able to. Never be able to, death again, tearing another piece from my life, tearing away at my life until I’m left standing on a jagged scrap of it, Fitz’s own scrap drifting like a withered leaf into the dark.

Buddhism, religion, I never even think of it. Does Fitz? Has he been contemplating his death? Doesn't each life grow upon the last in Buddhism, gain in wisdom and compassion? This is when push comes to shove for your religion, when you die. Will he be reborn, somewhere, as someone, the same soul? It would be nice to believe that.

Six years since we were together, since we held each other, kissed, touched, slept in each other's arms. Three years since we last talked. But he didn't care, it could have been three days. And I didn't care either, don't care.

There are footsteps above, coming down the stairs toward me, legs turn a corner, in pale green anesthesia scrubs, ghostly green, and a white coat. I glance up at the face before it turns to me, but I see no eyes. I see a skull's empty holes in a live face. I look down before it looks at me.

"Hi, Leon," it says, pausing.

"How ya doin'." I don't know who it is and I can't look at it again so I keep going as if in a hurry, in deep thought, preoccupied.

Another flight up and I glance back, but it's gone.

Talk to him, Dr. Lester had said, like nothing is wrong. It's good to talk to him. So I did, I talked to you, to the memory of you, to the hidden part of your mind I hoped was still there, that could hear and understand but couldn't reveal itself, in the illusion that somewhere in there you remained, locked inside a body that wouldn't let you out.

But I hated that body, Zach, that skin and bone creature that lived in my room. And I hated it most at night, its wet nasal breathing, every night, all night. So that when Mother turned out the light and walked down the hall, I was left with one sound. Not the quiet of the house, the murmur of them downstairs talking or watching TV, not the outside sounds of the dark neighborhood, the occasional car, people walking. One sound I was left with, the sound of that thing's breathing, trapped with the sound of the mucous in its throat, in the throat that you would never clear.

I hated it, and now I feel that hate in memories I have never before remembered, memories like the pictures of an old book I have never before opened, memories of ugly, angry feelings. You abandoned me in that neighborhood where I needed a friend, needed a best friend to be brave with, to explore with, to chase, and to follow. And in that family where I needed a brother to answer my confidences, to whisper secrets to, to hide with and giggle with.

Okay, sixth floor, now through the door, quick, casual, like you're supposed to be here. Quietly, look around, no one, just a somber hall, barely lit, a half dozen dark open doorways. And one shut, Fitz's. The nurses shut the doors of dying patients. Quietly, don't wake him, now close the heavy door, with its precise metal clicks.

The room is lit by the TV, the sound off. I pause inside the door, he can't be up. No, he is slumped to the side again, asleep, chest rising and falling, even asleep he breathes hard. He seems to frown, as if worried, his oxygen tube askew.

In the cold white light he looks so gaunt, a statue of what, not just death but something else horrible, not just a statue of AIDS but something more personal, not marble but plaster perhaps, or concrete, the skull outlined in its skin, dusted with white whiskers, his hair so thin, scalp gleaming, flickering in the light from the screen. Death by the light of a TV, at least the sound is off.

Again thoughts come, thoughts of you in such a way, more memory unremembered until now, vivid and shiny, of skinny arms and slack skin, as if draped over bare bone. Skin and bones, yes, Zach, you were skin and bones. Dying all that time, I see now. And I knew it, I see that now as well, I knew in my child's mind somewhere amidst the simple anger and fears. You were dying.

I switch off the TV and feel for the lamp on the bedside table. There is a glow from the window, the city sky outside. I stop my hand, there is enough light.

Poor Fitz, I want to sit with you, touch your shoulder, reassure you, tell you something. What? Tell you you'll be better, you'll go somewhere better, somewhere you can relax and breathe easy, somewhere you can stop this struggle, this losing struggle. Heaven, Nirvana, I don't know, but somewhere where you can be calm, where you can smile that slow rueful smile and laugh that confident laugh again.

And I want to tell you that I love you, that someone here loves you, loved you all along, never stopped loving you. Maybe not your mother who died, or your father who ignored you, and then banished you. Maybe they didn't love you or weren't there to love you. Or the wife you never had, or the lovers who came and went. But I did, Fitz, I did, and I do still, and I always will.

I watch the sad skeleton of his person through tears now. I feel my own breath. And now, again, I feel it, death crowding around me, as if a dozen dark-cloaked figures have shuffled close to watch, silent invisible eyes watching my hands, eyeing my pocket. I turn toward them, toward the darkness of the room, and they shuffle back into shadow. They will return the instant I look away, they know that, I know that.

I need to do this. What if a nurse comes. I want to stand and gaze at Fitz, remember him, think of him. But I can't. If you're going to do it, Leon, do it.

I find a syringe in my pocket, give a silent twist to the top of the container, let it fall with its familiar touch into my palm. Now the Inderal bottle, I hold it to the faint light to be sure, the Inderal first, not the digoxin, make his heart stop, not fibrillate. I hope I won't need the digoxin.

The dark ghosts around me jostle for position, I feel them at my elbows, crowding close.

Were they there then, in that children's room, that place unaccustomed to death, gathered round your bed that night, child-ghosts sitting cross-legged on the floor, watching you sleep, knowing I was awake? More and more of it rushes into my mind.

The metal cap flips off the bottle, falls to the floor with its tiny clatter. Stop, find it, don't leave it, there it is, pick it up. The needle cover pops off, save it, don't drop it. The needle gleams, a slim lance in my hand, it slides through the rubber stopper, into the clear poison, like water, inside.

His breath rasps in and out, the only sound now. As the clear fluid squirts in its tiny stream into the barrel of the syringe I glance down again, the breathing body, the mind unaware of me inches away. Think of what I am destroying, this subtle intellect, the years of knowledge accumulated here, of wisdom. Fitz was wise in his way, wise about people and love, wise about hurt and shame.

Doubt paralyzes me suddenly. Are you doing this because you're crazy, Leon? Have you twisted this around somehow into a justified act, and now, the culmination of your psychosis, the true confirmation of your psychosis, you're going to kill someone?

So far you've just been acting a little weird, talking too loud, jumping at baseball mitts, but this, this is the real thing. Would you do this, have done this, a month ago? This is the real thing, this could land you in jail, or in a bed at Southern State Hospital with some Arab psychiatrist asking you about your mother, this could lose you your license and—

Just do it, man, I feel the ghosts urging me on, nudging my elbows. Just do it for Fitz before some nurse comes in here and you lose your chance.

My hand finds the IV tubing, slides along it to the medicine port, now the needle, the other hand shakes as I try to bring the point to the little rubber stopper with its circle in the middle. There, okay, slide it through, into the stream of fluid flowing into Fitz's arm. Thank God he's got an IV.

Fear seems to rise around me, inside me, all through me. This is something I have never done, something I never thought—

Do it, man, stop thinking and just do it! I push the plunger and feel the steady stream of fluid flow into the tubing, do it fast, give it to him all at once. Don't anyone walk in now, not at this moment, this one moment I could never explain away. I listen for the silence around us, outside the room, Fitz's rapid breathing the only sound, my own heart the only sound.

Okay, it's done, stop, relax your hand. It's done, it's in, cap the needle, put it back in your pocket. My hands tremble too much to cap the needle. I turn and drop it into the sharps box on the wall. Turn again, back to the bed, and feel the dark ghosts scramble to avoid me, the room full of them.

I look down at Fitz and feel myself swirling in a vortex, a whirlpool of fear and death and horror at what I've done. I recall suddenly a mother brought in to the E.D. by police one night, who had just shot her two-year-old daughter, the woman a schizophrenic, gripped by a horrible delusion, a horrible hallucination that the child was a monster controlling her mind. The woman had come in before, trying to get help, living the urban nightmare of ignorance, poverty, drug addiction, mental illness and nowhere to turn. She had phoned many times, the E.D., the Crisis Line, 911. She had tried to open a crack in the iron wall of overcrowded social service agencies to get help. But there was no help for her, no real help that would listen and reach out and grab her and stop her. And the fear had grown and the confusion had spread through her mind. Until she had done it, had found a gun somewhere, borrowed it, stolen it, and shot her own child. And now I see her sitting on a gurney in handcuffs, rocking, moaning.

A whirlpool with Fitz at its center, and the doctor in me watches his chest and his muscle tone and his closed eyes. How much time has passed? Seconds, ten, twenty, while the molecules of poison flow silently with his diseased blood back to his heart and into it and swirl through it and rush back out, stroke after stroke, squirting down his coronary arteries and into the tiny channels feeding his myocardium, into the microscopic maze of capillaries, one thread of a tubule to each muscle cell, and click on to the receptors there to slow that cell, slow it to a stop, and then the next cell stops and the next, until the muscle filament itself stops, and the next and the next, a thousand times, a million times—

There is a catch in Fitz's breathing, a faltering of the rhythm, then a breath, and again. God, Fitz, please don't wake up, please don't open those eyes. Then it stops, the motion of his chest, the sigh of air moving in and out. I wait, feeling myself tremble, feeling the silent roar of death around me. Here is a heart that for thirty-some years has never stopped. Here are miles and miles of capillaries through which blood has always moved, red cells have always tumbled. And here is a brain that has never been without the oxygen and glucose for which it will now starve, now, right now, this second, this minute and the next and the next, the furious commotion inside this still head as its billions of ordered synapses swell, burst, and die. And with them the feelings, the thoughts and memories, the accumulation of thirty-some years of life, of childhood and love and warmth and humor, the subtle tracings of people and feelings, of voices and moods, laughter, anger, orgasms, moments of love and moments of sorrow, all of it, all of it dying now in front of me.

Fitz is silent, still, still as sleep, still as a rock, still as only one thing in this world is still, death. Where is your soul, Fitz, in that mask of skin and muscle over dead eyes, dead bone and nerves? I haven't heard it, felt it. Fitz, where is it, where are you? You need to leave now, leave this flesh that couldn't keep you alive, and go off like the others. I listen to silence now, total silence from this person turned corpse, silence louder than the whispers, louder than the voices have ever been. Fitz, where are you? Damn, don't just die, don't just let it go. Where is your soul, Fitz, I want to shout. I reach for his hand, already cool, already limp. Dead. I drop it and want to scream.

I bump the chair, moving backward. It's done. He's dead. I've done it, murdered Fitz, murdered my friend, my lover. I've committed a mercy killing, a true mercy killing, not just let someone go, stopped trying, let nature take its course. No, this time more than that, this time I speeded it up, pushed it along, reached down that dark tunnel and grabbed the black ghost there and pulled it, jerked it up the tunnel, hearing its laughter at my torment, at the silly anguish we humans put ourselves through when we speed up the inevitable, hearing its cackling at the posturing and arbitrary rules we place upon ourselves when in the end, in the end...

Okay, get real, Leon, for a minute. I glance about for anything I might have dropped, the litter of murder, then pop open the other syringe from my pocket, and drop it in the sharps box as well. The bottles will go where? Somewhere far away from here, somewhere like the river or a neighbor's trash, no, not even that, maybe the ED trash cans, which receive all manner of weird shit, each bottle in a separate one. What if someone sees you? Fuck it, you can get rid of the stuff. Stop agonizing.

I look again at Fitz, look again at the bony figure in the bed, and again memory rushes up in front of me, rises and bursts like a wave I forgot was coming, of your skin-and-bones body in the bed, Zach, the infuriating sound of your breathing, the rage of that little boy that was me, night on night, that trapped little boy who knew he might just as well have been strapped to the bed as the dark empty hours dragged by, strapped to his bed in that closed-windowed room with you, that sick mucous-breathing thing in the other bed.

I retreat to a corner of the silent room, the somber ghosts opening a path. Past the chair where I could sit, past the sink, to the corner where I squat, the walls firm behind me, the room dark now, very dark and still and silent, the bedclothes tented over the corpse of my friend.

I hated you, Zach, and hated you and hated you. I thought of ways of killing you, childish ways of killing you, pouring turpentine into your feeding tube, or lighter fluid and then holding a match to the end of the tube. I imagined an explosion in your belly and guts all over the walls, whatever guts were. I didn't really know.

But that was murder, wasn't it? A crime, I'd go to jail. Did kids go to jail? I didn't know.

Fear, hatred, something, clenches my teeth so that my jaws ache, digs my nails into my palms, makes me sweat and shiver at the same time. Where am I going?

Or stuffing clay into your mouth to choke you. But they would find out. A string around your neck, pulled tight, but I didn't think I could pull tight enough. I watched TV carefully then, watched how people killed each other. I noted who went to jail and why, on TV, in the newspapers, who was punished, and how they got caught.

I was a vicious, desperate, and wicked child, malevolent and scheming. I hated myself then almost as much as I hated you. I avoided the rabbi's gaze, remained silent and guilty at the synagogue, dreaded Sabbath services, dreaded the sanctuary where there were not just my parents and the rabbi but God, too, God who read my evil thoughts, who knew the terrible plot I hoped to hatch.

And then the end of it all, the climax of it all, the forgotten memory I know is there, waiting darkest and most malevolent, the final night when I lay hating you, the only consciousness in the dark room, in that silent house the only mind awake, perhaps in the whole neighborhood, the whole community of dark homes and sleeping people, I alone was awake.

I alone heard you retch and vomit in your sleep, heard you cough and gag, gasp and gasp again. I alone heard your struggle in the dark, your sleeping struggle, although asleep or awake the world was much the same for you. Wasn't it, Zach, wasn't it the same blank wall, the same empty unconsciousness? I hope it was.

I alone heard the ugly throat sounds of vomit in your lungs, of your brief struggle to live, to keep what remained alive of you alive still. Such a brief struggle it was. And my horror at how easy it was, at how close death apparently lurked, at the thought of all we had done for you, day after day, at home and in the hospital, and then suddenly in the night, suddenly in only a few seconds all that was destroyed, crumpled like cards, with the suddenness, the ease of a castle of cards falling flat.

Then strangest of all, roaring and snarling at me, frightening me, paralyzing me, silence. Silence so deafening that I covered my ears, silence so laden with screaming significance that I lay trembling. Call out, shout, jump up and get Mother and Father. Zach stopped breathing. ZACH STOPPED BREATHING! But something held me to that bed, something grown up and secret, like a mind within my mind that I never knew was there. It whispered no, lie still, don't move, don't speak, let this happen. The adult in me, or so it seemed, the calm thoughtful adult I had never before encountered, never met but would someday be—would I be that adult someday?—called to the boy of that moment and stopped his cry, his movement. It said let this happen. It said let you die, Zach. Let you die.

And the little boy that was me lay there motionless, silent, scared even to breathe, amidst a hurricane of thought, a gale of fear and guilt and mystery, because he had never seen anyone die before, never heard anyone die before, didn't know what it meant. He had never lain in the dark with a corpse before, a corpse of his own creation. Would police come and pound at the door? Would they know somehow, how could they know, but they always knew on TV. Would they take me away, take me to jail? What will happen to Zach now, that little boy thought. He's still there, lying in the bed. Is he dead? DEAD, the word seemed so odd, such a simple word for all its import.

A floorboard creaked and his eyes flew open and another being moved in the room, a pale form moved across the space from the door to your bed, silent with the liquid unselfconscious grace of an unfettered woman, unfettered by clothes except a simple gown, unfettered by hair let down, by Father who slept, by the knowledge that no one except herself was awake, conscious, watching, listening, in the universe, in her very small universe most of which was in that room at that moment and had suddenly hugely changed.

The graceful silent rush, the tiny cry and catch of her breath, the movement of a live hand grasping a dead one, holding it, feeling instantly the limp ease of its movement, the toneless weight of it, the skin that must have been cold, just a little cold in the few minutes that had passed, yet so cold, colder than anything else she had ever touched.

That ghost stood for a long time, then sat delicately on your bed and gently grasped you, pulled you close, limp and heavy, and held you for another endless moment.

Something wet on my hands, my own tears, there in the corner of Fitz's room. I should do something, what, get up, go downstairs, go home?

She lay you down and arranged your body, as I watched unmoving, afraid to move, eyes open in the dark. She arranged your arms, limp now for the first time in months, covered you, covered your head with the sheet, then moved to her knees by your bed, moved to a position of prayer I had never seen among our people, never seen among Jews.

I wished I could hear her prayer. I wondered at it, wondered at what words she used, at the God she spoke to, and what it knew of me, for it must have known what I did, or did not do, did not jump up and yell for help, did not run and get them when you choked. It must have known that I let you die, that I hated you and wished you were dead, thought for hours and days and weeks about killing you, about how to do it, plotted and planned your death a thousand times, and never with the excuse that, no, I'd never really do it, no, I'm just kidding, musing, wishing, but I'd never really do it. I never said that to myself. I really wanted to kill you. I really wanted you to die, to go away and leave me alone with my childhood.

She didn't know, this ghost, and Father didn't know and you didn't know, did you? But God knew, if there was a God who knew things then he knew about me.

She rose, still graceful and ghostly, rose and touched your face once more through the sheet, then turned away, toward me. My eyes slammed shut, and I lay silent, tense, soundlessly screaming, with the rapid realization of the trap I was in, the trap of my own making, a sudden prison I had made for myself, for how would I know when she had gone, she was so silent. How would I know when those eyes I held shut so tight could relax and open once again.

The smell of her came to me, then her touch on my face, her cheek next to mine. The covers moved as she arranged them, and then silence. Was she gone, could I look now, or was she kneeling by my bed, praying over me as well, praying for what? To the God who had just watched me let you die, who knew I was a murderer, or almost a murderer, having done all the acts a murderer does, save one.

But as I slid open one eye, clumsily slid back the tensed lid of one eye, there was just darkness, emptiness, and the covered corpse of you a few feet from me.

There is movement, the door opening, a nurse coming in. What am I going to do? Not a nurse but a slender tentative woman, Rita. How did she get up here? She glances about the room and doesn't see me, then steps to the bed and looks at Fitz for a long moment. One hand rises to her mouth, and then the other. She steps backward, peering about the darkness once more.

"I'm here," I say.

She doesn't startle, doesn't scream, but turns toward me. "Are you okay?"

I nod, rising. I know what happened, I want to say. I know what happened to Zach.

She reaches for my hand. "He's gone."

I nod again. We stand close for a moment looking at the sad figure in the bed.

"So skinny, Leon. What an awful disease."

I slide the oxygen tubing off Fitz's face and lay the bed flat. Then I straighten his body and arrange his arms, finally covering him with a sheet.

"Should we tell the nurses?" Rita says. "They know I'm here."

I look at her, struggling with the ramifications of her words. "They don't know about me," I say. "Did you tell them...did you say..."

"It's okay, Leon." She takes my hand and pulls me toward the door. "Just walk with me to the elevator. I'll tell them."

In the open doorway she stops, turns again to me, wide-eyed, glancing at my hands. "Did you...was he dead already, I mean when you came?" She stares at me.

I feel as if I am one of those clumsy ghosts, as if her gaze passes through me and never returns to her eyes. I look down at the floor, waiting for her to move.

"Leon?"

My eyes climb back to hers. Am I here, can she see me? "Let's go," I say as if speaking from one dream to another.

We pass the nurses station and Rita stops at the desk. She speaks to the ward clerk there.

"I'll tell the nurse," I hear the bored woman say.

Then the elevator doors glide open and we are gone.

I should feel relief, shouldn't I, and sorrow, and revulsion at the act I have committed, remorse, guilt. But I am numb and speechless and feel none of it.

"I'm sorry, Leon, but I was worried about you. You didn't want me to come, did you?"

"It's okay."

She grips my arm. "It must be the best thing for him that he died, right?" she says, watching my face. "I mean he didn't have any hope for anything else, did he?"

"Not in this life. He was Buddhist," I say, although I'm not sure why. Perhaps I hope there is something to it, some validity to Fitz's hope of reincarnation. Did he hope for it, still believe in it? I never asked him. Perhaps in Labor & Delivery there is a child being born right now that is Fitz, Fitz's soul. Or somewhere else, some nice place I hope.

"So were you with him when he died?" Rita says.

Now I look back at her, her eyes calm, worried. Can I trust her? Trust is not a simple thing, not the black and white it's supposed to be. I nod finally as the elevator stops.

Alone in the locker room there is again the rush of memory, an urgency to replay the images of Zach's death, as my limbs move through the motions of dressing. It is exhausting, as if dressing underwater. I want just to stop and sit, there on the simple bench in the simple barren room, this neutral room with no significance, no symbols of anything, just a space where I can sit and think, sit and remember. But she is waiting out in the hall, where someone might meet her, question her, smell her breath. I am fearful of the corpse I have left upstairs, of the chasm I have blasted in the stone wall of my physician's life.

I push my arms to move against the torpor of the place and emerge to her worried face.

We are almost out the door to the parking lot when I remember the medicine bottles. "Shit, wait a minute." The two glass bottles of Inderal and digoxin lying in the pocket of my white coat, hung in my locker which is locked, but still, so incriminating if anyone were to look, the murder weapon.

"What is it?" Rita says as we stand in the open doorway.

"Here," I nudge her outside into the dark. "Wait out here and smoke a cigarette. I forgot something. If anybody asks just tell them you're here with a patient and just stepped outside to have a smoke."

"Leon, what are you talking about? What did you forget?"

I turn back inside, ignoring her question. Fear grabs my insides like a paralyzing hand. God damn it, what a stupid thing to do. But still no one passes, no one enters the room as my quivering fingers fumble with the lock, then fumble with the bottles, pushing them into my pants pocket.

She takes my hand when I emerge. "Will you come home with me, Leon? You don't want to be alone tonight, do you?"

"Okay, my car's here. I guess I can follow you. Where are you parked?"

"Do you think you should be driving? I mean you look..." She is wide-eyed, uncertain, afraid to say the wrong thing.

I shake my head. "I guess not."

"Why don't we come back and pick it up in the morning?"

I stop, my thoughts tumbling, my car in the lot overnight, people know my car.

"Okay, bad idea," she says, watching me. "So I'll drive us home in your car and we'll come back and get mine in the morning. Will that work?"

I sit as if stunned while she drives. She knows what I've done, doesn't she? I haven't told her, but she knows. She knew before I left her.

"You were very good to Fitz, going to see him so much." She looks sideways at me. "And being with him when he died."

We drive down an empty street, storefronts dimly lit by the occasional streetlight. I stare outside wondering what to say, how to talk. Will I ever be able to talk again?

"He had a wonderful sense of humor," she says. "I mean I remember from when we went over there, to visit him that evening."

The image of Mother kneeling by your bed comes to me again, the feeling of lying there in the dark, feigning sleep, a child horrified, amazed.

"I killed someone once," Rita says.

I look at her in the dark. "What?"

"I killed someone once." Her voice is flat, calm. "A long time ago, or it seems like a long time ago, well, about twenty years, that's a long time."

I watch her, wondering at her words.

She glances at me and gives her quick nervous laugh. "Really I did."

"You killed someone? You mean another person?"

"Mm hmm, he was a horrible person, more like a beast. I've never told anyone about it."

Her words come as if from a tunnel.

"I was twelve years old, if you can imagine that. I mean if you can imagine me at age twelve. I was a smart-mouthed little brat, really skinny. I mean I know I'm pretty thin now but I was like a beanpole then. And talk about naive.

"We lived in North Carolina, Camp Lejeune. Ever heard of it? My father was in the Marines, a career staff sergeant. Which was kind of like being a career bastard, and he was good at it, too. But he was pretty good to us, us kids and Mom, a little rough around the edges maybe.

"He'd always be gone a long time. This was during Vietnam, and then he'd come home and he and Mom would get drunk, you know, they'd kind of go on a binge. I think he needed something to help him wind down, or at least he thought he did. Vietnam was pretty rough on people."

Again I see Mother kneeling at your bed, and the cringing child across the room, those few feet away in the other bed, cringing in guilt at what he did, or didn't do, the accomplice to death. And his surprise at her reaction, or lack of it. Any reaction would have surprised him at that moment of that night.

"—got along better when they were drunk. They'd act like they were having this big welcome-home party. Only it would go on for about three days. And us kids didn't know any better. They'd be happy and take us places, out to eat and stuff like that. There were four of us in this little base housing house, I mean four kids and the two of them, so it was always crowded and noisy and course it was always hot down there.

"I remember standing outside their bedroom door listening to them screwing. Us kids would stand outside and giggle and carry on."

She turns the car into Eden Park, down the hill from her house.

"You want to go sit on Chuck Rock for a while? It's a good place to talk."

She goes on before I answer. "But Mom was the alcoholic. He could stop drinking but she couldn't. So she'd—Oh, Leon, I'm sorry, do you want to hear this?" She touches my hand. "I just go on and on sometimes. I just thought..."

She parks the car, then turns to me. "I just thought it might help you somehow."

I don't know what to say.

"C'mon, let's go up on top of the rock." She climbs out, steps swiftly around the car in her agile way and takes my hand, leading me. "Camille showed it to me a couple years ago. I didn't even know you could climb it 'til she showed me. The kids call it Chuck Rock. I guess the name is from some video game or something. I hope no one's there."

We walk among dark trees by the pond. A ribbon of moonlight across the water follows us. The air is heavy with smells of shrubs and grass, cool, redolent, soothing. It must be three in the morning by now.

"I don't really remember her being drunk except when he was around." She is talking again. "But after they had one of their binges then she'd be back into it again, and it'd be a real struggle for her to stop. When I got old enough to understand what was going on I used to hate him for what it would do to her."

I follow her up the sloping back of a mammoth boulder to a flat spot on top. Below is the pond. She sits close to me on the warm stone.

"Isn't this nice?" She searches my face again. "So one time Daddy came back from somewhere and they had their binge but then they had a big fight about something, and he had to leave again before they got things worked out. I don't remember what it was about. I think she wanted to get us out of the base housing. You know, get a decent place in town, 'cause it was so crummy and crowded, but he didn't care.

"So she's back drinking and angry at him, and he's gone so she started going to this bar nearby. You can imagine there were a lot of bars around a Marine base. And guess what happens, she meets this guy. His name was Jodi Tomlinson, which I'll never forget, and he was such a worm. He liked people to call him Tommy, thought it was cute or something. He was a warrant officer—"

My thoughts turn away as she talks. That boy, the accomplice, lay waiting in his bed, in the now silent room, waiting for the ambulance, the police, sirens, serious men in uniforms with loud urgent voices, and grew more and more amazed that they didn't come, more and more amazed at the silence in that house that went on and on, undisturbed. Not even Father stumbling from sleep, angry and uncomprehending. No, the final incredible realization came to him, after how long waiting, an hour maybe, that she had simply returned to bed, gone back to sleep. How could she sleep?

"He was kind of fat," Rita says, "and had this hillbilly accent and he used to talk and talk all the time. I don't know what he did for Mom but she started hanging out with him and drinking with him. That was the worst part, he'd drink with her and we'd come home from school and they'd be passed out on the bed.

"I used to hate that man, Leon. He was a real letch. He used to try to feel me up all the time, whenever I got near him. And Mom would just laugh and ignore the whole thing. Course she'd be drunk most of the time, or else hung over and then she'd be angry at us. It was a terrible time."

She came to him in the morning, woke him very early—he did sleep—and told him of your death. And he pretended surprise, clumsy and fearful, a childish attempt at shock and sadness for her, for them both.

Father's grief was just as clumsy, although genuine, that of a man who has seen much death.

And then finally they came, first a single policeman looking about, asking solemn questions. The boy froze in fear at the man's glance, felt his mouth go dry, his voice disappear.

"Leon was asleep," his Mother rescued him. "He didn't know 'til this morning."

Then Dr. Lester who touched you, arranged you somehow. He hugged Mother who cried, then hugged Father, an awkward halting movement for them both. Then he kneeled by the boy, the boy that was me, and hugged him, too. He hugged him and talked to him. Did he know what it meant, this doctor who knew death himself. I wish I could remember what he said.

"I used to pray that Daddy would come home and straighten everything out, get rid of Tommy and get Mom to stop drinking for a while. But he didn't come. I think he got wounded and went to a hospital over in the Philippines for a while. Mom wouldn't tell us about him and Tommy kept egging her on and kept her drunk until finally she started talking about getting a divorce.

"A divorce." Rita turns to me, tears shining in her eyes. "This little worm of a man just came into our life and started ruining it, ruining Mom, keeping her drunk all the time, and ruining our family and doing it all behind Daddy's back.

"God, Leon," she says with a hand on my arm. "I've never told this to anyone before. You won't tell anyone—who would you tell? Who would care? Maybe the police. I don't think they'd even care."

The rabbi came, an old man who stooped over you, mumbling in Hebrew, ignoring the boy.

Then an oversized black station wagon arrived, with no windows in the back, that strange curl of metal trim where the window should have been, a decoration, he wondered, watching from inside the house, or does it do something? Two dark-suited young men pulled a stretcher from it and wheeled it toward the house, with somber deadpan faces, odd expressions on faces so young.

"Robert, he was the youngest," Rita says, "maybe six then. He started having nightmares all the time and wetting his bed. And Tommy would spank him in the morning if he wet the bed. That was helpful, you can imagine.

"That bastard deserved to die, Leon." She clutches my arm. "There was nothing good about him at all. He was mean and hateful." She gazes down at the water now. "So I did it. Daddy kept a sidearm in the closet and he had showed me how to use it. It was a forty-five automatic. So one afternoon when they were passed out on the bed I got the gun down. It was always loaded. I wore gloves so I wouldn't leave any fingerprints. They were these little knit kids gloves with sequins on the back. Funny, the things you remember.

"So I took Tommy's hand and wrapped it around the gun. He was too out of it to feel anything. I remember I thought about shooting his balls off. That's what I really wanted to do. I wanted to hurt him, isn't that terrible? But that wouldn't have worked. I had to make it look like it was either an accident or suicide.

"So I wrapped his hand around the gun, got up on the bed right on top of him. He was passed out on his back with his head back. Ugh, it was the most awful thing, Leon. Being right there on top of him, and he was naked and he smelled bad like he always did. I was so afraid he'd wake up. God knows what he would have done to me if he'd woken up. So I took his finger and wrapped it around the trigger and pointed the gun right under his chin and pulled on his finger until it fired.

"Then I ran out of the room so Mom wouldn't see me when she woke up. The other kids were outside playing. The thing I was most scared of was getting blood on my clothes, 'cause I knew the whole neighborhood would come running when they heard a gunshot."

Now she looks at me again, trembling. She laughs a nervous laugh. "But it worked. It worked like a charm. That was the loudest noise I think I ever heard, that gun firing, and I dropped it and ran out of the room. God, Leon, I felt so...um...I don't know, I guess exhilarated or something. I think I almost had an orgasm. I ran into my room and then into the bathroom to look in the mirror and make sure I didn't have any blood on me. I almost forgot to take off the gloves, if I hadn't seen them on me in the mirror. I didn't know where to hide them. And then Mom started screaming and someone was knocking on the door and then people started coming in."

She laughs again now, turning and squeezing my arm. "You know what I did? I put those gloves in my underpants. Oh, God, Leon, you can't imagine how I felt then. And there was such a mess in the bedroom. I only peeked in between all the neighbors and then went outside to keep the kids from coming in. So they wouldn't see it. God, Leon, I thought there would just be a little hole in his head and a little blood on the floor. But it looked like his head had exploded. There was blood all over the walls and the ceiling and everywhere.

"Poor Mom, she was totally freaked out. Here she wakes up from a drunken stupor to a room covered in blood and then all the neighbors and the M.P.'s all over the place."

For a few moments she is silent, remembering.

The boy watched out the window, knees on the front room couch, leaning on the sill. He watched you being taken away, zippered into a long brown bag, much longer than your body itself, long enough for an adult, he realized. His few questions were ignored and he watched to see how he should feel, because he knew he didn't feel the way he should.

"It was such an easy thing to do, killing that bastard," Rita goes on, "and now it's like somebody else that did it, some other girl that wasn't me."

She glances up suddenly, as if to see the effect of her words.

I nod earnestly and think vaguely of what I should say. Something to comfort her? Should I touch her, hug her, make a joke? I sit lumpified, congealed on the stone, nodding. It is so quiet here.

"So you didn't get caught?" I manage finally.

"Leon, what are you thinking of?" And the inquiring innocent face of that murderous girl, now adult, continues its rapid transition of expression. Now it flows from introspection and memory to inquiry of my own expression, to surprise, then puzzlement as she reads my face of which I have made no conscious control, of which her curiosity piques my own and for an instant I await the settling of her face so I will know my own. What does she see in me right now?

"Your face..." she waves a quick hand, "it's different, Leon. What are you thinking of?" She starts to smile, where seconds ago had been the memory of murder, of family tragedy.

"I don't know," I mumble. "It seems so quiet here, doesn't it?"

"Quiet?" she says. "Quiet? Leon!" she feigns exasperation, laughter in her voice, "I just tell you this incredible story that I've never told anyone before, the only real secret of my life, that I murdered someone, blew his fucking brains out, and you say it's quiet."

Now I feel myself smile. "Sorry, guess I'm all in a dither."

"Why did I tell you all that?" Rita says. "I'm sorry, it all just tumbled out, didn't it? I guess I thought it would help you, or something, after you...after what happened with Fitz."

Fitz, what happened to Fitz? And then I remember with a start. He's gone, isn't he. Gone from my life, gone from the world. I think of the nurses undressing him, latex gloved, sliding the clotted IV from his arm, removing his rings, tying a tag to his toe, naked, so naked, and slipping the pale cloth bag over him, from the small discreet stack of them in the back of the linen cupboard.

And gone, too, is his suffering, his struggle for air, his body wasting away, the pain he ignored so well, the hopelessness of certain death. Gone from the world, my friend Fitz.

"What you did was a good thing, Leon," Rita says.

I lie back and let the warmth of the solemn monolith under us seep into my skin, let the night air move over my face, cooling my thoughts as if they were the coals of a bonfire, or perhaps a small conflagration, now scattered, dashed into the dark, their glow ebbing.

And you, Zach, you're gone now, too, aren't you. Where is your voice? I don't hear it. Your presence, always with me in my mind, always here for me to talk to. You won't be here anymore, will you. I feel the sad twist of how alone I am now, how alone I'm going to be. I'm sorry, Zach, sorry you have to go. But I'm not going to cry. I'm tired of crying.

It will be dawn soon, its exquisite paleness creeping up the sky. And what will this day bring? I lie and listen to the silence in my mind. I find Rita's hand with mine.

About the Author

Samuel Finn lives in Seattle with his wife, two teenagers and a black Lab. He is a veteran emergency physician and works in a busy community hospital. He welcomes comments and questions about Heartbeat at finnsam@speakeasy.net.

Printed in the United States
1386900003BA/46-63